welcon

TILLY'S TAILS

by Kevin J Gallagher

First published by
Michael Terence Publishing in 2022
www.mtp.agency

ISBN 9781800943742

Cover design
2022 Michael Terence Publishing

Michael Terence
Publishing

Contents

Introduction

Hello!

I'd like to introduce myself…

My name is Kevin Johnny Gallagher, mostly known as KJ or Gypsy. The nickname Gypsy coming from my many years of travelling which included 14 glorious years in the USA mainly working the Californian coastal towns off the Pacific Highway Coast Highway (PCH) where I was in heaven working and running bars with my two reliable partners by my side - a 1964 half Ford Mustang 289 and a classic Italian Laverda motorcycle.

I'm of Celtic decent, Dad was Irish and Mum was a Welsh lady, so the passion for rugby and joy for life is always with me.

Growing up and just loving life with friends and of course, a dog being our mascot was always involved which always brought joy to us all.

Cooking is one of my main hobbies but life, in general, is my main interest and I am still travelling and meeting people that belong to other countries and cultures.

I now live in an ole smugglers town off the English Channel in Kent, UK called Deal that in its day was riddled with 'you name it'. With its 366 pubs, the military and miners' smuggling and whatever else that was going on. This plus the resulting banter inspired me to write this adventurous story of *Tilly's Tails* - a dog's-eye-view of those wild days leading to the (seemingly) calmer lifestyle in Deal today.

Watching peoples' laughter whilst telling me which part of *Tilly's Tales* they love the best and relate to makes my day.

When I wake, I look forward to beginning another day, then cook breakfast whilst listening to the radio playing tracks I could not live without. Music is a joy in itself. The joy of life, in general, is a gift and I hope you too enjoy yours.

May your god be with you.

- KJ -

TILLY'S TAILS

Tilly, Annie, come you two! cried out Auntie Emma, come, come to me. Smiling with happiness as she knew Aunt Emma went through it herself until she became free.

Staying at Auntie Emma's and Cousin Annie's has always brought a smile to my heart,

For Mum and my aunt knew it was best for me to have a break before the big start.

Nanny Sky will be here as she's on her way; she will be here very soon,

So, make sure your hair's all brushed, clean tongue and all is in bloom.

They heard the garden latch sound and all ears went up, hearts beating to a race,

Then the ole rat-a-tat on the door and then came the sound of paws to a pace.

Nanny, Nanny! Yelps, tails wagging, skids all running around, Nanny, Nanny Sky's here,

For this is the day to walk the long front and down past the winding pier.

Slowly things calmed down, the hugs, licks, tails still wagging when the neighbour Buster entered, not the brightest but loved by all,

A typical old English Pitbull, do anything for anyone, and all you had to do was call.

With the young ones running around, Buster had an idea. Bashful, shy and naïve as he was, he had an idea of what was going on. For he heard through the grapevine why Tilly was here and staying. And yes, he had always had a crush on pretty Tilly. He spoke underneath his poor-hearted thought's breath, oh I wish it was me.

No one's looking, she thought. So, she reached for ole faithful and she then took a slug out of her wee flask strapped to her collar pouch; of course, it was Plymouth gin.

But no one would dare say anything to Nanny by telling her that it was mother's ruin and to many, one hell of a bad sin.

Nanny Sky, another old wise Staff Pitbull herself, the governess's side all her life she lived and witnessed all from the mayor's stately house.

The dogs of the rich with their noses up, there for the shoots and for returning the pheasants and the grouse.

It was her birthday, you know, Bella the Beagle. She'd always been spoilt to the hilt. Ya, she got a new basket, toys, everything she wanted and all.

Lady the whippet said it was her birthday. But that's every day, she said with a laugh and a call.

We bantered for a while when Mollie the mix came in with Frieda at her side,

Morning Emma, I've- a tut out of her first before she spoke, oh, I've run outta nail varnish.

Frieda's sweet voice spoke, By the way, how is Tilly? Tell her we all send our love and tell her to keep her tail up and waggle it with pride.

That's not the only thing she needs to keep up, came a bitchy comment from the corner of the exclusive handbags, scarves, ribbons, varnishes and all that was for sale,

It was Fifi with the other King Charles spaniels from Sandwich having their weekly, itchy chat with Poochie and the other snub pugs all having their wail.

Nanny Sky stood up, brushed herself down with a good ole shake then walked over to the ladies and then to the watering bowl to have a drink.

Whilst Aunt Emma, smiling to all, looked towards Nanny's back and then turned to the youngsters with a wink.

Right girls, it is time for this long Sunday walk to see, tell who's what and all,

And when we get back, we will see who has the last call.

All excited, tails going, bags checked and all leashes in place, yes, all ready to take on the ware.

Let's just take them with us and then if anyone asks, we got them for their care.

Out through the kitchen door, tails, paws everything all a-go, oh how they adored this historical, magical stroll, then across the gardens, crossed over then down to the end of the patio.

By the way, where's the ole boy, Shep? Where's your granddaddy and Scamp?

I think he heard through the grapevine that we were to get together and he's headed to the golf course for a stroll with his buddy, you know the old mutt, Tramp.

Nanny Sky smiled and said, that ole, English playboy, you know something, he'll never change his way.

And tell him I send my love, that is if I don't see him through the day.

Just to feel the breeze blowing off the front and their thoughts in their hearts, they knew with the air's aroma this was to be a new start. Along Canute Road, through the estate and from all around you could hear the good mornings, smiles, hellos, stares,

And then from garden fences ole dogs, paws folded, tongues a-sagging there were the odd glares.

Breaking the air, how do you feel, Tilly? Annie asked with a soft pleasant tone, have you spoken to Dylan within this short while?

Oh yes, Annie, he's at the Gentlemen's Obedience Police Academy, she responded with a smile.

Nanny was eavesdropping and muttered to herself, Well I didn't know he was following that leg. In what division does he want to be?

Well, he's been chosen for the Police Drugs and Army team, but we will see.

Across Ethelbert Road, Aunt Emma's soft tone spoke, Right, young lady you need not bark a word but here we are just to walk. A stroll many lovers and all make through many a year along to put their hearts and minds at rest,

So, we may hear the odd words and get many looks, but we just take it in jest.

Along Deal's prom, looking aside with her old instinct, a little swig she managed to get away with and hide,

But she couldn't help feeling, watching her future family growing and all with pride.

Emma, a lecturer in Barkeruria, a lost Latin doggy language and now teaching at her own kennel club in this field. Now then, how are you coping with your first year, now running your own classes? It must be nerve-racking as well as such a challenge for oneself.

I'm doing fine, Nanny, and it is never a dull moment.

With Emma's total interest, growing up she always loved to learn and it was no surprise that she took up teaching. She was chosen for the Prince College of Training in Cambridge, which was a great honour and then she returned to her beloved Deal, a Kent coastal town, to teach under-privileged breeds of all kinds.

This is the road of teaching she followed up on and made such an example, they gave her her own school of behaviour. Ya, all sorts are graduating outta that Kennel for Mutts as many called it, but she proved those critics wrong you know, dogs with half ears, broken tails, missing teeth and scrabbled up snouts took pride in and let the growling-snarling manner of their past out.

By the way, the college is called the ESMSS, the Emma School of Manners, Scent and Standards, which is what the letters stand for. And will set an example for many doggies who just go around with a nasty frown. I'm loving every moment of seeing some flea-bitten, raggedy mutt take heed and listen that one day may take his or her standards to the next litter in our life and all will be well.

And I've taken two on, two who have assisted me so much, Nanny, as one's from the Dover dock streets and the other is from the back streets of the East End, both cross breeds so it helps the ones who think college is just for the Pedigrees.

Now, every standard of teaching in the manner and mode, they have both reached their degree.

Along the Marina they strolled with a rhythm in pace with the soft shingles that were dancing in tune with the water's race,

When they all just smiled with a tune which suited all with their pace.

As walking along, a call came out of Harold Road. Then came a bark of excitement, Buster, Tilly, Annie? They turned to see who it was. It's Bella with some other Beagles, Bob, Sammy and Honey.

Nanny Sky looked at Emma as they crossed the Marina and then they welcomed Bella and the others on board,

Whilst the young ones ran upon the front to find, chase whatever was in the overnight tide's hoard.

Sky, I must say it's wonderful to see you about again and taking this walk along, it's something that makes you feel reborn.

Yes, I must say it is a wonderful feeling, thank you and good morning to you Bella, and by the way congrats on your birthday of this Sunday morn.

The youngsters played as through the currents they waded whilst the ladies looked on, their thoughts just pleasantly carried along with their walk.

And they knew, all in all, if there was anything to settle then now, today was the time to talk.

You know what's going on as we've seen it all before and whose silver-spooned nose in this small-minded town will be up to imply.

So, by the time this day is over, we will have any question answered and then let anyone ask why.

How far are you going? Oh, down to Kingstown and it will give us time to let out what's to be said.

Then when it is all out and my feeling's content, I'm going to turn around after that and head home to that loyal basket of mine that people call their bed.

May I join you? Oh, please do. Bella looked at Nanny Sky and knew that expression she had on. She was out for scalps, and when she caught those culprits who were making Tilly's life sad, she'd hang them high. The two walked on with Nanny Sky muttering, I'd be honoured if you'd join me in this say.

The young ones a-playing, nanny reached to her famous collar stash, Care to join me? The question was a wink but it will end in a sway.

Another stride along the Marina, times like this when you can't help thinking a thought or two, then we will see names such as Britannia and Albion Road. I think of Effie the Airedale,

Sam the Boxer and who was that sailor dog who was with you? Bella smiled, Oh, Alfie, my, he was handsome to the core.

And with it all their memories and thoughts they burst out with laughter and bliss with a roar.

Looking over to the playing, now it's their turn and beside them we will be, and then through all that happens on their journey in life. Then we can only hope it is not sore.

Nanny Sky, is that the Goodwin Sands out there? The ones that the stories of the Romans, Caesar, the smugglers with their lugger boats crossing over them? Those songs they sang about the death that followed the curse of those sands. They charmed the ships' crews by their singing of ballads about the hidden gold, silver and the finest rums of the world they had stashed away. Yes, those sailors believed their soft voices were telling the truth and in they sailed to meet their fate.

They all just sat there along the front staring out with all different thoughts passing through their minds and hearts, most thoughts were upon thinking and imagining what it must have been like in those wild days of the sea life when beside you, you did not know if it was a thief or a mate.

Along the Marina, they walked, yet another bark outta Horsa Road, Frankie the Bulldog with Jack the blind Yorkie.

My, what a pair they are! They can tell stories, yarns, and many an ear listened to them in the old inns of Deal when new doggies just docked at the feet of their sailors who sat drinking, talking of their cargo and smiled to think with their thoughts of the pair and my they can tell a porky!

Morning Gals, is this the family, Sky? Yes, yes Frankie, you know my daughters Emma and Darcy? My, oh my, just like you aren't they, Sky? Yes, another pair of heartbreakers and as pretty - are they free? The ladies just smiled as a charmer he had always been. A legendary tag was left in many a gal's heart, they never married, yes but Frankie and Jack had lovers in every port and never, never were apart.

Even now still as old as they were, they'd see a pretty gal's smile and a swish of their tail the chit-chat of charm was on the start.

Last night sitting in the Ship Inn, there were yarns going on and gossip of a young lady in a little cluster.

Jack thought he'd mention this to Sky and just then Frankie curiously looked, Sky, don't mind me asking but is that Johnnie's boy, Buster?

Yes, yes, it is. My, isn't he the cut of his dad and seems to be as gentle as he was. But there was no gentleness on that terrible stormy night that took him away and peril in life he was endorsed.

That pup, he was only three months old when I last set eyes on him, Sky, but it stays with you when something dreadful happens and it stayed with me to this day about what happened to his father on that stormy night's course.

We'll sit awhile and Jack you can tell the pups stories of Henry the Eighth and Nelson's clips,

The mascots and the fruity stories who they saw come n' go off those dodgy ships.

Is it true Nelson's doggie had a lover being a French poodle? He kidnapped and bound her in the Star and Garter. And Henry, he loved the big gals who danced in the ole inn the Deal Cutter. They sat a-while till they heard their yarns and thought it over, well these banters, were they true or not? But the yarns were happy and they enjoyed listening to them and how and what they were about down along the Marina, then along onto Beach Street the banters were being told of the corrupt side lanes where the brewers, mills, naughty houses, where the dirty dogs of the night would dance and perform their ways in the naughty houses and inns along the streets.

They would act in this manner mainly for the admirals and captains and then for the pooches for bones, biscuits, anytime, anything for a warm night's room sitting by a fire just to reach their meats.

Down past Exchange Street, Griffin, Golden, Farrier and onto Coppin,

many a different look they got. But yes, they kept their tails a-bopping.

Here we go, gang! Into the town we enter where the greetings, looks, words will be, we can just wander, maybe a little shopping? We'll just see. Emma, Darcy, hello, hello came a happy welcome, Effie, the medley mixed terrier smiled, and waved oh, how happy, a joy to be in her presence, she liked to sit aside at where the pier begins and there was just the scent of all breeds of dogs spread along there which brought on a thoughtful essence. Into the town they entered when a call came out, Yahoo, Darlings, Tillas, Annie yoo-hoo!

They stared at each other with 'oh no' expressions on their faces and it matched their smiling thoughts of now what do we do? It was Birdie, the Standard Poodle with her forever smiling maids carrying her assets, yes of course all the top labels on show as they walked a few steps aside,

One must have all of the highest to set one's standards, so one stands out, and so one can hold her pride.

I've just left Posh Paws, hair done, nails a-gleaming, all four paws shining, and Lisa, you know, the owner of Mrs Lang? She had her top attire brought in and of course, she wanted me first to view it at hand.

Oh, and look at these etc, etc one must have all this when one is in such demand.

Did you know, darlings, that this afternoon will be another show of Mummy's- I mean *my* clothing designs on The Strand, oh and of course, I'll strut- I mean walk the catwalk.

And darlings- just before another word, Sailor, her fiancé pulled up with his chauffer. Good morning, ladies. A sigh of relief came about as this would help to finish her talk.

Morning, Darcy, Nanny my darlings of Deal and yes, here he goes with his charm starting with, Darlings, at least I must have a kiss to steal/

Birdie, my sweetie, oh, we must put it in the book. We have been called to Uncle Wellington's this Sunday. Oh, sorry ladies, but I tend to forget, so a charter has been made and then I can't forget and then there's no regret. Wellies lives in Kingstown, we must meet Sunday evening at The Castle House for the grace, elegance, fun and the beginning of many a romance,

With a taste of champers, floors for all dancers, then the smile whilst sat, paw-in-paw, the watching of sunset over to dear ole France.

Sailor, cravat a-tied, hair all groomed with teeth polished wide with a lifestyle only to live in bliss,

But only one was for him. As annoying as she could be, it was Birdie and that was his only kiss x.

Come, come, the Morgan was being loaded with boxes and bags by the maids. Wait a sec, let's have it delivered as everything's all just a clatter.

Yes, following their old scene as usual everything was a panic, another show with all in a scatter.

Both maids smiled at everyone, with a little embarrassment, they were regular poodles, Sally and Milly,

They both grew up and schooled, groomed, danced and cried with their best friend, Tilly,

Do you have the chance to speak in between all this? Are you okay? And can we meet at The Strand?

Yes, yes, I'll meet you whilst the walk is on; these were the words from Tilly, I'm so sorry - we'll meet at the band stand.

The chaos, at last, was over as they all smiled and waved then on their way they went. Darlings, sweeties, see you at the walk. Of course, Birdie, yes, she had to have the last say.

Along Beach Street and past the woodyard, the smiles from Doris as she was out for a quick stroll herself and they'd just reached Oak Street when the welcome smile brought all hearts to meet and greet each other. Hello, hello you all and this must be Tilly I'd say. A kiss to Nanny Sky and all and then again, they were all on their way.

Along Beach Street and then passing Chapel Market Street, Emma looked out as she knew there was going to be out there the small town's stare,

But a wink to Tilly's nervous smiles, all around there was no reason to feel or be aware.

Along they strolled and to the Pier they arrived and Nanny's thoughts were, mm, I think it's just in time for a sip of a wee dram, water of course was set in mind.

But a sort of hint of what was in that flask seemed to make your thoughts smile and be kind.

Looking out watching the water's sharp teeth snap at the Goodwin Sands, you could say it was their sort of banter and what was on remand.

When history tells a story if you didn't pay the toll to pass, then the price was their demand.

They snapped your ship, stole your cargo, all of what you had under n over the decks,

Then the truth lay at the bottom of its waters, yes, yes centuries and centuries of wrecks.

The views are as pretty as they were back then, aren't they, my lady Sky?

As the voice spoke, Nanny's heart and thoughts rose like a swan lifting to fly.

She turned, the others looked on when he spoke again, you still bring out the spring when you walk this way,

And the finches, sparrows, larks return to sing, how beautiful you still are I must say.

With a smile, Why Phoenix, and may I say you still are a prince and still such a gentleman's gent. A step back to look, why shoulders, legs, tail and nose all still straight and none too bent. The smiles all around as a nice aroma flowed like in an Olympic arena. Sky looked on. Oh, I'm sorry, Phoenix spoke, let me introduce my granddaughter this is Aseena. Salukis they were and as gentle as they looked from their glamorous head, hair down to the toe,

Their thoughts and manners were just as natural and graceful for them to show.

This is my daughter, Emma. Why, hello! And my granddaughters, Tilly, Annie and also a friend of the family, Buster. You know what happened next? One glance at Aseena and his heart was all a-flutter. Would you mind if we joined your good company on this pleasant stroll along the walk?

Well, we'd be honoured was the reply and we'll carry, reminisce old times and fill every second of this air with this pleasant talk.

She put her paw-in-paw like many a time they walked the prom as like the days that passed by.

They then felt curiosity was on the youngsters' minds of what was flowing, glowing around them and who and why?

Tilly and Keeley's friendship and bond of open paws made Aseena's feelings relax at last as she didn't know a soul,

As from a wee puppy she was moved from her home town for reasons of heartbreak that was hard for anyone and she paid its toll.

Slowly they talked as young ladies do of dresses, nails and crushes on their idols and of course who's who. Then they asked Aseena, would you like to come with us as we are walking to the Grand Parade? The grandparents looked at each other with a smile then leaving the Pier down past Five Step and Custom House Lane, yes, the beautiful fond memories of theirs still remained.

Nanny spoke, Do you remember when we were pups ourselves, we said that's where the demons, villains lived and there was a danger that we could be slain?

They walked on when Bella, Honey laughed, open to that innocent banter,

As Darcy spoke, Often, when I'm out with friends I tend to walk through there still with a canter.

Along Short Street and on to Board Road those sagas they talked about were being on the mode of temperance,

As wild as those nights were of wine, wench and song there was still a sense of pure elegance.

Phoenix with wonderful thoughts spoke of yet again ole myths of the girls so wild, and one of the wildest, the ghost of the crazy widow, Betty.

They say, Tilly, she's still seen walking through the market square looking into the inns, walking through the houses and onwards then to her own little jetty.

The girls looked on around then at each other with a funny, yet nervous twitch and now and then said, shall we or do we believe this? And with that thought they gave themselves a little itch. So, ladies, before we go on just how many stories do you think were shared over a glass of wine or their dogs chewing a bone, sharing their tales and secrets of centuries? No one really had a clue. But how many sailed apart and never to see that lover again and those secrets, Mm, if only one knew.

Aseena spoke, Keeley, Tilly have you grown up with all these stories? Oh yes, we must say, and many, times we went to bed asking ourselves, true or false? And even still we question those stories to the day. Honey with her sister said, yes, yes, we as well lay in bed by the fire, listening to our family telling us the ole stories until we hid under our blankets, tucked into our baskets with a little fear, but for some reason we were not frightened to the point that brought on a tear. Just then yet another bark echoed out from along the way, it was Charlie the head of the black labs from Walmer, and what does Deal owe you, Nanny Sky, for bringing the sun back and calming the Channel's rage?

Oh, just another spiteful saga and gossip, Charlie, of a small part of the town's silver spooner's page.

Please, Mon, come, come join us as I have my family out for the day and we have the table set there on the side, do you remember my brother from the West Indies? He's with me,

Clencil, what joy to see you again, as Nanny was first to approach the happy bunch, the last time I saw you was the birth of Jasmine your daughter, Charlie, she's over as well, she's here to tell the wonderful news as I'm a granddad to be.

Around the spread of grand welcoming food, the sound of yelps n barks echoed about and then a kiss from Purdy, Charlie's wife, fell upon Nanny's snout and then the look at Tilly from their daughter, Jasmine, as they knew each other from the puppy club, was so gentle. Please sit with us a while and yes, the young ones bonded as they sat on the side with gentle chats of their life whilst the elders chattered away and the happiness of welcome was within their natural culture and at the same time, there was always an instinct if there was a danger, and that came up with a little warn,

With their feelings of defence if it was necessary, they would watch over their litters, as they still called them that at times of speech, and now the next generation bringing the gift of life into their world, their protection was even more intense with a scorn.

We are all behind her, Nanny. So, don't worry about the spooners in the square. The reason Purdy spoke these words was there was a pack of hounds, local gossipers watching over from the summer shelter as they were sat with their parasols and jeering over and yes, yes, they had bitterness on their tongues whilst trying to outbid each other's words in what to say. And what did they know? They couldn't survive a second outside within the real world's ways. Right, Charlie and all it's been a-before the words came out of Nanny's nose there were heads, legs up all around.

Alejandra and Javier, the Chihuahuas playing tag and chasing JR and RJ the Jack Russells through the tables, stools, Coma estas? The words meaning hello, how are you from their native language of Mexico. Then a laughter all about when once more, Come, you all, we must make ground.

Jasmine with a rose in her mouth passed it to Tilly with a word and a smile with love and sincere, we will go through it together my friend; we'll get through it together my dear. A wave, a wag, a sniff, a pause the tapping of excitement from a band of content happy paws,

Yes, the odd glance back at the few spooners in with their temperance out looking with badness in their claws.

Aseena spoke, It's the same in my town, they will not bond together and help if there is the spite or heartbreak within the village,

But an error in one's life, oh how they dwell and make it into pillage.

Tilly smiled to Aseena then to Bella, Keeley, a boost, thoughts, cares were overwhelmed with the sheer contented hearted zest.

Another look and a smile from granddad Phoenix. Nanny and company, Buster's wag with a heart so full, this company made it only the best.

Not two steps passed when another welcome bark came from a passing car.

Heads turned up to music playing and to see whose bark came from the window that was ajar.

It was Meaka and Seceara, a pair of golden retrievers, two nurses who worked with Darcy, Tilly's mum who runs a home with an open door, smiled, waved as happy as can be, and a pleasure for all who met their ways and to be in their company.

Walking a little further, they met another grand figure in life, Gypsy, what to see you again a pleasure it is and I see you still have your Clandestine Firkin; do you still carry your finest sailor's joy?

The big husky, Saint Bernard mix loved for his voice, it howled on dark nights they say on the boats he sailed upon fishing. Whatever the weather they say his voice and presence brought hope as he would sing there is land ahead, ahoy.

Alfie, the mix always walked side by side with Gypsy, yes, a little extra to the stories again,

Just like Blind Eye Jack and co, their history of these two legends that's the only way to explain.

Even after all these times of ups and downs these assets still made one smile.

Walking on the front they were joined once again with receiving the welcoming sounds of Hello! from the everyday traders, the calls of the fishermen with their catch of the day, the sounds and cries made it into escapades. The merry cries from the fishermen, Herrings, monk, skate, mackerel, sprats and many of other fish,

All's here, all's welcome, come pick n choose your very own

catch of the day for your dish.

The twins Jack n Russell, Taffy the terrier, Tucker the westie in and out and through the lobster pots and boats they carried on with their inherited chores with a happy ambiance way,

Not to say a swipe with a rod or a broom from a fisherman to shoo the gulls away.

Passing the boats, a few questions came from the youngsters, Bella, why call that fish a skate when they don't have roller blades or whatever? Yes, this question came from you know who?

The others just looked and laughed at each other as they didn't have a clue.

And Aseena, why do they call this the Prince of Wales Terrace, whilst we are in the middle of Kent?

Bella looked on at Phoenix, laughed as their thoughts were left just as bent.

Yes, the sun kept its promise to shine upon everyone's dream that any cloud should dare show a dark side he'd chase them into the Channel to keep the rain away,

Whilst all smiles kept growing as the thoughts grew stronger throughout the pleasant day.

Towards the Castle they strolled when Effie the Kerry mixed blue came into view and smiled with the essence of such a group which produced a joy of shapes and sizes which brought her to a smile.

Hello, hello to you all, are you going to the fair? Questions all around, I've to take these Chiffon collars to Birdie's mum's booth so I'll join you along in joy for a while.

Past the Castle and on they strolled then onto the green where there were orders of command. No, no, my dear you have to walk with grace, elegance and then you have to make your presence known. It was a practice run for the show later that day for Birdie's mother's clothing and she wanted as always to make her designs stand. It was the sophisticated, chic Lucy the Deer Hound teaching the grace of the catwalk,

Now once again, Sophie, Millie you are Greyhounds show me what you got and Solar, you are a Whippet with the sleek class of your own, show them how it is done and Alice you are a Dalmatian, shake those spots as I want this whole crowd tonight to talk.

She looked to the left, India and Ellie, the glazing white German Shepherd twins they were and proud to shake their assets side by side to show off the chic clothing of Lisa's store. You know Mrs Lang who chose Deal, not the madness of Soho. Her class dressage made for the human mums to match the doggies' class leathers, collar bags, leashes, the make up all together it deserved a glow.

Glaring with essence, her eyes ajar, Tilly spoke, you like what you see Aseena?

Before she could reply, Meaka and Saceara show those coats and furs and make your goal sincere. It was Lady Lucy's order to the beauty of the Afghan Hound sisters to show their stance,

And as everything that surrounded them glowed, all you could feel was the romance.

They reached the beginning of the Strand and the stalls were busy with the essence of barks, calls from traders selling their home-made what-nots and the flamboyant aromas of air freshener scents, just a happy go lucky feeling to be around and it felt a joy to witness such an old market feeling when just then a head turned when she realised there was company about her. She turned her stern head and spoke with her stern as ever voice, Morning, Sky, it has been a while, hasn't it? Then a kiss to Nanny, a nod to Keeley and Bella, My and look who is with you! She turned then and gave another kiss to Phoenix's cheek,

Then she turned and just couldn't resist glaring at Aseena

who was just looking so meek. And who may this be? Came her stern, elegant question, please, introduce her to me as I find it my concern.

And straight away she knew this was the next Twiggy of the dog world and the modelling world she would spin and turn.

With a bashful, heartfelt glare, Aseena's eyes stared and fluttered and something stirred inside,

The look came again and she didn't know it but her whole life was about to become open wide.

Just then the more serene voice spoke and all stood to admire with a little fright in its sense, it was the voice and sternness of Katie McDonald. KM was here herself to thank her roots, the town of Deal where it all began,

Where in the Queens Hotel she met her career and all bells rang. Beside her, Carol, her hairdresser, ole Monty to her left, his smiles still as beautiful as his breed.

The Chocolate lab, oh a heart breaker if there was ever one and still has his charm like a puppy in need.

Then Lisa and Laundie, from U Beauties, the ultimate creators of the nails, skin and eyes and all that goes with a glow,

Then of course Mary from the Bear Necessities having the eye to make sure all went with a flow.

All the dressers, carriers, the works were busy here and there, in the amusement of the fashion world buzzing all aground,

For within hours the Dogs' Media from all over the world would stare, with eyes all around.

Nanny spoke to the girls to explain that along London's Kings Road, Curls n Twirls, Chelsea's Tails a Mane, Mayfair's Top House of Dane,

etc, etc, it's all hers, girls, that's the Lady who makes or breaks the Catwalk in the world of fashion n fame.

Does she own the burger shops as well? Came the question from you know who.

Nanny looked at Emma and Keeley, then to the girls with a smile and at Buster mm, he still doesn't have a clue.

Then with things getting in full swing a beep from his chauffeur as he drove off. Out of the Morgan stepped Sailor to get the male side of the show in shape and make sure all was ready for the road,

The Poodles, Ruby, Chester, Manny and Pepe with all the latest attire to pump the heart out of the abode,

Fredrick and Angelo, the Greyhound movers, the male side of the latest young swish attire with the matching collar studs and to show how to move.

And with their specially-created paw-ware only made by Shoes by Steve. The strange thing was, of all the cobblers of the London's high-end scene that made the Grensons and Barkers for the mega rich to prance around all on shine, she chose Steve's Shiners. He had been very loyal to the profession of cobblers and he designed with the blessing of a woman's paw, from a short-heeled Chihuahua to a long-legged Lurcher he knew how a lady wanted to walk and strut her stuff. Based on The High Street of Deal, Louboutin for the ladies and his Padded Paraders a beautifully cut design that really took strutting for the guys to the next level to fit in the groove.

Mrs McDonald smiled on, then with all her calmness turned and took one look and saw Aseena's elegance and grace,

Once again, she walked through the crowd to Lucy, her words pierced into her ear, Get her! she spoke whilst giving her a kiss on her snout and an embrace.

Then all changed, Mummy, mummy, yes you guessed it. Birdie's arrival all the glitters and sparkle were on the walk,

Mummy these are my friends, Tilly, Keeley, a little look at

Aseena, Mm. Then on with the talk.

All around them it never stopped. The clothes kept changing, the crowds praising and the catwalk kept showing all the way. The sun kept her promise, smiled with glisten and the show went on all day.

The adrenaline pumped, all the hearts within the spectators, designers, the models the whole media surrounding walked, smiled and shone with the sun,

Even the looks from sullen bitches couldn't touch or ruin the feeling of the fun.

The girls were just a-glare looking upon all the action going on and mostly Aseena. She glared at all and was in full bloom just like her mother was in her beautiful career that still was the talk of the day.

Then came a note carried over from Lola you know, Mrs McDonald's private side with the silver tray,

Nanny turned to face and receive the lady, nodded, smiled and tried to look not surprised. *Mrs McDonald's request asks that you all attend tonight's BIG -TOP-VIP PARTY*, and Emma saw the note and giggled, in a way, Mum, you know to go there and be requested is the only way.

Emma's eyelashes lifted with a smirk and Bella's elbow into Tilly's side, they were waiting for Nanny's response and to answer the offer from the host and how would she address? She nodded, replied with a smile and said, we'd be honoured. Lulu turned away then Nanny turned to the gang with a look, now then you lot, how do we get outta this mess?

Nanny with a nervous question, Phoenix do you still have your Tux? Honey, Bella do you have-? Before anything else could be said, Let's sit down and talk this down as we are all limited to time. Just then Aseena spoke, Can I make a suggestion, Nanny Sky? Quaint little Aseena spoke, if it's okay with Grandad. That's Phoenix by the way, this is how I'd like us all to imply. My Mother's collection of her elegant evening gowns, hats and jewellery, they are hidden away like a sad hibernation that has never been woken and they all long for the world to see. We shall all go back and bring life back of her memories, back at the Manor, room after room once filled with maids, a butler, the fires will glow and the sound of laughter will match the sound of room bells that used to ring,

Like in days of a butterfly hatching a young heart would bring all the walls to sing.

All eyes fell upon Phoenix as after listening to such words falling upon him, his authentic heart just sank; how could we not have such a night?

How could he turn down his own thoughts when the stars will shine so bright?

I shall call Margaret and Crawford to explain and express my sincere apologies and expect a house of mayhem and to make sure Crawford doesn't call the doctor to warn him that I've lost my mind.

And have a padded cell waiting for me; no, he wouldn't be that unkind.

After the call, the Chauffeur, Frank, made two trips and looked in the mirror at Phoenix for it was Margaret the governess of the house he had to face,

Then explaining what was to happen, she welcomed all with a rare embrace.

Led by Aseena, the looks of excitement flashed like lightning on a summer evening's storm,

Then with a nervous nod and hello to Crawford, Phoenix was trying to act norm.

With a shock to the ears and eyes, a smile from Crawford, Sir shall it be the white dinner jacket or the tux to suit the event?

Phoenix explained the evening, Then I shall leave it to your choice to make me a Gent.

By the way, Crawford, I have a young gent; will you fit him out as surely, we have his size?

As he, this is Buster- Crawford, he gave one stern look with that famous Crawford glance at the poor pup and then once again, up and down he looked and then Grampy spoke again, He will be escorting the ladies with me and we can only compromise,

Come with me young man, we shall start with the hair then down to the bow tie.

Buster didn't know how to respond but only sheer excitement and to be treated in this manner. What joy he thought and Crawford himself with a staring feeling, if he wasn't enjoying this enlightenment then he'd only be telling a lie.

By this time the girls were getting excited as just to think and imagine what was ahead of them. The optimistic eye of Margaret glanced at the apostolic eyes of Nanny Sky who was standing with the girls who were so excited that you could feel the walls of the house's happiness returning which brought back such joy, then the stern order of Margaret's, Right ladies, you all follow me.

All the girls couldn't help but feel the glow of love as they near enough flew up the stairs with Aseena leading and expressing her long-trapped feelings that she wanted– needed to release and then to feel the time was now to feel and be free.

They were up the stairs in a flash and then flew down the landing, led by Aseena as they reached the beautiful smoked oak door and then came to a halt with a puff and a pant as Margaret arrived with Nanny aside,

Then putting both paws in her apron, she pulled out a bundle of keys of all sizes, took the shiny elegant one out, put it in the keyhole and opened the door wide.

A minute's silence as curiosity entered all those who didn't know what to expect. As Margaret entered the room the rest stepped in to witness the beauty of such passionate colours of joy, love, that all you could hear were sighs, awes all around. Margaret once again took charge as fiddling through the keys again found the small one to open the cabinets made from the finest, elegant woods from all over the world. She opened them, then no one really could make a sound. For there in front of all were the choices of such beauty from the glittering shine of jewellery from all over the world.

Rings, necklaces, earrings made from diamonds, pearls, rubies, emeralds that you would want to pick out of the hand-carved cabinets and hold with both paws to embrace.

Whilst all stood there in glare at the sparkling, precious gems, Margaret walked to the adjoining wall where in the centre were the most elegant French doors made from every shade of glass with the patterns of flowers graced with all the birds harmonizing with flights of song. She just put her paws between the ones ajar and opened them to expose a sight of such beauty that no word from any language could explain. Dresses made from satin, silk and velvet, every type of cloth from around the world made to dress Queens and Princesses filled the room with such grace.

Tilly chose the silk which glistened like the love within one's array. The elegant shawl of lace carried off her shoulders; she just couldn't help but sway around with a flow.

Next Annie stepped out in satin and Auntie Emma couldn't help but raise her paws to her cheeks, my, look at my Cinderella, how she carried the dress with the grace of a spring's waterfall, with a velvet serpent's scarf with twists, as she walked with a glow.

Aseena graced the air within silk and satin and lace in a gown only a panther could carry, for she knew in a way tonight was her night and the media would talk and watch with an eagle's eye.

It is time for you three now, this was the stern voice of Margaret, Now let us see the flutter of dressing for you two, Emma and Sky, for the eyes will be on them with the angelic appearance and to answer the questions of who, what and why?

She must have been a beautiful woman, Margaret, Aseena's mother that is, came the question from Emma to have all these beautiful needs.

Yes, yes, she was and her husband, oh! He loved her so and when he would return from other countries, he would bring these beautiful gifts from his business trips from all over the seas.

As they picked, chose and dressed they too felt once again like innocent girls dressing for their first ball and to be able to choose from all these beautiful materials, oh what excitement!

The windows were left open and the local birds came in to help with the dressing and sing as the afternoon turned to early evening the maybugs hummed in tune and glowed with enlightenment.

This shall be our night, Mum; this came from Annie her daughter. I wish Darcy was here to see her daughter. She was at home looking after Tilly's father. Invites like this do not come every day do they Mum? That is why I say this can be our night so this shall be no masque, no shadows, no masquerade, to hide from. For whoever's love is for who their choices will be made.

Girls, girls, please, please your attention. The excitement was rising from all. Margaret spoke again, I've asked Teresa, Becky and Barbs the trio who run the finest hair salon there could be on the High Street in Deal. Teresa, the daughter from a family of smugglers that go back to when the town was no more than a few boats and sheds. Her dad's breed was of Scottish terriers of an ole hard race, ya, they smuggled, pillaged the world and then one day his breed anchored ashore the town of Deal and it is said his ancestor set eyes on his love for life. Marcia was her name. Oh, how she broke the hearts of many a wild dog of the traveling seas; she sang with a howling tone that calmed the wildest beasts out there. Then generations later in life her mother was singing one night in the Pink Flamingo on stage; there she was when she glanced across a half smoked-filled room. She set eyes on Tilly's father. She just gave one glance and the arrow, the arrow of love was bolted from the slender Afghan beauty, for it was love at first sight.

Mutt or Pedigree, large or small whatever the breed you were from you could not help but feel the presence of the bond between the two that night within that drinking kennel club. A private location on the front on Beach Street, an abode that carried tails from way back and one would have to be known before you were given an entry into that light.

Marcia with a voice for the ballads of the songs she sang to these snarling hard mongrels and all was a sound to charm any storm's fire. Her instincts saved and praised many a heart and that is what she became, a legend of the town.

Teresa followed in her mother's ways but with the gift of the touch of her paws not her voice, with the gift of seeing what beauty she could create out of another dog's coat and turn it into a satin gown.

At Teresa's, any beauties' gossip that was going on from around the town, if you didn't hear it from Teresa's located on the famous high street then it was not true. That salon goes way back to the days of when and where. Heleena, you know Lady Hamilton's doggie and side kick who travelled everywhere with her wherever that Admiral went, well she even used the Salon.

She was often seen being escorted by two big bulldogs, Nelson and Kitchanna, two big galloots you would not mess with to say the least, anyway she was kept in a cottage, you know one of those kennels in the courtyard of the stables behind the Clarendon Hotel where when the mist fell, if you didn't watch your back, it was over, gone.

Launa, Becka known to all will be arriving first for she will wash and provide the creation that would seduce the devil himself, she herself heard within seconds of the news as she's the owner of Laundromutt, explained where the grooming will begin to suit the finest of coating. When they were puppies, Becka played chase around the fishing boats with Tilly, Keeley and the other puppies of the town. They would then sit on the front combing each other's coats whilst chatting about their dreams for the future and how beautiful those dreams were, just like the feelings of the world's different seasons, a wonderful feeling to have and share.

Anyway, as soon has Margaret called and explained about everything that was going on, everything was laid down and put aside and then the call was made out for Betty and Barbs, a pair of feisty spaniels, whose clients- yes, their clients of then and now, were Her Majesty herself, the whole pack of the royal Corgis.

Some of the jealous stylists from here and there believed this story to this day were just ole porkies!

Yes, more banter which I'd say is 50-50 true or false you know Megan, like the beautiful long-haired Corgi. You know you will see her paw in paw with Max walking St Georges Garden. Well, she is the daughter of royalty. When the Queen herself was visiting the barracks here her head Corgi, Ivan, nicknamed Taffy had a major affair with Megan's mum, but it was kept top secret for some reason.

Still Nanny's thoughts opened again whilst talking the walk and she embraced all the emotions from every word that came to light.

The girls blossomed more from listening to the crosstalk whilst the guests got clipped, brushed and had their eyes brought out like the distant stars beyond shone so bright.

Tilly, please come I need to speak to you alone, Nanny spoke. Tilly's smile turned to be aware.

But her natural instinct was to trust Nanny for what was to be said was only words of care.

She looked into her eyes and said, look, myself and Phoenix have chatted about a concern of ours and we want to invite your mother and young Dylan to join us for tonight's grand ball. I called Darcy to explain what has happened in today's drama and she would love to come to this evening's event. So, we called Gene, my cousin and she will stay with your father till we return tonight.

But with Dylan. Only if it is your choice of feeling it is to be from your heart to call. Tilly's smiles turned to embrace a light that would brighten the dungeons of hell, her dreams in hours all becoming true.

Oh please, please Nanny Sky, I can only say from my heart how I want to thank you. With a full hug and a gleeful smile, she turned to the others who were trying not to nose. And with this news it felt like a dark winter's evening feeling of gloom had just turned new.

But they knew from the body language, it had to be something to expose.

Tilly, you must not call Dylan, don't, you must leave that to Phoenix to honour the invite for all the young hearts and old are joining together to bring in a glorious night. Nanny walked to the doorway with a content gesture that it was time for a wee tot of lady's lift as everyone's lips were now dry. She smiled at Phoenix to begin; he turned to the sofa, sat aside to lift the phone and made the call. When the other end answered and heard the invite the whole world for Dylan began to sing.

Crawford, Buster's brave question came out, you know Nanny when she mentioned Teresa's gang arriving? Well, the stories I hear from Uncle Popeye the boxer, Teresa's daddy and friends used to use Pinkie's parlour and Kane's curls where a lot of things went on. And by the sound of it, it just wasn't a clip or a brush down you could get; it was the full works whatever that means? But whoever went in came out with a song.

Buster, young tongues shouldn't blaspheme in such a manner, looking around no one was listening. Silently spoken, Ya-ya, Pinky, she ran it with an iron paw and yes, she does have another name.

Landan Lorraine was the other title and she ran it with her long-time lover, Kanga Kane, both English Bulldogs; you could leave there and think you were insane.

DFLS they first called them at first then they fell in love with the town's history as Kane was an ex-navy man, scalping all his fellow sailors all around.

Then they bought Number 1, Broad Street, not famous then but they built the landmark, made a name and stood their ground.

Ya, when they had some of their famous chums down from the back lane, Hoxton, you know the famous East Enders.

You could say every Staff-English-Bull-Terriers, Dobermans etc., who had a name was in Town would meet for those benders.

It was best to keep away really, I told myself as you didn't know who was who? Kane, Landy often invited me time and time again. Yes, yes, I admit I went once and my, what more can I say?

And maybe when you are older, I'll sit you down when I've got time, and I'll tell you all about those days and what happened along the way.

You know, like all about those old banters. Some say that it was history repeating itself. Little things like just one night a glance across a room she set eyes on her own lover, who remained that until this day. Who, Teresa? Yes, they worked there as the heads of grooming, yes, all those stunning beauties and all the beasts, but always held their own and were respected for all for their treats.

Now, ole Kane still clips at the barbers listening to the yarns and loves to reminisce in those he can trust.

Because you never know who's listening or asking what. Plus are they out prowling to bust?

Pinky, now she's mostly at her London pad where she loves listening to the proper banters, not the nasty tail taggers who always lost out and wanted a bit of that wild lust.

The barbers, yes, yes it will carry on with just its loyal regulars in company, talking and listening,

And then you had the public, you know, visitors peeping through the windows just to think of those wild days and what was going on in that house of sin.

Pinky's? Oh, my word, no way could that be happening now, the ole laggers with their nasty tongues would have it burnt to the ground,

And they knew their Smutty mutt husbands are safe now under their eye, as now it's all sound.

Margaret's appearance broke the silence, Gentleman, please the ladies will be dressed within the hour, your attire! Buster making a glance at Crawford sulking, startled, excited and as expected you can guess the rest.

Crawford sensed this, looking at him sideways, privately storing his knowledge, smiled with this and he will hold the rest until the time was right and out would come the cream of the story and the best.

Margaret's mellow mode sensed there was man's talk and knowing Crawford like she knows the cranks and grannies of the ole house she knew only too well he had the pup hooked.

Anytime, anywhere Crawford would call the new pup at the manor, Buster if he heard his name and he would be running to him and have him booked.

Just then the large sound of the door's charm bell rang through the hallway and harmonised the floor.

Crawford still smiling at the curiosity of Buster's thoughts made his way to the door.

Lifting the old latch and pulling the door ajar to find who has come to call, a glare a stare.

The slight, nervous figure of Dylan with Tilly's mum who stood there proud and feeling a bit aware.

Standing proud dressed to the hilt he held his own as he stared up at the respectable presence of Crawford the first intro to the household,

Evening sir and you may be? A slight pause then Dylan spoke, Mr Hamblin is expecting me and this is Tilly's mum. Just then Emma was on the balcony and just looking over seen her sister and called out, Darcy, we are up here. Buster noticed the arrival, Hi Dylan, this helped him relax more around the abode.

A glance once again glaring around the grand house one couldn't help but feel the love from the beauty of the past and present surroundings of true love that made the warmth so bright,

I shall escort you to the lounge, Sir, where Mr Hamblin awaits your arrival. Smiling walking with Buster at his side, both dressed to the hilt they smiled to lift the light.

A stern stop, Crawford halted, turned to the two, as to say wait here you pair then walked through the large open double-doored room to the gent who they'd soon come to admire.

The slender gent stood, glanced over, looked at who's to be introduced. Dylan looked over and just couldn't help to stand with admiration at the structure of the gent's attire.

Dylan looked sideways at Buster with a check out expression which they both knew was nerves and knew there was no danger but the feeling was of just normal tension, turning around and walking back to the doorway, Crawford spoke, Mr Hamblin will see you now, and with his hand waved him in, trying not to laugh as now there were two of them, and how did this come about? And how could he break their bond? This he just couldn't mention. Leaving the doorway, Crawford took a look back but couldn't help but bow his head with a straight smile that directed at Mr Hamblin who picked up on this and tried to look away from the grin.

He turned away, picked up his thoughts, looked at the pair and just knew where to begin.

Buster, still excited from his day of learning about fine dressage under the careful guidance of Crawford and Mr Hamblin's presence, his thoughts as a young pup's future changed with all what's happening and he embraced it with essence.

All excited again Buster couldn't help but speak first, Mr Hamblin, this is my friend Dylan. Looking at each other Mr Hamblin knew he'd got two young gents who would and want to listen.

Evening young man, proud and feeling welcomed, the barks, chit-chat began of what and when. Areas of careers they wanted to follow and all, then the Academy and acceptance was mentioned, well you can just imagine how the positive reaction was from Mr Hamblin to hear this and Dylan becoming a cadet.

Yes, yes, I know the Don- Lieutenant Harding- yes you can tell him I send my best wishes, yes, he repeated, tell him that we have met.

Smiling once more again at each other when Crawford appeared once again, Gentlemen the ladies are ready to be escorted please, you are all expected so please follow me to the Hall,

Just then Margaret was with Nanny standing there then making their way down the staircase, announced, Gentlemen the ladies are ready for the Ball.

Margaret, my Phoenix spoke, yes, yes, I know but Nanny and the girls talked me into it and someone has to keep you all in line, yes, I shall join you in this Gala, this ball, our SPHERE, now Crawford-before another word was said it was, No-no, I shall be here to protect the abode. Someone has to be here, keep the fort, protect the castle, I shall be here to hold.

Nanny's smile to Margaret, then to Phoenix, back and forth with a hearted understanding of their close bond,

It was just so close, warm that all they have been through their eternal friendship holds together and it feels so fond.

Nanny, Phoenix, Margaret, thinking and reminiscing of their younger days-when their thoughts turned to look to the top of the stair as the apparel of beauty in silk n satin. They just looked like swallows and falcons in their elegance of flight.

The ladies floated down the staircase as this will be the emergence of their beautiful night.

The ladies floated on as the memories of the clothing once worn through thoughts of love was back on show to give the world a belief, and to lift anyone's dreams of love, and to believe in it and its happiness will however beat its enemy.

One feeling could again believe in joy after being set in the presence of this feeling of excitement for within this small, close love they share within, will be for the whole world to see.

Teresa, she stood there one hand on her hip, the other on her lips took a step back and sternly looked at their creative beauty and, Oh yes, yes, it's precise.

Becka beside her, herself being a Mommy glanced with delight then smiled at the birds of paradise.

The hallway embellished and Nanny chatting away glimpsed over Dylan's shoulder and up to the top of the staircase,

Then her thoughts set on Dylan's eyes as to say, turn around and see the genetic of beauties that's open with their embrace.

Floating down the staircase, every eye was on the carved like statuettes bringing enlightenment once again to the whole house as how it used to be, when Tilly didn't want to give away her feelings of joy to her sweetheart who stood there dressed in clothing so fine.

Oh, her heart came through her smile then travelled through her body which then glowed through her view and to be in such company. And there in all Dylan's presence, there he stood, and how proud she felt to see him stand in line.

My, oh my, Aseena, were the first words from Phoenix, and out came his thoughts of his beloved loss when he lost his daughter and now right in front of him was his now granddaughter's beauty that was once carried by her mother had now matured into blossoms galore,

He presented himself and gave his paw out to greet her smile to see life once more my, how he felt just to adore.

This gave a break amongst the group as Tilly was next and Dylan's walk across the room to put his paw out to step her off the staircase,

All excited and with a nervous manner, this could only be greeted within one's beautiful embrace.

Smiles filled the hallway, even Crawford managed to break one, with his arms behind his back and he stood watching the house enlighten with feelings of warmth as of before.

The chauffeurs who were in their short chats looked on with

their polished carriages awaited at the door.

Boleros, shawls being placed over the smouldering shoulders of the ladies, first Phoenix's manner placed Nanny-Margaret's and the youngers looked on with a careful eye and then lifting off the hangers they gracefully carried the girls' wraps then placed them over the birds of paradise, wings.

With all what's going on the gossipy blackbird peeping through the window was ready to fly forward, oh yes with all these new tales she's flying off as she sings.

Boarding the cars and on their way, they couldn't help but show their excitement of thinking of what lies ahead. What is the evening going to bring? Only minutes away and we will all see.

They pulled up, doors being opened then just stepping out and embracing the air and the enlightenment of the lustre around the marquee.

Just outside nods started, curious gnaws and stares came from all angles as from where and who are these beauties? The excitement, you didn't know which way to turn.

But it was a blessing for this episode to begin and yes, the older ladies watched these young beauties being ogled by their ole men, then they looked back at their hubbies with a burn.

Paw in paw they entered the beauty of the evening's beginning, one just couldn't help but just glare around with happiness. Hello, Phoenix, evening Margaret. Well, Sky, it has been a long time hasn't it? Greetings coming from everywhere, turning to Phoenix once again, I'd never have known we'd know so many folks here Nanny, as Phoenix spoke,

Maybe the town heard we were all coming, That's why so many are here, came his reply, nervously said in a joke.

The youngsters really didn't know which way to turn as their adrenalin flowed from their eyes, but by the time this introduction ends the doors to the world's roads will open with a step for them and the eyes of windows to life will shine so bright. There was so much going on and of course a voice echoed out,

Darlings why sweeties you are here? A slanting glare at the girls, I do love the dresses, who or do I know the designer? By the way I'm to take the first walk, just then she spotted the media, Sorry dears but I got to go, looks came about laughing oh, take no notice of her, came a stern but harsh expression of words. It was the hostess, the lady of the night approached with a greeting smile, she glanced back over her shoulder at her daughter then forward again, looking with an understanding expression at her guests.

With that stern welcoming smile, she greeted them again, I'm so glad you could make it as to give such short notice and for you to honour our requests.

Come, come I've a table, it awaits your company to welcome you. Mrs McDonald then turned to lead the amplifying guests through with the onlooking curious crowd of VIPs, Margaret nodded with her impressive smile to Phoenix and Nanny could only bring a grin to them both as they followed their host, all along many guests looking on with curiosity to who are these guests being led by herself through the walk?

Only guests could enhance their thoughts with guesses, and then by the time the night was over, then, they the media, etc then they can all talk.

The table set into the VIP section, nods going again as Mrs McDonald waved her hand as to say this is your domain for this evening and this is your head waiter Giles, please do just sit and enjoy.

The personal capture of how they felt could only be said through their orated presence with the gents removing the ladies' shawls, taking their seats and then their first order being taken with all smiles to employ.

After settling down then looking around, Phoenix knowing the ole faces glanced about the VIP section to who was here. Waving with a slight lift of his paw and a nod from another table, nodding back he spoke to Nanny, why, look over to the left, there's Frank the Knash!

Buster heard the name mentioned and with his close interest with old ways said to Mr Hamblin, Sorry to interrupt but I couldn't help but hear the name but is that the name involved with the robbery of the Great Pedigree Chum Train Bash?

Trying not to look over, he replied, yes, yes, my boy do not look over but the ones all around him, the two big mutts, they're his sons Leo and Bobby, the other, the other big galoot, Teddy, yes his notorious brother, they say he's the one who wiped out the Alley Cat Gang, back in the east end.

Four on to one, mm? And you know whose territory that is and was, don't you? Whose name came up earlier when we spoke about Pinky's Parlour and who is her friend?

There's not a day that passes when arguments don't break out at every private Kennel club or a Speak-easy back-alley snug that it was them who pulled it off. Frank the Knash of Deal and Dean O'Dando of Hackney with both famous gangs they pulled off that famous raid.

But in respect to every Mongrel, Pedigree from the Ritz or corner basket, would hang their tongue out and no one would say a word whatever the grasses were offered to be paid.

And you know the well-known pair of detectives, Nosy Ned, the German Shepard and Mushy Martin the Golden Retriever from the famous department, the Mixed Mutt n Mix Squad.

They believed they had enough evidence to charge both gangs but when at the Old Bailey the verdict not guilty was given, nobody could believe it. All that work with other officers' paws from all over the world who gave a hand. In torment a few photos were sent of cans with the serial number from that stash were found empty next to a cocktail bar in a Brazillian beach bar and a few in Montecarlo Mardi Gras, the sales reference numbers on show, with a note saying, 'wish you were here', that was one sign of that wad.

Phoenix's expression spoke for itself as he was smiling from ear-ear. Now then, see the table next to them? That's Rosie Lee and Debbie Dee, the Cockney Cockers as they have always been known. They ran the Bull Dog Inn down in Camden Town, well they broke every heart from north-south. east-west, every dog who thought he was a swayer or a swagger tried to hit it off with them. And believe me, there was plenty of them with swish, waggly tails and the ones who saw themselves as the tough ones, ya? with their bobbed-off tails and pointed-up ears. They tried as well, but noup, no chance.

And of course, you've heard of the secret Diamonds of Deal, haven't you? Well, see the lady at the next table with a bunch of beauties? Well, that is Emma Emuzzia, the daughter of Bent Nose Bertie. Emma owns the wonderful store, Barkers on the high street. Well back in Mayfair, there were a few charmers to say the least and Bent Nose Bertie was one of them. At its peak, four main holdings owned by Sheiks in all had guests staying with them from all over the world and with them were their beauties parked on each paw. Well at the end of their stay, the whole of their assets disappeared, never to be seen again until now and then a beautiful Amulet worn at some exclusive do would turn up around a beauty's neck.

The old banters from the ole dogs from down Soho and so on. Well Dotty the Doberman married to Bernie the Pit Bull who ran the Dog and Duck, she still barks the banter and still swears to this day that Rosie carries a photo of Frank the Knash in her purse. They had something going they say from a long time ago. Anyway, then one day whilst Frank was out on his afternoon stroll through Hyde Park, he set his eyes on Valarie, the Afghan running off her leash with her hair flowing wild with the wind, you know what some still say? There and then it was love at first sight. And after that day in the park, he never set eyes on another doggie, and she never gave another a glance.

Debbie Dee fell for Oscar, a gentleman if there was ever one. He's the black cocker who flew in the cockpits with his owner in the day of the Spitfires in the Battle of Britain. He is such a gent and they too have a beautiful daughter by the name of Minnie who was born through their wonderful romance.

There was silence for a while for everyone's thoughts were on Rosie and her heart, was it broken or not? How does she feel now just glancing over at his table, would she want to still be at his side?

But are the memories enough of those wild, wonderful days of open doors that you never knew what was to come next? And life's offerings you took them with a pinch of salt and let it just glide.

It all changed when the girls burst out as they spotted the Director of Zakannie, all around the table three yards away, the girls were near enough screaming when Zak himself was there in his mum's designer outfits and he wore them well. Georgie, the daughter, yes, she was there as to say lights on and cameras should all be on me. Annie the mother noticed the media trying to click, click their presence but they were moved on straight away.

The son and daughter loved every bit of attention just like Birdie and all but the mother with her laid-back Italian mode of life's simple gifts wanted privacy and had the media and all brought down to bay.

Their Father, Merventi? Well, he's the brother of their sister company, Bonemani you know the one? A little more on the private side of the high customers' fashion needs.

The public found it hard to believe when they announced their background, and when they came to light. Italian yes, but the town's name? Bolognese. Mm, I thought that was a sauce not a place or a breed.

Margaret tapped Nanny; you know that generation both thinking the same. Why isn't the father Merventi sat with the family mm? A bit of a player in his day I've heard. Still is, that's where the boy gets it from, as they say, like father like son.

Valeciehi they say was her name, a beauty from a village high in the hills where the grapes grow to make the wines of the world sparkle and taste like the juices from heaven. Her father's from the ole families. You know the ole ways. They say he had warned him look after my Princess, my daughter or you're done.

With all what was going on, lights, flashes, and all, Zac-looking around just stopped and stared when he set his hunting eyes on who do think?

Yes, Aseena of course and within this mass group of the flamboyant names, with the class of the richest, most famous involved in the fashion world all watching each other's styles, movements, eyes on everything of importance, they all knew it was Aseena's turn to shine and will she be the new face? They will be after her to promote their attire and one's mind has to be thinking as you did not have time to blink.

Annileana, the mother with her eyes like a hawk took a glance in the direction of who he was looking at. What had caught his eye? But she herself couldn't help but stare at the natural beauty of Aseena's presence; no one really could keep from glaring for who is she? Who's her agent? All the questions from the Fashion world were out and who can answer these? Either way everyone knew there was a new star on the walk.

Ladies and Gentlemen, please take your seats as the show is about to begin. The hustles and the bustles of the starlit show opened with a feeling of Gladiators walking into an arena all feeling it is my day today. The announcer introducing the next models of whose company's trendy styles will take the awards tonight, and at the after-dinner party, whose designs will be all the talk?

Oh, how the night flashed by like an electrical storm across the open African plains. Mouths gasped open whilst viewing another's style, the girls still in a whirl with happiness of witnessing the whole essence of the night. Keeley spoke, Tilly just think this happens every day and night over and over again. Wow, what do you think and feel? Could you handle it? No way. I love this introduction and what a sight to see and feel but- Just then a flash of lights and the blare of music started; another of the top breeds hit the catwalk like a King or a Queen walking down the Royal Aisle to be crowned,

and if the audience, the media, everything and everyone that could move didn't respond to a designer's clobber on show, you know if the crowd were not standing, roaring and applauding your name, then the strutty head honchos would stomp like a spoilt brat then he or she would stand all day and sort of smile was given and frowned.

A stern voice spoke out, is everything to your liking may I ask? Phoenix, the gentleman that he is, stood up and Dylan watching him like a hawk, stood as well. It's the host, Mrs McDonald checking in on her guests. Yes, yes, I must say. She smiling had one thing on her mind and you know what that was? A quick glance at Aseena with a nod and followed by a smile she then concentrated on her table guests, and who may this handsome youngster be? Tilly smiling at this comment looked into Dylan's thoughts and proudly blushed for now the truth of him in her presence was known.

A shake up came then with a slight tremor of an earthquake. A stampede of paws from you guessed it, Birdie. She'd just come off the catwalk with the stylists and all, still trying to work on her. Reporters, viewers flashing their lenses, Wide eyed Winston, or Frenchie he's also known as, with tell-tale Anginatina the terrier at his side jabbing down anything she could comment on. The pair of them worked as free agents to the main Magazines, The Bitch, The Cat Natter, A Dog's Coating, yes you name them; if the price was right, they would sell any story to the highest bidder and the gossip was then all over the media to be shown.

Darlings, were you watching? Did you see me? If anything, it was a bit of a let off as it broke the chit-chat as just then she was called back to the walk, they all started to laugh amongst themselves including her mother as they all knew that was Birdie's way and she wasn't going to change.

Birdie's group skid-dawdled back to the stage all in all and left everyone with a smile for you could only laugh at this manner as there was no harm in many ways; it's just that's the way her world was and for whoever was in this business if you took it too hard then it was time in life to make an exchange.

Jamie's Jostles, the jean specialist, his rig-up was next, and the girls were in their element again, as who was walking the strip but Dashing Dean who for the past season took the walk by storm.

Many in the business of the rag trade often gaggled on that DD as he was known and was actually Jamie's son, oh really? Yes, he is, it's a fact and his mum of course is Anginatina, you know the one? She's married to Tramp's Tailors director Boris the Bloodhound. But of course, the scandal of gossip in this bizzo was known to everyone as just norm.

Right, how's everyone feeling? This came from Margaret's stern voice as she had to admit this had been such an experience and had done her the world of good to break the build-up of everyday life at the Manor and meeting up with Nanny as well.

It's been a godsend, and just to think all this began over a stroll along the front, and now where will it end? I can't see it forever ending as it's only brought happiness to this new bond of friends, to where their whole world has become the stage.

And what lay ahead of the roads to their future world will only grow from day to day with this intro to a world of adventure whilst others may just want to take it day to day with simple age.

The final flash of hosting the final catwalk was to show the wares of the House of Dane's formal and evening dress. This really brought out the element of Margaret and Nanny's smiles as to embrace the joy and enthusiasm of such designs of beauty which brought out the feelings of clothing that can walk and talk for itsself and who was to carry it to its value? The gathering of their evening's experience in this trade of such competition so far was just beyond their thoughts were, as said, this runs on every day to reach its element of the fashions that are new. The next announcement from Giles as he approached the table was, Please, ladies and gentleman follow me as dinner will be served in a short while. They all looked at each other again as to reach their evening's joyous next step as to feel and say what next?

They were led into a large room full of every character there could possibly be out there. It was a sort of social gathering and an introduction one could say before the main dinner was to be served. Phoenix gave a pleasant happy smile to Miss Harris, or Margaret may we say, which was returned openly from their own mind.

They have witnessed so much through this world together that life's whole chapter could be written about and around them. And for this evening's offering to joy has done the world of good to all, Sir, Lieutenant is it really you? Startled by the voice behind him he turned around to witness a huge ageing structure of a dog.

Well, Scooby, Sir, was the reply. They just looked at each other with a joy of life's memories and one said how long has it been my friend? The others looked at the bond they were sharing but to be honest the youngsters looked on to say to each other, what is his kind?

Scooby, a huge half Rottweiler and half Bull mastiff and still at his age a fine structure with a gentleness that life could offer just through his smile. He then introduced his wife, Sir this is my wife, Elsie. I've heard a lot about you Ma'am, was the response said with a gentle look. She turned and gave a glance at her husband with a oh yes what have you been saying? But she knew as from the day she set eyes on him, he couldn't say anything bad.

There was never any badness in one's tone as it just was not in their hearts, there was a wonderful essence that the guests witnessed through these friends lives' experiences. And how did you meet and how do you know of each other? Came a question from Dylan's curious mind. I served under the Lieutenant, came the answer before anyone could blink. This brought Buster's ears up as once again anything to do with the manner of the stories of war, then he had to know how or what had happened. Yes, we went through the battle of the Boniezers, in Dongolia. What, you were there, Sir? Yes, we were with that group that rescued the village of Dogglelar and if there was an ending to anything in a saga in one's life, that battle when it was over, I was glad.

Please, follow me, Giles spoke again. Giles, Grandad asked with a glare, Sir, would it be possible for this couple to join us at our table? I'll pay. No, Sir, there's no need to say that but yes, yes, I always put side chairs to each table just in case. Would you care to join us Scooby? He looked at his wife and the smile on her face answered the question. They followed in with the flow of well-being.

Now what brings you here Scoops? That was the nickname of the big fella. Well, Polly and Jarvis, Polly is our daughter who owns the restaurant the Whip-it-up and they are doing the high catering dishes here tonight. Tilly couldn't resist but to speak as she was listening. What the Whip-it-up as it's the trendiest doghouse there is in Soho.

Yes, my dear that's our daughters, named after her mother's breed, of course the slender side of us. Elsie being a Whippet with her slender figure, Polly took after her, looking at the size of Scooby it was a godsend for a girl.

Oh, how the evening flowed with so much joy, everyone shared their views of this or that. The food, you name it, it just didn't stop from bringing total delight to all. Then after dinner, another announcement was called to light, all snouts and ears were up, Ladies and Gentlemen, will you all join me for the final part of the evening, please join me at the grand ball where we can all waltz and whirl.

The ball was as grand as the word could say and they danced as the bands played to suit everyone's play, oh how it made the evening even more to be full of grace, beauty, whatever beautiful word you wanted to say it fitted the ball, then once again the host approached with the question, Sir, Madam I hope it was to your liking? Mr McDonald wasn't sure who was the wife of the Lieutenant. If there was one. But Margaret seemed to be at his side.

And she replied, Yes, yes thank you for the invite it has been as perfect as to say. Sir, may I ask a direct question to you as to do with the company I hold? It would be a great honour for me and my team to offer a photo shoot for the young lady to introduce her to our fashions within and wear ours with pride.

He turned to Margaret who now had Nanny beside her as well as if to say how shall I answer this? The ladies turned to each other and then back to the host and said this is fine by us, but it is the young lady you need to ask now. You do not mind if I approach her as I would only do this with your consent? Yes, you may and with good courses you must say as what words you use in this manner to the young lasses, the words you use must come with good thoughts and not nonsense to fill them with delight. Thank you, Sir, ladies you can trust my heart as this is something I am aware of and what to say.

As her thoughts came to her heart and mind she thought of way back in her life the promises she was offered in this business that had been the ruin or the making of many of beauties of the past in this world of glamour. She was close to taking the wrong road when she herself was taken under a good person's wing and saved her from the heartbreak of promising lies. From that day, she then promised to protect the innocent models that would be exposed and she had done so to this day.

She turned with a modest gesture and then from the top honchos she made her way across the floor to where the young girls stood in their dresses of beauty and they stood as proud as they glistened and shone like stars on a summer's night.

Aseena, yes mam, was her nervous yet excited reply, Tilly holding her paw as the two youngsters shyly looked at each other, can we speak? I've spoken to your grandfather to ask permission to speak to you openly as I feel this was right. Well, myself and my designers have agreed that we would like to invite you and a friend to a photo shoot as we feel that you have everything we want in the new faces to address our clothing's name to make it equal in every manner to express its beauty in its natural ways and you have the beauty to show it as dawn brings out the morning's breath of a new daylight.

Her Grandfather was looking over with a careful eye but his instincts were clear and relaxed as he knew she was in safe paws. She looked around and you could sense the body language of her feelings and smile. Yes Mrs McDonald, yes, I would love to, as long as Tilly can come with me? Of course, she can, of course, we will make arrangements and will notify you ASAP and, on that day, we will have a car sent to you and the possibility of staying two nights or so. It depends on how many shoots there will be, okay?

With this Mrs McDonald turned to answer a call from another guest and just said, Enjoy the evening, ladies, enjoy. The two just smiled with such glee that made the whole room shine with their body blossom of happiness. Let's dance, Tilly, come let's dance. The rest of the evening was something that you would only read about in fairy tales, happiness and security could be here and it could be in the palm of their paws to begin.

They danced to the music that charmed the beauty of the ball. Even Margaret's defences came down as she waltzed with Phoenix, the champagne flowed like a shower in springtime, each song that came up they couldn't help but return to the floor and then the announcement came, Ladies and gentlemen please can we put our paws together for the host and the staff of the night and for the grand hard work of putting such an evening together, please. With this everyone stood and clapped until there was the echo of joy all about.

Now the conductor spoke, And for the last dance please take your partner to the floor. Everyone around the table rose. Tilly's eyes lit up as Dylan escorted her to the floor as they walked behind Phoenix escorting Margaret, and the music brought them into the final bow and this evening would forever be in their hearts and with this they would always sing.

As being escorted to the main doors there were barks and banters, including hugs to embrace a wonderful evening, were all around, then of course those words were in the air, Darlings, darlings how did you like my show? Yes, it was Birdie, wanting and seeking all the attention and getting it, she took a little glance at Aseena as she had seen her mother pass her something after her evening's embrace. What could it be she thought? But there was no badness in her heart just a spoilt girl in all.

Mrs McDonald's sights really couldn't help but watch every move Aseena made as it was like a spring flower just rising after a winter's sleep. Phoenix strolled the hallway to thank everyone he knew and to the delight gathered everyone together as the youngsters were still excited and barking away. Margaret, her name was called out, the car's over here, she then gave everyone the orderly bark and they made their last move. Phoenix looked once more to the hostess and with this they waved to say everything will be fine and with this they left to the sound of an array of birds singing a lullaby to say oh what a wonderful evening and goodnight.

The chauffer smiling with a glance at the mirror watching the pups play, they just could not stop from yelping on about who they met. And what they saw. Never in a century would they have thought this would happen to them. But it had and now where will this path lead them? What adventures, what stories will they tell in their later days of what happened to them whilst just one day out strolling? Maybe one day they will talk to their own grand pups all about this saga. The thoughts were non-stop but no one knew really that after tonight their lives would never be the same within this life's flight.

The next morning arrived and the girls rose from their baskets with delight and made their way into the kitchen where Bongo the Bulldog was trying to separate the huge bones ready for the annual chew for the old friends of Phoenix's pride. They had a monthly meeting at the Manor to shoot their old banters of yester years. He gave a morning nod to Aseena and her guests who were all now sat about the table. With so much adrenaline going on with the dresses and so on it was best for all to stay at the manor last night.

Morning, ladies, did you sleep well or did you sleep at all with all that drama last night? The young pups just smiled at each other and then back at Margaret, who of course was back into her actions and spoke, You girls must be hungry? With this they sat down and yes, off they started again about the last night's event. It is only natural this was to be and Margaret let about their banter.

So, young ladies, you have been invited to a shoot then? When will this be may I ask? I'm not certain but I think it will be at the end of the month came the reply spoken with excitement once again.

Keeley spoke all excited, So you are going to London for a weekend then? Yes, and I just can't wait. At this time, Phoenix strolled back in through the doorway with his elegant smile. London did I hear? Yes, yes grandad, that is where the photo invite will be. Margaret looked over her glasses at his reaction and paused for a while as he caught her look. He knew it was a please keep quiet look and he just smiled to himself with his thoughts within and would speak of the question later in the day.

Breakfast, Sir? came a stern look over her glasses again. She placed his bowl down upon the proud old worn table with his slightly warm milk just the way he liked it. Are you two going to training classes today? Keeley asked her cousin. Are you on the course as well, young lady? Grandad wasn't aware Tilly was at studies as well. Yes, I am she replied a little nervously. We are both at the Royal Academy of the Police and Army College. This is my and Dylan's dream to become bomb and terrorist sniffers for the masters section and if we graduate from the scent and smell course, we will be on to the next step to reaching our dreams. But the main thing is we graduate from the finest college there is in the land for these courses and we are on it.

Yes Granddad, you don't mind me calling you Grandad do you? We are now onto the underground phase and it is really interesting to capture the difference of scents below, you would never imagine what scent belongs to what if you were not aware and the only way to learn is from the ones who have been through all this from the past and there is no better lecturer in this field than who they were being taught by.

They have the history from wars of the world under forests of Burma to the cold depth of the Falklands etc, etc where you could not imagine scents could be or come from. But you could not help to ask, well how this scent could come from this or that? That is what the lecturers were out scouting for, who will ask the proper questions that one day may save the lives of so many innocent comrades and the public walkers and ramblers lives will be kept safe. One's instinct has kept others alive with passing on their skills that they learnt themselves and with all this being taught with eyes and ears up with fascination would one day be the saver of many and can live a life of happiness along one's way.

Tilly spoke, How did you sleep, Dylan, last night? I slept in the guest parlour but I silently popped down to the under kitchen where Bongo and Bozso and many of the staff would gather after a long day's brass and the scents that flowed around the room from every corner would fill any contented beast's ease and thoughts. I popped down there as many of the old staff were friends of Dylan's father who helped run the feeding chambers at hard times and was well loved by all.

They looked at Dylan in a way as to see if he carried his father's instincts. As well as working down the mines he too was a member of the anti-sniffers squad and what a member he was. Anyway, he sneaked down the staircase in silence as he too could not hold onto his tongue of what he witnessed on the night on the town. He embraced the talk to the pack huddled around the open fire where centuries of all breeds talked of hunts, etc, etc and now he himself told the banter with eyes staring and ears pointing up.

So many questions of the town's behaviour were discussed. Lads, you name them they were there, the whole evening's action was all mentioned. It is hard to believe that a show of that line would attract such interest and I learnt so much of what power is about when known and who you know. Crazy just crazy.

Bozso got up to stretch his long old legs and asked, By the way how is your father doing? He's fine, Bozso, and how come you were invited to this VIP gathering in the first place, Dylan? Well, we were out walking, and it all came about when Aseena and Tilly just by walking along the front only that morning got introduced to some new folk and just like that they become great friends and the excitement of meeting, chatting built up and the next minute they were invited to the evening's event. Still if only they knew what that night was going to bring into their lives was no one's belief. Put it this way with who was there, and who knows who, you could say it all still seemed hazy.

Tilly mentioned it then to Grandad, Last night we mentioned to Aseena that it is our open day each Monday and she has an interest in our course and kept mentioning it to us so I spoke to Dylan that I may ask her to come along today. So, early this morning I reminded her and she still wants to come along if that is okay with you? Of course, why not? Was his reply. We have to go home to pick our bags up with our college tack and then head off for the day. We need to be there prompt on time or else!

Grandad laughed out loud with memories of being a graduate and the discipline set, so he then said, When you are ready, I will get Henson the other driver to take you home and pick your stuff up and drop you kids off as it is on our way to the market stores if that is all right with you? Of course, that would be perfect. Out they passed and headed over to pick up their attire.

Out of the car they hurried, in through the door, Hi Mum, Dad. A run around picking their stuff up and back out of the front door with, Bye Mum, call.

The day passed on and the speeches and all went ahead but the thing that really set Aseena's heart pacing was how to pick up a scent of distress under the stress of action. There were 11 objects put in different areas of danger and in action it could blow the whole neighbourhood apart. Rupert, the tall, elegant Rhodesian Ridgeback was on the floor pressing his scented snout could not help but notice Aseena's beauty and presence and like a prince on a day of a jubilee, he had to put an extra show on and now and then gave a peek over to who was watching. And sure, enough it was she.

Applause came from all around as he got the main object and gave it an extra point to say, Here it is everyone. Oh, how dashing he was as he strutted over to the lecturer's stand with congrats coming from there as well. But in reality, he knew Dylan was aside there watching on with his guest. Wiping down the sweat and sipping on a cold bowl of water, he looked aside to sort of say, Oh, hello, Dylan, I did not see you there, and straight away he coped it on. Hello, Tilly, how was your scent card results from the last test? Looking a little confused she coped it on as well. They were better than I thought, Rupert, and by the way this is my friend, Aseena, she as an interest in our topic and wanted to see what all the training was about so we have brought her here today to see for herself in reality, after we discussed so much last night at the banquet we were at. So, it was great for us to have time to bring her along.

Just then the large sound of the class was over by the famous ringing of the historical bell.

Well, what are your thoughts on this morning's introduction, Aseena? Gosh you need to be aware, alert every second of the day, haven't you? It is not just your life at stake, came Dylan's reply but everyone and everything about, and around you. You let your snout down and it is over. You cannot react or over-think as it can take the main scent of what you are looking for away. There are things you would not discuss with a friend in today's lesson, Oh, by the way we were looking for a bomb of a certain make, model. How can you explain that to someone? They would honestly think you have lost the plot.

Tilly took a glance at Aseena's response to the statement just made and she kept looking back at Dylan with a, well where did that come from glee. But it is the truth, one error and it is all over; would you like to come again, Aseena, as we would have to put your paw mark down as it would be a check-up and recording of course. Oh yes, please do so, I would love to see the reaction of one's thoughts of within team working across the towns or out in the wilds. It must be forever interesting as to what will one learn next in such awareness of all around you and what is there. Change the subject, Aseena. I think also there could be someone else with his ears up in the air listening for your reply so he could give you all his charming talk and best shot.

Back at the house, the excitement of the day's adventure came out the second they entered. And how was your day? It was a question from Margaret as this was new to her and her concern was understandably there. Grandad, well he knew Margaret had to know what is going on. And a slight open laughter came from Grandad as he could not hold his enjoyment of his type of humour. You would never believe what I witnessed and- just before she could ramble on, Grandad in his slender stand spoke, The post this morning, well, we had to sign for one addressed to you, Aseena.

Looking confused- she was more innocent really than confused as she clasped it in her paws and placed it beside her. Grandad knew what it was, as a call from a certain lady that came to him regarding his granddaughter and it was very professional and caring to do it this way but the caller knew well which way to talk, if she's out to get what she wants and once again she's someone who does not listen to the no.

Yes, the others were looking on as they were as curious as Aseena to know what it held inside the sealed envelope tied with a ribbon of approval and that alone was enough to make thoughts flow into a matter of, open it! They settled a while and just talked about the adventurous day at the base and of course the Major listened and watched the body language of his granddaughter, to see if there was interest in the course. Yes, he did see it, as she just flowed with curiosity of how to pick the certain scent up and how important that one sniff meant to making the right move that would save so many lives and assist in stopping badness spreading through everyday ways of living.

He was just going to speak on the thought of asking, would you like me to talk to the college? When Margaret entered with the orderly word of dinner as she told the guests to return to the house after college to have dinner before going home. Margaret looked on to him with that famous glance. So, he stopped again with thoughts of just let her sleep and think, as with her mind running with so much going on and then she herself can answer which road will be the way to go.

Morning arrived and yes of course a curious vibe flowed around the walls that carried historical ups and downs that made the beautiful current of feelings through the everyday pattern of the abode. Aseena had time to have a little think to herself on all that had happened in this short time, but the main concern and interest was of course the letter. Everyone's thoughts were, okay but what is in that letter?

Aseena entered the warmth of the kitchen and around the table-counter the looks back and forth were, tell us Aseena! And out it came. I've had an invite from the studio for a four-day shoot, everyone. Jumps of excitement were all about and of course, concern and worry from the elderly and then the stern look from Margaret came from over her magical glasses whilst dishing up, as don't forget she had been Aseena's mother, carer, everything imaginable in her life she had been there for her and now this chapter to begin, well what can one say but the famous sentence-words from Margaret, Aseena, I'd like to talk to you after breakfast, please.

Aseena glanced over to her Grampy for a backup plan of some sort. But even Phoenix dared not question this order as you could call it as he himself had been ordered to one of these one-on-one meetings. So, he the master of the house, no way would he dare say a word so whilst the plates and so on were being taken to the washing station, looks were cast over each other's shoulders.

Aseena knew where she had to go, for all her life up or down, good or bad news was discussed in the front room as that was the heart of any memorial times of discussion that for some reason ended up clearing any unwelcomely words that passed through the air.

Leaving the warmth of the ever-loving kitchen, the eyes of her grandfather looked over with a concerned but a fun stare at Aseena and tried his best not to laugh so he gently turned away pretending that someone was calling for his advice on some matter. As he knew well, Aseena was to ask does he know what the call up was about? But being the wise ole gent he just gave her a curious nod of good luck.

She made her way down the corridor with looks from staff in all with, yes, the nods of good luck came from all around. Margaret made her way through one of the side exits that for many years were used for secret escapes from the dark side of history's tales in all but they did lead from room to room in a quarter of the time.

Standing stern with herself she straightened herself up, took a deep breath then knocking on the door of the front room she heard Margaret's, Come in, orderly call, and then just letting herself in she was welcomed with the soft-hearted voice that the whole world loved of Daisy, Margaret's sister. Her soft black velvet coat echoed the presence of her voice to everyone she met that stayed within their hearts forever. Hello, my love, were her first words that brought such a smile to Aseena's heart and thoughts that all worries were relieved with the greetings.

Aseena's front paws came out to be clasped by Daisy, Come, come let's talk. Oh, the feeling of just being in Daisy's company was a joy and as they sat, Margaret spoke, I've asked Daisy to come and discuss her career with you, Aseena, for as you know she walked the catwalks from London to New York and who could advise you more on how to take the right road, as you know Daisy talked and walked it.

I just want the best my dear were Margaret's nervous words as she did not want Aseena to feel she was imposing too much and she wasn't, it was just her nature to feel she needed to protect her so in every way. My dear Sis tells me of the invite you have now after the success of the feedback from the party the other night. It is from Katie McDonald herself then? That was the next question asked. As soon as her name was mentioned to me my thoughts came about. You have the whole world ahead of you with a person like that at your reins, Aseena, but do not cross her in any manner, promise me that? Everything that is put in front of you must be read and explained to you, okay, and most of all signed with witnesses and all proof will be shown.

Now, stand up for me and pose in your own style. These were the gentle, orderly words from Auntie Daisy. Daisy's presence could not have been better for how Aseena's feelings were running. I sensed and prayed to myself this would happen, were Margaret's joyful thoughts and one howl in the winds with a message to Daisy worked. Margaret looked across to her sister just with a thank you smile and it was returned with a no problem nod.

Aseena please, when you are just going to step backwards lift your heel it will give you a better straight pose, please. It had started already the advice as with both paws on her hips like it comes naturally to the dominant ones, Daisy kept sending out orders as to how to walk and strut to entice that walk along in front of the onlookers who want and will be out to criticize anything they can pick up on. It was almost too clear to see this natural bond and understanding as of Daisy's history in this hard, beautiful choice of work so the next question will be, will Daisy be joining Aseena on this entry to the modelling world? Plus, how far will it go? And what would be the host's reaction when setting eyes on Daisy, walking through the doors of her own showroom? The beauty that walked away from her so many years ago and did it her way to reach the catwalks' peak where for many a year her name just glistened with beauty.

Just then Pepper, Daisy's long-time lover came through the doorway, he, too carried a story of his own. A tough character known in every port of the world but once again he too had eyes for only one. From the day he set eyes on Daisy his joy and love had just grown.

The next morning arrived and all was at bay. Aseena's first words were to say thank you Margaret, thank you for what you did, this was embraced with a hug of such feelings that filled the room. I've spoken to Tilly to explain that I've asked Auntie Daisy to attend us to London and she is even more excited than I am. I brought it up to Aunt Daisy the first chance I got and without a doubt Daisy took my offer. She will be staying at her friend's in Convent Garden, oh that would be Nadia the Irish red terrier.

These were the words spoken from Margaret explaining that it's her sister's best friend who modelled with her and whose cousin lives at the Bungalow on the front, you know where Meana raises her feisty daughter Poppy, they too are involved in the modelling world and mainly sheepskin, cashmere and the tweed attire for the wealthy that can afford that kind of haute couture you know. They are very close knit with whom they call Nanny and Nicky Bampie who run and hold the reins of that domain as they chose the Bungalow many years ago and built it into their own castle, the Happy Keep it is known with a history as long a Great Dane's leg.

Meana kept her Irish roots of heart from the land to explain what natural talents can offer to the clothing world. You know wool and all the rest of wear and tear that looked the part at shoots, hunts, gymkhanas and all the balls and dances, the body of a good strong dog showed the rest and sold itself, so if you looked at all her creations, all from the heart, and then looked at Poppy; another heart breaker with dogs from all over the world lining up trying and pleading with her for a date and with the words, Oh, please, just one date I beg.

A week or so passed and Nanny Sky was out walking with her human partner, Shelly, and they popped in to visit Darcie and on entering through the door they met Tilly first. Oh, hello my love, how are you Tilly, with all this commotion going on? How have you been feeling? It is a huge change that will affect every part of your body, your thoughts and your emotional depth opens with excitement. These were the words spoken by Shelly whose whole life was around childhood of all breeds as she was the midwife at the barracks for the base's horses and dogs.

She noticed then Emma's presence when she popped into the kitchen as she had a batch of leeks given to her from the allotments whilst passing and she thought who would want them? Do you want these, Emma? Oh, thank you were the words coming from yet another happy flow throughout the kitchen. By the way, Tilly, how is that young handsome pup of yours doing? He is doing really well, Nanny; Dylan's been called again to meet the board of control of the bomb squad and this is not even halfway into him qualifying, Nanny. It all seems to be happening so fast, were the excited words from Tilly. And you know with all his hard work it will show.

Turning back around she spoke again, I'm meeting your mother this morning, Tilly, to go over the dogs' brush project. What's that? asked Keeley curiously as she was visiting the house of joy. This is what they called the house where Tilly and generations had been raised. Nanny Sky then carried on telling Keeley, Oh, it's a small very successful cleaning company that we set up to give the best clean overs for the high-end kennels and apartments owned by the wealthy business successors living here now. We kept the name quiet as it was our choice to do so. Well, they are now asking us to consider managing their locations to tenants and all as they now have our full trust and it is they who approached us. It is a wonderful feeling to have this and now we will discuss it this morning to see if we want to advance in this stage.

A little silence and thoughts from Nanny Sky and then, Tilly would you come along to the meeting as you always discuss the layout of baskets in general and for you to look at some of these places for us if we go ahead; that is maybe you can consider a managing position? I'd be honoured, Nanny Sky and where will you be meeting Mum? It will be at the Forrester's Rib and Bone Café-bar on the front of Beach Street as they want us to carry on our contract with them and the owner, Maggie the Irish Miniature Bull Terrier has praised us and other landlords in the town they want to be introduced to us so it has just come together that the Forrester's is the ideal spot to meet at and we can discuss the matter to see if it is time to make the business grow.

There is so much going on with so many positive views, Nanny, and after so many years of just holding out with visions it is now coming together to all who believed in the light for the future here, anyway we are discussing it to go forward. So much has happened in such a short time and who could have seen this coming with Aseena and all? Let us just keep in this positive manner and outlook, okay?

There was a message sent by the Howling Bark, a local newspaper, one of the reporters would be popping in as she has just been told that Nanny Sky mentioned the meeting at The Foresters so she sent it by bat with a plea, can she sit in on the meeting? She will come here first and you can take a stroll up along the way and have a mummy chit-chat.

A rat-a-tat on the door and it was the lady herself and she arrived with a smile. Then Dylan arrived with all this chaos going on; he just popped in and was welcomed with a, Good morning, young man. Dylan was on his way to the barracks and popped in to see his sweetheart, Tilly. Molly's here, the reporter that is, I can't stay as I'm a little late. He then shouted back to Tilly, I'll see you tonight! And off he scarpered with a rapture.

Morning my love, you are blossoming like a flower in spring's finest morning, Tilly. How have you been? These were the words from Lilly, a beauty from Spain's troubled times of the rebellion of the attack from the wolf packs of the dark mountains that invaded all the beautiful villages of the southern ways of music, love and life that Lilly's parents stood to guard and lost their lives by doing so. Lilly was only a puppy when she was found and the plan was, she'd be smuggled out by a pair of shepherds and their sheepdog, Mario was his name.

They were to meet a boat at the Lake of Light that would lead them onto the link to the English Channel and then their destiny was to meet the fishermen at the border of France who were to smuggle her out to Kent with six other puppies where they were to be met to start a new life. Well at the lake they were ambushed by the nasty Dogfish Gang who raped and pillaged anyone or anything that moved. Anyway, it was said that the whole lot were wiped out and a small raft of reeds she fell upon floated her away and the current took her out and drifted by fate, to safety.

A week later, a lady was walking along the shingles off the Pier in Deal and heard a strange weeping in a bundle of mixed odds and ends the tide had brought in and there she was. She carefully wrapped her in her coat and led her away to safety where she has been ever since. Lilly and Tilly have been lifelong friends with so much they have shared and now another amazing part of life begins with an introduction to another chapter.

Lilly's mummy is Tilly's godmother so you can always feel and gather the bond that is there between them. So, when out strolling along the front and passing the Pier, Lilly stops and silently says a little thank you to a location, she has always been very close to in her heart. When walking past the Pier and on along the front you just can't help but gaze with thought of how once again the banters of the days that these historical buildings kept so many secrets within their walls. It is just a lovely way to unwind one's thoughts and mind.

They reached the Forrester's and just strolled in to the welcome of all the landlords and so on and within minutes it was business talk. Margaret introduced Darcie and so it just flowed into chit-chat of what was necessary and expected and what was vice-versa. It was just natural to the way one would want a meeting to go with just using common sense, without some ass rabbiting on about this and that with nonsense talk from ones behind.

Right, it's been a pleasure to meet you all. These were the words spoken as Darcie stood up. If you all put your cards and names down here with our Assistant Manager, Lilly, we can organise a visit to see what has to be cleaned and managed to your liking and our service will begin from there, if that suits everyone? Thank you, Margaret, were Darcy's next words, and left them to it as you know what landlords are all about don't you?

Out they walked, and whilst looking about they couldn't help but notice James the Greyhound; another one who fell for a local gal here. He was sent here from the northern land for a big race and set his eyes on a beautiful, full bloomed Lurcher named Louisa. Once he saw her, they said it boosted his stamina and ego so much that they reckon it was the best race ever as he outraced every dog by four lengths in all!

He told his owner, I've done enough for you over these years and now it is my time to walk away and that was many years ago. He is now the local bookie who also owns The Beer and Bone where Tilly's father used to drink and a well-known watering hole that goes way back to the Black Shuck Days. Many, many a banter of the passing hoards from the ships afloat were talked over a beer and a bone, that's where it got its name from, I think. It was said that there was a secret tunnel that led straight under the Black Pig.

You know the butchers off the high street, opposite St George's church where all the big bones and cuts of the finest steaks are supplied from? The hound dog who runs and owns it, she is the seventh generation you know and she has another litter of puppies that are in practice to follow her path in butchery. Anyway, they said it was true that the tunnel was still in existence but what would it be used for now I wonder? Who knows, was the simple reply. Anyway, it was said by many a local Mutt and Pedigrees that it was a curse if you purchased your supplies of meats and bones from anywhere else, you know.

One tale was said that on one winter's morning as a storm broke out, a howling sound could be heard from as far as the coast of France, that the crew were doomed. Why? The tense question came from the onlookers listening. Well, the Captain's cook ordered a batch from the side dealers just thinking it would put a nice shine of coins in his collar pocket and just then, the Black Shuck could be heard. What does that mean, the Black Shuck?

All the dogs' ears were pointing up, as they listened with a glare. The Black Shuck, a mythic hellhound of medieval England said to portend your destiny if upset and it is said on clear nights sitting on the front just where the few fishermen who are left meet, you can hear the hellhound crying out opposite where the Queens Hotel stood. Why? was the next question. Because underneath that hotel was a deep, dark, cellar where the hellhound lived for centuries. The fishermen, marines and miners used that spot and many a times leaving alone they said they could hear heavy footsteps and breathing and although many a night the fighting between them over a local gal or a dispute of some kind they would make up and buy a last night toddy for the one they were fighting, just to walk home in company to their own kennel.

Ways of living changed in many different levels of life. The Marine barracks closed, the mines closed and the fish swam elsewhere. Locals found it hard to adjust to different breeds moving into their territory with no time to gossip and banter on about what size fish they caught on that morning out or what mutt got fighting in The Wagging Tail, or who was told to get out of the Ship Inn for fighting or cussing. But even then, the youngest puppies talked in a strange way when they mentioned the story of when the Queens Hotel burnt to the ground. From that horrendous night, a banter would go off by saying the fire was started from the Black Shuck hellhound's scream and it started that fire with rage and anger for the return of its rightful home and to whom it belonged and should be returned but alas it was the gossip and a part of Deal's show.

Lilly, Tilly what would you two say if we were to take on all those other locations in the conversation earlier? The girls were interrupted by Darcy, which in turn interrupted the talking within each other's thoughts as they had done from childhood as Lilly stared and glistened as Tilly explained about her body and changes due to her condition.

Tilly's eyes brightened each time she spoke of a movement inside her and it was a wonderful thing that being surrounded by the love from every shape and size of breed about her from a waggling tail to a pair of loving arms from a human, it all mattered.

Anyway, think it over and I'd like you two to put a charter together for me on all these cards and addresses, okay? And how we would go about it. The two young hearts looked at each other with joy because of this request that had been asked of them and off once again they started barking with the joy of their own views of play and which way about this they would go.

Time moved on and after a short while a letter arrived at the Manor via Betty the Blackbird that had to be signed for again and was addressed to Aseena's attention. Signed by the kitchen hand, Meaty Molly as she's known as she was waiting for a delivery of ground beef and who was forever in need of a yarn, she found Aseena who was getting ready for a chat about her grandad's experience in warfare as she had not stopped talking or asking questions about military after her visit to the college and it was felt Grandad may be trying to coax her to follow up on this career but which one would she choose? Who knows? And which one was the safest?

Anyway, about this letter; Molly was waiting for it to be opened for she too had a passion for fashion and all the talk of the London show but of course this was awkward for Aseena for whom would she choose to go with her?

After reading the letter openly, Margaret looked at Chit-chat the chaffinch who sat on the windowsill to listen to any gossip or mail and she flew straight over to the Parkway where the large old vicarage house stood and landed on the kitchen windowsill. She gave a little tune out to let Daisy know she was there and passed on the news and all the details from the telegram given to Daisy in that beaky chat and of the date of the Main Event in London which was to be held on the 14th of September, which was only two weeks as of today.

Back at the Manor, a quick message from Aseena was given this time to Stanley, the Song Thrush who was Betty's husband who sat on the back of the chair next to the window peeping out on what was going on. Yes, it was a perfect timing as Stanley came flying across the town and noticed Tilly with Dylan outside the trainee barracks with a smile that would shame a Cheshire cat.

Hi guys, was his quick intro. Sorry to bother you but I got a note from Aseena. With knowing what it is about I thought I'd let you know, Tilly, that a date has been given for the London trip. Don't get me in trouble by telling you of this news, okay? She also wants to get hold of Daisy to ask her as she wants her to go with her. He was watching Dylan's reaction on this matter of him listening to other news and spreading it about. Stanley with a little bow of false embarrassment gave a quick smile and said, Right, I gotta git so bye and I'll see you soon, and off he flew and within seconds disappeared without a trace.

How are you feeling about this trip, Tilly? If Aseena asks you to go with her to London with all that is going on and so? These were the concerned words from Dylan. Oh, I'm fine don't worry I'll be fine. You know Daisy will be with us, don't you? And she's Margaret's sister so don't say anything more. By the way how was college? was the next question asked. Dylan explained that he had been picked for the undercover training as well for the Army which had been his main drive but either way it was great news all around.

Dylan, I must say can you just imagine and feel what she, I mean Aseena, must be going through now? As it is now reality Dylan and you know I have to be there, don't you? As she would be there for me even though we have only known each other a short time. By the way using that word "She" She's the cat's mother you know?

Tilly looked a little confused with the question and just thought a while. Then it clicked that it was Nannie Sky who would say this if she heard a certain tone in one's voice. Tilly just smiled it off and they were both off on their trot.

Aseena contacted who she needed to as she had organised a meeting on Wednesday morning for a chat and that morning had arrived and Tilly was welcomed with warm milk in the kitchen. Molly said that Daisy was there already and in the front room as it had to be somewhere to talk without being disturbed.

On walking through the door, Tilly was surprised to see Nanny Sky there. Welcome my dear, with a kiss on the snout from Nanny Sky. She explained that she would be in London at the same time as she would be visiting Oscar, Nanny's brother in the East End so it would be company in a way for Daisy as they went way back and also Nanny's natural medical experience and street smart to the history of London's ways would be such an asset, plus guess what? She knew Mrs McDonald as she was at Daisy's side when she walked away from her offered contract that long time ago.

This had really come as an act of fate for this to happen for Aseena and who was around her life, as look at it now? After all this time for it to happen, Nanny Sky and Daisy are to meet Mrs McDonald and Aseena to maybe the door to her becoming a top model.

Just then a little smile came from Margaret as she entered the room and looked over to her sister then noticed Nanny Sky just taking a wee dram of- I wonder what? Outta her famous bot.

The overall planning was discussed and the best way to travel they felt would be best by train but no doubt something would change within the next two weeks going by the everyday saga of this escapade. The old friends were talking as they left the youngsters to chat about what and who? Daisy, thinking of the last time we were about with the Mrs McDonald it was not the best one was it, when we got up and walked away. But now, how can this have come about? It is fate, isn't it? And for us to be going with Aseena, well it is not that we were invited with open paws, was it? The two just looked at each other within a few seconds silence and then both burst into laughter.

Margaret then got back with her ways just to ask, Are you staying for lunch, Nanny? Yes, I think I shall as who can resist the splendour of your offerings? So, the rest of that time was left to the busy chit-chat run about the house from the charms of the everyday life that brought joy to all who witnessed it, company and all.

After the sharing of their times in all, it was time to make tracks for Nanny who got up with a little shake and said her goodbyes and to say, I'll see you soon and if you hear anything else or something comes up then let me know. Oh, and while I'm thinking of it, where will you be staying, Daisy? Think it over and let me know if you want to stay with me at Oscar's and I can put it down with the rest of this charter.

At another planned meeting for the Dog's Brush, a nice vibe was building between the girls with ideas and so. Excited questions like from Lilly to Tilly, what do you think of this as a logo? etc, etc? You could tell their hearts were in it. Since the time at the Forrester's meeting, Lilly and Tilly could not let their creative hearts-minds shut off from the challenge that Darcy had given them and they loved every minute of it.

The feeling of the company started from their imagination coming into reality had given them the main drive. This can and will be a very successful business and we can do it; you know that don't you? What some of the older folk need to know is we want to hire new young staff and so- so that we can train them for our standards as some staff of the old ways believe that their way is the only way and that is that. If this goes ahead which I have no doubt it will, we can discuss it then with the board in charge, okay? Okay was the adventurous reply from Lilly.

Dylan's first results will come through this week, Mum and that is of his first test and it is the bomb test team that he adores so much. I myself can't get the cleaning-managing company out of my mind, to tell you the truth, and a few instructors noticed that there was something on my mind as of my studies of being observant.

I sat down with my main instructor himself and told him my status and guess what? His childhood was very unsettled and his mum raised him on her own with a set of seven others in her litter. He said, you are gifted, Tilly, and opportunities are with you to choose with loved ones. I was lucky to have a neighbour who cared like a father to me as his son was my best friend. I wished I had the role model of a father, like you have to support you and help you choose.

Well, what more can I say? He has said his thoughts and that he wants to keep an open door to my entry into the Drug and Bomb Act Team and if ever I need to return, the door waits for me to open it. He wants me to rest and decide what is best in all matters.

Well, I could not put it better myself and I'd like to meet him sometime, Tilly, if that is okay, to thank him for his support and understanding to you both.

Only that afternoon there was a meeting with Dylan and when Dylan walked into the office, he could not help but notice Bob the Bomb, his instructor was alone. Sit down, Dylan please, and then out came his speech of what Tilly told him and then his advice to her that he had given. He stood up to congratulate Dylan on a few things in life and then the result of the test! 100 per cent pass with a lot of advice from the top dogs in the line of duty, plus his congrats on the status of Tilly.

That night after explaining to Tilly and the whole gang his results, he was then congratulated again from all over and then smiled at Tilly and said, Fancy a walk? And they just strolled along the front and spoke of their childhood dreams and the talk they both had with their instructor and their future plans after such a little saga of their own in such short hours and the great advice given to them from good hearts may have now set their future plans ahead.

They sat at one of their favourite spots where they loved to just sit and watch the fishermen prep their next sail and chat amongst themselves in all and they also spoke of their family history. Dylan's family mainly all from Wales and Tilly's from Yorkshire who made the famous treks from their homelands and many a local chat back then in their native homelands was about the conditions of their mines. Between the danger and coal dust both was such a threat to their lives as both families were from the coalfields trade and a good wager was to be in Kent. So, they believed in a better way to live, they packed their personal belongings which weren't many and set off on the long trek along the buckled and cobbled roads in all and then reached their destiny where they built a whole new way of life and to where they made their bed.

The next few days everything was better than they thought as the response and demand for the girls' cleaning service was just beyond and so they called another meeting. Lilly got up and spoke of a subject that she felt had to be said as it was good timing to talk about careers and so that if it is as successful as we feel, it will be right to bring young staff on board to be trained? A few nods came from around the table plus a few trying to keep a straight face as they were not used to this serious chit-chat.

I and Tilly would like your honest opinion on our introduction and offerings of service for the Dog's Brush? These are our leaflets, cards, costs etc, etc they are all done, so give us your honest view? Well after all the talk and show of their designs what more could a person say? You two have put some work into this haven't you? And we would all like to thank you both. Lilly mostly wanted to get this out before the London trip and not leave any confusion and crazy thoughts all in a rush.

Yes, the time had finally arrived for, you guessed it, the London Trip. You would honestly think they were leaving for the departure to another part of the world with all the attention from around the gang at Teresa's, and local stores as of course news got out and no doubt by the local magpie and blackbirds' gossip columnists, you know? They met in the morning at the front of St George's Church on the high street.

Anyway, it was out there with a lot of flare with its view of what exactly was going on? But it's best to keep them guessing was the old saying. Luck had it that Pepper's brother, Big Bozzo, had a reunion with his ole team from his kennel college days in London that weekend and also, he had a delivery to pick up two days after, so it fitted ideally with the traveling status, so he would let the girls travel with him as he would be there a few days or so. Anyway, he would be escorting them to the Kensington Kennel Club where they had been booked in for their stay in London to whatever date they wanted.

Oh, the excitement and joy around the house's atmosphere was just enchanting to say the least. Daisy arrived at the Manor a little early just to make sure the necessary items were within the package of whatever the girls were bringing with them. And with a little running around they were in the loving kitchen with thoughts flowing like a spring's stream and of course it was a little awkward as to who was going. But it was understandable and hopefully who was on the invite was not their say.

Margaret was standing with Grandad and most of the staff, and friends were beaming with joy and of course worry for what was ahead for Aseena. It was of course Margaret as of from the beginning of her life she had been beside her. But knowing Daisy, Nanny Sky and Tilly would be with her was everything and also don't forget the big galoot of Bozzo being in their company was even more relaxing but alas it just came natural of her nature to worry for that was Margaret's way.

They got their bags on board by the staff and all and the waves and cheers never stopped. You would honestly think we were emigrating, wouldn't you? was Daisy's laughing question under her breath. And to be honest, it is a good job Margaret is off the scene as do you honestly see her being around the types of breeds and ways of what we are heading for? The five just laughed out loud and it started to sink in that here we are on our way and the girls just sat in awe watching the scenery of the everyday way of life that surrounded them, away from the Manor and the small town's gossip. Look at that Tilly? etc, etc like a tennis ball the questions kept passing back and forth from the two young girls whilst driving along with Daisy, Nanny smiling on to Bozzo, the trip was just the beginning of this time in life that not knowing would be a major change in their lives and how it would open up one's door.

The lights of the big city were shining out as they drove closer to the centre and their eyes were openly ajar. Turning here and turning there they were now in the middle and watching how active the ways of life were for many and the private thoughts were amongst their minds and then the turn into the road and the big gates with flashing lights saying: Welcome to the Kensington Kennel Hotel. A glance about when they pulled up outside the doors and the concierge came walking over with a stern look as if to say, Who are these when they are about? Then Daisy spoke before Nanny could let fly as her natural days of fame came back to her. She mentioned, we are guests of Mrs McDonald. And sure enough how quickly did the doors open up to the floor.

Walking through the door, Nanny with her straight temper was taking a little glare back over to the introduction and tutting a little, well, in my day this would never happen. Anyway, the young girls looked about and what would you expect from the young hearts but watching the beaming action of people going here and there, Sir, Madam being repeated and with Daisy's smile one could not help but notice, I think it was her memories of her time in the high light, who knows? But it was a grand expression to see.

The concierge walked them to the reception with a few glances at Aseena. One in particular who was at the reception and giving a little flash-talk of who he was, which in return thought he'd get the highlight treatment. Tilly picked up on this and just then the valet-ushers were ordered to take the guests to Level 3, Rooms 8 and 9 and with their cases picked up and a please follow me order came next from the valet. Oh, how you could get used to this, came a funny chit-chat from Nanny to Daisy, with a smile to the girls whilst whisking along, leaving the reception area and they were just at the door of the lift when Aseena looked back to the loud bark, talk coming from around the desk.

The door of the lift opened and the excitement entered their hearts again and then Tilly looked again and couldn't help but notice Aleena's stare back over to where they just left. She looked at Daisy who picked up on this too and then the please follow me chat came again.

Up they went and then buzz, the stop at Level 3, the doors opened and another order and a little do-dally walk of excitement within them followed along the hallway. The door opened and the introduction came, This is your room, Miss

Stenhouse, and I'm sorry Ma'am, your name? Oh, the look again from Nanny. Ah, thank you was the quick response from Daisy. Then if you care to follow me next door.

The girls turned and as entering their room a loud bark of Wow! came out as how else could they respond to what they walked into? Everything a girl could dream of in a fairy tale image was laid out in front of them. They walked to the window balcony with a glare out across the action of all the city of London could offer. The ushers were waiting aside after unloading but the girls didn't know why and what they were hanging around for. Then Daisy walked in to check and tipped them both, Thank you, Ma'am, and away they went. This of course set the girls off in a fit of laughter as their heights of the trip just kept building.

Just then a tall slender Red Setter tapped on the door and near enough walked herself in with an introduction of herself, Good day to you. I hope your trip was a safe one with no interferences? I'm Stella Unsworth, Mrs McDonald's personal manager in all. I'm just checking all is well and to let you know Mrs McDonald would like to meet you again before the tour of the studio in the morning, so she has booked a table in the Sunshine Room for dinner tonight at seven if that is fine, shall I confirm it?

Just then Daisy walked out of the bathroom and the two looked at each other with interest. Hello, came the next word and the manager could not help but stare at Daisy's presence. Nanny looked on at the pair of them. For some reason she, the secretary felt that she knew her and after giving the acceptance of the invite to her for 7 o'clock, the lady spoke again, I hope you enjoy your stay with us. Making her way to the door, she could not help but stare back as to think where do I know this lady from? Her heart and thoughts could not relax enough to give her an answer but sure as a little more time passed, it would come to her before she went insane.

The girls were excited with the buzz of what to wear? rolling within their thoughts. When Daisy spoke to them both explaining to them a word of advice in what sort of manner to act on in tonight's intro. They knew of the status of Daisy and not having seeing this woman for so long but the two of them were mature enough to understand and if anything, this was one of their main highlights of the trip to witness this themselves.

The only concern Daisy felt - and this was where she wanted to explain to them both, I hope you feel Aseena, that this will not affect your outward look in this type of career if you do decide to follow up on it? If so, I'll stay away and keep to my room. You will do no such thing, Daisy, if you don't go, we don't go and that is that.

The four just laughed out openly and started then preparing for the night ahead of them. All the grooming and plaiting and of course the right artier of dress flowed and filled the room with their excitement, when Daisy said a few words, You two step back please? Smiling and gleaming from ears to tail, they stood proud and oh yes, came the satisfied words from Daisy's heart. I must say how beautiful you look and a shame your mum's not here to see you both.

Then a shy yet embarrassing reply came from Tilly, You two look glamourous yourselves, I must say, as the pair chose an off the shoulder 1920s style attire to introduce themselves to the night's host. The four then checked this and that and back to front, nothing was missing and then the time came to say, Right ladies, the time has arrived and from the minute we walk out of this door, it will be either make or break.

Down the hallway they strolled with other guests with a natural expression as to look on and wonder with their thoughts of who are these two beauties? And over their shoulders they looked and the guys got either a nudge or a stern stare from their wives-partners and all as to say, I'll speak to you later but overall, it could not be helped.

They arrived at the entrance to the Sunshine Bar and once again the looks onto this beauty were just ecstatic and Daisy spoke to the maître-de and introduced themselves as, We are guests of Mrs McDonald. And as he checked the list, his eyes could not help but lift each time a thought of he'd seen them all over the years? But just setting his eyes on Aseena, he just could not help himself but to join the queue of admirers. He then ticked his list; the nods came in reply and they entered the bar in awe of feelings of Gosh! Oh my, what can you say?

The girls just adored the aroma of excitement about them, whatever it was this was new to witness for their memories of a heart's beat they could not help but feel they were girls and that to be treated as a lady was adorable to say, looks once again came across the floor for who is this? Then those famous words even though it was someone known to them were, Oh, darlings, hello again! Yes, Birdie and her ways, she looked at the two younger guests up and down and said, Love the dress, to Tilly and then the I'm a bitch tone, Oh, is this a work from Mutts and Tux's may I ask? No, in fact it is one of my works came a stern reply from Nanny as she gave Aseena a little elbow prod and a wink and of course Birdie then caught the eye of another guest and called out again, Oh, Darling, great to see you etc, etc.

Just then a slender voice came open to the air and it was Milly and Mylo, It has been a long time, Daisy; You are looking well. The smile from Daisy was just immense as this amazing pair were the first designers to introduce the Catwalk to Daisy's first steps that after that night in The Canters and Trots Club in Manchester, she never looked back and it made the two designers' names even brighter for who they found that made the fashion world shake.

How long is it since you last saw that couple, may I ask? Was Ameena's curious question. With Tilly listening on, it was the wedding of Prince Charles and Lady Diana. We were being asked to dress the dogs of the day and how grand it was. You know how often we hear the name Lean Berger? You know the creator-designer of the luxury beds and blankets and rugs, carpets of the real Dolce and Gabbana style? Well, that's their father, if I may say so. Lee the Lean Berger, a tough breed I must say again and a strong survivor and one of those breeds that out lasted them all and a legend to many and by the way, they are not a couple, Aseena, they are brother and sister. One of their father's other business's is the beautiful rugs and on the high street back home in Deal and he lives over at Broadstairs.

Just then another thing caught the attention of the girls; it was the voice of that tall, slender dog who kept popping up and now here again miles away from the last place he was here. Who is that may I ask? One of the girls asked. Well, Milly was back talking, Well, strangely enough, I can help you out here on that question. Where you live, not far away there is the family of Lord Gawain Douglas whose daughter is the owner of that butcher's shop in that lane across from St George's Church on the high street where some very old wives' tales come out of, The Black Pig, and Lizzy is her name. Well, that is her brother, Jamie. A playboy along with the name he carries, may I say.

It goes way back and at the Royals' wedding we got introduced to this Lord Gawain Douglas which carries a very Welsh name I must say. Lee used to use the Beach Club at the same time and knew this playboy's family. What more can I say? What are those words? Like father like son, but you know what towns are like for gossip but still it doesn't stop you from being aware.

How could Lee know a lord from Wales in Deal? Well, the eccentric moved and settled here just like Lee's Hun background family. They escaped the invasion days as once again his ancestor fell for a local beauty and that was that. He, his ancestor that is, slipped away one night away from the raider's gang who were planning to attack Sandwich Bay and disappeared into the night and as they searched for him, they naturally thought he'd been slayed or drowned. But he was kept under the fishing bay lobster pots, nets where they could not pick up his scent as of all the smells in all. That must have been a smelly place to be kept? But that is what you do when you fall in love, anything!

He stayed there undercover until one morning the invaders felt it was time to move on and they set sail and the rest is history. You see that is where his feature comes from as of his breed, they were bred for guarding cattle and sheep and of course their masters and anything under their care. That place seems to come up in a lot of subjects, doesn't it? What, the Beach Club? Yes, it was a bit of a playboy's hangout, if you could get in that is.

So, what's the punchline with Lee then? Where and how did he meet his love, his sweetheart? Well, it is said how he met Haley, that's her name by the way. Apparently, he was on his way home from a night out with the pack, as they used to call them, when he noticed a damsel in distress along the dingy, wild, Middle Street in its day. Anyway, he came to her rescue and it is said he gave a stray German shepherd and three mutts, who used to mug along a good ole whooping and it all started from there. It is never ending, is it with all the drama along this town of Deal? It is a wonder no one ever wrote a book about it all, came the words out of Tilly. After that drama, on that night, that was that, and they have been together ever since they met.

Then came the time for it to happen; Daisy and Mrs McDonald's introduction after all these years. Nanny's heart was beating, looking on with suspense. Aseena was in a conversation with a make-up artist who in fact was a friend of Becca who she was at college with when she was learning the steps into the hair-fur foundation, when this make-up artist found out from chit-chat, we are from Deal in Kent, she asks me do I know Becca or Angela? Yes of course I do, and they have done really well for themselves as Angie owns Dapper Dogs and Becca owns Laundromutt, the best of classic and creative styles in Kent.

And of course, off it went with the doggie snarl-growl and chat as they called it. With all the chat going on, it gave an immense feeling to chill out from the feeling of the tension of all that's been going on around them. Oh, by the way would you please tell Becca I send my love and give her my card?

Just then, Mrs McDonald came through the dressing room door, and spoke first with a question to Aseena, It is such a pleasure that you could make it today and I hope all is satisfactory with your rooms that is? These were the words of introduction from Mrs McDonald. Yes, yes everything is wonderful, thank you.

Just then another introduction came as Daisy turned around, hello, Kate, it has been a long time, hasn't it? As Mrs McDonald's instinct of voices, she still couldn't focus straight away on who had spoken. Then realised who it was, Daisy, Daisy Stenhouse. Daisy, what are you doing here, and what can I say? After explaining to her who she was to Aseena, do you think a woman of her status could concentrate? No, she stared and glared like an eagle in full flight watching and just could not help but feel her thoughts wanting to embrace Daisy for I feel it was losing her all those years ago and not being part of someone she cared for? The years of seeing Daisy's career blossom into what it reached and not being a part of it must have been hard. In business, feelings can reach the part you may not think is there. But it is and don't forget it but there is always time to make up. As life is too short to carry bitterness that one day you will face yourself and only feel regret.

All the lights, glamour of the night got better by the minute and laughter and smiles with introductions carried on without one fault to the evening. But do you think Mrs McDonald could keep her eyes off Daisy? No, Daisy was in a deep thoughtful chat with the photographer that opened Daisy's skills all those years ago. Sean The Shot as he was known. He was a Kerry Blue, a terrier from the native land of Ireland and as natural as the land he was from, he could summon what and how a model wanted to expose in every feeling of body language, his or her ability to show off.

Oh, Sean, what more can I say but to meet you of all breeds here of all locations! Daisy explained the reason why she was there and as Sean looked over to Aseena, after Daisy pointed her out, he just said Well what can I say Daisy? She will take the walk by storm. Do you know how many of the bigshots here tonight have asked me, Who is she? But now knowing she is with you and explaining everything to me, well? And you know who could be involved? How do you feel on this? She's watching, Sean, came her reply and gave a kiss and a piece of paper which of course was her number to call to discuss their concern and matters.

I knew I had seen or met your Mam before when I first got introduced to you and it has been on my mind since. It was Stella the agent of Mrs McDonald. I could not get you out of my mind and then it clicked who you are. I admired your career as far back as you could imagine, by the way, and what got me interested in you was my mother. She's Annie Craven. What, the promoter? This was Daisy's reply. She often spoke of you all of my childhood and she told me how you used to share a flat in Soho all those years ago and it was just amazing. She told me when you got chosen for a New York show in all and what I should do? Was the conversation, shall I go Annie? When not a day later, Annie herself made a major breakthrough as she got chosen for the same trip by the Dogs and Hog's promotion of the Howling Mercy Band. That was it, we set off together and left all those young mutt's hearts in tatters.

I can see your mother in you a mile away, I must say. I will never forget the expression on her face when we were in New York and the two of us in a city like that, well what can one say? The only match of expression to match it was when a feisty terrier from Scotland- What, Andrew was his name if I remember? Well, that is what makes these old banters so gathering in thoughts? I must say Mrs Stenhouse- Please, Daisy, Daisy, you can call me. Well, Daisy that scoundrel of a loving mutt, Andy, followed my mum all the way back after he met her and that is my father, Daisy.

Daisy just embraced the young feisty lady in front of her like a grandmother would do after being apart from the next youngest litters of the ones she loved. I never seem to be able to get away from the drama, do I? It is only to be admired how a person comes out of it all, is the only thing I can say.

Can we keep in touch, Daisy? Was the question from this ladylike character. Of course, and what is your mother doing now? Oh, they bought a smallholding in Scotland and live the life of simple leisure. They just harmonise in their own company and I will let her know ASAP that I've finally met you. Please, we must make it to our table as I've just got that look from you know who?

A little laughter came from Daisy as she glanced across the busy floor and slowly walked across to where the host-guests were waiting. Please take your seats and join us and I must say what a grand place to choose, Mrs McDonald. Yes, it is grand, isn't it? Came the reply to Tilly. One must say what a very mature thought of Tilly to ease the introduction at the table. A big change from when the old days of the church hallways when we were changing behind old curtain rails, isn't it Daisy? And the company at the table looked around confused and startled from the host's words and glanced without a clue.

The food came out like a feast to royalty and was shared

openly as it should be around any gathering of hungry mouths to feed and as the tastes filled everyone's thoughts and the plates were empty, Mrs McDonald made a gesture, Please, I know you have had a long day with traveling and so but would you join our company now to finish the evening on the roof of the Lovers Bar? As they have a pianist, singer and what a beautiful evening to sit and chat overlooking London's city and the Thames River to finish our night.

They rose from their table as in the days of the lords and ladies and made their way to finish the evening's success so far. Following the chaperone, he escorted them up the staircase which seemed to be more fitting than the lifts for some reason. Anyway, Nanny Sky lovingly slipped her paw through Daisy's and just strolled with the wonderful company. Stepping through the doors onto the rooftop's bar, the first thing everyone seemed to do was look at the stars and how they glistened the night into full bloom. Oh, how I wish Dylan was here with me now, Aseena. They just smiled away with immense comfort in all.

It could not have been two minutes after sitting down and the pianist started playing and smiles within their company blossomed like daffodils smiling to the primroses on their first spring day. Then Aseena looked up and across from her seat to see a woman raise a glass to her? She just naturally nodded to her with curiosity to who it was. Then looked to the woman's left and who was sat there but the gent again of the short intros in certain times and places they have seen on sight.

Daisy, don't look straight over but do you know who the lady is directly in front of us at the table with that guy again? Why that is Lady Marietta, she is the longest person in the tradition of Irish folk to carry the titled name of Marquessate or Marchioness that has been carried on since Irish folklore began, a rebel if I may say so. The owner of the sheepskin-mohair, clothes fashion attire we spoke of a short while back. My, is she a real lady? Yes, she carries her hereditary and proud of it, that goes back for centuries. Then, just like fairy tale stories go, she was at the castle of lords and ladies when she was introduced to an English titled gent, the Viscount Nickiadados, Bampiena, Batomianio, a real English gent,

Folk back yonder were on their guard for her to marry or even think about it, to an Englishman. But she would not lie to her heart and why should she? She changed many ways of thinking and made the road open to many new-minded Celtic women of the world to talk, and she proved it right by sharing her love and they have done everything together since. The younger guy is of course the great grandson of that family I told you about back home in Kent.

To be honest, I do not know why he is sitting with them. She looked back over with a glance again and this time Daisy was watching. Nanny looked on and as tough as she is could not resist in putting her paws down with a grateful smile and said, Gosh, Daisy, I'm glad I didn't miss this dear; I know we have seen and done a lot but this is only imaginary at our age and what a way to bury a burden, if those are the right words to use. And as Daisy spoke a short sentence to Aseena, who was beside her, Well, young lady, all this began over a stroll along the front. It makes you wonder, doesn't it?

The rest of the evening just went with a flow and the chat went easy, to say the least, when Stella spoke, Right, I must leave you as tomorrow's another day and I don't want to be to burnt out with this evening's amazing time. Whilst I remember speaking earlier to you, Aseena and Daisy, I shall meet you both in the reception room with our guide and the day will begin from there.

Everyone then felt the same with wonderful sighs from all of a grand time of the night they have had and rose to say goodnight, then one by one stood and thanked the host and with looks back and forth, Daisy to Mrs McDonald, Aseena to the table opposite, and many wished each other well and may your god be with you in this world.

Walking through the grand surroundings back to their rooms, Nanny suddenly stopped and came out with something that entered her mind-thoughts, of, Wait a sec, Daisy, I thought we were to stay with Nardia at her Convent Garden pad, not the Kennelton Hotel?

The four of them once again looked around at each other and thought the same. But like the Seven Wonders of the World, it would take a long time to solve this question and maybe time would tell?

The morning arrived and the first thing Tilly did was to call her sweetheart. Dylan, Good morning, I wish you were here as I miss you, Dylan. I too, was the reply. Tilly called from the hotel and explained all they had witnessed so far and the hotel in all with the way they had been treated after they found out who they were guests of. She mentioned the beauty of the rooms but most of all how they finished the evening off. Do you know what they played last night, Dylan? Our tune, our song. There was this pianist on the roof top terrace bar and it could not have been a more beautiful evening.

She then explained the details and the rest of the saga and then a knock on the door came. It's Stella, Tilly you know last night when I told you it will be 10 am, that I will take you on the tour of the studio's etc? Tilly picked up on something here as a do me a favour? Yes, Stella forgot what time with all the drama going on with meeting Daisy and the rest of the excitement, it had slipped her mind. Not like her for she was accustomed to functions with thousands of guests but this was different, it was personal. Anyway, she forgot to mention the time. Oh, yes Stella, it will be no problem we will meet you at the reception.

Who's that? Came the question over the phone. Dylan, I've got to go as I've to get the rest on the move because of the crazy day ahead of us, Bye and I'll call you in the morning, okay. On the other end, Dylan just gave out a little laugh as he hung up as he knew well the mayhem of what was going on in the Big Smoke.

Morning, Nanny, sleep well? No, I did not! Came the reply to Daisy. Do you remember my last question of the night last night? I still can't work out to myself how I did not realise it earlier that we did not go to Nadia's but to the hotel. And you know how switched on I am in these situations? It was all the excitement of the trip in general and with another back-chat reply over her shoulder, she explained the morning plans given to them of what is ahead.

Do you want to go with the girls? I thought of it and yes, why not? It will do us the world of good to see the offerings of the photo shoots and all the new types of camera tact they have? It will be interesting. I still can't get over the response of this Stella lass and who she is. Can you believe it Sky? Even Nanny herself knew Daisy was excited by calling her by her first name. She just gave a little chuckle to herself.

All's well ladies? They were in the reception and quickly she introduced Hugh, the overall minder-chauffeur extraordinaire who could not do enough for a person and today he had four! In the car they sat when through the mirror glance he spoke, I understand you are all up from my part of the world then? They soon responded to his voice as he told them he was based at the Marine Barracks in his day and all his time was with the stables and oh how proud he was looking after all of those horses. Beats looking after ole mutts like us then? Of course, this reply came from Nanny as the laughter filled the car and another back glanced smile came from Hugh.

Shortly after, they arrived at the studios and out they stepped into the car park and in through the two large doors with Welcome above its entrance, Welcome to the Flash and Dash Studios. The whole building was all about action and the guests adored and embraced every second of it but when Aseena took a look across the floor, when she heard the words shout out, And Action! a voice shouted out then, Flash, the camera's at work, the fur on her neck stood up and shivers of excitement from tail to snout just ran through her as she saw the Afghan Hound strut her stuff down that catwalk to reach the end, twirl and back again, she knew there and then this is the world she wanted and with these thoughts she embraced it all and let into her heart to soak.

Daisy picked up on this straight away and so did Stella as they looked at each other with a smile as right at that minute came another voice of welcome. Yes, herself Mrs McDonald. How are you all feeling and are you enjoying yourselves? Oh, we are having a wonderful time, just wonderful, thank you so much for inviting us here. It was only obvious the girls were enjoying it all, it is every youngster's dream to be within such a place.

A strange kinda humble look came from the host to Daisy and it was returned with a smile and a nod. I honestly feel that this has done the world of good for both their souls, young lady. This came from Nanny to Stella which gave an even more welcoming feeling about.

Over a little break it came out, a question from Mrs McDonald, Well, Aseena we have discussed a matter of a photo shoot as of an introduction tomorrow with Kara and her team here just to see how you feel and take to it all. Yes, a look came at Daisy again and she just smiled on as Aseena was near enough leaping about with Tilly beside her. Well, that answers that, doesn't it, came a contented smiling face of Mrs MacDonald. Now it's time to leave here and see some other parts of this City that we can walk to.

Here and there they visited with adrenalin and excitement and then just turning onto Bond Street, the awe once again in Aseena's thoughts and expression were just beyond. Daisy looked on to her and just smiled. Nanny Sky spoke openly, She really is a beauty, isn't she? She got it from her mother; you should have seen her; what a beauty in every manner. What do you mean should have? This was Stella's question and it was answered by telling her of that terrible accident and then her grandfather, etc raised Aseena without her. No wonder you are protective over her.

She took a little glance at Aseena for care in her thoughts, and this was a good thing because she would be watched by another eye in the presence of her life. The girls were in awe and could not help but stare with so much joy and excitement as the names, Asprey, Chanel-Dolce and Gabbana, Louis Vuilton and Tiffany and co were just lit up all around them and once again Aseena's dedicated thoughts just said one day, one day, Tilly, they will open their doors for us to greet us to spend our dosh within those big names along them instead of one of those doormen giving us the look like go away you little mutts, go away, shoo!

Just then a panic shout out came and a scuffle, some type of disturbance and all they heard was, My collar, my bag! Two ladies had been set on and their possessions grabbed when all they heard was, Set, get them! A handler officer released his dogs, a Doberman and Jack Russel and belting down the street after the culprit, they tackled the bounder and Yep, they got him down within seconds and got him pinned in a way that the dogs had not witnessed.

Of course, Tilly's interest in her career was lit up and when they walked down, they had to go and look at the scallywag who was by no means a nice picture. They heard some of the crowd mention, Why that's Galoopo, a mixed mutt with more scars, bites and half an ear missing. He's the head of that gang. What, outta the Tower Hamlets neck of the woods? Yes, Bite Me Now is the gang's name.

Anyway, the authorities have been after him for ages. They say his ancestors in and around London go back to Patch; you know the dog from Oliver? Sorry, Bullseye is the dog's name owned by Bill Sykes. Anyway, that was his great-great granddaddy, so it doesn't say much for him, does it? He's a four crossed from a Staffie-terrier-bulldog and a boxer.

Nanny Sky's ears went up a bit when the Staffordshire name was mentioned but it was all in fun. The mutt looked on at the girls and gave a snarl, What ya looking at? And then gave them a growl.

He was then muzzled up, tied and bundled into a van and off he went. He was able to peep back out of the window whilst being driven away and the handler spoke, Don't let him bother you okay? We got him now. No really, I was so impressed by what I saw. She introduced herself and told them of her boyfriend and their future work back in Kent. That was a great tactic how you got him down. Well, we call it the trip and mix, Aussie, also known as Whoopa, that's me by the way, the Jack Russel he gets in under and nips the ankle then I get beside the foe and we just flip 'em over and that is that. There is no way up and cross-legged and it's all over; they are just bent.

Well, there is never a dull moment to the day is there? If you want to Tilly, we can send details of our tactics to you and your boyfriend and let's keep in touch, as it would be very interesting to see which section you both take now you are through into the main gates of BDSS. The Bomb Drug Special Services college how that was my dream to get to that squad; did I ever tell you that, Auss? Ya, every day since I've known you Pontco. That was the nickname of the Doberman; Danny was his real name. Anyway, we must move as there has been another call. Bye, take care.

Well, what can we say about that drama? No one's hurt so let's just put it down to entertainment for us? It had to be a statement from Nanny with her humour and off they went to the next adventure. But they did realise how quickly all of that had happened and it was everyday it happened. When they saw a person walking down the road, coming out of one of those stores with a £10,000 diamond dogs' collar around their neck and barking about it. Keep your jaw shut is what I'd tell them; don't be heading out barking off and bringing trouble on yourself; you just have to be aware.

They got back to the hotel and if anything, being in this type of company was really helping Stella to let go and enjoy herself. It was quite clear that it was meeting Daisy and then acting in this hosting manner assisted in all ways.

Well, just to let you know we are booked into Jawbreakers tonight, said Nanny. What, the rib house? Yes, we have been invited by the owner who was at the gathering last night. They want us to join them whilst you are on your visit here. After calming down, they made it back to the hotel and up to their rooms and even the older gals found it all exciting with the drama and all and yes, there was more to come.

Chilling out for a little while, Nanny asked Daisy, Well, my friend, how are you feeling about being around Mrs McDonald? They still call her that after all these years whilst not in her company. It is much better than I could ever imagine. I think it is just maturity in both our lives that has helped ease any tension. But do I, or would I trust her in business with Aseena? I just don't know. I have to ask myself, if I'm asked to manage Aseena's career, would I want to? I just do not know, Sky. We will see after the visit here and how I feel and when we return home and relax a while, then ask the same question. Plus, we don't know yet ourselves, or herself, does she want to follow up in this career? And it will all come out after tomorrow's shoot on how she feels.

But Nanny herself, not with any modelling work within her, knew the answer to any question on that term, after witnessing the adrenaline of the young lady and this way of living; from its clothing to just walking into the limelight, of who is involved within this fast-paced crazy way of how to make a living, instead of being inside a nine-to-five job of being under the thumb.

The evening arrived and once again the build up to preparing it all made it even more exciting to say, the girls got fired up with this and that and knowing they were heading for another hip joint was even more of a boost to say.

And then a knock on the door and of course, it was Stella who was once again as excited as the guests and in her life, she has met new friends within business, but this was more than just a business sect, this was an enjoyment in her heart, and she enjoyed the outlook and its way.

Big Hugh added to the excitement with his humour and manner, escorting the ladies down from the car park to the entrance of The Jawbreakers, and once again just walking in with being hosted as the special guests, stood out to them. Hugh himself wasn't going to lose out on this chance of a feast of munching on those famous ribs, so he just walked in with Stella and all and not a word was said. It did stand out a little to see this rather well-dressed handsome gent walking along with this bunch of gals but it did not take long to figure out who he was just by his presence. It really wasn't the scene for their host to be there and quite frankly it suited it better as they could really chew in, including Stella and what a feast it was. It was the best of Cajun.

After the experience of everything and more they received at the Jawbreakers, they were invited to see a band that had been at the party the night before and Stella, being so known to the scene and the in-crowd, was approached with invites, as of course the band took a fancy to- I wonder who? Of course, everyone around the town was talking about the beauty with this new face about, and who is she? stood out a mile.

How do you fancy popping over to the Barking Mad Bar? This band's invited us. And it was the two elders who answered first, If you don't mind, we are only here once, aren't we? So come on. Once again, they reached the door and the owner spotted Stella and the VIP treatment was given. The owner was a member of the rock band, the Dogs of Darkness who Stella had a great part in bringing them to the light of the clubs and then onto the fame of the world music scene. At their peak, they headlined the Big Festival, you know the one? The howling hounds, the biggest of the glam rock days of the Dogs of Hell.

In they went and amongst the crowd Aseena could not but notice that one dog who for some reason kept turning up and once again he was looking over with that hello look on his snout. Daisy noticed this and took the leash in her paw and spoke about what was ahead of them the next morning. How are you feeling about the shoot in the morning, Aseena? She just turned her thoughts away and replied, How were you on your first time, Daisy? Buzzing is the only word I can use. Well, I'm the same and just can't wait; I just can't wait to see and feel how I'm going to react to it Daisy.

Stella was listening in and just then Tilly called Aseena to the dance floor as one of their favourite songs was being played by the cover band. Walk This Way just came blasting out and off they strutted, taking the floor by storm. I was quite surprised at the mature manner with which Aseena answered your question, Daisy. Yes, and so am I lass, so am I. The two of them with their experience of all they had witnessed between them, looked on at the girls on the floor and I'll give you one guess who was in the middle of the pair? Yes, Nanny, for her passion and joy for music was to say the least. What more could they ask for with being treated this way and how and where it all came from and what will it reach, one could never predict and it was best left this way.

In the presence of all this there were flashes from the spotlights and this brought out the inner side of what was building inside Aseena and once again it was spotted by Stella and Daisy, as they looked on, and the two started talking again and just could not help but say, She has it all, hasn't she? She will take the catwalk by the tail and who's to stop her may I say? And this is where it all began.

It was just the joy of it all to let their minds and thoughts mingle within each other's and that is exactly what was needed, to be relaxed and feel at ease. But one thing the two older girls did cut loose on that night, yes, the cocktails and to the surprise of the others, the joining of the band on stage with their version of Simply The Best that the whole club enjoyed.

The morning arrived and yes, there were a few sore heads but nothing on a scale that could not be handled. Surprised, yes, but entertaining it was.

Tilly made her way into her room where she had a little privacy to herself and eased into her conversation over the phone, Hello Dylan, how are you? We are only three hours away from the shoot and I'm excited for Aseena as she really is blown up for it. She told Dylan about the Jawbreakers invite, but did not mention the band may I say? We will keep that quiet, Tilly thought to herself as she did not want to send the people back home the wrong impression. Also, it could be a good weapon for bribery in the future, couldn't it?

I've really made another great move at the college as well Tilly. I've worked with two different handlers and both say my nose is just natural to its theory to what it's looking for. With sensing the bombs, I can pick its presence within seconds; this was active to say the least and I'll tell you all about it when you come home. By the way, when is that? We will be home by Monday. I'm saying Monday just in case they ask us to stay over for the weekend showing, as there is a big one on. Plus, it will be easier for travelling, as that is when Pepper will be going back home. Okay, tell Aseena my thoughts are with her again, okay, love you. Speak to you tomorrow.

She placed the phone down with a smile and her thoughts were all at home until the bedroom door opened again and Aseena's adrenaline filled the room with Tilly in a way trying to calm the tone a little. The time just flew by when Daisy knocked on the door to have it opened by Tilly. How is she? Were Daisy's words as she left Nanny in their room to chill down after the night before. It is best for this light episode to be focused on Aseena and not a crowd that includes Tilly as well. Ready? Was the next one word shot out from Daisy, here we go, let's do it! The two walked out of the room like a fighter ready to do battle for the world title, walking down the hall as if to say, well here I am and from here, will it or will not come to grow?

They reached the studio and Stella was there with her open welcome smile, Everything okay? Feeling, okay? Daisy took a look at her as if to say, don't you dare mention last night! But it was all in good spirit. Aseena, this is Louisa and her make-up team. A few nods came about and then the artists cut loose, bring this out or lift that up, and shots from every angle were being taken to the extreme whilst orders, looks and views were being fired out from all over the studio.

Don't get annoyed was one glance from Daisy's expressive frown to Aseena when one orderly photographer told her to look this way, darling. It was the darling word that fired Aseena up but she soon calmed down and let her instincts just do the work. She's a natural, isn't she? Were the words from guess who? Yes, Mrs McDonald to Daisy. Yes, she is may I say, and you want her, don't you? Yes, I do and there is no way I will use any words like and I'll do anything to get her. I've learnt over the years about respect, Daisy, and that's a promise. Daisy's expression without using words was enough to answer any question there was to ask and Mrs McDonald picked up on this. The cameras started to slow down so it seemed and the bodies of the team just broke out with applause all around.

Amazing! Fantastic! Congratulations! The compliments just came streaming in from everywhere and I have to say if there was any question to be asked on any doubt, then after that show they were left upon the shelf. The adrenaline was still pouring from Aseena. She looked straight into the camera lens, didn't she? Were Stella's words. And all around her just looked on and flowed. She then turned to Daisy, as if she was the one to impress and score the winning goal for the FA Cup and the whole team was for you but you wanted that coach to embrace you.

After that performance, lass, the questions are answered by yourself and the only one left now to answer is, is this for you and do you love it? And we already know that don't we? When we get home, we will discuss how the feelings are then as you will have time to unwind, talk with the ones you love and trust then we will see about what lies ahead of the long and winding road and will it be true?

Walking off the main floor from the main studio, Stella approached Aseena with excitement. I just wanted to say that she thought you did a wonderful job and the tongues did not stop from waggling whilst watching you and I, too, found it amazing to watch you. Before we go haywire talking, we have been invited out again tonight down to an old location in Soho which has a lot of character and it is based on Twiggy and I know how you feel about her and what she stood for. Once again it is a private function, so shall I tell them we will be over? If anything, Daisy was more fired up about this invite than anyone else, may I say. Oh yes, we will be there. And with this, Stella gave a glance at the few people who were over at the entrance just on their way to leave and waved and nodded to let them know their invite had been accepted.

Let's make it back, okay, and grab a Dogallatte? It's a famous coffee drink created by the café back at the hotel and we keep saying we will pop into the cafeteria at the hotel, so let's do that? Before Stella could say anything further, Daisy spoke and said, We will see you tonight, okay? This was a professional tone as if to say, you are not welcome on this chat, and she took it very well and got the hint.

On arriving back, the welcome came from the hotel's host at the doors as they were becoming well known and liked by all the staff, but it was only natural that this was to happen, due to their personalities. Hi, Mat. Oh, hi Daisy, Tilly's in the Coffee house as I saw her go in a minute ago, ya. I called her to give her the feedback from the photoshoot and I know she can't wait. How did it go by the way? It was Melissa the female host and of course a girlie thing like this was the main topic of talk throughout the Hotel in all. Amazing, just amazing, Mellie, I need to speak to you when I can, okay? That was Aseena,s quick answer, as she could not wait to see Tilly and open up and she literally flew across the reception leaving Daisy trailing behind.

In she walked and both Tilly's paws were out with a welcome as catching her with that adrenaline still running was great, because it gave her feelings an escape route to express herself and all that she felt inside. Daisy went straight to the counter to order and turned to walk over when another voice came about. It was a guest of around the same age as Daisy and of all things, she recognised Daisy from her modelling days; yet another one. What's going on here? Is it a time capsule of some sort? Daisy thought to herself with a little laugh.

She explained that she was on the photoshoot of the famous culottes worn by the Gracy Twins for the Paw and Pad, a small independent clothes shop in Tiger Bay, way back when the fashion exploded into that era. Who can wear this with a style to carry it? Thought the owner. That was where Twiggy took the part because her status and shape and the dog beside her,

her Afghan Hound, slenderness and the rest is history in the style which brought on a style to a mint.

How time has passed with so much history we have witnessed since those days, haven't we? I stayed in this business because of the travelling with the styles to match the different countries and generations, I just could not resist the offer from an independent editor who hired me to travel wherever she and her magazine went, I was beside her.

And yourself? All I remember one day a shock newsflash came about that you retired and walked away from the catwalk and all? Yes, I just had enough and I fell into a chilled mood in a town off the English Channel and wanted to find myself, as it was important which way I was going in life. I walked away from the highlife as it was leaving me in a blur.

Just then Daisy got a message from an ole pigeon who you could tell had seen the life of this city and told a few banters in all. 'Allo, my lover,' in his cockney slang, I'm looking for Daisy? Yes, yes, how can I help you? Hi, I'm Harry, I have a message to say. Pepper, he will be travelling back to Kent on Tuesday and if you are all done, he will pick you up here at around ten o'clock, okay? He tried to call the reception to get hold of you but each time you were out or busy, so I told him I'd be over here with the recipe choices, with menus for the Feast in the Fair here on the bank holiday weekend. I've to give these to the chefs here from the Cosy Kennel and the Pointed Nose private clubs, to show approval of their choice to the house here and this is the best way by beak and wing and for me to bring it over, then they know they have the news they need.

Why is Pepper in one of those clubs? No, no he drinks with us at the Hair of the Hound which all the staff use when they get off their shifts. Anyway, Stanley the Sparrow he's the grub-snail catcher with the garden staff here; let him know if you are clear and he will come over and tell me without any delay, okay?

By the way, between you and the young pup with you, you are the talk of the town. It got out about the photo shoot and who you were in your day and what you did by yourself by standing up for what you believed in. They love all that here as they are all from struggling tight litters with a dream and vision and stories like yours keeps their hopes, dreams open.

Just then a whistle in the wind came and Harry got it, I gotta go Daisy but it's been a pleasure meeting you and if you leave Tuesday, have a safe journey home. Bye! and off he flew.

Daisy walked back into the lounge to tell the girls, we need to slow down a little and focus on when, in reality, we have to go home, okay? I just got a message that Pepper's driving home on Tuesday so that is it, okay? We have to think before saying yes to anymore invites, okay? With this, who walked back in but Stella and it could not have been a better time as Daisy told her there and then they must go home on Tuesday and do not take any more bookings of any sort. Okay, was the reply as she knew it was on the cards. Whatever it was, she felt it already, she did not want to hear those words to be honest. A bond had grown with them and it was a close one; who knew what it would grow into?

I've to call Dylan and let him know we will be home on Tuesday. Just has she stood up, she felt a wonderful feeling within her body and Daisy noticed this. Are you okay, lass? Yes, yes, I am Daisy I am. If anything, I feel an immense sensation that I've never witnessed before. Come with me, Tilly. And with this they made it back to their rooms. You must rest, lass; I know you wanted to go shopping but we have another three days to do that, okay?

As she took Daisy's paw, they walked over to the lift and she walked Tilly to her room and she near enough took the door off its hinges. The excitement to get to the phone and I wonder why? Dylan, Dylan is that you? Yes of course it is, who else would it be? He replied in humour, how are you? I'm fine but, how are you? You sound like a pup on Christmas morning. Mentioning puppies, she spoke of what happened earlier and what she felt about and inside her and the amazing sensation from her tail to her snout, she felt like she was in a heavenly trance.

She explained everything to the hilt and then explained that they were making tracks and plans now that they will be home by Tuesday and on will they flow with their romance.

Aseena was back then and she could feel a very strong sensation within her presence around the room and it was not long before she was told of the feelings that Tilly had felt. You could see she blossomed with her friend and everything was put down in body and thought as this was personal and that is how they are, a bond of help and love. And for whatever the future brings within the paths of their lives, the love and friendship that had been built and grew still stronger by the day, would pull them threw anything that life throws at them because they had each other and this would guide them through life's problems and their spirits of life above.

The rest of their stay was just as rewarding with more than they expected and desired, plus their offer to this big city's ways of manners and happiness was greatly welcomed with open paws with who they had met on this wonderful trip. The one thing that did surprise many was the open offering that was given to Daisy on the Monday morning from Mrs McDonald herself and that was could they meet alone for a coffee? And both sides watched with anticipation from all angles of the hotel, from cleaners to the head, all eyes were fixed.

Then after the two sat and talked the smiles were clear that things of the past were to be let down for it was best to do so in life. The patio doors that led from the café, they led to the Hayes Park and the hotel were allowed access for any hotel guests to enter across the small bridge over the stream into the famous grounds and when the pair rose and followed each other out there, that is when everyone stopped still in what they were doing to look on and how everyone's thoughts were mixed.

Don't ask how or why but Stella was standing beside Nanny Sky and looking out they witnessed the two embrace and join each other with a stroll through the offerings of the park and smiling contentedly then turned around and looked back to the hotel they could not help but notice a package of eyes glaring at them and then suddenly turn away and walk about pretending they were at their own business of everyday news.

How could you not help but laugh out after witnessing this end to a saga that no one could predict, and what would the odds have been for surely it would be as strong as who shot JR in Dallas or any other soap opera out there now or then? It surprised many to say the least the outcome but let us just say it is nice to get a positive result with so much going on around them. Shall we make it back indoors? Yes, let's do that, and they gently strolled back across into the hotel with a welcome of nods and nervous you could say smiles, from all who were leering on. Can I get you ladies a drink at all? Yes, you may and with this they sat at a high table and sipped on classic Martinis and kept glancing about all inside and not giving away one ounce of what was said out there on that walk, no, not one ounce to any clues.

Are you coming with us tonight, may I ask, to the bar down in Soho? Yes, as it is your last night, why not? Right then we'd better make tracks, Stella, as I've to get ready for this evening and we are no youngsters and need the extra chiselling. That is one way of putting it isn't it, came the reply from Nanny Sky as she glanced at Daisy and then back to the host, okay we shall see you tonight.

Okay, okay you are all keen to hear what went on out there aren't you? Were the words spoken by Daisy. Well, you are all going to have to behave along the line and maybe in the future I'll tell. But as for now my lips are sealed and will stay that way. The eyes of curiosity stared on as they made it to their rooms and a quick bump into one of the gardeners gave Daisy a flashback. Oh, please, can you tell Stanley the Sparrow to tell Pepper that we will be ready for him in the morning at the hotel front, to return back to Kent, okay? Yes, I'll do that right this minute as he's on break and will be back at the kitchen hall. They all looked at each other and realised that this was their last day and night but once again after another positive gathering it all looked bright.

How are you feeling about going home, Aseena? This was the question asked by Tilly, as they were getting prepared for the exit from this Masquerade of shows and poses within their stay.

I feel that when we return, I will need to answer my own desire and heart, Tilly, and I will be asking a lot of questions but only I can answer them in the end and I've answered a drive within me of what would it be like to enter this world of modelling and the desire is still there and the question to answer to myself will be is it home or away?

The evening arrived and to walk into the club-bar-showroom and see the takings-shots and captures mainly based on Twiggy' s earlier years to show the figure of expression was enough, to say the least, for one's own answers. The expression on Daisy's smile was immense and of all the things to happen but whom did Mrs McDonald walk in with from the stage door, but only herself, Twiggy! The guests around the table were just ecstatic to say the least and it brought even more of a bond to the new and old friends, as once again glazing eyes of passion were shinning like stars on a summer night.

Nanny Sky had to say, Daisy, I honestly feel this could be one of two tricks and the first is this drive for the youngster to dwell upon on her travels home, to feel she must return herself to the big smoke, or is it sincere and a truthful gift to us? Time can only tell us this one my friend, was Daisy's reply, only time will tell.

Just then out came a cry to all, Darlings! Yes, you guessed it, Birdie, yes, she's on the floor; even Twiggy herself had to smile as she has had this misfortune, if you could call it that, of meeting the young lady in the past with others, so it could only be taken in fun.

I shall miss you, Aseena, came the words from Stella. And I, too, was the reply, believe me I will. They had to keep a little hush-hush as don't forget what this invite was all about in the beginning.

The evening carried on with such fun even with the parade of Birdie. Yes, it was a tremendous aroma to be in. Are we going to keep in touch, Daisy? This was a humble question in a tone from Mrs McDonald but it was answered with a positive reply. Yes, we shall, of course we shall.

As the evening moved on, we do need to make a move, Daisy. By surprise this came from Nanny Sky. Maybe she knew the long journey in the morning was going to be an emotionally tiring one plus knowing if one more martini came her way, there would be many more!

I just want to say thank you so much, Twiggy, for this evening and the questions thrown at you, may I say, were a little awkward to say the least. No-no, you must have got it yourself in your day? Yes, I did, I did! And as the two burst out laughing, she managed to get a little whisper in Daisy's ear, watch out for her, Daisy, watch out, for she will be in high demand. She knew well what she was talking about as she stood up and looked around with her historical glance of their company and a vision in sight for what was to come.

The morning arrived and all about the hotel was a feeling of a sad joy from the staff as they did not want to lose these guests; they had become more like members of staff than paying guests. Mind you, wouldn't you lay it on the line if the offer came your way with all the expenses taken care of and told please, please enjoy your stay with us and anything you need, etc-_etc, enjoy.

They made their way out of the doors with the porters beside them with their bags and then met big Pepper who stared on with a gasp out of his truck window, as from Managers to chefs to porters all joined in on their departure with hugs and smiles. He looked on surprised in a way as they clambered in with a little hysteria in tune from his fare who, without even thinking, he will hear no end of their venture and this he will employ.

Bye-bye, the waves and thanks were all about when surprisingly Mrs McDonald herself turned up with her daughter at her side.

One couldn't help but look on to see Birdie there; Come on, that's not her, is it? So, whatever it was all about, smiles were all around and the waves of arms and paws were all open wide.

It was kinda quiet in the front as they drove out through the traffic of London's ways, with hoots and cusses from all angles with even a few cab drivers hooting at the truck as they recognised their fares from the past few days. See ya next time, me ole cockle! Was their famous cry and they waved on until the big motorway was in sight and on their way back home to Kent, where no doubt questions and all would be flying at them from everyone to find out what happened? And now what would be happening next?

As in a town like where they lived it is everyday life to find out what is one's bizzo and the more one finds out the better it is. Feeling okay Tilly? Was a light question in her ear from Aseena, as they held paws and smiled to each other with the past few days' actions still running highly within their hearts and thoughts. Fine, Aseena, I'm fine and I'll be even better when I see Dylan. Nanny heard this and gave a smile to them both.

Well, my ladies, may I say there was a lot of chit-chats everywhere on the subject of you, lassie, being in town. You were beaming, Aseena. Pepper's strong Yorkshire accent spread a hearty feeling of warmth in that crammed truck cab, and no doubt Margaret will be howling into my ears of my side of what I did and seen?

Never mind you telling her anything, came the reply from Daisy and laughter filled the little space they had until they saw the sign: DOVER 14 miles and Nanny said, not long to go now gang.

And for some reason it stayed quiet till the first drop off happened and it was at Nanny Sky's home where out she stepped to hear all the barking and banting from the neighbour's around her domain and then she called out, speak to you in the morning, Daisy, okay love? and off they drove to the next drop and that of course would be Tilly.

Daisy stepped out first to let her paw out to bring her down with gentleness and standing there with a welcoming smile was, of course, Dylan and with him a surprise, Lilly. Welcome home! Came shouts from around the garden next door as over the fence was Hilary. She's a Connemara Collie and a midwife since Darcy's generation anyway. She was visiting Rosie, the chocolate lab who has had problems with her legs since way back.

She too was involved in the catwalk business to promote the style of her coat as there were not many about in those days. You were either a black or a white lab not a choc.

Anyway, Hilary spoke to say, Thank God you are back, Tilly, as who do think would not shut up about you and this trip you were on? Yes, Rosie she was talking about of course. Word got out that you were escorting Aseena to London and she too knew Mrs McDonald and she has asked me to make sure I speak to you directly to pay her a visit when you get back. This brought an open joy of laughter from Daisy as she too knew Rosie well and could be a little bit too silly.

Hi, Mum, was the blossoming voice spoken to Darcy, with both paws out she embraced her joy of life like a mare cleaning her new born foal. Darcy of course heard of the movements of Tilly's joy from Dylan and could not wait to see her in the flesh to discuss her daughter and here she was now back home. Indoors they headed with waves again mixed with, see you soon calls, as Daisy got back into the truck and Aseena sat in the middle. She looked over her shoulder to Pepper and they both smiled in a contented manner as they looked down.

Daisy spoke first with a funny tone; this is all because of you young lady. It is, isn't it? laughing with a little embarrassment, you could say, she replied with a contented smile.

Then one more drop-off for Pepper's long drive and that was to the Manor where Margaret and Grandad awaited. The doors and ears will be waiting with open jaws and paws as it seems to have been a little quiet in many ways since the young lady's absence and it does seem to have been a good while.

As they drove up into the courtyard Margaret stood at the doorway with granddad beside her and the hefty figure of Pepper got out to lift the young lady down from the truck but he was too slow, for the youngster was half way up the stairs into the embracing hugs of her loved ones and just could not keep a second's silence in explaining what she had just been through and witnessed.

Pepper put her luggage down so that it could be picked up and Margaret spoke out, Anyone for tea? They were going to drive straight off, but Daisy thought quickly, that it may be right to fill Margaret in on some details of their saga to give the house an idea of what Aseena would be trying to explain to them all.

They sat for just a while and said what they needed to with a lot of laughter about in their tone and Margaret was so impressed and thankful and Daisy said there and then, Right, I need to get some rest. And they said their goodbyes and then back on the road they hit.

Well, I cannot thank you enough, Pepper, for what you have done as it has taken so much stress out of the traveling side of this trip. No problem, lass, if anything it has been great company for once and I'll call you next time I'm heading up to the 'smoke'. They both laughed as it was the truth to say the least in what he said. They arrived at Daisy's and gave a quick hug and 'byes and Pepper had his entire cargo unloaded with success.

Inside her own home, she just put her assets down after shutting the door and with a sigh of relief thanked the gift of life that it was over and at the same time, she did not know it would have been such an adventure herself and answers for her own heart and soul that she never thought would come to be and here, in just under a week, the whole lot was over and look what has happened in that short period, who would have believed it? And with paws to fingers and thumbs crossed, all this will even get better with all the dreams of everyone involved it will all be blessed.

Back at Tilly's, the whole saviour of life was buzzing and it was not surprising why. With a new generation on the horizon, with new careers and another surprise, Bailey, Dylan's brother would be arriving from Wales in the morning. He had been on tour with the Sheep Shearers, a group of half a dozen who worked touring the world on expeditions of sheep shearing. They had been in Australia for six months then to Ireland and then back on the mainland of the UK and he being a dissentience of Wales from his folk, who made the famous walks back in the day to Kent for the hefty work down the coal mines, he felt comfort at home there.

He and Dylan, they were very close as the bond of

puppyhood had been very adventurous and happy and that made this sit in their hearts. He told his brother he had a guest with him who was an American Cattle dog who applied for the position with the team and after the interview, they had to take him on for trails and were all so impressed that it was a very easy decision to let him on board.

His name was Rusty. And a mighty big pleasure it is to meet ya, buddy, as I heard a lot about ya and your mam. He, being a real, typical southern boy, you could not help but fall for his manner that fitted in well. He adapted to the chit-chat all around him from the close-knit family and felt at home himself with that bond of love that was so easy to feel for this had grown since way back in generations of struggling for a better life that there was no way you could put a price on this loving hoard.

Dylan, do you think it would be better if we stayed at The Bone and Bowl? As it's the two of us by the way. Nonsense you will be able to stay here, even so we can test it for a short while until you see what is next in line? Anyway, so much has happened, Bailey, that you would never think could have in just twelve months or so. And most of all, you're close to becoming an uncle! What do you think of that then? You know well they will be ruined by me, don't you? Yes, yes, I know with the two of them bringing laughter about of their banter.

They shared a hefty feast that was renowned from Aunt Darcy's dishes called the Chew Brew Chomp. There is not to this day a dog or whatever animal that has disliked this dish and it was made for sharing as once again, that is what dining is all about and that is to share.

May I say, Ma'am, that's one mighty dish ya made. I'm a gonna lick that pot out if I git the chance, may I say. This brought laughter about once again. Now let me just show you before we go out onto the patio, where you will be staying and I hope you don't mind sharing the doublers baskets with Dylan?

No-no, if ya seen where we had ta put our paws down on some ranches, Ma'am, along the line a heavenly lay down such as this is just what they say is Heaven. Once he started with his tongue wagging there was no end to him and shutting his bark up. Yes, well we would love to know and listen to some of these tales if you dare!

Morning arrived and a flow around the house was of natural everyday love and banter and of course the main status of Tilly's condition and what went on in London, plus what happens next? Dylan was on a stroll with his brother along the front as they needed their time to chat and both sharing what was on the line of their future in a different style but both in their contented ways, it would be a great adventure for them both.

When Dylan told Bailey about his acceptance into the 50/50 training squad, both drug and bomb sections, you can just imagine how excited he was for his brother and especially now with a whole family on the way. Do you want puppy's broth? And where and when will you meet your match, Bailey? Who knows that, Dylan, who knows? Both thought about that question for a second and then they just burst out with laughter aloud.

A major change since our days walking along here listening to the banters of the Deal luggers and what they had hidden on those flat-bottomed tiddlers? And the fishermen and their chat over their catch of the day and the ones that got away. Speaking of that, is there anyone still fishing here? Yes, yes you have the small knit family still in action as a part time living and solo fishermen casting off the Pier and just sit there to get away from everyday ways plus, they still sit amongst the shingles with their thoughts in all.

We often spoke of that was not the life for us, was it and now look where we are, Dylan. Where did the time go since those puppy days walking along here where it all began with those everyday adventures and ideas of becoming rich? And to say of those thoughts we had, yes, we were very proud.

Where you say a love in my life, I can never forget Poppy for look what we used to get up to once again in those puppy years, how we survived I just don't know.

But it was all about the walk and talk and the lessons we learnt from for our hearts and thoughts and which way and where will they go?

She knows you are back, Bailey, as Tilly was talking to Lilly about their business plan of the Dogs Brush Cleaning Agency and your name came up and somehow Poppy was with her and heard the banter. She's been dating one of the Alder family. You know those Alsatians over in Walmer? A real nice wagtail as I met him at one of the classes 'on the drug aroma and scents of the inner and outer buildings. He is training for the Dover team and going all out for it.

Just then on their way along the front, Phil the Dill, the Doberman, you know the landlord of the Claredon Collar Club, a location where these boys had their first drink, learning the leads of life. Anyway, he saw the pair and invited them both down for a few bevvies on the house as a welcome home and Dylan's congrats drink.

We will pop in tomorrow. Wait a sec, lads, we have a band on Friday so it will be your choice on what night okay?

The two strolled along in awe with the delight of each other's company and reached the gates of the old Barracks and just got chatting away about its history and then just made their way back home where they gave the odd bark to whoever knew them and so on.

They arrived back and with the greeting of the house as usual, Dylan told Tilly of the invite by the Pincher, as she called him. She just smiled as she thought to herself, Oh my, what is gonna happen on that night? Will it carry on into one of the ones that the youngsters will rant, talk about in the many years to come of one of those crazy days of dismay!

The Clarendon, Collar, Kennel club had a history that went as far back as you can imagine, being on the front and all. Generations of breeds arrived in style and fell out of there with questions of what happened last night? But, oh well, there's another day to chew a bone as the old saying goes.

The two strolled back and Bailey opened the door and met Rusty. I'm sorry to have left you, Rusty, but I had to talk to my brother and catch up but I did not want to ignore you. No problem, ma boy, me an ya Ma, sorry Tilly's Ma, had a good ole chat on cooking and the old dishes the dogs of the fishermen-smugglers would eat. I explained right from the beginning of ma family who were with the first to land in the New World, the States that is and what they ate in all travelling across the land to make a new life for themselves. As history goes to say, ma family were with the cowboys who travelled from state to state and built the ranches to where it is now. Anyway, we're gonna have a Cajun dish and we bin over to The Black Pig and met the lady there who you told me about, ma boy. A mighty fine daughter she has, ma boy, mighty fine.

They all laughed about how Rusty fitted in and you could tell Darcy took to the lad like a son from her own litter. Right, let me show ya where you two will be at boy! And with this the movement of the happy house was all about again with smiles of contentment, excitement and getting feisted up for whatever was ahead of them. But first of all, like traditions of all their cultures there was one thing that had to be done and that was to dine!

By the way, I've a message from Aseena, Tilly. Phoenix, you know her Granddad, he wants to say thank you to all for the tremendous company and advice you gave his granddaughter before and on the trip to the Big Smoke. Rusty looked confused a little on this so Dylan explained to him that the older generation knew London by that name just like a southerner calls New York. Anyway, Dylan told his brother and Rusty about the girl's trip and kept it as short as it could be and how it all came about.

And there's me expecting a town with a few sprats swimming about and everyone in their baskets by the time of 8 o'clock. I wuz mighty wrong about that, weren't I? Yes, it is really strange, lads, how something can happen so quickly. Just like that, a simple introduction and it all started from there. She has become a wonderful new friend to Tilly and so much has happened since they met up that it is hard to believe myself. But who the hell knows what comes next around here?

The fiesta, as you could call it, matched the company and they shared their banters and hollas throughout the night until it was time to let nature take its course, sending them to dreamland and each one just followed their snout to their baskets and said Goodnight! It didn't take too long to pass out with so much contentment within their hearts for the company they were in and the next thing they knew they were awakened by a bark of, Wakey-wakey, breakfast is up! And of course, the feeling of happiness flowed around the house that chased away any thoughts of fear.

Mrs Gooseman, the blackbird who's been the local postie for half a century dropped an invite from Aseena's Granddaddy for the festival feast and famous race at their Manor, as a goodwill gesture. She passed it over to Darcy who was at the kitchen table and commented on the letter by saying, Oh, stepping up in the world now I see, Darcy, after she had a nose in what the invite was all about.

Darcy just laughed it off and then Tilly walked in and it was passed on to her. This has arrived for you and that was good timing as I need to get a message to Aseena about Friday night and if she would like to join us on that social meeting and catch up. So, she scribbled a note and just caught Mrs Gooseman on the way out, off on her rounds. Quickly, Mrs Gooseman had to ask how Tilly's condition was and was she feeling well? A lady's thing you know and a way to get any gossip in hand. Oh, I'm well; I'm fine and thank you for asking, she answered with her smile.

After a little morning shake about, she watched Mrs Gooseman fly off to her next delivery nose about. She is something special, isn't she? A laugh came from Darcy as she asked how her daughter was feeling? Darcy's thoughts were open and she muttered to herself, A Grandma, me? A nod of the head and a wag of the tail and then back to business. A bit of a lad this American pup, isn't he? And for him to be here now with all what is going on. Yes, at the same time Mum if it wasn't what is going on with me, there would be something else going on and that is what makes a town like this a good play to make your grounds.

It did not take long to receive a message from Aseena to reply to say she would be meeting them and just couldn't wait to meet the other members of the family and friends. And this time it is local which Aseena has not witnessed herself by the way, and to my knowledge of first introductions, for many they are the ones that seem to bring on the stories that stay in the chatter minds of many. Yep, a good ole banter and I feel there is something of this week's excitement that what happens this weekend is going to be one that will remain in their thoughts and hearts and their memories that will stay.

There was another meeting called together for the girls with their business plan as to their outlook and wednesday arrived and their survey had come back to them on all the feedback and future locations that want their services and the response had been amazing which sent a great feeling within their group. With excitement, Darcy spoke, So we all agree that it is to be called the Dogs Brush, yes? They sat about around the tables back at the Forester's Arms where Margaret looked on at the excitement of those open thoughts of setting about their own business and of course thoughts of herself starting up, came back.

Ladies, can I mention something now and only now? They looked on and it was all about communication with each other and to keep it that way. You must work as a team, okay? Her stern voice spoke from experience of how to hold your own. What do you think of our logo, then by the way? She laughed and said, I would prefer if you had a young handsome beast strutting his stuff in a manner to excite us all rather than that one! They just laughed as well, as they knew only too well that was the type of answer she would give.

Right, that is that. We now want to all agree on what date we start, rotas and the whole time we have to suit ourselves and to make this our business okay? Margaret, being one of the oldest traders in this town of ours has seen many, many companies and ideas come to life. And she looked over with her stern, yet wise expression and knew these girls had got it, as a person may say, yep, they will make it the best in town.

The days building up to Friday were set mainly in the buzz of the company beginning and of course the London trip and all around and of course the news of the girls and Bailey being home. Darcy thought this one out and decided to let the youngsters have their way and not join them on the town as she did feel a little too much if her eyes were on their behaviour and of course her daughter's condition, she would certainly be a Grandma in her tone. So, she contacted Nanny Sky, Daisy and Margaret from the Manor, as she had known her since childhood as her granny was best friends with her and helped through the days she first joined Phoenix and the position to take the house and all its habits and bodies on, so it would be nice for them to meet and discuss the next stage of the road to

Margaret of what they witnessed in London with Aseena's adventure and future with full eyes down.

That afternoon, Aseena called in just to check, What are we to wear, Tilly? A girlie thing of talk over, you know? And they agreed casual-to-smart coatings would be all around comfort to suit all. So, so much is going on, Tilly, I don't seem to know whether I'm coming or going. These were the words from Aseena, discussing what was happening since their trip. I'm still in a little bit of shock and I've popped down to Becca today to have a trim-clean up and she told me she has never had so many questions thrown at her about our trip! They just laughed to themselves of all the drama and talked of the gossipy tongues of the day.

Then came the morning of Friday, no not the 13th but in a way, there was a strong feeling of the word in their thoughts from the old and young it could be a night of dismay!

We first met at the Ship Inn along Middle Street, a natural thing for us to do as the couple once again had known us all since our puppy days, Ray and Penny in a gentle manner gave us the boot when we tried to get served and act like adult doggies but alas, away we were sent.

Ray asked Dylan about the twin course he had just been accepted to, as his pup was applying too and Dylan grew up with him. A shake of the paw, he congratulated him and then over his snout he looked at Bailey and added, how are you, my boy? He knew how different the two were but could not help but like them both but thought now what will the Town Cryer be calling out at the dawn of the next morn after these had finished with it? And most of all he just heard his son get talking to Rusty and his interest in the States, he had to join in and talk his Mum out of his shift, so he could be with the youngsters on the loose, to an open thought of just be aware?

How could she deny him as we have all been there once?

Will, that is his name, by the way, I'll cover you if you want to join their company? It was the barmaid's call out so it did not take long for him to agree on that term, then a drink in paw and the banter on its way.

We promised Rusty we would take him about so we are popping over to The Forester's to introduce him to that pack of characters, the Hair Bear Bunch as known to many around the coastal towns. It was a sort of smuggling code name from the ole days, by the way, Rusty that is where it came from. That is what I've heard anyway. Don't you just luv it? Ye ole names ya have from way back ma boy, ya, I just luv it.

This was the chat from Rusty as he was telling Will about his location back home in the States as Will was telling Rusty that he wanted to work the Route 66 one day and that is where he wants to travel to in his future plans.

They made their way over through the narrow stretch road and onto the Marina where the Foresters sits and in through the door they went. A few sturdy looks came about, mostly from the regulars recognising Bailey being home and the big Galoot of Rusty and it did not take long for him to bark and it was clear with his accent it would be picked up on and yes they did have eyes set upon them with an open stare.

The flow just carried on as it did not take long for the locals to take to the Yank as they would call him and a few glassy-eyed local barks came about when talking about a Yankee yellow belly on their tongues. Yes, a bit too much wee dram in them I'd say. But Rusty being a southerner he would not take offence, anyway plus he had Will beside him who knew well who to keep a good-hearted new friend away from, and the craic started onwards into the night.

Some of the old mutts loved telling Rusty the banters of the smuggling days and the hounds that knew well where to hide the stashes of their master's packs and hoards, hidden away even to this day and were never found. You see on your walk and so check the street names off the front like Copper-Silver Street, why are they named that?

A little silence in thoughts, even with Dylan, and so and yes, Rusty copped it on that there were a fair few extra tales added to make the saga stretch but it was all in fun to make the night a good one when they found out a little bit more. Bailey copped this on and enjoyed staring at the ones who were telling the tales and gave a gesture, don't go too far as to make fun of their guest but they too took to the guest as they knew well, he was all made from a good stock.

So, after their wonderful introduction it was once again time to move on and they took him along the front, down towards the middle of the town explaining to him the buildings of where all the stories and legends began, like pointing out the Goodwin Sands and its greed and takings by storm and nature and this brought on his thoughts again into shock.

They enjoyed the craic explaining to their guest just like generations before them about their ancestors' history and ways and it was important for these local characters to carry on the stories of hundreds of years of history and yes, many a banter was based on the smuggling or whatever that made the town unique.

Just then when they reached the Bar 81, a flock of local girls with two midwives, with them. Lisa-Bella spotted Tilly, about having a hen night or a dog's dunk known by many a local. Tilly, she was the talk of the town as well by the way as word was about of her condition. Oh, how are you my dear after that trip to London? I remember my first litter, Bella said with a gentle sigh, don't worry my dear all will be well. Then one of the younger dogs spoke with a sniggery, boozy attitude and Dylan was just going to say something when she just touched his paw with a please, glance, don't say anything my love and his rage calmed down but he did give the bitch who spoke a good stare and realized who it was. Yeah, one who had a long crush on him and had her eye on him for her own but this was not going to make things better for her was it?

There were a few older mutts passing by and heard this bad barking type of talk and a wink came from a stern ole terrier, Frank was his name. Leave 'em at it, I'd say, and don't try to understand them, ma boy, it will only leave you in disarray.

The boys looked on as they too heard the nasty words and were ready to say something but after the words from the ole terrier, they looked at each other with smiles and laughter on the advice they were given and for some reason totally agreed and thanked Frank for his concern. They arrived then at the Pelican Pub and inside were a few military sniffers who were telling their tales in all to a few younger pups who once again had their ears up for some ole banters when they realised who'd come in.

They noticed Bailey being home and the girls out as well with, of course, the beauty of Aseena in their prescience. So out came the male strutting as you may call it to put on the charm. Please come and join us for a while before you paint the town, a little laughter came from the gent who spoke, who also happened to be an instructor of a legend at Dylan's college.

Updated chat came out and they knew of the results of Dylan's trials. Tell me, Dylan, which way will you go now that the two choices are with you? This came from Sky the Light, an Australian sheepdog who was brought over when a batch of Royal Marines were on tour in Angola with an Aussie unit and she loved working with a Welsh border sheepdog. She then fell for the love of her life with a dingo-like mutt and the rest is history. She got her nickname from her reaction of picking up a scent of whatever she was told to find and her eyes were like lightning but dogs learnt quickly not to get on the wrong side of her as her bark was as fast as her picking up a scent.

They discussed the choices and Dylan loved those banters of advice and then Bailey joined in with his intro explaining to Sky that he had just returned from down under and how much he adored the open life of the country and just before Sky asked what unit he was in, she then noticed the shearing type paws and remembered he never joined any corps, it was only Dylan going into the line of duty.

They were just going to say goodnight to move on when Geeta spoke, Tilly I just can't help but listen to the chit-chat of the meetings you girls have had over the new business and feel I'd love to discuss working for you in some manner? Of course, we can talk. What are you doing tonight? Come, come join us as we are celebrating a few things in our lives that have happened and with Bailey being home too there is a lot to chat over. They said their farewells to other guests and headed for the door and with Betty - she's the landlady, her elbows on the bar's counter thought to herself, a sense of history's wild days is felt here of this little buzz heading down to the town and her daughter, Sally being with them. Oh my, what will the morning banter be? I just hope it's not dismay!

They walked on and the laughter just carried within the air that blew from the south of the Channel and let's face it they had a lot to laugh and smile about, hadn't they? They reached the Pier which once again carried so many banters and so, and pointing out to Rusty its stories and who apparently lived underneath it, And even to this day, his head pops up now and then to give a cocky wink to the gals or poke his tongue out to the guys but it's true he does exist. Greg, the one-eyed croc is his name and those who have seen him say he must be at least a 50-footer. We tried everything in the book as kids to catch him as there was and still is a good price on him but no luck came our way, even as naïve an American can be for believing, Rusty could only laugh this one off.

Mind you, I think we should pop into the Royal Hotel just to explain to Rusty that this was, if you wouldn't mind me saying, a bit of a playing field, for you could say the most famous naval officer ever. Yep, Nelson himself. What? Horatio Nelson the 1st Viscount, the Duke of Bronte? Well, your history is well on him, isn't it? Yes, I studied naval history as my daddy wanted me to go to sea, yep, an ole sea dog he was. Well, Rusty, my dad is ex-naval and mum too, these were the words out of Will; maybe that is why they hit it off so well straight away. Anyway, Rusty, Lady Hamilton? She was Nelson's kept woman as you may say. She was kept in a little cottage over there, you see it is just a large car park now but in its day it was all houses, then flattened in the war by the Luftwaffe.

Right through the road where we walked from the Ship, that road used to go right through that car park onto South Street. He made many promises, Rusty, to her. And nearly all those promises were made out and around the royal Hotel's bar or main bedroom, may I say. Mind you I have to say some of the ole dogs' tales reckon she was a bit of a doggie collector herself. Mostly sturdy officers so who was laughing at who? A mighty playing town ya have here don't ya? Yes, you can say that and that is just one of the legendary tales my friend and no doubt you will hear more, Rusty, believe me you will.

Like for instance I seen you looking at Margaret the landlady from the Foresters who was visiting the Pelican and who she was weighing up. Margaret the longest-most character landlady in this town's history and she has seen it, done it and watched its ways and changes time and time again. Geeta, you see is her step-daughter. Many, many years ago whilst on holiday, vacation you call it, she was in Thailand and a couple she became close to as she visited the area often. Anyway, there was a bad time in changes and gangs of rebels overthrew the government and took Geeta's parents away to be slaved in a bad part of the town but within the mass mess, they managed to pass Geeta to

Maggie who somehow smuggled her outta the country by pretending she was Margaret's pet and took her under her wing and raised her like her own. Geeta just somehow fitted in Margaret's shopping bag with many other objects and as she put her paw out to touch her folks through the cage, they were set on and she never saw them again until 30 years later after somehow, they too were smuggled out and to witness the reunion was an amazing sight. She knew straight away who they were and just could not wait to embrace them both.

Margaret was listening and watching what we were talking about as it was in her genes to be wary of one's behaviour towards Geeta. Anyway, Geeta's reunion was a beautiful time in her life to witness and you see that is why she gets along with all shapes and sizes of the breeds in this town and she's close to Lilly as once again, look at her background and it's the same story and the only difference is that it happened to Lilly in Spain and the special love these girls have is loving to each other and stronger still.

The evening carried on with the feeling of a great bond of new- old friendships beginning and even sensed there was love in the air for some but for whom? Who shall it be? Who will follow this destiny of love and their fate? Only time will tell. And now the wind's changing with the fall drawing in, carrying her stories from many parts of the world of love and life. It will be each other's destiny and their story in life of their own fate.

The evening just flowed with the harmony of the company's new and old love and has they walked into the Clarendon Hotel they were welcomed by Phil the Dill, oh yes in his bow tie and all he welcomed the guests with open paws. He introduced his wife, a pretty Springer called Mia Tia. Born overseas as her Daddy was an officer's seadog, one of the greats -well they say the best snout in scenting. But that is still argued over. Anyway, being the lady she is, she put both paws out to greet the girls as Phil planned this for some reason. And it was only seconds before it was found out why. Phil the Dill had a sorta nervous, tension yet excited feel about him. He called Dylan and Bailey over to one side cleverly to tell them something. He told his manager to give the guests the best seats in the house and the boys could assist in bringing the drinks over, but there was more to it. And it was talk of the way the old town was and telling something to a mate.

Look lads, I didn't know myself as I would have changed us meeting up to another date, but anyway there is a large reunion of a well-to-do group here to party up and discuss business and memory matters. The two looked at each other in confusion to sort of say what was it to do with them? Phil the Dill spoke out as to who it was. Well, The BLC are here, the Barka Larka Club. It's a shake paws club of Lawyers, Kennel property investors and councillors all belonging to the gun club, etc, etc and they all had their doggies with them as the shooting club was held on that afternoon. They did ask could the dogs stay? And the Mrs said yes, and didn't think anything of it. When I came down the stairs earlier and saw the pair of Shihtzus loverty and doverty together, drinking their honey laced milk I nearly died in my steps. I looked around and saw Henry of the Hunters, a well-to-do Bloodhound and many, many others of all shapes and sizes and all other top dogs, my heart started pounding as I tried to keep my cool not let on to anything.

Will looked at Rusty who was looking confused and explained to him what the tension was about. You see, Rusty, there was a club here in the town that was used by every local social breed in history; it was called the Seadogs Club. This was a club house that for centuries belonged to the Sailors, Miners, Fishermen - you name it they met there. Anyway, behind their backs the BCL Club tried and succeeded in buying their club house and changed it into a bloody yacht club, for what? All the locations over at Sandwich or wherever, they took our club that had been the stronghold for any main chit-chat for two centuries and more and they knew what it meant.

It was that hoity-toity, toffee-snouted sausage dog; you know the one we used to call beaky? Well, his owner who owns all that land and so on and also belongs to the council planning board, he talked his owner into it and did it out of spite because he was not big enough to meet the Rowing Rovers team. It was not personal as he just was not up to standard to be able to do the job that would save lives, etc, but because he could not have his own way, he acted as a brat. Right, how are we going to get around this one Dylan, without causing a bite or a bark out of this lament?

Come on, come up with something. Just then who walked in, paw in paw, but Poppy with her new escort, Wilbert, the German Shepard. Dylan looked at Bailey to say remember him? Yes, I do, came the reply. Does Poppy know whose family he is from? Does she know who his Daddy is? He is only the chairman's dog of the Barka-Larkas, you know. Yak, you know what it must have been like for the boys to see the girl who grew up with them on the paw of you know who? And when Bailey saw it, well what can one say? But the look from the two lads said it all.

Phil the Dill tried a fast one and said, shall we go over to the Bar and Bark on the High Street, as the Dog la Doodles are playing and maybe we can have one there? Dylan did think that logical and agreed and said, Okay, let's pop over and see Marian. She's got the place now, Bailey.

Walking over the old court yard, Dylan was watching his brother's reactions just to see his temperament when who should they meet but Aussie and the Huskies, all members of the Seadogs Club. Phil the Dill nearly came to having his own litter at this point and barked a quick jest out, Hi, guys, we are gonna have one over with Marian at the Bar and Bark to let her know Bailey's home and to see the band, do y'wanna join us?

Ya, by the way this is Rusty, he's over with Bailey and he's from the States. Why howdy ya all! And it did not take long for them to enjoy his manner.

Enjoying the company and music, the bunch of breeds carried on just chatting, reminiscing about old times and laughing away and Phil gave a nervous glance at Dylan and said, I'm just going to pop out and see if the coast is clear. Then he slipped out of the side door.

He arrived back at the hotel just to see how things were or to see if there was any sign of the guests leaving, as no doubt he felt how long would it be before word got out who was over at The Clarendon and what was gonna happen? Well, that was shortly to be answered for who walked into the Bar and Bark but Bert the bulldog. He was the head bouncer of the Seadogs Club and proud of it.

He was in the Ship Inn, his local when Loopy the Lurcher came in and said, Hey Bert, I just passed the Clarendon Hotel and you will never guess who I seen all dolled up to the tee, only Yakan with another Pup, Wilmer.

Well word of this manner spread like wildfire and more and more doggies of the night became a pack and they in no way were going to ignore their chance of catching them all together again. Yes, they got more of the local honey booze of haven down their long and short necks and the feisty bark came out and yelps and yells filled the room and there was no stopping it now.

Many a mutt came flooding down to the Bar and Bark that they were flowing out onto the road and by now all fired up. So, led by Skipper, the other bouncer of the town and Bert, it did not take long before Bailey and Dylan were in the middle of the pair. Tilly looked at Dylan and with a naughty smile winked as to say, Go on, ma boy, give 'em what they deserve. Even Rusty picked up on what the score was about and with Will, he got all excited about this big bash on its way, like a saloon style bash you could say.

But this was one that would have tongues wagging and go down as one of the memory brawls and gnawls that was going to go paw to paw.

Now all Phil the Dill could do was look at the heavens and say, Well, here it goes, as he had seen at the door Bert the Bulldog shaking paws with the bouncers. And one was Percy, the son of Sambo the Snoozer, you know he used to be the head honcho of the Pink Flamingo, and yes, a local head on mutt, this kinda bond and loyalty was good you know? Bert gave Aussie a nod when he saw him with the huskies walking up to the front door and then Percy looked at Dongo, the liver and tan Doberman, and their thoughts were, Oh well, it was good working here whilst it lasted you know, that is if the job was still there after this night of bliss.

Good evening, sir, I understand you have a booking for our establishment's dinner conference at 8pm? Phil the Dill's snout dropped to the ground and it had to be laughed at you know when he realised who the booking was for; only the vets that Tilly and all belonged to and only yesterday morning she was there having her scans and the laughter of bark chat was of such joy as they had known Tilly since her birth herself.

At the Animal House Vets, there had been times in so many of the dogs' lives that had been so important to each one, only a diary could tell of them as from an examination to give them a pass to enter certain training lines of duty one had chosen or even to pull a splinter out of one's paw, just wonderful memories for many. Like many a story, such as the one when Stephanie Fox, honestly Miss Fox a vet? had to go to Bert's brother's allotments to examine a whole wipe-out of chickens as a vixen got into the coup and like a vixen does, she killed every single one of Benny's flock, his pride and joy.

And after the verdict of what happened, she had to sign the statement for the owner to take to the police as proof of what happened.

How are you supposed to keep a straight face reading the report on this case, signed by a Mrs Fox? Anyway, they are here for their yearly thank you dinner for all their hard work. The director led them in and proud he was of his team. He sort of sensed something was up when he saw certain mutts fisted up and a lot of movement going on. Hi, Phil, how have things been for you since seeing you last? Jeremy, a tall gent who idolised his team's hard work and it was great to witness a dog and human's connection in everyday life as it was and it showed here as proof of man's best friend. Mind you after the night ahead there may be a few questions to be asked and it all would not end with a kiss.

Phil was interrupted earlier by Brad, of Brad and Van Howling, you know the hubby of Becca of the Laundromutts Grooming. The pair are always in such demand and Jeremy got them only by a cancellation. Anyway, Brad called in earlier with Paul, you know, Angela's other half? She owns the Dapper Dogs Grooming. Anyway, he was assisting Brad to carry their kit in to set up as it was another surprise for Jeremey's staff for entertainment whilst they dined.

But who knew the entertainment was to be something of another type of style to suit their enjoyment whilst they wined?

Betty, yet another beagle, who has been the head waitress-host at the Clarendon for many a year, came over to greet them and Phil smiled to her and she knowing him thought, okay what is going on? As he notified her, Betty, please take our quests to the Snoutilliers Bar and tell Lilly the head barmaid that the first drinks are on the house, okay, and we will call you and the guests to The Long Tail Table Room in a short while.

He thought just off hand if he could get this room over the

other side of the hotel before anything did happen, they may not witness anything as he knew well it would not be long before something kicked off and who knows Phil the Dill just might run a mile.

Anyway, she led them across the hallway into the Snoutielliers Bar and who was in there but Poppy with her date beside her. Nods came about and condolences to Poppy as it was Jeremy who had tried in vain to save her cherished mummy just a while ago and everyone loved Meir, the pure Irish red terrier from the homeland of Ireland. Poppy was born here who once again, he brought into the world. Nanny Ryan and Bampie Bateman you see would not allow just themselves to be there for the birth so Jeremy sat with them and oh yes, it made a story for the chatterboxes of Deal, something to natter about. Next to them was Mr C R Robinson, the lawyer for all types of cases who in fact was on the defence team for the great pedigree romp and then down to Bonzo from the Bar-studio 21 on the front, that time being accused of stealing the prime bones off the Princess Anne yacht when it was in harbour here one time.

Anyway, a nice kinda chap. Evening Jeremy, were his first words and then just the banter of everyday life in general. Your table is ready, Sir, and this was for Mr Robinson as once again he was rewarding his staff for all their team work. It will not be long for your tables to be ready, Sir. That was for Jeremy's attention, and a thank you gesture came from him.

Yes, it was at this point at the other section of the Hotel that was boiling to the point of who would throw the first paw? Or who would take the first bite? Then who waddled in but Nellie, the old landlady from the Black Lion on the High Street now the beach, with its beautiful gifts on show for many. She was with some of her old staff, including Goffer the greyhound and Sparky the Staff terrier. Yep, members of the Seadogs Club and Nellie had her Patio shut down by the council for a shake hand-paw deal from that bloody Larka Club. And when Bert was coming back from the gent's pool and they saw him, a chat came out and you can guess what the main subject was.

And that was that, they walked down the hallway down past the murals then into the Blue Collared Coat of Arms Bar and as soon as many of the other dogs noticed who was there, by now the adrenalin - if you can call it that - was up and ready to go. The disco just started next door with Stephen Woolf's Born To Be Wild opening when bang! Aussie had some pointer by the bob of his tail, the first bite struck out. There were collars, hair, fur, teeth, you name it all over the place. Yelps and barks could be heard from as far down to The Royal Hotel; visiting guests all over were asking what the noise was outside? And many a landlord said oh, it is the local firework display for the life guards but word got out to them what may go off.

Head-to-head, Bert the bulldog was having it out with Roderick the Rotweiler. Dylan's skill of boxing was up against Sparky the Spaniel and Bailey was up, toe to paw, with the massive Goliath, the Great Dane. He was giving it his best when Zappa the Hungarian Vizsla joined in and by now the whole building was in uproar and guests from all around came to see or left in fright for their life.

But who walked by with her paw within her partner's paw but Poppy and she took one look inside and saw the love of her life with this big galloot of a giant and looked at her date and just said a quick, I'm sorry and off she ran, up over a few scrapping around on the floor, onto a table and leapt onto the bar, and as she ran across it, knocking a few glasses here and there and up she jumped and with both paws around the Great Dane's neck down he fell like a mighty redwood tree, he tumbled down, ya over and over the blows, bites came to an end and yes, they got their revenge when the cheers started to go about and the finest line came from our visiting guest, Rusty, by saying, My that was a mighty good fight, ma friends! And after that workout, who needs a gym?

Looking about and around him, Phil the Dill had one thing to say after the storm, Now we can let it lay. Whilst all the scrapping was at its peak, Martina and Stephanie from the Animal House vets were in the ladies' powder room and Lucy was in there with her friend Denise, a beautiful Afghan Hound with the slenderness of a snake made out of silk; she was a practice Veterinary Nurse as well and after being introduced, she just hit it off with the girls. She turned around quickly and thought I could play a fast one here, and gave Keeley a nudge in the side which made her a little confused. What brings you here this evening, ladies? They explained and asked, What part of the location are you dinning in? The pair knew it was in full pelt back in the Collars Bar and would need assistance maybe to stitch a tail back on or a snout to straighten.

Anyway, Keeley knowing the Clarendon so well got the girls talking into walking back their way, and so they did fall for it and down they went walking and getting closer to the battlefield, they noticed and heard a lot of hyped-up, yelped-up scallywags with bites and bits missing and running about like packs of hyenas after their prey.

Well, reaching the main entrance they took a quick glance about and thought, what in God's name has happened here? Stephanie said straight away to Martina who is a head nurse at the surgery, Go get everyone, never mind what they are doing just tell Jeremy what is or has happened and we need help! In she walked into their dining area when the main course was being dished up and straight over to Jeremy she said, Please, I'm very sorry but we are all needed, Sir, as of something has happened and Stephanie has told me to come and get you all.

Catarina, one of the other practice Vets, was so proud her brother Jenearno was over from her native land of Italy and she stood up whilst introducing him over from Milan where he owns his own practice. He was talking of his warm welcome from everyone and the friendliness from everyone and how everybody seemed to get along in the area. Catarina was looking at him so proudly as he was her loving, handsome, younger brother whom she doted on.

After listening to what was what, he spoke out, I'm sorry everyone but an emergency as come up and we are all needed. All looked about and confused, they all stood up and followed the rest to the gladiators' arena as you may call it in its day.

All dressed up for entertainment and not expecting this would be the centre stage act, their natural skill came to them all as they spread out. Louisa, that's James the Bookie's sweetheart, yet another nurse in the human field was assisting putting a pug, Wilson's the name and a feisty one he is. She was trying to sort his ears out and James getting his hand in was thrown a quick sarky question. Had any bets going on, who will beat who? He just laughed and replied, I brought my girl Louisa out for our anniversary of romance for all our years together and this is how it's rewarded? He just laughed it off and said, Believe me, if I knew this was going down, I'd have made a fortune.

With it all, to tell you the truth, it had to be laughed off because what else could have one done? The situation now was the clean-up plan. Denise was nursing Zappa the Hungarian Vizsla and she just took one look into his eyes, as she had his paw in hers whilst stitching it up and that was it, it was love. And then Keeley spoke, Oh Denise, you have met my assistant teacher then? He is the expert in Howly-snoutery. another lost language spoken between packs that travelled and hunted through Europe.

He was just coming through the door to meet Keeley as he said he'd meet them for a drink and walked through the wrong entrance when he was caught by the scruff of his neck and got swung around in confusion, another nip on his butt and that was that. He got stuck right in the middle of it all and of course as smart and handsome has he was, he stood to the side of the dogs of the day and yes some may say he should have walked away, but he joined into the whole tune.

Karen, Alison, Jack and Marlina were spread all over the room with Lin-Megan and Julie at the bar asking for some liquor bottles to use for putting on the dressing and yes, there were two cases of Champers on ice whilst working. Yes, it was Phil's quick thinking with some amusement in it. Carol turned to the other manager of the Animal's house team to say, Well, is this the dessert we deserve? With a little laughter in her voice. Catarina just noticed Becca and Angie walk in and with total confusion and shock on their faces. She spoke with the humour in her voice, Well, it looks like you girls will be busy for the next few weeks? Give me your cards and I'll pass them on to our new patients.

They were down visiting as they said they would pop down as they were going to enjoy the music given by their hubbies but the funny thing was, Phil spoke to Jeremy to give his approval just then to sing a few satisfactional songs to ease the tune of the room and looking at Van Brad, he started with A Little Help, a cover of the Beatles and then led on with Wild Thing from the Trogs. There was a fair bit of different views and feelings when that came out, but it was to mostly everyone's mode whilst they got on with the task of cleaning up.

Jeremy pulled Phil aside to let him know that Chris, the attorney from Robinsons was there and the clan from the Barka-Larka club was trying to get him to sit/speak as a witness. And he asked them, witness what? They thought that introducing themselves would say it all. Phil just smiled in jest and who walked in that second but Chris, Hello, all is well Phil? Of course, just like the old days, isn't it? Not knowing the fact but Chris was the son of a Miner and whoever was local would understand that word Miner, linking it to the Clarendon. Ya, it was the main hang out for the Miners, dogs who pulled the trolleys and carts through those horrendous tunnels of coal. Ya, many a head-on pomps went on there with the doggies of the marines, but they always left in a mood that suited them all.

Just then Mia Tia came in with a tray full of whippetters winkies, shots to give a little boost to the staff and was talking to Aimee and Carol, the pair of managers who set the floor rolling again with, anyone up for this round? Smiles and cheers were about and Van-Brad started another tune. Catarina a little embarrassed by it all, apologised to her brother who at this time was chatting away to Haley. She, another nurse of all practices was deeply involved in stitching a tail back on that belonged to Prince, a large German Shepard and with the hype, music and the shots being dished out, he was in holding up his tail and staring into this pretty local's eyes but not knowing except for his sisters look and stare that something was up. Haley was the daughter of not only Frankie. Yep, the head honcho of the Great Pedigree Chum Train Robbery. She honestly laughed to herself and said, yes it had to be HIM and she thought after this night's escapade she would tell him later and not spoil the drama of such a night, as Betty brought over another bottle of ole Sparkly to refill everyone's cup.

By this time the main drama was over and if anything, the laughter with the music and requisites did make up for it all and no major injuries were sustained really, just broken snouts, ears sagging and tails a little less wagging for a while but the Barka Larka's club? Ya, their egos and up-market barking had been shut at long last.

For many, many a year the loss of the beloved Seadogs Club left a handle over their feelings and at last it was now left in the past.

Lucy, the tall slender lurcher, sister of you know Susie, the ex-model, spoke as she spotted Dylan, Tilly I just walked in by the way to ask for you. I understand you wanted me to speak to your friend, Aseena? But I was away before you left for London. All the chat was going on and then Bailey turned to Poppy with his paw out and with a smile said, Well, now what? It had to happen when we were about, didn't it? What will Bampie say or Nanny? I bet I'll get the blame for all this.

They just laughed it off and joined in just chatting when: Well, howdie mam, you must be Poppy by the way? Yes, it was Rusty; he himself had just had a brush down off Angie from the Dapper Store, and then spoke again, you are as pretty as I imagined from all the talk about you along our travels. He, being that naïve way of expressing the truth didn't think it would embarrass Bailey. But he did have a little drooping in his gums and eyes whilst looking at Poppy's response. That was a mighty fine brawl, if there was ever one, Bailey, I'll talk of that one in the saloon back home, when I get there that is.

He strolled off talking away as a southerner does about everything really in general when a smile came from Poppy that answered any question. Yes, she still had eyes only for one and he stood right in front of her. Just then, who came across after having his tail straightened, but Wilbert. He just smiled and as a gent, he put his paw out to shake Bailey's and wished them well.

Strolling amongst the warriors of the battle, there was still an adrenaline in the air with a very happy-go-lucky aroma to it, kind of strange I must say for such an immense battle. But it may be the feeling of victory that still flowed around and it did keep everyone's feelings on a high.

Are you okay, Dylan? Yes, yes, I'm still a little bit buzzing but you know what doggies are all about? Tilly just smiled with a reply of my hero, my prince and it was spoken with a happy smile with it.

Look, Dylan, it is just not going to happen, is it? It is quite clear who she was talking about with those pair sitting down together? Yes, it's Bailey and Poppy of course. I think like we said before, just leave it to themselves to sort it out but those who know what love is and its mysterious games, they know they will never love another. Just then Emmeline spoke, you know, Becca's sister the midwife. Are you okay, Tilly? It was obvious her concern as she knew of Tilly's condition and with all this palaver, she wanted to make sure she was well. Yes, yes all's well thank you.

Then it got back to the reassemble of everyone's business, until in the end, Becca's hubby had his tack all wrapped up and loaded, he did get a few barks to carry on but Phil the Dill did slice his paw across to tell the band the night had to come to the end. Everyone carried about and did the best they could with a few surprises up in the light. What with Denise and Zappa, Haley with Genaro and all the visitors if you don't mind. What would come of these pairs? Would love be in the making? Only time would tel.?

The show was now over and the final farewells were on the call with hugs and embraces enclosed with laughter as it was still in the air of their victory at long last. By now the vets' squadron had departed, alas with the rest of the guests and Bailey turned to Poppy, saying, Can I walk you home, Lass? Of course, you may. Don't forget, she only lived up along the famous front and with such a beautiful evening, it all could not have been better.

Aseena spoke to Tilly and said, what have we not witnessed, in this short time of knowing each other? This was said with laughter as Dylan was listening on and then butted in, By the way, Aseena, thanks for your help when that Spaniel's mate joined in. She bowed her head shyly as she looked on at Tilly's surprised smile as Aseena spoke again, you won't tell my grandad, will you, about what I did to that setter?

Aseena was discussing the brawl with Rusty who was walking with her; I hope you don't think wrongly of us around this part of the world, Rusty? Oh no, Aseena, if anything I thought I was back home when it broke out, the fight I mean. By the way, that is a very pretty name, what is the meaning of it? Or what history carries with it?

Well of all times to explain. My parents were full of joy and very adventurous and travelled the world and loved India. My granddad loved it there as well and a wonderful friend became a great friend in their lives and his name was Syede. Well, his wife, Sehara, had a daughter who they lost but they believed in her short life she brought great joy to the time she spent in their lives. Well, her name was Aseena and it means in a Sanskrit origin, fulfilled, and in a native part of Canada it means Female Wolf. And then a traveller of India who fell for a Turkish beauty said in her language it meant beautiful. So, I was named after their feelings in all.

Rusty was gobsmacked by the explanation like that and what could you expect? I've had wonderful feelings past and present to guard me and my passage in this life, Rusty, maybe tonight was one of them?

It stayed silent for a minute whilst the two of them thought of what was just said, and then burst out with laughter. Bailey approached the pair and said, there is a beautiful full moon outside on the front, fancy joining us? They laughed aloud whilst unwinding to Phil the Dill's one liners of his view of the night, with a snarky spin in his voice, he barked out, yes, yes you all go out now and leave a poor mutt alone and cold in the backstreets of Hell, yes you all do that. Rusty, I must say, took heed as he was not used to Phil's ways of humour and felt sorry for the poor hound and was just going to bark out, oh let's stay and help, when Mia Tai, his wife, spoke with the few words, oh come, come now, you beaten wee pup and I'll get you a bone. Yes, they all smiled with the words of goodnight, etc, etc and waved on to the staff that were left or who were about and walked out after a night that was never to be forgotten and no doubt by the time morning arrived, there will be extra banters put on a wee bit?

Out they walked and sat amongst the top shingles whilst the bottom shingles were in harmony, humming with the current of the mood of the English Channel which you could never predict. But what was in tune was its mood and it was grand in harmony with the youngsters and surroundings. Out and about, there were barks and shouts of good night coming from here and there when Safi and her sweetheart, Barney, came out with, we showed them what was what, didn't we? The group looked at each other with a little shock as how sweet Safi was and everything about her. They had never heard this type of bark out of the wee gal. Even Barney took two steps backwards with laughter over her words. Goodnight to you all and off they strolled.

Rusty, I don't know what you are like on breeds of history and so on, dogs. But Safi? She is from one of the rarest breeds left you know? There is a bird here called a magpie and renowned for stealing colourful objects and storing them in a secret nest. They are black and white in colour; well Safi is a kissy-stealing-setter. You watch her habit if we see her again and watch what happens when she meets other crowds. There are only a few left and she is one of them. Wow, yes, I've heard of them from Celtic myths and history books, Rusty just looked on in despair.

They just sat there and shared each other's thoughts and Tilly spoke of her nice gentle thoughts of the past and said, Dylan, Bailey, do you remember when we were pups all the fishing boats were along here? Poppy spoke then and said, Ya, I remember, like that storm when we said if we were stranded out in the storm over the Goodwin Sands in our own Lugger, would you two come out and save us both? The two brothers even then as young as they were said, Of course, we would. Staring strongly at the brothers, the young girlie pups said, you would swim out to save us, yes?

Bailey with his charms spoke, Of course, we remember and we still would stick to our promise wouldn't we, Dylan? They laughed amongst themselves as Lilly said, look, now there is only one fishing boat left in action. Oh, how times have changed!

They all stayed silent with their own individual thoughts of their outlook of now and then and what is to be. But who knows that? Only fate can tell that tale. Keeley broke the silence then with, Aseena, since you returned from the trip to London have you given any thought of what's next?

She gave Tilly a quick glance and said, well, so much has happened and really, I have not had time. Dylan and Lilly picked up on this and sensed something was going on, but felt it best to keep quiet until they knew more themselves. Poppy sensed something as well and said, Bailey I must be getting home as Nannie-Bampie will be wondering where I'm at and we don't want them on the prowl looking for me do we?

Laughter was about again as they stood up when Bailey said, Rusty you wait here my friend as I walk Poppy home, as she only lives up the way and I'll be back. Rusty then carried on with, how are you getting home, Aseena? Oh, Benson will be down in a little while as I called him. Okay, I'll be back in a minute, Rusty.

Just sitting against the wall looking over towards France, Rusty spoke out, A mighty fine evening, Aseena, wasn't it? They laughed about it to themselves and Rusty had to say in his sort of shy manner, Aseena, would you care to take a walk with me on the next time you are free? She smiled to the gent and as Benson arrived, she passed on her details of how to get hold of her and that is what she exchanged.

Bailey arrived back as the ole car drove off with Aseena giving her graceful wave of her paw and a smile before disappearing out of sight.

Well, my friend that was a night not to forget, wasn't it? A little silence then laughter as the two looked at each other. Do you remember when we were in the wilds of the bush and all seemed calm when Dolly the Dingo spotted me going down to the stream or pond or whatever it was for a drink, when I bent over and she screamed and yelped at me to get back? She rushed over and grabbed me by my tail and hauled me back when I came close to snapping at her in thinking is this some type of joke? Then that large head rose out of the water and it was the biggest Croc you can imagine could live. I never thought for one minute that was gonna happen, who would?

Anyway, that was the same as tonight, who would have thought all that jazz was on the line? I can see Poppy's your love my friend and always will be, that is what I want to talk to you about and this is the right time as my feelings are true. We leave in three weeks for the next episode of the tour and how would you feel if I asked Poppy to join us and she accepted?

Well, in his southern twang he replied with, it will be a much better face to look at than your ugly mug, wouldn't it? The two laughed with Bailey saying, I could not leave her behind knowing she wanted to come with me. If she didn't, then I'd understand. But Bailey don't mind me saying, she has to want to go for the joy of it, not just to be with you, okay? Bailey looked at Rusty and he then looked back with a stern expression of don't mess with the girl's heart. Mind you, after what I just witnessed, you may be asking someone as well to join us, what do you say? Maybe, my friend or maybe not.

They laughed it off and stood up, had a little shake and made a move along the front. Fancy a little historical walk? Yes, I'm still too high to go home yet.

Well, they strolled along the front, down past the Pier and passing each building, Bailey would tell of what the building was or that empty shop there was used for gutting fish, then saying,

That row of cottages up along the front? Well, that is what they called the tackle row. All the bait, weights, reels, rods, contacts for boats going out, whatever you needed that was the place to get it. Now they have been made into houses that someone comes down once or twice a year to visit and that is that. No life for its walls to enjoy and listen to the barks and chats of a happy surrounding at all, with all the joy of a new day's life to start. Their walk finally came to an end when they reached where they were staying and with a sigh it was, I'm ready for the sack now and I'll sleep well after that escapade.

Waking in the morning, the main conversation was of course last night's episode, and by now it was known far and wide between the postman and of course Mrs Baldwin the Blackbird, everyone knew and if she didn't know, no one knew.

Over breakfast, Rusty said, Bailey, do you remember the end of last night and I'd walked with Aseena? Well, I need to get a message to her and what's the best way do you think? With the happy house they were in and all the action going on, he gave a little whistle and with the kitchen window open, a hop came about after a fluttering sound of wings. Yes, Rusty this is Kevin the Robin.

Straight away he got tucked in, I heard about last night, mate, core I would have loved to have seen it, they reckon it was the best and it will go down as one of the classics! I wish I could have seen it. He took a look around and hopped aboard the table as it was always a joy being in this presence in the morn of gossip, don't you think? With this, he turned and looked at Rusty and introduced himself, Alright matey? You must be the yank they are talking about?

Ya, I'm the one, came the reply. You could not take offence at Kev's words as he told it as it was and it suited him and everything and everyone around him.

Bailey spoke then, Kev are you anywhere near the Manor

today? In fact, I am as I've a registered letter for the place. Why? Well, this young man wants a favour and can you pass a note on? Yes, I sure can. With this he stopped a little longer for more gossip and took the note off Rusty who asked, could you please make sure it goes to Aseena? Sure, will matey, I sure will. And with this he said his departing words, then up over to the window sill he bopped and off he flew with the news that may serenade.

Tilly was busy with some odds and ends when she remembered something. Dylan, what is on your schedule today? Nothing really why? Well, I've another meeting at The Foresters with the girls about our business plan and it is looking set, I supposed, to meet Mam at Manes Market at 10, but Emmeline the Midwife is popping in to go over a few things and she wants you to be there for some details she wants to explain, is that okay? Sure, of course, I'll be here. Why a different Midwife, Tilly? Is everything okay? Oh yes, she is to do with a fast delivery if that happens and what to do and act until the Midwife arrives. Anyway, it won't take long and if you want you can come to the meeting at The Foresters? He thought for a moment and with a little fun he replied, what, with the whole lot of you howling with ideas, etc, etc? I think I'll give it a miss! This was said with a sense of laughter that the whole lot who were sitting in the kitchen munching away understood and even Rusty picked up on and knew.

Kevin visited here and there and hopping across the gardens, he met Polly the magpie with her sister Dotty. Yes, they were of old times and they were there to give a peck massage to Margaret and Daisy who were stretched out on the lawn adoring this treatment of every four months which was or is in fact their heaven. From head to tail, pick, peck, pick, peck this old art of fur stitching and removal of old unwanted fur, it felt like silk spread across one's skin and no words could really match its feelings to one's body and mind. They just lifted their paws to wave and give a little smile to Kev's question, as go to the Manor with any news that he carried and hopefully, like most times, it was good news that he brought.

He flew up onto the balcony and with a little whistle to Aseena who was in joy in her room with her thoughts when she heard Kev's call. She walked over as Kev was removing the registered letter from his underwing and the message from Rusty, he gave both to her, smiled at the note from Rusty's thoughts then with more of a stern glance looked at the sealed one for she could see and sense where it came from and with it, she stopped and looked and stared.

Want me to stay, Aseena? Yes, do please just for a minute. Okay. Don't forget, Kevin had known Aseena since she was a puppy when she was orphaned, even to the situation of letters from her parents when they were away on business, he'd for a short while comfort her with stories of happiness from around the town on those days she was not allowed to go.

Anyway, you have opened it now and I have an idea of what it is about and who it is from and well? Take me out of my suspense, tell me? Is it direct from Mrs McDonald, Kev, explaining that her team and herself mainly would like to offer me a contract on terms of trial to model for them and can I give them an answer within a fortnight? A little silence was there and Kevin, with his whole experience of the world, as he was a feather dresser for The Birds of Paradise Boutique in both Studios of London and New York. And after calling it a day, which no one really new why, he chose a postie's position in Deal for some reason. Anyway, Kev responded with honesty of, once it is looked over and all is fine how could you turn it down if your heart, passion wants to take that line of work? How could you turn it down?

Just then, Margaret came strolling in with Daisy all fluttered with smiles and all and chatting openly about their ordeal with

Polly and Dotty. Oh, until next time, my dear, until the next time. It was quite clear it was talk about the massage when Margaret spoke again. Kevin and Margaret had known each other since his childhood and she knew something was up. Still here, Kev? Why I was just on my way, girls, did you enjoy your Peckoony? With his sarky humour, I'd better get out of here. With this he just hopped up onto the shelf and whispered into Daisy's ear, Speak and listen to her for me, okay? As she just got that letter. Strangely enough, Kevin, we were talking about the ordeal in London just a minute ago. Thanks, Kev, she replied and off he flew.

They pretended they didn't know anything and Margaret said, Aseena, the Peckoony, we will book you for an appointment once you have earned a session and you are entitled to it I must get you a booking with us in the future, young lady. She just smiled with a nervous little reply, thank you, I can't wait.

Just then Aseena looked at the pair and spoke of the letter, Please Margaret, Daisy, I'd like you to read what Kevin has brought me. They both looked at each other with concern then back at the youngster in front of them. She opened it and spread it across her desk so they could both read it together and did so.

Well, first of all, how do you feel about it all? Excited I must say, Daisy, very excited to the least. I want to go over it with your grandad and his lawyer to confirm its intentions and, of course, how Grandad feels about it but to me it is all done but we must have it looked at for the better.

No doubt Aseena was straight on to her friends to whom she found should know and Tilly was the first in line to be told, of course it was only seconds until she told Lilly and that was that. Bailey was listening to the chit- chat between the galls and gave Rusty, who had just entered the kitchen, a little glance and told him of the news but said, If you do meet Aseena, please don't mention it, the letter that is; let her tell you herself, okay?

Becca was the next to be told as of her bond with Aseena as she trusted her; it was known she groomed Aseena since she was a puppy and talked to her of all that was going on in Deal, and the town's ways that she was kept away from but not for any bad reason, just safety and the question asked from Becca of her before the letter arrived, that if the contract did come through would she join Aseena? As once again she grew a bond with Becca. But it was asked in excitement but at the same time it was something to think about, wasn't it? It is not every day you get asked to travel the world and get paid for it, is it? Aseena, I feel we need to keep this as quiet as can be, as you know the jaws and tongues will be wagging but once again everything must be hush-hush until all is for sure.

Nanny Sky was chatting to Auntie Lilly, the owner of the Best Warm-wrapper Blankets In The World on Queen Street. Anyway, the chat was over as she was telling her that Margaret and Daisy would be trying to get her to join them for a peck down.

If she agreed, Nanny Sky would agree but not within the garden for all eyes aglee, just Molly, Polly, you, me and the girls and no one else to see.

Sitting at her dressing table, alone with her thoughts and just taking a little glare down on the table at the letter she had received when a reassuring voice spoke out behind her, It is all a part of growing up, my dear, and decisions are to be made whether they are right or wrong; these are the times in life of learning. Aseena turned around to see standing there her key anchor in all the paths of her life so far and apart from Margaret, it was her grandad. My dearest, you have a gift just like your mother, of beauty, and to carry it with grace and everything life offers this is one of those choices and if I was in your shoes, once it is looked over, which no doubt it will be, how could you turn it down?

To be paid to travel the world and learn of its ways of crafts, arts and cultures and so on. Gosh, I wish I had your beauty.

A gentle, beautiful smile followed after this little speech and Grandad spoke again, I was proud of your mother and she will be now looking down on you with this choice in your hand and she knows, like myself, you want to go. So, fly my dear, fly with your heart in your paw and gather the world's knowledge. Then sarcastically, he said, Oh and its food of the countries you are a guest of Aseena, you must learn its food dishes and bring back the joy of cooking to me! I had to go in a dirty old truck staring at every shape and size of a mutt getting ready for the front, the front in North Africa where we were first based. Grandad served with the Snouter m'Gowta Bomb Disposal team in the war and that is why he mentioned the front and Africa.

You, on the other hand, will be traveling in style, of course. Who will you take? As after this little reading of the letter, it says, you will have a choice to take a companion with you. It will be tough, Grandad, as now had you said a part of learning in life, Tilly, is to become a Mummy and Becca has a son and hubby of her own and it would be quite selfish for me to ask either one of them. How about Nanny Sky or Daisy? She said this with Granddad's humour and looked from the corner of her eye to see the reaction from him, once she mentioned those two names.

His response was, why not the pair of them? I'm sure this Mrs Macdonald would not mind. She delt with them in London, didn't she? Oh, whatever the times in life were, there was always Grandad as he brought the best out of the subject in mind. Just then, Margaret walked in and with a stern look at Grandad, he knew it was time to flee so he just embraced his joy with a simple kiss and off on his commitments he went.

Now my dear, you have a lot of questions to ask and answer,

don't you? And no doubt in my mind you were waiting for our discussion on the topic, or subject shall we call it? Without a doubt in her voice, she said straight away, If only I was in your shoes or a lot younger than I am now, what would I do? Times were so different back in my days, at your age, Aseena. Now the world is so open for all breeds in life and you have a choice like this.

Aseena was a little shocked by the positive outlook of Margaret's words as she had always been so protective of her, but even now Margaret knew Aseena was a young one ready to fly her nest. And knowing it had a guidance of flight like this to begin with, that was why she was fully behind the call. Believe me, Margaret was so quick in thinking about major topics and the safest road was the one she would choose. So, don't worry this was well thought over in her mind like a wise ole owl. Still, she was only what she was and her thoughts were, my, if only I was a younger soul than now and seeing and being around you, Aseena, all her life and now the door is very close to opening to an adventure like this. She let her silent thoughts travel for a little while then jokingly had a little giggle to herself with a frown.

Back at the Forrester's Inn, right then what is our next step? These were the words of Darcy whilst standing up to get herself a drink at the meeting. Morning, Geeta, she had arrived to get the location of the pub open for normal services. As busy as she was, she heard the conversation and the question, just ask. Can I say something on the question just ask? Yes, go ahead please; it is nice to hear views. Well times now are not like the old ways that you can do whatever you like and in a good way it is better for the workers. Anyway, make sure everything is legit in every way, etc, the right way. Insurance, law, etc. Make sure it is all legal and that is that. You have a fantastic plan and don't let any stupid matter mess it up, okay? My being here at this pub, I've witnessed and listened over the years the creations and ideas of business and seen the biggest of them all fall under one thing, the law. They thought they could pull a fast one and make a few extra bucks and ended up with their backs against the wall. Just do not try and pull a fast one and that is that.

Tilly took a look at her mother then at Sally who was the most experienced of the cleaners and had asked to be allowed to this meeting as, she too, heard through the grapevine of the girls' plans for the new company that was to be called The Dogs Brush, and they were picking only the best to make their name the tops, and they would do so. They let Sally have her say and with the experience of years working with everyone and knowing the field of work needed to do the job, she spoke with great thought.

After she finished, around the table there were nods of agreement. She is right you know, that came a whisper from Tilly to her mum. Yes, let me get a drink and I'll be a minute, okay? Sitting comfortably, her head was going back and forth to listen to the girls' excitement and why wouldn't they be? They had the courage to get up and do this and now it was reality. We have a policy, Sally, even though we have not begun, we will speak our policy to you. With its honesty and open thoughts and minds it is strong with our feelings and we know your feelings of joining us, so here is my offer, we need a port, a base-office or whatever you want to call it. How do you feel about assisting running it with the policy that you are able to be out there on the battlefield, if needed? The delight of this option came straight out with the reply, when do I begin?

You could not help but feel the contrast of each individual and a belief in what was ahead of them and it was all local, to say the least. Right, everyone agrees, Sally, for you to come on board. So, then there was a quick round of applause.

The chats followed on and then to the main question and that was for the day they could start this adventure. Then Auntie

Emma spoke of a different subject, you have all heard the latest news on Aseena, yes? Hush, Auntie, no one's to know. Nonsense, let me tell you now at Teresa's they are arguing about who will decorate Aseena's hair when she goes to her next shoot and The Tail to Paw are in turmoil, with The Wags Tail, the lady's clothes shops, over whose dress she will wear when she arrives in London.

Oh my, come, Tilly, one can only laugh at it all and it is not every day these things happen, is it? Well, she still is entitled to her privacy and that's that. Has she called you? Yes, she has and I'm meeting her in the morning at the Café On The Green where we can just go for a stroll and discuss anything. How are you feeling about it all? It is obvious how proud I am of her and it is a tough call to make in your life just to say yes and head out into the world of fame, fashion and all. Well, at least we will get maybe invites for the Emmys and Oscars award parties?

This triggered Tilly's humour and she just smiled from the reward of everyone's life was opening with joy. Becca will be with me as well as she wants to ask a few questions but we know really what it is in aid of. We are now at a stage in life where we will make decisions, Emma, just like you and Mum and your friends did when you were our age. Some are great and some errors were made but only time and life solved these difficult times out and then there were happy answers from the turn out. Emma looked at her niece in a way like, well, where did that manner come from? And then thought her condition in her life was making her talk and feel this way and a good job it is doing too, one must say, to let her voice speak with a sharp sting.

Molly, can I have a quick word with you about transport? We will need transport. Yes, we will and I may have the ideal answer for that. It's Adelealoola. You know, the daughter of Anosha and Dosha, the poodle cross setters from Deal Mutt Mobility Motors, a classic customised bike and now cart shop. Their shop is at 28, Queen Street. Customers have ordered their Motors from all over the world as of the beauty and skill in their design. Well, I mentioned what we are doing and she showed me a design that she created with Neil from Curwen Cycles, that's her uncle you know. You know he's based on the north end of the high street? Well, Adealoola has a tremendous passion for mending antique and classic furniture chewed up by doggies of all shapes and sizes. Some houses she has to visit, she finds it awkward to get to, you know down some back lane etc. So, she told her mummy that she and her uncle she adored, Neil, designed a mobile scooter and a trailer to fit on the back with a classic bike aboard with all hooks and so on to fit all her tools on. So, with both bikes and trailer and all, no place is out of the way to get to.

Well, she said we can on trial, borrow the other two she made and if it is suitable for us, she will build more for us with a payment plan. Perfect! Tell her yes, we will take them on and she mentioned- wait a sec, make sure the other half of the staff, partners do not have the keys as I don't want to see any of them parked outside the Runny Snout or the Broken Tail and yes, this was said with a grin.

Back at the Manor: Aseena, one must say congratulations my dear, congrats, this came from the voice of Crawford of all figures. I must say when you walked down the stairs on the night of the party, on the introduction, I knew it was to be. You carried your mother's beauty as a woman of love in all. They would be so proud of you, one must say. And your grandfather- it was never grandad or granddaddy, it had to be precise from Crawford, which suited him for all he stood for, as strict as one could be, he had always given Aseena that extra care as of all she went through in life at such a young age. One must ask, will you be leaving The Manor and living elsewhere? As one must know you are in safe hands and paws.

Times up Arthur
Justice For the Judge Please

Deal's Boned Cat 'n' dogfish Hot pot
Yum 'n' Yums!

What does he know?
Hudson's the name,

The top team Dylan-Josh-Martin,
Lamb Pate
Beef Pate
Chick Pate
Smuggler Marrow Bone
orders
to go
ole Swag bag.
Deal's Human Mail Letter's
Nice Letter bag!
Heavy Long bone bag!
Postie's Secret Smuggling bag.

No, Crawford, I'll be staying in hotels I assume when we are on tour for photo shoots and shows and then on my breaks, I'll always take the long, winding road to the place I love and call my home. One must say it is interesting isn't it my dear?

Just then, Margaret came through the door to see Crawford pass a little something into her collar box. This will protect your dreams young lady. He then turned around and made his way out of her room with a glance at Margaret's glare. He is a big softie at heart, Aseena, you know that don't you? Of course, as he has always been there, hasn't he? If I was naughty around the garden sheds etc he always knew where to catch me, didn't he?

The two laughed to each other, sharing these thoughts. Now then, let's see what he has put in your box? Unfolding a beautiful soft handkerchief, they found two items: a brooch of a beautiful butterfly with emeralds and rubies spread through its wings and the body seemed to be woven from mohair that must have taken so long to stitch together; the other was a swallow made out of some sort of dried flowers stitched together and covered in small birds, with eyes of tiny little sapphires of such blue, you would think they were carved out of the sky on a summer's day. With them both was a note explaining they belonged to his grandmother who travelled the world and fell in love with India, there was for some reason many beautiful captures of names or something of joy, etc relating to the country of India. It had to be related to memories of wonderful times and that they carried the names forward. What else could it be? Either way, it was all to do with joy. They read the note and found it quite touching. I think I embarrassed him and that is why he legged it out of the door as soon as Margaret entered on the scene.

The Swallow was to wear when travelling, to protect one's soul and the butterfly was to wear inside for protection when one was embraced in functions or whatever the occasion. Both would chase away any bad feelings that tried to enter within one's heart. I've a message, Aseena, from a youngster asking for you to take a stroll with him? A fine chap I must say but I think he may be a long way from home. Margaret looked at her with curiosity to see what she would say. He is downstairs, Lass.

Just then, Crawford noticed him whilst chatting with Grandad and made an approach. May I help you sir? No, I'm being taken care of as Margaret has gone to notify Aseena. Grandad and Crawford looked at each other with the expression of what is going on around here? It kinda reminds me of what is that program you like? Taunton Abbey, with all its affairs and so on.

Grandad could not help but burst out with laughter at Crawford's words and just then Aseena came down the staircase. She looked at him and he apologised for calling so soon but he explained, I just took a stroll out and came across the Manor as Bob was chatting to Charlie the chaffinch at the entrance gates and noticed Rusty, hi, hello once again and in such a short time and he did say why not pop in and introduce yourself? And this is what I did by chance. She spoke of how nice it was to see him again and said with a little embarrassed look in front of the two older folks looking on, please, let me show you about. With this he could not help but stare at the times the history of the building had witnessed and the times through history that the house must have seen.

Would you like to see the gardens? They are my favourite parts of the estate as my memories as a pup here was no end to adventures and the stories of who lived down in the dark parts of the woods, ghosts and ghouls. With jaws as wide as an entrance to a volcano's mouth and when angered they would rage with screams that could be heard as far has the village and everyone would hide from the growls.

He looked closely at the beauty beside him as they strolled the grounds and watched of course from a distance by a pair of curious old folk with their ears pointed up, eyes glaring over when Margaret entered the room and startled them both, Admiring the gardens are we? A little shaken, they replied with, yes, Margaret, we were just discussing how well the flowers blossomed this year with great pickings in the allotments for the gardener's choice to enjoy their work in all. Yes, I thought that is what you were both doing, Margaret carried on with her everyday checkings and just laughed to herself at the old boys' antics and made her way off to another part of the house.

The two youngsters carried on walking when Grandad spoke again to Crawford, as to say it seems to be moving so fast lately, doesn't it my old friend? I feel it is for the best as well, as it seems happiness and adventure have been set and offered to them all. Grandad was very shocked, listening to Crawford's reply as the two still could not keep from looking out across the lawn.

Rusty, how did you find the episode at the Clarendon Hotel? I'm sorry if our fellow country folk startled you. He once again turned aside his look and just could not stop from laughing, as back home in his native Southern side of the States, he witnessed enough to give a decent reply.

She then spoke of her feelings of what she had just received and the meaning of the news, as in a way to warn him not to expect anything with their future. This in a straight way was the first sincere answer to herself that she had decided to except the offer to go. Please, please, Aseena, don't feel that there should be any obligation on my call as you know I'm to head off on tour with Bailey and the band. But can we keep in touch along our travels, as there is such an easy way to communicate now isn't there? Why, I would love to as this way we can explain what is going on in our lives and where we are in the world.

They just laughed about when Aseena broke out with an explanation to explain to Rusty's next question, asking what the pens in the woods all battered and torn were for? Well, for generations going way back, a tradition on any well-to-do Manor was the gathering for the shoots. Just then, a large figure of a man stepped up with his dog, Treacle and spoke whilst giving Rusty a glance sideways. It was Skip, Rusty recognised him but where from? Then the fight at the Clarendon, he had hold of certain spectators, you could say. Skip was the Manor's Gamekeeper and retired to the cottage down onto the stream side of the bridge.

Hello you two, how has your day been? Once again like the rest of the main guards in line, his concern was Aseena and it would stay that way. Everything is grand, Skip, and I'm showing my friend around the site of the many secrets and all. He nodded his large head with a concerned look that was funny for how many of these glances had Rusty got within minutes of his call. By the way, Rusty, back to the question, the coupes and cages were all for the finest pheasants and the other game birds such as the partridge and grouse.

Let's take a stroll back as I'm meeting Tilly for a girl chat and to discuss a few matters. If anything, it is good to let off a little steam to another and mine is who do I choose to be by my side? As the company have allowed me to take a friend, companion with me. I feel it may be a bid to make me more at ease to take their offer. But even so, it is a tough call to make. Maybe it is a little bit of fate as I can advise you on one not to ask, Poppy. Bailey has asked me would I mind if Poppy could join us on tour and I've spoken to the others and we have all agreed it will be fine. You can see they love each other, can't you? Of course, Rusty, and knowing of them from their feelings, and now sharing time with them you cannot help but feel their bond, can you? And you know it is true. The thing is, Rusty, you would think we have been friends for a lifetime but we have only known each other a short while before you guys landed. It was my grandad and I just walking with our thoughts along the front when we met Nanny Sky and they spoke to each other and I sensed affection from them both for each other, and wondered what was the glow? Anyway, we must make it back, Rusty, as I've a stack of odds and ends to sort out and who I've got to call.

The next morning arrived and Aseena was just dropped off on the Strand to meet Tilly and she could not help but feel the adrenaline of her thoughts that just a while back across this open stretch of green is where it all began. All the excitement of this new life and friendship that the small group had bonded with and the different roads that they would be taking was just immense to say the least.

She then just walked over and reaching the Café, Dylan was just leaving Tilly as he had a meeting at the Academy, so he walked Tilly down as it was on his way and then, once seeing Aseena arrive, he made his way off with an embrace to his sweetheart and a smile to her guest. Bye, enjoy yourselves, and away he went.

Morning, Tilly, how are you? For some reason, Aseena had a little nervous feel about her and I think it was just so much going on about her, she hadn't had time to just shut off from anything at all. Anyway, she sat down and told Tilly of her guest yesterday and how much she enjoyed the walk and chat they had. Oh yes, I see, Tilly replied and spoke in a curious way. Shush, will you, we hardly have said two words to each other and he like myself will be heading out into the world. So, you decided you are going then with those words you just said? Yes, and I'm so excited, Tilly! They sat down and it all started to flow out, about their feelings and adventures in life that were staring them right in the face. You know it was you, if anyone, I would beg to come with me on tour, to keep me in the right line of light but we both know this is impossible, don't we?

Yes, yes and it is only normal to feel the way you do, Aseena. What I would do to be given the chance of something like this in life, but my life and love come first. Even Dylan has said to me with open paws, how am I feeling about it all? And we laughed about some answers I gave him. But once again, Aseena, the joy of becoming a mother and my own business with the girls and the choice of my life, as she calls Dylan, everything is like the beginning of a dream becoming true and you, Aseena, have become like family. And now, Aseena, there is your adventurous journey to begin as well. We both have roads to follow in life and it is now with us both. The girls just sat and embraced the words they had shared.

Just then, a happy-go-lucky voice came about with, these are on the house, ladies! It was the famous Boney-Mahoney-Bones laid out in front of them, smothered in hot butter. My, Tilly, you are looking well? It was Pete, the owner of the café he worked so hard in building up for this recipe of soft or hard, large or small chewies, did the trick of that. And who is this may I ask? This is my friend, Aseena. Before any other word could be said, Peter said, oh, you're the one who's breaking all the hearts around here? I knew you would keep yourself for me, I knew it all along just like the rest, isn't it, Tilly? She just smiled and explained, this is Pete the owner, Aseena. His joy and humour that kept everyone happy and not be offended as if they took offence, then their life must be very boring and their thoughts of happiness and fun must be small!

I've decided to ask Keeley as she has the sense and adventure to hold her own and she wants to do things in life, Tilly. I can talk and relate to her as I can with you and Becca. I think Becca is planning to try and sell her pair, Hubby and Son, that is so she can come with me. She made a comment to a customer of hers and asked her, would she have an interest in buying a ready-made family for a while to see what it is like to be a Mummy? Then she told her of the offer she was going to be asked and trying to find a way about it so she could go. Yes, yes, it was all said in fun speech but once again we have to admit, it is a once in a lifetime to be asked to go out in the world to visit and work in different countries and get paid for it, isn't it? I feel it is the best choice you have made but I still think there is a better choice for you.

This got Aseena's mind roaming into who? And then asked Tilly of her choice, and directly, as Aseena's curiosity was answered with Birdie. Aseena walked straight into it and after her little silence she just burst out with laughter. So, when will this begin, Aseena? When do you intend to leave for London for it is there you will start your training surely? I have to give my answer within two weeks for the Yes or No and then all the legal procedures will be set, so I don't know how long that takes. But I'm calling them in the morning so then it is in their hands for the date. It will give time to sort any matter out here and get organised.

Tilly thought she would have a little dig and said, Aseena, when you say matters, do they include the likes of Rusty? Oh, shush will you, Tilly. In fact, I must find out when they plan to leave, as another adventure begins for them doesn't it? Poppy, do you think she will accept Bailey's offer and go? Yes, I do and I do hope it is the right one as it is something she will find a totally different way of living all together. She will not be waking up to warm milk, etc-etc every morning and doted on because no more than yourself her grandparents have raised her and adored her all her life and with living along the road with a band and all, it is a different kettle of fish. Well, she is not going to find out if it is for her if she just sits down after Bailey leaves and then wonders what her sweetheart is doing out there.

I feel Dylan will be talking to his brother with a strong tongue about his offer to her. If he messes up, then he will not be welcome back here, will he? It would not be safe to return here, Aseena, for his own good and he knows that. Well only they can answer their own fate and destiny and that is that, but I think it will do her good just to learn more of what is out there in this beautiful world of ours with wonderful moments in life that we can all share.

Back in the town at Teresa's Salon, Susie and Elli the three-legged greyhound, were having a weekly trim up and of course the gossip was all about the local gals and what's going on around them and what joy to these tongues to lick up on. Susie, having been such a beauty in her day, who they said was the longest legged lurcher you could imagine, they said in her heyday dogs from far and wide would beg their owners to walk along the front, if they knew she was out walking and follow her track and tail just to have one glance at her pins. But did she know how to hold her own or what, Elli? Well, she's her best friend from God knows when.

That time of the terrible storm, they still talk strongly about. Well, she was their full in paw to assist her love when the boats went out to save who they could. Yes, he was the head honcho of the Dogs Head life boat that went out that awful damned night that managed to save so many a mutt that was forever grateful to those brave lifeguards. Anyway, they managed to save every one off that wreck and then pulling in the boat over those slippery shingles on that night of a dreadful storm, she tripped over a block of some sort and got trapped in the cable that was pulling in the boat from the cap stun, and that was that. It was a hard decision that had to be called from anybody. But the cable was pulling her along down through the shingles when it was the decision to take her leg off or she was a goner.

She survived the ordeal but it haunted Patch, an ole Yorkshire Collie who did the walk from his homeland beside his partner an old miner. He blamed himself for the accident, as if he had not been out there on that boat, she would not have been there and it would never have happened, but she explained over and over she was the daughter of a Sea Dog, from generations of rescues hard core doggies and she would have been there anyway. They saw it through all the tears and stayed together with joy in their hearts. If anyone was to look for them, you could guarantee you would find them in their local, The Pelican on Beach Street. By the way, you know the Pet Food Express on Stanhope Road? Well, that is their daughter's store; she's the youngest from an eight-birth litter you know. Dot is her name and her son, Pete, and they run it like a dog chewing a bone. Yes, James, you know who I spoke of earlier from the bookies on the high street? He's from that litter has well, Dot's brother. Out of that litter all but one settled in Deal with stores here and there, they always remind me of happiness when I hear that song? Shiny, happy doggies, holding paws, as they are always smiling.

Well, it is a town that has tales of many and they are never ending, aren't they? These were the words from a visiting Cocker Spaniel who was having her hair curled and nails painted for a function or some sort of invite. Yes, you will find this behaviour in many coastal towns as don't forget there were ships of nonstop hoarding of their cargos from all over the world and the adventure and excitement was tremendous to say the least. You can just imagine, can't you, what it must have been like being at sea and then landing back on hard soil to cut loose and then go back to their ship and then head out to the open seas again, shining.

The Cocker Spaniel paid up and wished everyone well in the salon and yes, the eyes and tongues were waiting to start and as soon as the door was shut, off it went and it started with Chi-Chi the Chihuahua, with a tut of did you see how she had her nails done and the colours? I don't know with all these changes going on, how does she dare to go out in public like that? Then of course Shoo- Susan, not Sue, etc but Susan the Shitsu, spoke Teresa, darling, what kind is she? You know what I mean, to go out in public like that? Teresa looked over to the other members of staff with a hint of laughter in her throat and said, She is an American Cocker Spaniel who has come here to visit her brother for his annual event to honour his father. A little silence came when she replied with, what, Rupert? Yes, Susan, Rupert who lives on the front of Beach Street.

Well, the air changed as she and many others had the hots for him as he was an officer in the American side of the Sniffers and Rescue team and very wealthy too. They say he has a chic kennel pad in Santa Monica, right on the beach front and he flies back and forth to live that life of the up-market type. His folks sent him to the highest of Dog's Duty Degree colleges in New York and London for the best there is to offer. No worries of the cost or expenses for the way of living out in the big world just given a do as you please type of open bank account. Teresa really went all out and how she held back the laughter was anyone's guess. Chi-Chi, with a little tremor and stutter in her voice, said, Oh, please, please, where is she staying? You must invite her to tea with us at the Lady's Afternoon Club. Rupert, by the way is a well stuck-up bit of a vagabond but couldn't help it in a way, as of his upbringing, but even so, no one is better than the next four-legged, hairy dog, are they?

Back at the mad house of happiness, Dylan arrived back from Collège, Tilly, everyone sends their love and best wishes, okay. Oh, thank you and please, Dylan, return my thoughts to all. A few were asking, Tilly, will you be returning? But I mentioned that you were told to take matters a little easier but don't just shut off, they all started to laugh at that, as they know you too well and that is not going to happen, is it? I didn't mention the cleaning company okay, as I don't think it is for me to say. Well, I don't want to explain as it will never end trying to. With this, they both started to laugh.

By the way, Dylan, your Mum called up to say your aunt and uncle will be down on Friday. What Bailey and Hollie? Yes, they are coming down for the weekend to visit. Bailey heard this as this was their mum's brother who he was named after and yes, their favourite uncle for what's hard to believe was it was their uncle not their cousin. As yes of course he still acts like a puppy and gets away with it, as of his charm and so.

Alison, Dylan's mum who is loved by all as she's the head nurse at the Retrievers, Rescue, Retires kennel up on the hill on Kingstown overlooking the views of everything you could imagine A wonderful place to just take a stroll or just relax at will to one's own thoughts. You see it is a location for ex-service dogs but it is such a beautiful location that there are ones that will pay handsomely but must behave in the manner of the kennel's rules not theirs. As the way they want to as you can get some of the officers' dogs that can strut outta line at their own will and snout about but they are put right back into their basket if they think they can run it their way.

I was talking to Grandad this morning, Aseena and he said all the legal matters with Mrs Macdonald and her lawyer has been confirmed on the legal procedures and the contracts have been agreed. There was one problem they would not agree with until Grandad stood up and started to walk to the door. It was over a contract that had to be for Keeley as well because he wanted her protected, as if they got you to sign and thought now, we have what we want we don't need Keeley now and tell her, right on your bike young pup, get back to your pad. But it all changed when they knew Grandad was serious. Just as we were going through the door, he even had me convinced.

She, herself nodded to her Attorney to agree, it is up to you now, Aseena, to make up your mind fully on this matter to your future and career. So, we want an answer after your final thoughts, okay? And we will then call Mrs McDonald and give her the news so that is that. Thank you, Margaret, just one thing again young lady, don't overthink things and complicate anything to yourself, just go with your heart and feelings to what you really want, okay?

As Margaret was walking away back to more chores that

seemed never ending, she took a glance back and watched Aseena squint her shining pearl eyes and give her ear a scratch whilst just thinking of the words just spoken to herself. Aseena's thoughts were of excitement in all and she got straight over to Keeley to let her know that she must give everything a thought over and did she want to go? And can she? Aseena explained to her the contract had been made and all was now the go-ahead and then they would be away.

They were in their element of thoughts; well wouldn't anybody be with such an adventure ahead of them and not far away either. My grandad wants to meet with your folks or if not just yourself or maybe a lawyer? It is just to explain, Keeley, the contract and just to go over any legal matters that may concern you, okay? He even said that if you want to let our attorney take care of everything and he has done that already just as a stand by, but if you want your own just let me know and I'll tell him, okay? I don't have one and my parents as everyone knows is Mum all in one and she would respect it if your lawyer would take care of the matters concerned as she would get confused and in a panic; that's Mum all over you know.

The days passed and it seemed never ending on getting legal things in line so no complications were about when a call came to Aseena whilst she was with Tilly. Hello? Aseena, is that you? Yes, was the reply and who is this? It is Stella from the catwalk and how have you all been since back in Kent? As mad as ever as there always seems to be something happening like a soap opera! A little laughter came in with a personal word as well. Aseena, I've missed being around you girls, do you know that? Meeting you, Tilly and Nanny-Daisy with all those years hearing about her and then of all times to meet her in person, well, what can one say? Aseena replied with, we often talk about our time in London and you are always in our chat and thoughts, Stella, oh thank you and the rest.

Well, the reason I'm calling is Mrs McDonald had a meeting

yesterday with a very well-known photographer. You know when we were in the private little gathering on the top of that hotel?

Yes, is that where the band played?

Yes, that is it. Well before we went up, there was that group sitting across from us.

Don't ask me if I remember their names as there were so many introductions, was Aseena's reply.

No-no but anyway who was in that group was Rankin. He has now approached Mrs McDonald and asked to shoot you. Sorry- so sorry, Aseena, to use those words it is what we use in the business for a session. He wants the shoot to begin on your first introduction from our company. That is if you are coming to join us?

Yes, yes, I am and myself and Keeley can't wait.

Who?

Oh, sorry, Keeley is Tilly's cousin as we have discussed who is best to join me over and over. I'm with Tilly now do you want to speak to her?

Yes, please came the reply.

Hello, Stella.

How are you?

I'm fine, my body's feeling a little strange with a lot of movement and so.

What do you mean?

I'm pregnant, Stella.

WHAT! Came the surprised shout.

Yes, I thought you knew? Well, you know now and that is why I can't join Aseena.

I miss you all, Tilly, and I was just telling Aseena who has approached us for a photo session.

You will have to do us the honour of joining us here has our guest, Stella, sometime in the future when all has calmed down okay?

Yes, yes, I'd love to and that is for certain.

Okay Stella, I'll put you back over to Aseena as I must go.

Do you know who this photographer is, Tilly?

Yes, I've seen him when the TV is on and when top programs come up of photography and major photo shoots like royalty and so on, or a judge to win a contest, photographers get all fired up if it is his name. Aseena is mentioned? Well, say no more?

Oh really? But why me is my question?

I think to be honest when some real new hotshot comes up, they want in. Just like us lot looking into Al's cake store on the High Street when he brings out the new special for the day but he is not as good as Al's cakes though. My favourite ones are the marrow-boned butter buns with the vegetable-fruit-multi-mixed bonanza bowl from Amy and Josh Prentis grocers shop on the high street. once again, their secret recipe is hidden for nobody to know but many to taste.

Anyway, here's another of the old stories-myths. Amy, she is the ancestor of Bronxsfill of Broadstairs.

What the ole pirate of Germany?

Yep, that's the one. When the bond was so strong in Royalty between Germany and here, he was a son of a Prince of some sort who for the likes of many a story fled his ship for the love of a local gal he fell for but his blood family denied he should be with her. Anyway, he fled the ship with an elite crew who were loyal to him and set up the Dealy-Dover smugglers' ship that looted and stole the best veggies-spices and of course rums and other remedies of taste for everyone's thirst.

Aaimiee-Royal-von-Jackson would become her name if she took the title of way back but that is not her nature; just call me Amy she has always said. She has a loyal team herself. Just like many a thing or tale around here there is a saga or story behind the name like her doggie Josh. He is a breed that's supposed to be extinct. He is a Jagder-Griffon. Despite its name, which means literally, a wire-haired hunter, it is reported to have been from a large livestock herder from Austria, similar to a Briard. He is thought to be related to the ancestors of the Leonberger. Who knows, anyway he was found in the streets of Austria with a number on his collar, Number 7. Amy on holiday asked the grim-looking one-toothed menace, where are these doggies going and what is the number for? With a snarling reply he said, Ya don't wanna know me darling! Ha, Ha, ha! He frightened poor Amy but backing her roots she held her ground and offered a healthy wad for his leash and she walked away with him and away from that gruesome back market.

And there is Scot the Scotty, yes, a typical terrier who will hold his own; he, once again has a story behind him of his ancestry. Way back, King Walloopa of Walmer had a problem with a terrible gang of rats who jeopardised the whole castle and told the King, leave or else. So, one day there was a traveller who stayed in the woods next to the castle and one night two poachers were out and saw him sitting by the fire with his doggie, Daloola, a Jack cross. Well, the traveller fell asleep and the next minute a snarl and snap and it was over. A pair of dirty fat rats tried to steal their takings of a brace of pheasants or whatever; anyway, she had the pair upside down in seconds and just gave a little smile back at the traveller as he was awoken by the crack.

Well, the pair of poachers worked for the King and thought, hang about we could do something here couldn't we? So carefully they approached the traveller with an introduction of, hold sir, we mean no harm. So, they sat and talked of many a thing going on in life when one mentioned the problem at the castle of the bullies and for a handsome price to you, we could introduce a plan to solve the problem. He was introduced by them to King Walloopa the next day and they gave a demo on Daloola's skills and that was that. That is how Scot's life history began here just like many.

Daloola fell in love with a local Jack Russel, Rumpo and they created the best clean up clan there is to this day. So, Josh and Scot hold their fort off with Amy to trade the finest of veggies and fruits that are so fresh and the best and ready to burst.

The weekend came to an end and Kev the postie gave Aseena a private call. A beautiful spring morning when her bedroom window was ajar, he hopped, then whistled over to Aseena and said, got a minute?

Oh, hi Kev, how are you?

I'm well as usual. He hopped onto the dressing table chair and said, Look I was at the Lawyers' office, Williams and Barnes, and dropped off a packet from London from guess who? Yep, Mrs McDonald's attorney and I know I shouldn't but yep, I had a peep and after all the jibby-jabby words it had a date, the first of May they want you in London to prepare you for your training. How about that then?

In fact, Kev I feel better now as I've a date to focus on and now I know, thank you Kev.

The lawyers will just go over the necessary facts and then call you which will be I'd say around Friday, okay? But do not tell anyone, Aseena, as I'll be in such trouble okay.

Aseena managed somehow to hold her tongue and Friday arrived and whilst playing tag in the garden with the gardener's grand pups she was called through the window by Margaret, Aseena, can you come in for a moment as your grandad wants to speak to you.

What was ideal was Keeley was with her as she had stayed the night.

And you too, Keeley. Grandad, he is in the lounge okay.

They looked at each other and did sense a vibe of some sort. In they walked and,

Aseena, Keeley this is Mr Griffiths.

Hello, sir-

Please if you don't mind, looking at grandad for approval first, call me Michael.

Sitting down they were both looking at each other as that age does for some reason, when Mr Griffith spoke again,

Ladies, I've received the contract offerings from Mrs McDonald's lawyers and I'm not going to beat around the bush so now it is time to say yes or no, ladies, you are either going or not as I've the date they want a reply by.

Aseena already knew this date but kept it quiet.

It is the first of May and that is in three weeks' time.

We have decided we want to go and we have got so much to sort out like new photos for the passports etc, etc.

I've gone through every detail and it is all legal to status. The contract is for both to you as Keeley, it covers you in all areas. They explained what they meant in this to protect her and she was nervous at first when they said her contract, but after explaining, it was clear to do so for all.

All papers were signed with grandad as witness as well as acting agent. With both ID paw proof signatures down, all was done so Mr Griffith folded this and that, placed them in his briefcase and away he went with a smiling nod.

Like young girls should act they were bouncing about and headed straight off to tell Tilly and so on. Margaret looked about and stared at Grandad and spoke,

Well, she is off then? How are you feeling?

Well, it is only natural how I feel but it is exciting as well isn't it? Our little beauty to walk the catwalk of the world what more can one say? Do not worry, Margaret she will be fine plus do not say a word but I've hired a top dog who will follow her in every matter there is out there. Whatever the matter, Margaret, he will be there and kept in safe paws.

You are always one step ahead, aren't you?

He just replied with a little smile and got up himself and said,

Fancy a stroll yourself Margaret to see what has blossomed this year?

She herself just got up brushed her apron down and the both headed out, with Margaret wrapped in her shawl.

As a little time before that was mentioned about the visit coming to town of Dylan's relations. It went amazing as of the open bond they have always held and his cousins. They are at the same age and so much going on in the line of careers and so you would not know which way to look.

Auntie Alison was grateful to see her brother as well as all the banter and laughter of memories. Just then Bailey called Dylan aside when the mothers were chatting in the kitchen.

Dylan, Dad's asking for you again as he is confused. When you went out for a drink and he asked would you get him one. Sam, that's their dad's name and many say he's the joy of life to be around with his shining black coat and matching eyes. The Black Dive he was known as, he was a joy of all doggies. He used to belong to the rescue dogs' team. Well, an ole dated disease that hits the old sea dogs who had battled the storms and waves saving lives when needed, his day job was a doggie puller of the coal carts out of the mines when the donkeys and so were too big. He never complained to anyone, like dementia attacks humans this cruel disease that effects doggies are called doctatailier. It confuses the mind and so.

Anyway, he loves still to tell a banter or so especially when all the pups are about. You just have to be patient and listen with thought if someone has it when they talk and bark to you. And the whole Town would listen to Sam whatever. Tilly always knows it upsets her sweetheart and to comfort him when leaving him after a visit or so.

Anyway, as Dylan walked into the backroom his dad started off again. Right, me handsome, with his Devonshire accent, he spoke again, Did I ever tell ya about the Spratwafflers and the Walmer Rodents? Ya did they used to go head-to-head or what? Smiles were all about as they knew the story inside out but some of the visitors had not heard the names. So, with curiosity they looked on and sat at his side to listen to the story.

Well, the north end of town where it was a no-go for us to enter was the home of the sprat-wafflers, a hardy-hearted gang of fisherman with a glare and glee for anything that swam or crawled out of the Channel or along its coastal banks. The other end if you go up south only a mile or so is the beginning of Walmer. It was the camp for the Walmer-Rodents; both gangs were as bad as the other, like stealing each other's lobster pots and filling them up with empty bottles of beer and so one would blame the other.

Then on market day either end of the town at the pubs, one called The Crawly Crab, the other The One-eyed Bass or The Staga La Loo La, these were all pubs along the front and it would only take a little time until it went head-to-head. My, would they fight or what? Paw to fist, bite for bite, the humans and doggies would cut loose on each other that you would not know who was who or whatever. Then when it was all over, they would make it back to their boats as it was too dangerous to go home and face the Mrs, they would sleep it off.

When they'd wake in the morning, they would set their nets

or pots for another day's catch.

This went on for centuries in all and it would not be fair to say who got the better of who, but if you went along Beach Street there is an ole building now made up into a beautiful second home for some rich kid or so, but that building was the Sailors Rooms Hostel. You would just give what you had for a space to sleep; many made sure their dog was beside them because you would not know what you were in for, as many woke to find themselves on a ship heading for countries no one had been to. You were a part of the crew or if not, you were thrown overboard for not listening to the order given.

But back to the fights who knows really who took the glory?

In Walmer where all the fishermen's landings used to be is an outstanding building that has been the saviour of many, the RNLI, the life boat station that holds once again so many banters and it is said that half of the team in the ole days were yes, Spratwafflers and the other half, Walmer-Rodents. But really if it's for saving lives who cares who you belong to? Chris and his glorious team of locals no matter what the weather, they are the team that make all the rescues.

The building? It's been there since 1856 and it boasts 28 gallantry awards you know? That is just for the government records never mind others. With those names, Sprats or Rodents, they too were members of the crew and I think who called them those names were the families of the smugglers you know. They would rattle on with the banters of shipments etc of all those fine wines etc they brought in. Plus, they would banter on who caught the biggest fish and the fights and so between the two clans. Then they would return to all the rest of the attire and news of their cargos and where they were taking them to. You know there was never for some reason any trace or sign given of their loads and it was all left with no clues.

Julie, she's the lady of the shop at the station who runs it day n night. Well, she's the great-grand-daughter of Wilf the Wolf? Is she really? Well, this character was the one they say who got thrown overboard because he wanted to release six young boys and girls they had working on a run-down ship and the captain used them to smuggle the tobacco into the town in disguise under their child-puppyhood innocence. Well, after they threw him overboard, he and his dog, a bull mastiff called Wolf swam back and climbed up the side of the ship and released the children and brought them to the shore where Andy's ancestors were waiting for them, he is one of the life guards you know?

Anyway, his family took them through tunnels that are still there under The Stags Head into a few cottages, and between the other members of the family they pretended they were their own. And that was that. I don't know if it is true or not but they say Wolf was so big and strong he had the children on his back to swim them ashore. But your guess is as good as mine. But that is where Wilf got his nickname from, Wilf the Wolf.

The other members of the crew all carried a story or banter of some sort but behind it all there was a reason or meaning to them. Like Chris for instance? His forefathers were wild to the last and his great-grandad used to wrestle with Wilf the Wolf for show on open days. A dapper of a dandy he was then just like many of the other wild ones. He was showing off his bruises and cuts of the many assignments he got whilst out saving two-legged or four-legged victims out of the Channel when he looked over and there she was in full bloom, Lilly La Lover, a beauty if there was ever one, a cherry picker. What? Oh, sorry that is what they called the local galls from the Walmer area.

Lilly, you know from The Loving Blanket and Dry Cleaners Store on Queen Street? Well, she's from that family going way back and carries the tradition on with her granny's name. Lilly was her great-grand-nanny and kept traditions going for many a year. Anyway, as I was saying, Chris's grandaddy fell for her there and then, that is how that family chose here as their home and have been a part of it ever since.

Lilly is Daisy's mummy, isn't she? The lady who went with Aseena and Tilly to London for the modelling intro?

Yes, that is right. It just goes on again to yet another adventure as did you hear?

What?

Aseena will be leaving for the London contract in a short while.

How do you know that?

Oh, this is still a small town if you want it to be, don't you worry! And also, Tilly and the girls, well they started on Monday, you know, the Dogs Brush Company, gee it is all happening, isn't it?

Talking of news and banter where do you think all this gossip and banter is coming from? Yep, Teresa's Salon and the Laundromutts, the best place in town to get the best there is out there within at least 20 miles. It matches their service to the hilt as no one can match their quality in general and that's a fact.

News spread like there's no tomorrow and the stores in the town were soon at it with whose dress she will pick. It will be my dress she will wear on the date she leaves, and she will wear the diamond collar. This was the call from Mr Fry of A. Simmons, jewellers on the high street, blah, blah, and Polly the Collie, you know? That is Steve's wife from Timpson, it's mentioned about that she has designed a pair of shoes for her hubby to make with such passion you would honestly think they were the twin magic shoes made for Dorothy from the Wizard of Oz. Yes, they are all at it like true grit.

Tilly is that you? Have you time to talk?

Yes, Aseena, how are you with all that's going on?

I'm at my wits end with organising this or that. I am not too happy with the photo on my passport, I must say, it does not give me much credit.

Listen to you and your tone! You will be sitting next to Birdie in a short while with that outlook.

Oh, shush, will you? I have heard great words spoken of the business and how well it is doing and I'm so pleased for you all.

Well vice-versa, Aseena.

Yes, Tilly, that is the reason I'm calling. So much is going on Tilly and we will all be going in different ways soon so I'd like us all to get together this weekend coming. It only hit me last night whilst just lying-in bed, myself and Keeley leave for London; Bailey, Poppy and the rest leave to go on tour and you with the new business, it is all happening so fast, so let's have a get together, okay where shall we meet?

A little pause and Tilly said, I know let's meet at Cin-Cins, you know the bar down in the alleyway off the High Street that links to Middle Street. Okay, they have bands there so we can have a good ole time in all.

Are we gonna ask any adults to join us?

I don't think we should although we love them all we won't be able to talk of such things openly.

Yes, that is a good call.

There will be one tough call to make, Aseena, and it is your shout. Birdie is down next weekend, as whilst cleaning at the Pedigreeder Hotel, Susie heard the receptionist say to staff guess who's booked in for next weekend? Yes Birdie. Susie just laughed with Emma but very professional didn't say anything as you don't know who you are talking to or who's listening.

Do you think we should invite her then?

Let's think that one over okay? There will be a get together for all ages of friends and family next week but let's have our own little meeting first. By the way Tilly you mentioned The Pedigreeder Hotel?

Yes, Aseena, we have that in our contracts as well now. We really are making a name for ourselves.

That is great news, Tilly, I'll see you on the weekend okay.

Calls to one another were made to meet up next weekend but they wanted to keep it small.

Dylan was getting ready to leave for yet another assigned meeting when Bailey announced to him, I'm making that call this afternoon, Dylan, the one to Poppy's family. I just want to explain to them my intentions and well-being. I know what they must think of me of my past but I did no wrong broth.

You try telling that to a stranger when their flesh and blood is hurting because the love of her life chose to leave? You know who you are dealing with don't you? They have a lot of connections, Bailey, old connections if you know what I mean?

I seen coming outta their domain, Frank the Crank and his grandson, Cleo -da Leo you know?

Once again, the head honcho who has always been the main suspect of the great pedigree train robbery, what were they doing there?

I just don't know but it is said they, that is Poppy's grand-folks have a place in the capital the locals call the lock up. Hardy ole mutts of all kinds have been seen entering that domain and not come out, and who invited them there?

With a tremor in his voice, he waited for the answer. Dylan was watching his brother's body language and went for the jugular vein, Yep, Frank the Crank.

Dylan found it very hard not to burst out laughing for it was all made up and said to himself, what he would do to be there on that visit just to see the face of Bailey watching them. But this would be one of the classics of tricks they had played on each other whether small or tall.

It was only the matter of time before the news got out and

we all knew that but it was surprising that the public of the town held their manners and stayed away from the Manor. Really, I think it was the grandfather being a well to do figure that folk tend to fear in a way, anyway that did not stop the Dealites trying everything possible to get a bit of the banter of what was going on.

Dealites?

Oh, sorry that is the name that the ole smugglers in all called the pretty gals of the town. It's said it came outta the Deal Lugger.

Where?

Yes, yet another ole inn that the bad boys and smuggler dogs of the sea used. That was the hang out of the Tide and Time Brewery workers and how it got its name originally. They supplied their fine ales and so to that location and after sampling the tastes, who knew what would happen next?

In those days, there was no holding back and they say owners and their doggies would be going head-to-head and they would be left with their lugs hanging in all shapes and the doggies drinking the beer not the water off the floor and also their bowls being filled with ale and they could hold their own and they would drag or lug - that was the name then for dragging their daddies or partners back to their boat or home that they were staying at.

They say you could tell where someone had been, including the police. They would show a blind eye to it that you would see a big galloot of a mutt or even a small terrier dragging by the leash their partner along the side roads till they reached their domain. Yes, and the saying was, oh guess where they have been and what they were drinking. Again, the time and tide has got the better of them. Outsiders thought of the poor fellows it meant they had suffered at the hands of the cruel sea but it was not, it was the devil's water of course,

So now you know where the name came from, the Deal Lugger. I thought somebody told us a little while back it was a flat-based boat they used for smuggling to go across the Goodwin Sands?

Na, don't listen to that ole garbage. You know the Ship Inn again on Middle Street? Well, have a chat with Oscar. He's a Scottish black cocker spaniel who smokes an old clay pipe that was made for him. He will tell you some proper ole banters. You supply him with a wee dram and he will talk all right.

The morning arrived after a few days passed that Bailey dropped a note and a card off to Nannie-Bampie asking permission to visit them on the matter, to introduce himself and his intentions of asking Poppy to join him on the tour of Ireland, Wales and Scotland and to say she would be in the best of company and health. They got back to him inviting him over for a chat and that morning arrived, today.

Tilly, do I look okay?

She checked him out and put a few hairs back into place where they belonged and took a step back to have one last view.

Right now, don't go overboard with excitement explaining okay as you do because they may think it is just a big party on tour. Mind you they won't be far wrong, will they? Anyway, good luck.

Walking a little nervously up the front he stopped and thought oh, they look pretty. They were the wild flowers growing on the front out of the shingles so he picked a nice bunch for an introduction not knowing that plot belonged to the house he was visiting and they are Nanny's favourite pride and joy for all to see. Well can you just imagine Nanny Ryan's face when she answered the door to see him standing there with his paw out saying these are for you. With her Celtic humour all she could do was laugh inside and she then invited him in.

The meeting went better than he thought and he did not feel

threatened and by the way there was no invite to their place up in the smoke, that's London by the way, so it did look like his world was looking bright.

After a real nice time shared with Poppy's grandparents, Bailey mentioned that he was to pick up a few odds and ends from the The Wagging Tongue, as they hosted so many bands there and there were a lot of ticks and tags left behind. So, Long Nose Larry who runs the joint mentioned it to me that by chance I want to look through them I'm more than welcome.

Fancy a stroll? As they were making their way over, the pair were walking across The Coach and Courtyard now the car park behind The Clarendon Hotel, to hear a call out. It was Becca, her studio was there in the courtyard over on the north side and she spotted the pair. She had one of the dogs she'd just groomed and was a little nervous in the area as she had just moved into town and did not know her way about. Anyway, she had a booking for her nails to be painted at Teresa's so she was taking her over to introduce her.

I got a message from Aseena to let me know about Friday so I'm looking forward to that to say the least. Just then a splendid bark came out of the busy area, it was Sailor, Birdie's fiancé.

Well, what a splendid sight to see! Hello, my ladies.

You could not help but like the gent and his manner but who was with him but that stranger who kept turning up at places where Aseena was a guest. Becca picked up that something was not right and stayed talking a little while when just then Grandad walked back as he forgot his neck purse and Sailor showing his manner greeted him with,

Good day, Sir, and how are you?

I'm well as expected, with his elderly mannered voice he asked, how are your parents and so?

Oh, they are fine.

Give them my best wishes, will you?

Yes, sir I will. But he looked at his guest with him and the guest bowed his head after seeing grandad. Grandad just gave a stern look at him and even Sailor picked up on this and said,

We must hurry as we have an appointment. And off he walked with a little glance back.

Grandad you see was on the jury board of the courthouse when it was active and he was also a stand-by judge and proud of his position. Well one of the worst cases of his career involved this bagga -bound who was within Sailor's company.

Are you okay, Grandad? came the words from Aseena.

Yes, my love, I'm fine. After your appointment fancy taking a little stroll to the front and have a chat for a while?

Yes, Grandad let's do so.

After Margaret's and Aseena's appointment, they left the dentist with an all clear from him to say keep biting and chewing. Off they set and walking across they met Grandad. Margaret had shopping to do and told them she would meet them at the front of the Pier at 12.30. Grandad put his paw out and escorted his granddaughter to the front. They sat upon the bench and luckily enough the one he used to sit on with his daughter was empty so they just sat and he said,

Well, Aseena this is where myself and your mummy used to sit and when she told me she was ready to follow her heart in her career and now you, well how the beauty of life grows!

First of all, Grandad, that person with Sailor? I sensed a dislike and can I tell you something, I've seen him about at events I've been invited to and he was even at the main one in London and my senses tells me to be aware?

Your training of reading the figure has served you well. You see you know the Law, Aseena? Your father always had a great interest in law. Well, you are the same my dear and when he asked me about the fraud involved in a major case that was going on with stealing ole dogs because of their inheritance and savings, etc, etc, you were sitting next to the fire listening and you interrupted and said that was very bad to do, especially to the old doggies who served, that is right you remember now. do you?

Yes, and I still feel the same as then, Grandad.

Well, that stray with Sailor, he was one of the criminals involved, Aseena, and money was placed into accounts overseas which led to him but someone said he got away with it as he grassed the others up. No one knows but I know someone who is still following his case and you mark my words he will get him if it is the last thing he does.

Sailor was not involved, was he?

No- no not that lad he would never act in that manner.

Good as I could never forgive him if he was but what was he doing with him today?

That I'm not sure of but the building they came out of, that is the investments of Canning and Scanning of fine meats in all with different offices on different levels but there's only one exit out of the building. I'm saying they may have been leaving at the same time and that bagga- bond's office is on another floor. I know by off chance Sailor has an investment in one of the companies that tests all the quality of the meats. They are working on a new program with such high standards and it is tested by their new highest scanner. The Scanner program is Sailor's project and that is the new advertising work that is shown all over that banner.

I was worried a little when Sailor said we have an appointment before darting off, that concerned me.

Yes, once again you were observant and I may give Sailor a quick call just to have a little bark with him you know? Anyway, don't bring worry to your heart, keep that pleasant, okay. Come on let's walk up and meet Margaret as we will be waiting for her instead of her normally moaning at us, where have we been, blah/blah. We can give her a taste of her own medicine.

I'll leave that to you, Grandad, came Aseena's quick answer to that response.

Becca made it back to her workshop and yes, her thoughts were in a curious mode and why wouldn't they be, knowing the question she was going to be asked by Aseena. But just then who did they notice but her hubby and son making it across to meet her for lunch and she glanced at them and just smiled with her love for them both.

Mind you if the right offer came within the next few days to take both of them off her hands, who knows? She may be rolling.

Back at the Pedigreeder Hotel, sitting at the bar counter chatting was Ruthless Ruth, the Rampur Hound talking to Lanney, The Llanidloes Setter over a Hotter-dogger Martini. Both of them were hard, menacing lawyers and chatting away to the legendary bartender Bertie and for some reason Grandad's name came up over some case or matter. And just then Bertie mentioned,

By the way, girls, I suppose you heard that his granddaughter will be leaving next week with that modelling contract and on Friday I've been invited to pop down and have a drink with Bailey and the rest of the gang as a farewell gathering at Cin-Cins before the formal family farewell party. Come along with me if you want? Just then who sat behind them at the high table, yes, Birdie with ears pinned to the chat. Yes of course she was listening in to their chat and got thinking.

The Friday morning arrived for the gathering at the Cin-Cin bar for their get together to say in a way goodbye for a while to each other. Tanya and Andy the owners of Cin-Cins made such an important feeling to their guests and that is why their location was chosen, plus of course how many hounds from miles around have tried in vain to get Cat's number? Cat the purring heart breaker, the bartender known as the Nine Hearts, not the nine lives as it is said a cat has. That is how many hearts belong to her from all the hungry hearts of the hungry doggies of Deal. Anyway, they knew just by leaving Tanya and Andy in charge, so they could just leave it in their paws to make it happen and yes it would be bowling.

Splendour from everyone who came from everywhere, Poppy stood so proud with Bailey as it was all over the town by now that she was to join him on the next tour, she was in her element standing beside Bailey who kept glancing over to Nanny and Bampie now and then as they were their guests and stood talking to Grandad and Margaret. Jeremy Pearson and the crew from the vets were there as well including Teresa and staff and yes, you guessed it, she was checking out the girl's hair and so as she had them in and out all day plus Emma from Tamarisk Ladies Clothing was checking Aseena out as she had one of her dresses on and she sparkled with glee in it.

It is going to be an interesting outlook, isn't it, the next few months ahead? Came the words from Nannie Ryan to Margaret who replied with,

Yes, my dear it is going to be interesting.

Grandad was talking to Bampie on near enough the same subject as it seemed strange but it was both their granddaughters leaving.

On that night back in the hotel room there came an outcall.

Darling, Sailor I do so crave for a sandwich so let us pop out for a snack down in Deal please?

There is plenty in the fridge or let me order you one from the chef downstairs?

Oh no Darling I feel like stretching my legs.

Sailor sensed something was up as she was dolled up to the hilt and you guessed it, as they took to walking down past the Cin-Cin Bar, and chose there to dine. Sailor copped it, the minute they walked in and was a little embarrassed by it all. Birdie spoke with her slight barky tone,

I didn't know you guys were out, type of chatter came from herself; everyone copped it on.

Andy and Tanya glanced over at Tilly as if to say well, shall we let them in? But they knew it wasn't worth saying anything to her as they knew her so well.

I thought we were going to keep this to us youngsters tonight, Tilly?

So did I, came the reply from Keeley. But it was Bailey who invited the other guests, but why?

Just then in the corner it was noticed that there was a load of instruments set up and over the microphone came an announcement from Bailey,

Ladies and Gentlemen, thank you for coming here tonight and as you know so much is happening within our small group it is hard to explain to you all. But we would like to offer our entertainment of the band to you all as we will be going back on tour in a short while. So please all the members of the band would you please come to the stage and get in tune to entertain this gathering of friends and family and let's play some rock and roll!

The members moved through the crowd and started to warm up and there were some funny-looking shapes and sizes to wonder what will they come out with? Billy the bulldog one hell of a drummer, a pair of grey hounds, Josh-Jacob the brothers on lead and bass guitar. Hairy Harley the golden retriever cross on Sax. Cilly the Collie on the keyboard but the strangest of all, a pair of hairy Dachshunds, Bach and Dudley, one with a trumpet and the other with a clarinet sitting on a large triangle, hand made to sit on and swing to the tunes whilst playing. And with the tone of their paws, they would click the triangle to harmonise with all the other instruments. With this collection it was just interesting to see and hear what type of tunes would come out of this ordeal and would it be a ball?

Oh, by the third tune that was it! The house was full of the happiness of in-tune music of blues, jazz, rock and roll, you name it, it was coming out to suit all generations and to see all shapes and sizes dancing in every shape and form was a sight for sore eyes. Bampie grabbed Margaret and did the Greyhound Jive. Grandad grabbed Nanny Ryan and did the Irish Jig and it just carried on into the night.

The finest element of all to me was Max, his brothers Murphy and Charlie and nephew and niece Freddie and Connie, the black Labs were asked to come out of retirement as they were the Pawpers, Soul Singers, to join Brad who was up on stage with the rest of the band and man could they sing in soul or what.

Bailey was in the bank that day for a meeting with Brad the bank manager for a loan to try and buy new instruments for the tour and had invited him down to the Cin-Cin Bar. Bailey, not realising or thinking, didn't know Brad was married to Becca who owns Laundramutt. Anyway, the smoke-filled bar was ablaze with passion as the band had steam-like sweat dripping from themselves whilst playing the finest howling songs of soul that kept belting out.

Not a bad sound, is it Bamps? Came a question from Ruthless Ruth who turned up with Lanney. Not bad for a bank manager with a guard dog from the docks etc is it? Let's not talk too much business and shop with such an evening's event ahead but just to let you know, I've brought Lanney, another lawyer with me for you to meet and yes good news, we have more than enough information on the case we want to build on that chap who robbed all the folk around here of their life savings. So in a short while I'll be in touch with the whole complex of what we got.

Nanny Ryan came to Bampie's side just to ask who that was when the pair walked away and he replied with,

Do you remember the case we often talked about reopening on a private investigation, the one with the entire pensions stolen? Well, that is the pair of lawyers who have taken a great interest in the case as I'm almost certain her granddad was one who lost his life savings.

It is of interest to me as I was on that case and often wondered who was the baggerbond with inside connections who was in one of those shake Paw-hand clubs who let that scallywag walk from court even knowing before-hand the verdict was in his favour and he'd head for the Caribbean and bamboozle his lifestyle on those takings.

The party carried on with true grit and what more could be said for the ambiance of the night's gathering, even how Rusty managed to get his big bass on the performance where with that soul sound it was needed. Brad walked off with a sweat of sheer enjoyment and on an immense buzz told Bailey,

Look let's see where you are after your tour and if it is still up to this standard of quality to entertain, we will discuss finding a sponsor, okay?

That's sound Brad, that is a real great compliment and I will certainly keep it in my heart and mind whilst we are on tour and I will tell the band as well.

Poppy, Poppy! Came Bailey's call out as he was buzzing from the evening's compliments and paw-in-paw they approached Bampie who was in Granddad's company again and was first to speak,

Well, I must say that was very enjoyable and you make sure you keep it up. Poppy was just glaring back and forth at the pair and Nanny Ryan just looked on with a smile.

It gives a much better feeling of contentment now doesn't it knowing the type of company they are all sharing and I feel better in all manners of mind as your Aseena goes one way and our Poppy goes the other way but it is their turn in life to wag their tails and sniff the air elsewhere isn't it? These were the words spoken from Nanny Ryan to Margaret and Bampie and could not have used better words to explain how they felt. Yes, they would always be puppies in their eyes but alas we all have to let go sometime in life and it may be hard to do but alas it's life's road which can be steady or like those famous words to that song, The Long and Winding Road and taking that route, it takes a while.

What have been nice over this evening are the worriers, the older generation have got to know each other in person and it has been nice to watch them chatting along and smiling sincerely. Mind you when you think about it the music that made the night was their era wasn't it? With a few updated tracks blasting out, most were from their memorising years of wonderful memories that bring out so much joy in a person.

Still on a little buzz, Bailey walked over to Brad and said, maybe now you will give us that dosh for new gear?

Laughing away, he replied with, Yes, no problem, do you want used notes or a cheque?

By the way Brad, I didn't know you were married to Becca? Each day around here it opens more doors in life of learning.

And I have to admit with nights like this that we have given people it brings more out in me to try and reach my way in music with so much passion in my life that I feel it is yearning.

Makes you think doesn't it, sweetheart? These were Brad's words spoken to Becca, because don't forget she was going to be asked to go with Aseena and this would have taken her to God knows where in life. But na, their happiness in their life is grand and there is no need to complicate anything there. Closing down the evening - and it could not have been better for those personal mysteries of family guessing of who's who and now who knows, they may keep in touch when we hit the road which is now coming to a countdown isn't it? By the way, do you remember when we were out that night and we sat on the front talking of this and that and you noticed that ole ambulance parked where the fishing boats were? Well Bailey, see that big geezer over there talking to Jeremy the Vet, he's the one who owns it okay. Christ of all people he was talking to was the vet and I wanted to ask him about a bloody ambulance.

Anyway, whilst everyone is in good spirit why not ask now was Bailey's thoughts? Nods were coming from here and there as Phil the Dill was in the party don't ask how but he was. Hi Phil was Bailey's chance to introduce himself as he was talking to the gent in mind.

Hello Bailey came the reply, great show I must say. Thanks for the invite a bit of a change from the other night I saw you isn't it? The Vet looked at Phil the Dill with a pause as don't forget what happened whilst they were at dinner at the Clarendon, Phil copped it on and noticed someone else and pretended he was called.

Oh, Hi Charlie, how are you? And off he scarpered.

Hello Bailey this is Lenny the Lobster who was the main roadie with bands he toured with like the Animals and the Wolfhounds and many more gigs from the hippie days.

Hi Man, how are you? Was his intro to Bailey.

Can I ask you what it must have been like at that time, Lenny? Traveling with so many bands and all?

Cool man just cool.

What was the best band you toured with?

Yes, all the questions came out when once again Bailey thought about who this is and what is he doing here? Anyway, Bailey asked about the Ambulance and his interest in it and yep guess what? Lenny only turned around with his kicked back tone and said I'll take you man on the road with my background you can use it to your advantage plus it would be great man back to my roadie days and where are you planning to tour and when?

Bailey explained to him where they wanted to tour and the gent replied, Okay, okay you have a deal man, I'll sit down to go over what's needed for the road and here's my number call me tomorrow and we will talk about what we have and haven't got?

The emotional chat started to flow out of thoughts like I can't thank you enough, Tanya, no thank you Bailey because if you were not leaving, I'd have you in here every night. Andy jumped in to say look you guys this will always be your hangout with the doors wide open for you and the others so if you want to promote any bands then let us know and it's done.

Andy it will be a while before we play here again so Russel came up with an idea. Once a fortnight, we will contact you with an update by video or whatever you call it?

Russel's a computer geek so he knows all about all that and you have your large screen so there you have it. Yes, let's do that for cert.

Well the days seemed to pass so quickly and they had their family farewell dinner gathering at the Hungry Mutt And by this time you could tell the bond growing between the parents-carers, you know for the likes of all the families and so on. It is grand to witness as now they can share their news on what is going on with us lot?

One main thing I need Aseena to do before next Thursday, that is the 24th we leave isn't it?

Yes, came the reply back to Keeley. What is it you need to do?

Well down on the front of Deal Castle is where Dough–Dough's Terry has set up the best pizzas in the world, not just Kent but the world. I'd like to take you down and try my favourite one or you can choose your own one, okay?

Chris is Terry's sidekick a wee Scot who knows how to put together a speciality I adore, it is called the Snoutty-magowti-malabony Pizza. Only they can make this you know and so if I let you try it, after that wherever we go in the world on our missions and tours, we will try pizzas and see if they can match theirs.

Tomorrow is a clear day and we want to sit out on the front to enjoy the pleasant view and air and just chill out. Dylan and Tilly, plus Bailey and Poppy will be joining us as it is something we have loved since we were pups, so it is on okay. I look forward to it because since meeting everyone it has been nonstop and everyday has been another adventure along the long and winding road.

The next morning arrived and my it was a beauty if there ever was one. Emma, Keeley's mum got someone to drive over and pick Aseena up at the Manor and take her down with Keeley to the front to meet the others who were there waiting for them. The welcomes were all around when the intro came,

Right then you lot what is it to be then? This came from the Host Terry and he was ready to shout out the order to Chris and out it came after explaining what was best to try. And it was just a little paradise of their own to munch, smile and have a little petty argument of what is the best from this abode.

Within this little group, Aseena wanted to say a few words in a manner of just to say thank you to you all for this and that and how much can I say in words that I can speak from my heart? I just want to say thank you. Just then Chris came up with a quiet plea,

Do me a favour? Just tell the gaffer my creation is your fave, okay?

Terry was looking on and as soon as Chris made it back into the operation zone as they called it, guess what? Yes, the same plea came from him. You could only laugh at their commotion as this had gone on for years and they still dwelled on the results.

The funny side of this was, as good friends as they are, if one gets more glory for their creation and tastes to the snout and a doggie to partner swears that one is better than the others you can guarantee it ends up with insults.

The next morning arrived and Dylan was explaining to Bailey that he was taking their grandfather out this morning as he was meeting Monty O'Dunky on the front at 12 for them to chat and just sit a while and let them reminisce their memories as it does their grandad good to assist in bringing his memory back. Monty was still the full shilling and since they were puppies, the bond between the pair of lifelong friends had always been there and always would be.

Many people asked how he got the name or the handle some say of Monty O'Dunky? Well at the time of the war when the military were pushed back deep into France with his Battalion of the Snouta-Nouta-Muttouter-Corps, they were in a part of Germany and a nun and a nurse, one Norwegian and the other German did not believe in the third movement of their then leader and broke away from the nation they loved with three youngsters.

Well Monty knew well what the circumstances were and took that chance and carried them away and they were forced back to Dunkirk. Well, that night of so much drama when all the fishermen from around here the town of Deal and for miles and miles of coastal towns, they got together and brought the whole lot back to the coast of Dover. The nurse and nun helped load and assist in every manner they could and keeping it short they made Kingston their home and were welcomed by all for their bravery and still talked about to this day.

Feelings are something natural and yes, Marissa the nun and Monty fell in love, and you know Missy the Newfoundland and with the beautiful black woven gown coat? Well, that's their daughter if you don't mind. The nurse? Gertrud's her name. She fell for Nanny Ryan's best friend who makes the Golden Shawls at The Old Barn, they renovated into their workshop with all the gentle, soft wools of the world combined. What's his name? Oh yes Reggie-Reggie the Rabbit they called him that as he was so fast in school at running. Then you had Harley, you know the hairy one who plays the Sax for Bailey's band? That's their son who all still live in Kingstown.

Yes, and one of the young ones who they smuggled in, what is her name? Oh yes, Tonya, Tonya the Terror. She got that handle as she's from Norway and who came from Norway? Ivan the Terrible so they put that name on her. Don't ask me why or how Trotsky her doggie got his ways from, because if there was anyone so kicked back then that's him. He just believes in feed me-love me and that is that, but there is a problem. He's a Jack Russel and the gang down the northern quarter as some folk call the area, what's their name? Oh yes, The Jack-Holliuns want him for their gang as he's a big one isn't, he? But he told them, Man you think I'd leave my mummy for you lot living in a boarded up run-down kennel you gotta another think coming. You lot carry on trying to catch a badger or rabbit I'll stick to my medium done steak my mummy knows just how I like it done.

My, Emma, with so much history of you knowing these loving stories it is a wonder you don't write a book about it all.

One day my dear maybe one day may I say. With this they all just harmonised in wonderful thoughts as it was only natural with all what was going on with so many thoughts rolling around in everyone's hearts so they just lay back and let pleasant thoughts just ease the day away.

Just as they sat there with gentle thoughts flowing about their minds a well-spoken lady strolled up to them with an introducing smile and looked about the group and said, My what's going on here then?

Just beside her was yet another kinda strange beast of a doggie, the most laid back of a four-legged figure you could imagine to meet. Aseena looked on as she spoke, well, muttered, Hello, young lady, and you must be the young lady the butcher Bonko was talking about, he was telling me you are heading to the bright lights?

A little confused, Aseena replied, Yes, I am. My name is Pip and this is my mummy, Sarah. A few little nods went about and the two trotted off on their daily stroll along the front. When out of range to be heard, Aseena asked, Who is that may I say? Tilly thought she would tell this banter as she often spent time with Pip as she was great friends with Tilly's mummy.

Well, Aseena, be ready okay. You see Sarah, that's the human's name, she was a very high-up attorney at Barkinham Palace Kennels at the time Charles was playing about with you know who? Sarah's position was all the legal advice and social business matters going on about them. Pip is her side kick.

Tilly was waiting for the question of yes, what is she?

Well, she's a cross between a Welsh Corgi and a Jack Russel known as a Kojak and you know she was the escort to Lady Di's side-kicks. Anyway, the media and so on got out of paw and the government were in a very hard position in their league and knowing these two gals knew everything of the behaviour of the next of kin head honcho of the country, knew something had to be done before waggy tails and tongues got out. So, they say a rumour got out that there was a hit on them both but it was essential that no one would squeal.

News travelled to the undercover team of this hit and with an amazing plan with the underworld dogs of the mining tunnel team they were smuggled out and no one knew of their well-being. But one evening in The Ship, an ex-SDS doggie got barking about this and that and told some younger sniffers drinking away, of their background. But in due respect it was kept quiet. Sarah's family bought that house on Middle Street just down from the Ship, you know the one? It belonged to that bagga bond of a human actor.

Sarah's family if you really knew it was the undercover unit. Anyway, who knows? But they were safe in many ways as long as their secret was kept quiet. David who lives there now is they say Sarah's brother and you know the gossip of Watson? That Springer, cocker Spaniel crossbred playboy of a hound who's dating Luna, the Poodle-Cocker crossbred playgirl who are once again like another pair of Bonnie and Clide's, they are all family and that wild breed inside them. Their history must be kept silent within the shingles of the town of Deal.

Only a day passed on and sitting down on their favourite bench Tilly spoke,

Dylan, I feel my body and mind growing into such a wonderful chemistry and bond and I just want to say thank you my love, thank you for just being here for me.

Thank you, Tilly, for saying that but I would never be able to choose a more beautiful place to be than beside you.

Oops, I just felt another kick, she replied with a loving glance at each other they just smiled away. Is it next Monday the band leave for that wonderful tour? And how do you think Poppy will cope with it on the road? I honestly feel it will be the making of her and also, she is from Irish stock and they survive through anything thrown at them. And also, it will be the full test of their love but to be honest I don't think that needs to be tested, do you?

She looked at Dylan and knowing him so well she knew he was thinking of his brother and his obligations that he had to prove after asking his sweetheart to join him on this tour.

He'd better not let her down, Tilly. I mean that; whatever happens out there on the road he'd better not and if for any reason he has any doubts in his heart or mind then let her go.

That reminds me of obligations I need to call Sally and Lilly that we have another office to view on the High Street and who can go and view it?

The business has really picked up, hasn't it?

She just smiled once again with a response of pride. When are you back at the barracks next, Dylan?

Wednesday morning as I've to meet another instructor to explain to me another course of scents and views of reading the individual whatever shape, breed or size; call their number before they call yours is their old logo?

The Wednesday arrived and Dylan arrived at the barracks looking the bee's knees. He gave a few nods entering and the sentry nodded after checking once again Dylan's papers.

Just one thing, sir, can you direct me to section D+1?

What? You are meeting The Firm are you?

He sensed a little teasing in the manner given but still felt a little bit on the nervous side as he looked back at the guardsman. Reaching the door, he gave a little knock and was told to enter. Welcome, sit at ease, please. As he sat, he looked up to find six staring at him and looking up-down at the paperwork then back at him.

A tall type of mixed terrier stood up and barked out, we all here agree we are very impressed with the views that are coming back to us over and over. So, we are not going to beat about the bush, we are here to offer you the position to enter the S-B-D

Squad directly as of today. We want you to think it over until Friday and then give us your answer please?

The meeting was short and sweet and then the departure came and the room started to empty when a bark came out with a sort of caring order to it. Don't ask why but Dylan felt this as he turned to see who spoke and there was this stern Jack cross looking at him and then asked,

Please let me introduce myself. My name is Betty and I'm on the board of the mentally-social side and have you got time to have a brief chat?

Yes, I have, he answered curiously.

Well, I'd like to welcome you on board first as I do not think you are going to turn it down just like your father.

What you know my father?

Yes, I served with him and what a wonderful proud time it was.

For some reason Dylan's ears went up and flashes of his father's tales came into his mind and he interrupted the speaker with, wait a sec are you Betty? Betty the bomber?

Yes, I am and how did you know that?

Well, when my father was in better health, he would often talk of his assignments and one he often repeated was the operation in the Middle East and going through a remote town on full guard and covering each other's backs on each side a strange scent came about and all you could hear was, get down now, take cover! And just then a blast of explosions and open fire came from every angle. There was so much going on but don't ask how he often repeated but everyone made it through. And he always said that one bark from that Jacko-Corgo, a pretty-tempered cross with her red coat and wiggly hips saved everyone's butt. And from that day onwards she was one of our team and wherever we were assigned to Betty was within and beside us and we built and matured everyday together, even though she was the only maid on board we would like to tease her and she took it in her stride with ease.

Well, I'm dammed how did you put that together knowing who I was? Maybe -no sorry, I now know why you have been chosen.

Dylan asked an honest question, did you know who I was before meeting me today?

No, I did not, even with your surname in front of me I did not cop it on but now after speaking to you in person I see him in you from the tail to the snout, just so proud of standing in all. Tell me something what is your father doing now?

Dylan bantered away when just then Betty spoke again,

Dylan, I hope you do not mind me speaking of privacy? But our section has to be mental as well has physical to see if they can cope in difficult matters. I hope you don't mind me asking but you are going to be a dad, aren't you? I'm speaking of this as I'm a mum myself and you know who is one of my sons?

Who is he? was Dylan's reply.

Why it's Barney the Bombo.

He's your son?

Yes, he is so now do you understand how I know and feel about mixed mutts in all? Give my best wishes to your girl as I know she was going along with you and if she wants to come back in onto the course, she is more than welcome okay.

They were then interrupted by a caring but stout order in a way by a whippet with two paw bands wrapped around her front legs. Dylan knew what they stood for because of his grandad's carer who came to visit.

Betty spoke with a gentle bark, we are needed in the Pad and Gnaw room immediately. Right Dylan, I've to go but please consider our offer, they are waiting for recruits like you.

As he walked out in deep thought the guard post dog just said a few words to Dylan as he was leaving,

Whatever you got boy you make sure you keep it okay because it takes a lot for that breed of a woman to please as she's one tough cookie. What you in for? By the way I'm Taff so if you do join us, I'll be seeing more of you.

Dylan looked back at him, a sleek kinda German Shepard with a pure Welsh accent so it was no question where he got his nickname from. Dylan just thought to himself I must have had and been though as many meetings in these past few weeks than in my whole life put together. He walked over to the bench where some human folk were sitting, nurses, looking at the way they were dressed; some veterans in wheelchairs and a bunch of guide dogs of all sizes.

A stern Irish terrier spoke, I just seen ya come outta there, ma boy. We are all retired out of there and see the lady there? He pointed to the one mentioned, well she got together a long time ago a pack of the human species and us that bonded into a social group and it is wonderful, we all get along and shoot the breeze and reminisce of our times and we love to take a walk, a stroll along, whatever suits us, we served our time and they respect us for it. Some have found it hard to cope and understand this civvy life. But if you take a look again and chat to the high nurse their and ask her can you take a walk through the corner ridge memorial hall and see the history in there? It will give your young thoughts a real open mind and give you an idea of what happened and what you can do if you want help if you need too.

There was a real nice vibe around this group and with that question said to me about the memorial hall I had to go down as I knew it would niggle at me if I left it, so I just walked over and introduced myself to the nurse in question.

Excuse me ma'am, I was talking to the Irish terrier as he

noticed me coming out of the barracks and he mentioned certain history stored at a museum called The Corner Ridge? A little silence whilst glancing at me then a stern look over her glasses came next then a question,

And what is your interest in such history as that?

Well, I've just been offered to join the corps and I've been given a little while to decide. But I know the road I'm going to choose ma'am.

Another little silence and then a patient spoke, Nurse, can I? Wait a sec, stay there and I will be with you in a minute. She walked back over with a gentle looking gent with a pure Yorkshire accent,

Hello me laddie, I'm Nurse Sally's hubby, just then she looked over those glasses again and he just smiled back to her.

After a few questions the gent told Dylan that he was the Host to the museum with knowledge like there was no tomorrow.

You caught me at the right time as I'm just in between this and that so I will take you down okay. After exchanging names, he replied, Dylan, that is a very Welsh name you carry, isn't it?

Yes, my grandmother was from the Welsh Valleys like many around here came for better ways within the coal mines.

Yes-yes, my family had to leave their loved ones and homes. You may be able to tell I'm from Yorkshire and back in our time it was tough so there was a choice to leave our homes or suffer with pain. After our family settled it was like a puzzle of just coming out of its box for the first time. Pieces everywhere. Some joined the coalfield, others joined the fishermen and then there were the ones who joined the military, but there was a problem. When the wild days of the pubs were here and dances and so on and an argument broke out over a pretty lass etc and yes, a few barks-words were said that led to you being cobbled by the collar. what side did you take? The miners-marines or the fishermen? Either way about it you were seen as a traitor so after all the scuffling you may have ended end up fighting again when you got home or saw family folk. A big fit of laughter came next as you could see his memories come flooding back with glee.

We strolled down along the way chatting about this and that and I told him most of what was going on in my life with family and friends When we reached an entrance to an ole church, its double doors had seen many a day of history and as Larry, that's Sally's husband by the way, opened up and a crank came from the ole door has he turned the lights on. A silence was about but a presence of history whirled around from corner to corner. Then Larry walked me through and all I could do was stare at the building's kept history and all I could do was listen to his words and wonder to myself who in God's name could go through this and come out sane?

After shutting the doors, I kept silent as to what I had seen in those captures and cases of what one can do to each other and hoped that I wouldn't witness that on a scale like that. We walked back on down to reality and reached Larry's home and he invited me in and I only stayed a while as I explained I had to make it back.

Walking into the aroma of a happy house, all was rolling as Sally was there after getting a message to try and make it up to view the office location and she did it on the way down as Tilly gave her the details and left the rest to her. Tilly was first to speak after Dylan said hello to Sally and a few of the other team members.

That is another contract office, Dylan, that we got. Dylan are you okay?

Yes-yes, he replied a little startled and still a bit shaken up after his little ordeal he was in thought but he came to his senses once back in the company of his loved ones. Bailey was around earlier and said it is confirmed it is Monday that they leave. Also, Keeley popped in with her date of leaving as well and that is the Thursday that week. So how they spent the week was a very social side of sharing their company and love. Bailey even had a face on dinner with Bampie and Nannie Ryan and no doubt there were words on that patio concerning their granddaughter? But it happened with good intentions. The mayhem was all about as the band put their final assets together and yes, the Ambulance was all fitted to the core for a journey of their adventure out in the world of music and bars was ready to commence.

Just then Bailey arrived back down as he needed his birth certificate as ID.

Hi, Dylan, the reply was quick and with a question, Got time for a walk along the front?

Yes, I do as it will help me chill out.

The two headed for the door with Tilly looking on but she knew what the score was. They just walked along and Dylan told his brother about his ordeal of what he witnessed and who he met. It was not like Dylan did not have any idea of what was out there in the field of action but his meeting with the old folk-nurses and Larry and being asked to join the section all came at once and it was a lot for anyone to take in.

Well, here it is Bailey when you go up to the happy house it is to pick Poppy up to leave her grandfolks and are you ready for all that?

Yes, more than I thought and don't worry I won't let you down okay or anyone else, that I promise as I'm standing here now.

This is a journey within a great pack of all kinds and there will be a few stories to tell the next time we meet up and that you can be sure of. Plus, you will be an uncle has well.

Christ, I thought of that and it will be strange as we have all grown up so fast and look what is happening in all directions. It will be amazing the next time we all meet up and see where the road of life as taken us and there will be so much to say.

With this a little silence was with them both and stayed that way with thoughts that were tense.

Bailey, I just want to tell you what has happened this morning.

To blend with even more drama, he told him of the offer to the squad and the position and then mentioned where Larry took him and once again his experience of walking through that capture of history from two wars and many other active parts of his regiment that he had been honoured to join.

Dylan said, I think Larry was just giving me the up on this and what can happen at any time anyplace if you are called up. And if anything, it was a very respectful thing to do. Not to frighten me or any other category but this is the line of duty, Dylan and can you or would you want to be a part of it? My response of body language said it all and I thought it was a brave thing to do. I'm joining but if ever I'm called up and anything happened to me then you will be the first to step in line and take the family under your paw, can I hold you to that?

Yes, you can and you know you will never have to doubt that my brother, never.

Just then a bit of a natter bark came about them. It was another legend of this baggabond town, Bruce. Bruce the brown broken-tailed fish catcher. He got his owner into so many scurries in his day over stealing the fishermen's catch. A fish-eating, stealing Labrador.

The biggest upset to this day still talked about was the Big Catch Tournament on the day the biggest rivals of all between the Spratt Wafflers and the Rat Rodent's best men. Bruce that day on the Strand went down the front and snagged the two best fish out of their baskets and legged it and the prize of the day went to a DFL. No one could believe it of all the fishing history and these two head honchos had won that championship for thirty years they lost it to a DFL and how? A local doggie of their own stealing their catch. Well, what could one say? Any time they wanted to wind up those two ole local fishermen a local blighter would mention that day at the Walmer's Strand.

Bruce's mummy or partner shall we say was from Glasgow, a proud Scottish Lass and they added to it that she got a hand out to make the damage that day. But na' I don't think so. Mind you many a time if she was in The Dog's Bone or The Smelly Mutt Inn, she would start a little song of Flower of Scotland if either one of those fishermen and their dogs were in and Bruce would start howling to the tune to really rub it in and oh what's his name, that landlord at the time? Yes Dozzer, Dozzer the dozzy dog of Deal that's what they called him. He would look across at the pair and then they would notice and start humming the tune and a few local mutts would join in to wind him up by singing that tune, yes that did the trick ya and every time it got to him, yes, they felt a little bit clever.

Oh, with so much going on I forgot I said I'd meet Arthur and Daley at The Hope and Lane Coffee shop, as you know well that is wherever I've been I'll always try out the town's coffee hang outs but I can't find a spot to match how they make my coffee to suit me. When I'm walking up the High Street come rain or shine my highlight reward is my coffee there. Don't ask me where the name comes from but it suits me and my moods. You see what was always on the agenda, and still is, that we get our coffees from The Hope and Lane to meet Lulu and Rory and of course Oscar, then head up to the front to meet Clare and Paul, Arthur and Daley's Mummy and Daddy. Why? They own The Sweet Retreat, the best doughnuts in Kent and they make them. So, put two and two together and what do you come up with? Heaven.

So, can you see how we have so many treasured memories to carry with us wherever we are these memories would help us to get by, these simple treasures make one smile. Mind you there is one problem, once you start eating those doughnuts it is non-stop so forget the diet that is a no go. Daley used to and still does quite fancy himself as a dog whisperer to the ladies but we know they were always after his mummy's doughnuts and that is that.

The rest of the remaining days were left in the paws of each individual to lap up time with their special ones between Nannie Ryan and Bampie, Margaret with Grandad, Keeley with her family and so on it was time for their own personal comforts together to share. There was a lot of love and if it was all put together in one pot and sealed you know? It was so affectionate that we could make a fortune if we could seal and sell it but no there was no price to put on it but it would stay priceless in our hearts to get us by whatever happened.

A lot of chit-chat was barking along with Bailey and so on, when a message came by to him from Kev the postie.

This is from Harvey as I passed him in Kingstown when delivering and he told me if I see you to get in touch ASAP to go over all the instruments as a last check point okay?

Thanks, Kev.

And off he flew on his missions of letters and Bailey said his farewell thoughts to his childhood pup friends and had to scarper off to meet Poppy down at the vets for a few jabs and all. This was on Bampie's terms of course as his organising status was always with him and he was not having his joy to life going around the country with a load of mutts of all shapes and sizes without being jabbed you can count on that. Not offending anyone this was to be kept quiet as the boys may have taken it the wrong way. You know when things were swinging and you found out by some dog barking out with booze that Poppy was not allowed to go if she was not jabbed up to the hilt, they would feel a bit on the insulted side either way you looked at it, it was dodgy grounds to walk along when barking up the wrong tree or sitting on the wrong mat.

Walking up and chatting about Monday a few emotional thoughts were talked over like when they passed the bandstand and started to reminisce, just sentimentally feeling the time had come for these partings and the heart started talking. It was Poppy's first time really away from her abode and it was not like the old days of across the seas, never to be seen again but it was the first time.

They strolled along just in thought and then arrived at the Animal House Vets and of course all the happy vibes flowed about the location.

Right let's get this done you two. This came from Megan of course and it was a nosy chit-chat as ever and she asked for them to send postcards to the practice to let them all know how it was going along the road on their travels.

Yes, yes of course I will Megan, said Bailey nervously, still a woose and afraid of needles, something that had just been with him since a pup.

Anyway, it was done with now and they were on their way back.

Now I've to go and meet Harvey as we have to go through all the instruments and tack okay.

Yes, where are you meeting him?

At the ole Barn that belongs to his family, and yes and I've to meet Keeley as we have promised to meet up with Tilly and some of the girls along the front.

A little peck on the snout and off they set on their merry way.

Arriving at the ole Barn Harvey was already there and in his cheerful ways he too was getting excited about hitting the road in a few days.

Harvey, can we have a brief chat?

Looking over his shoulder he saw Bailey sit down and so he made his way over to him. Sorting out the amps, cables and so on, he said,

Look mate we go back a long way and I don't want things to step in our way so if you feel under any pressure that Poppy is on tour with us then let me know, okay?

Don't take this the wrong way Bailey but I'd be preferring the view of Poppy than the ugly mutts we have with us.

With this they both burst out with laughter and could not stop and then carried about on the times of past memories.

So, when is it we leave again? What date?

It is the Monday, a week after Aseena leaves, I think?

Don't complicate things just say the date. It seems like complete utter confusion is all around and I don't know whether I'm coming or going.

This brought ease all about as they all felt the same as everyone had something going on and all leaving about the same time.

The girls met up and it was time for Keeley to make an announcement as she was the one who felt nothing like this could happen in her life and now she had it all and what a feeling to have!

I just want to let you know that we have another little gathering-

What another one? This came from Tilly as she asked what this one was for?

Well, it is for the folks to have a little social mix over a few jars and have a chit-chat. Tilly don't you remember the last time when one of our mothers ended up dancing across the floor with the largest Irish Wolfhound whilst drinking tequila and it made a lot of say?

A silence swirled around and about with the youngsters' thoughts and we've all been there on that main subject, parents' days, whether being dropped off at the dance for the first time or being picked up by your folks with friends looking on. Those memories all hung with us and to think oh no, not again.

The girls had their gathering and started to make their way back to their own kennels.

Tilly asked, how are you feeling, Aseena?

To tell you the truth, Tilly, I'm buzzing with excitement and I'm booked in for this and for that. It is going to be one hell of an adventure, Tilly, I know. I still wish you were coming with me.

Well, we all have a road to take, Aseena, and it is going to be a long one for us all to travel but an adventure I must say.

Do you know something, Tilly, I'm really looking forward to meeting up with Stella, I think she is more excited than you on her end?

Well, I still can't believe that you are moving to the Big Smoke and to think it was not long ago we were with Daisy on that train, and on the roof of that hotel. Aseena, I want you to promise me one thing?

What is that Tilly?

If you have any doubt and feel your tails against the wall walk away, promise me that? We will all be taking chances and so on but you most of all. You will be surrounded in every angle out there and there will be a lot thrown in your face but face it head on, okay? There will be downfalls and leeches of life about but just brush them off, and if you need me then you call, just call.

It stayed silent for a few seconds and then a big break of a nervous laughter broke out and it was back to the mayhem of all the thinking and so on and they got up with a brush-down and a check-out on each other.

Tilly made a brief comment, I may be giving you these coats soon if I get any bigger you know?

Walking along and laughing again at their own nervous jokes it was all a cover-up of their slight nerves on edge.

It is an awkward question but do you think you will want puppies of your own, Aseena?

After asking the question Tilly thought she may have pushed her a bit too far with a question of the sort. Looking at her sideways for a reply Tilly saw something in her eyes of her loss and how tragic it was in her young life to have been taken away from her beloved parents but with the love of her blood, she was surrounded by those who meant well and were responsible for the well-being of a whole pack, it would be a long way down the long and winding road before that came into her thoughts and also it would be with whom? There was going to be so much traveling to so many countries and where would it end? She would take this with all paws on the ground and stand proud and tall.

Tilly made it back to the house as the rest made it to their own domains and walking in, she mentioned the gathering for the parents.

Are you going, Mum?

I will if the boys are playing?

I think so.

Then count me in, was her reply. It is all happening, isn't it?

The blarney was flowing and questions flying from all angles but that was nothing unusual as it was such a happy-go-lucky abode and chemistry just flowed from the building and that is why it created wonderful results that helped one's thoughts look on the positive side to many lines of duty along their way.

The evening came of the gathering of the parents and Nanny Ryan and Bampie Bateman were chatting to Becca and Lenny and nods were bopping back and forth and the boys brought a few instruments with them just in case a little jam came about. And yes, it did once it came about in chat about the type of music they would be playing along the tour, a real social gathering and it felt just right for all just to lie back when the songs commenced into harmony.

Whatever breed was within them the harmonizing suited the feelings of their emotions. Smiles and expressions flowed about and it helped in every manner as don't forget this was the first time the partings had come about for some of the families.

Don't worry my dear I'll keep an eye on her for you. This was a gentle intro from Larry the Lobster to Nanny Ryan and she replied with a little nervous edge,

Thank you, Larry, thank you.

The smiles captivated the rest of the evening and the singing came to its end when they all said their good nights and goodbyes with sentimental thoughts but once again it was not at a status that they would never meet again.

How are you feeling, Tilly?

Yes, I'm a little sentimental but that is the way we girls are with our feelings of parting. Also, the Vet told me that my moods will be all mixed up in air so don't be worried about these episodes that I will witness.

Dylan just embraced his sweetheart as they were all saying their goodnights, etc and put his best coat around her shoulders as they all shared their wonderful thoughts from the rest of the evening and made their way out onto the Pier's front where many, many partings and arrivals had occurred for centuries and generations from the past and present who sailed out from such a small holding compared to many ports in all.

I have often thought to myself walking along here if only those walls of the buildings opposite each other could talk and tell a yarn of what they witnessed, how many questions would be asked but how may they be answered? And then thought how many of those wild nights of what went on, it's a wonder one's not insane!

Well, the Monday morning arrived and that night Keeley stayed at the Manor as it was best for the two youngsters to be together to get used to it ASAP as it would be that way for many a times of their young future. Grandad and Margaret, well they wanted to keep this really on a private matter just to share their times and thoughts and the staff were in a very emotional mode as don't forget many of them, even the ones who had left the Manor's employment grew up sharing their lives with Aseena, so they gathered to wish her well on this adventurous career into the limelight of fashion and the open door to the world's ways in all.

She takes after her mother, doesn't she, Margaret? This came from Charlotte the second maid to Grandad and Aseena since her puppy days to when she decided to become a mummy herself two years back.

Many emotional chit-chats commenced from their thoughts on their memories as Margaret walked and just raised Aseena's paws to embrace the love she carried for her and yes, the tears become clear and Grandad, well what can one say but the beauty of love flowed from very part of his old body but he did have Margaret's emotions to hide his in. Once again, Grandad in his very professional manner was watching as a car arrived to take them to London to begin this saga and knowing security was there right from the beginning was a sight for anyone's eyes. It was a sight of contentment for Grandad and Margaret as they watched the car pull out of the driveway onto the London Road and on their way they went.

The driver's eyes rested on the two passengers but with a concerning glance. Aseena looked on as he spoke,

Hello, once again young lady. It was Clancy from the second drive of when Aseena was in London with Daisy and so on. It looks like we will be seeing a fair bit of each other in the near future as I feel I may be assigned to your whereabouts on a daily basis, Lass. Anyway, welcome on board. I was debating whether you would take the offer when you were up the last time. I did not know whether it was a bit too loud for you. Myself and Reggie the Mastiff had a little bet on the side yes, or no? So, it looks like he has won a drink off me as he saw something that I did not. Anyway, he is all excited about you being around our company and like the last time he saw you, he sees you as like one of his own litter and it will stay that way. Don't be annoyed with the pair of us looking over you but that is what we are paid to do, okay. Explaining this straight away gives a yes or no outlook to make it much easier for everyone to get along. it does young ladies, believe me it does make it much easier to work as a team as with getting out of crowds, locations, etc, etc. My life is yours and when I know you are safe within my presence then it is a wonderful world. This has given me great pleasure ladies to introduce just a simple standard that is so important to us all.

With this the girls looked at each other and the understanding of the talk of this little private introduction had been sent.

Driving along the roads out of Kent, it did not take long before the phone started and as Clancy expressed himself, they had a feeling who was on the line. Yes, you guessed it, it was herself touching base.

I'll tell you a little secret, Aseena, herself, she's superstitious. Why's that? Well, whenever a new client joins us, she calls within the hour to see if that client is onboard and if so, is he or she content?

Along the way chatting they realized they were getting closer to the city the brighter the city lights got. Yes, exciting thoughts running through their minds and hearts and then driving into the busy roads with hoots, horns coming from all sides the girls kept looking about and holding onto their paws the car pulled up at a cool side of Pall Mall where Clancy pulled up to say,

Right, you two this is going to be your nest/base or whatever you want to call it this is it.

Then the two peered up at the building a little nervously but more excited to think here they both were in the trendiest area of the Smoke and it all began here.

I'll see you in and these two approaching us now are the local management but the first lesson to tell you, they are Mrs McDonald's message carriers, okay?

He stayed a little silent to make sure the girls understood what he meant. Then as they were escorted into their apartment, they flurried all about and yes, their adventure had just begun.

Look, I'll leave you to it but listen to me, Mrs McDonald wants you at the studio tomorrow morning so don't let me down by not being ready for me tomorrow morning, prompt at 9 am okay?

We promise, Clancy, we promise we'll be ready.

A smile from Clancy as he headed for the door with a brief glance back at the pups in awe and just kept smiling to himself.

Well, here we are, Keeley.

How do you feel, Aseena?

Let's be honest it is not every day that two 18-year-olds are given a place in London, is it? And here we are in Pall Mall amongst it all. Let's look at the bedrooms and who wants which one?

What would you expect but excitement from them both and may this positive response in their young hearts stay this way forever?

The morning arrived and there they were prompt looking with a glare at Clancy as they both got into the car. Clancy had a natural ambience about him that made the girls feel secure within his presence and that is why I feel Mrs McDonald chose him over many others. Anyway, the first question came about as,

How did you settle in and sleep may I ask?

Fine Clancy it felt a little strange listening to so many movements so early in the morning but that's the city, isn't it?

Right then, she's waiting for you both at the studio at the North End as she wants you to meet Graham, Gray the Ray, they call him. He has had that handle on him since God knows. I've known him since the Bowie scene and he has a wonderful scope of vision into colour, even black and white he can match the shades and shadows to complete what needs to come out. A very quiet private person, Aseena, with an art of creation of clothing as well. You should feel proud to be introduced to him so early in your career and your introduction so early really but I think I know why. Your exposure, Aseena, of slenderness will bring the light out in his work with the lens. You have all that, young lady.

It is a wonder, Clancy, you didn't get into the side of the lens?

This came from Keeley as she liked to listen and what Clancy had explain to them since picking them up yesterday, her voice seemed to be happy with photography.

Maybe your skills are unsung?

Walking through the studio doors the awe of the status of being in this element was like lightning striking the only tree left on the earth and seeing its vaults travel through the ground lighting up everything in its way. In the reception hallway there was a small group standing chatting when this wonderful gentle person turned to the two young girls with a delightful embrace in his welcoming eyes,

Welcome, please, please come in. With this he put his camera down on top of a high stool and then stood in silence for a second and then muttered two words, oh yes, yes, come, come my dear.

With this, the two girls just beamed with a secure immense feeling and Graham spoke again with both palms spread on his hips monitoring with looks from up and down he asked,

Aseena, please stand on your toes and stretch your legs until your paws reach the ceiling and Keeley put your paws on Aseena's hips and lift.

The girls were excited about this but once again Graham could do this and that and that's why every agent in this bizzo wanted him. He brought the best out if it was there.

Keeley felt a strange feeling move within her imagination as of her thoughts and she said there and then,

Aseena, please lift your left hip up to reach out please?

Just then Stella walked in and with such a buzz she flew across the floor and welcomed the girls on board. A tut came from Gray the Ray with a mutter of, Women! I just don't know. But once again that was his humour and it suited him fine.

Now stop the hugging, my dears, you'll have plenty of time for that after the shoot' Keeley, please with that expression in tone, I'd like you to focus on straight away what enters your mind as of how the dress code and colour would feel right on and around Aseena, okay?

With this question, Keeley could not help but feel a wonderful creative feeling that embraced her thoughts and replied with a, Yes, okay, answer.

Straight away she walked over to the many rails along the walls and started to view with a stern expression all the designs on display' not knowing or realising who was looking on? yes, herself the head honcho, Mrs McDonald and there was a normal expression from her which caught Stella and Graham's thoughts of what is this all about? They had to smile themselves has witnessing this as they not seen it before but it was lifting to view.

Anyway, being a little nervous, the girls looked about them from side to side and Mrs McDonald spoke quickly,

Please, do not let me hold you up in any manner. And she then took a few steps backwards to watch on.

Right, do me a favour, put this on against the light wall, Aseena, and stretch out bringing your legs together into making a twin shadow. With this Keeley spoke again, what do you think Gray?

With his famous Oh yes expression he made straight away for the lens and click, click, click was the only sound you could hear until it felt that they tired the camera out with exhaustion which was a tremendous feeling for all as this art work to be witnessed right from the beginning made it easier for all sides to work together. The photographer to the model and staff it was just natural to embrace their feelings in a style to share.

Stella then stood aside upright as she was introduced to Keeley.

This is my friend Stella, Keeley, Keeley, Stella, a it seems to rhyme?

Smiles and hellos passed as this was a quick introduction to each other and yes, Mrs McDonald looked on for some reason.

Enough of that please, back to the floor you girls.

Yes, Gray the Ray had a buzz on as he always said, it is one in every million that opens his eyes to beam with rays of delight to enjoy his job so much and Aseena has it.

Mrs McDonald stepped out of sight and walked upstairs to the lounge-studio overlooking the floor and Clancy was there getting himself a coffee and as he turned around, he saw her looking out over the darkened windows and couldn't help but speaking out.

You did well there, finding that beauty.

And that she is, Clancy, was her reply, a real beauty if ever there was one. Do you know what I'm going to do my old friend? I'm going to stay out of sight and step in only if I have to. After that experience over meeting up with Daisy after all times in life, it happened now when I've realised that we all have to stay back and let reality take charge and watching their style in all I'm not that inclined to expose our cut of clothing like I'd like it to be shown. Together these two can. So let's put the ball in their courtyard Clancy and that is that. You will keep me informed if needed, yes?

Leave it to me Ma'am, leave it to me.

They then just took a seat and watched the art of the floor bring joy about with pleasure and how well they did it with natural movement from the eye.

Back in the ole smugglers town of Deal things were jumping as ever with the company of the other gang getting ready for the next departure. Bailey's plans held together with this and that and another short meeting in the quietness of privacy with Bampie. Over what? Who knows? But it was the Tuesday and they were seen over in Sandwich and as saying nothing passes without someone's snout in the bizzo to find out another one's business, who saw them? Why of course it was Jimmy the Jumper. He was born from local terriers who must have a history from being around here longer than any mutt's tail. He owns shine a light that cleans windows with a flash. Why he watch's everything there is my friend and if you want any gossip spotting then ask no other.

The Wednesday evening arrived and it was kept personal with each one of the bands choosing their loved ones to be with before their tour that would leave in the morning from the courtyard of Cleo's. She's Denzel's mum the renowned family of the legendary Rottweilers of the boatyard owned by Kyla, the daughter of the old-time shipwright family whose name goes back to when that ole Admiral, what's his name again? Oh yes Nelson used to have his wicked ways around the town and he would have Cleo's great-great grandfather and his buddies walk the lady in waiting and her doggies back to that cottage behind the Clarendon Hotel and then back across the town where other dogs of the town and night would look on but dared not mutter a word or bark a bit to anyone inclined of what was really going on, they just told a banter that was surely a lie.

With so many banters over the years and the yarns out of the pubs or wherever was it true what they said that Kyla's family going way back when Wales and the rest of the Celts were at civil wars with the English folk, over Laws of paying tax and all that they were real rebels of the canine world and fought outta the valleys and made the small Dinghies called a Coracle - Cwrwgll in the Welsh lingo that go back to 2,000 years ago.

Anyway, they would row down through the coal-filled valley towns with a pair of Rottweilers down to Tiger Bay where the utmost sight of industry would be in action from flour mills to coal to everything you could imagine would be shipped out to supply the world of its needs and they would collect needs for the rebels from the owners of the business's then out of the morning's dawning light they would row back up to the needy who were fighting for the rights of the lives of Wales. Then one night once again a grass gave vital info on the raids to the law and they lay waiting as they were 8 to 1 outmatched at the foot of the Taff River that flows into the bay, the flood came on and the shout out Attack! And doggies from every working shed etc came out onto the ambush. It was a battle never forgotten and still talked about all over the valleys and Tiger Bay and if you go into one of the old pubs left in Cardiff you would find pictures and newspaper clips on that part of history. Plus, the ole pubs there you will find an ole Mutt sat at the foot of their partner or the bar telling a tale of those troubled times and of course a few extra banters added and it would start with the heading of the Edwards family.

Well, when they made their way back to the Valley's town of their home, the King's hunters in their packs were searching and haunting every kennel in every village with rape and pillage in their minds so the small pack of heroes had no choice but to leave their beloved towns for the safety of their village folk and set sail out into those coaldust-filled rivers that led to the Bristol Channel then out to where they did not know what lay ahead of them. And some how they followed gossip that came out of many a mutts snouts.

They followed those larger boats along the English Channel, a few landing in Portland looking at filled towns along the way, Margate, Ramsgate, Sandwich and somehow for some reason one calm night they could not sail on because of tiredness, they landed upon the shingle-filled coast of the town of Deal and looked here and there and settled for a night's rest as their aim was Dover to sail away to another country for safety, but for some reason they felt an embracing feeling in the air and this town of Deal became their destination.

What these dogs felt was a bond of the same instincts of roots of many other breeds and it did not take long to realise what and why? Many, many fellow Welsh-Yorkshire grafters took the long, long walk along those hard cobbled ways to the towns of Kent for the coal life and its following trade. So once again take a glance at the names over the shops on the main streets of the Kentish towns, Welsh or Yorkshire titles and that is the reason for it.

Anyway, back to the Edwards' gossip. On the Victoria Road, before it was built up of houses, well that was the huge boat yard and one of the main yards that made Deal the busiest dry port in England. Many, many an argument was raised on how it could be the busiest in England compared to many a city such as Bristol, Southampton etc, but it was. The Prospect House on Victoria Road, well that was the head living anchor and business house to all the goings on around that neck of the woods, even the true banter of what was going on in the Deal -Walmer Castle's cellars, what was coming in and out, by none other than the King's royals and doggies? But it was all to do with making a penny behind and under the taxman's books.

The owner now of the grand Prospect House senses and feels the presence of the wall's history and says it often brings a smile to his face of the one word that came out of there to describe its history; that word is fraud. The whole town was based on one way of making a buck and each banter like the pair of Yankie doggies who lived up on The Marnier whose daddy and mummy are Andy and Donna.

Norm and Storm are their names and Norman is dating Coco the Shih tzu who lives in the miners' cottages with her mummy, Jannette. You know how they used to make a living? Well, they are a pair of Chinese crested hounds and a very strange kinda dog for one's eyes to witness for the first time you see them. Why? Because they are bald. Yep, bald as a coot's butt. Anyway, they used to dance as a pair in the Ladies Desire club? You know the building on the edge of Dolphin Street? Well, that club was for all the women of the town to let loose after all they had been through, they had to somehow let go.

So, who got the idea one night after a little of that special brew from Mexico, yep no other than Frank the Crank introduced this place and the women of the town thanked him for that. Well Norm and Storm used to dance the tables and the ladies just loved to view and touch them just for curiosity for once again they had no fur. One night Coco saw more than just a dancer and that was that; yet another tale of distant banters of one's heart falling in love and staying in this hell-bent wild town of pillage.

Times are different now, aren't they? Mind you if you gotta sense with reading creatures ya can't help but feel the presence of a pirate or smuggler's breed coming out of a doggie walking along through the shady side streets that were once lived in by none other than a one-eyed dodgy mutt watching your holdings or a well-groomed, blossom-coated lady of the night offering the delights of her company on a bitter lonely night. Many of these sorta houses-kennels in the town now are closed of their history and kept for second kennels and a weekend breaking spot. So, you do understand how many a mutt's characters and features of the town have disappeared into the Channel and their past ways as of the corrupt features of the broken snout, or one ear missing, or a bent, broken tail or whatever are gone. Now it is a diamond collar type of doggie for the likes of Birdie or another well-groomed coat, clipped Pawdy -Mourdy-Barka by Becca at her salon or Tereasa's parlour but the town holds its presence with essence that makes many a doggie's waggy tail the happiest in Kent and the coats with the best, shiny updated looks.

They all had their personal meetings of another farewell as the Thursday morning songs from the blackbirds etc harmonised together with all the other sounds that made up the Courtyard where the gathering was held to part from Deal for another episode of music to be shared around the many a wall of bars, halls, fields and ears of all shapes and sizes to fill with enjoyment to share. The emotions were high as it was Nanny's first departure from Poppy on this level and seeing this posse spread around the courtyard like a pack of hyenas in and out of this contraption of an ambulance loading their objects of music and all with excitement gleaming from everyone getting ready for the roads. All you could hear over was, have you seen my-? Have you got my-?

When Larry the Lobster comforted Nanny Ryan with, don't you worry your little heart my dear, don't you dare. The hugs came about and Bampie Bateman put his arm out straight where Nanny found comfort and she looked about as if to say the sooner they head off the better it will be for all.

So, Dylan managed to have a last say with his brother,

As you know what we discussed and it's a promise, Bro, and you stick to that promise okay?

With this there were steps back and forth as to step out of the way and waves to friends and a smile or a hug was all around. It was as of this town's history of centuries of partings in all and this yes, yet another one.

The final hug embraced one's feelings and then they all mounted their transport that would become their homes for this wonderful adventure and then out onto the main drag they drove with waves still commencing from the vehicle's windows and out of sight it disappeared with a little hoot in the distance. Looks came about again to each other who were left in the courtyard and nervous nods comforted the parting for the mummies and all.

Right, let's make it back, shall we?

The linking of arms/paws were a nice sight again as they strolled out of the courtyard and on to the destiny to their homes, Nanny strolled along under the embrace of Bambie's feelings whilst Tilly smouldered from Dylan's affection and this was a wonderful joy for each other.

Dylan spoke to his mum to say it was better to have left their dad at home earlier in security and comfort. He would only want to get about and it would not surprise anyone if he had tried to join the journey by mounting the Ambulance or so on. So much had happened in this short while that one did not know if one was coming or going? This came out of Dylan's snout, talking to Jasper, his long-time friend who said he would come down and get things organised and on their way, so he did,

You didn't want to go on tour this time mate?

He then turned to his sweetheart and replied, No Dylan, I've got a more important band on the way myself mate due in a short while. He turned with a beamed expression and it did not take long for Tilly to realise what was what and started to smile with a caring thought to Lilly and whispered silently to her,

Congrats and well done. How long with you Lilly?

Their chatter carried on and of course what they were talking about was something they had very much in common and realised they could support each other as it was both their first time.

I've heard a lot about Dylan, he's been chosen to enter into the bomb squad I hear?

Yes, and the police depot, that is what Jasper wants to apply for.

Their banter carried on and Dylan described a little on the procedures in all for acceptance into the introduction,

So, if I can help just ask me Jasp, okay?

Thanks Dylan, thanks mate.

Lilly just to let you know we have a new venture on our plate.

Tilly explained about the business they had set up in cleaning and then told her about Aseena and Keeley with their contract. She knew of it through the town's chit-chat but Tilly was telling her things like they would beam into us at The Hope and Lane, as they were living in London now.

Anyway, cutting it short, once a week they will contact us on video from all over the world and this afternoon at three they are touching base and you are welcome to join in and listen to their chatter. In fact, why don't we head off for a little shopping of our own then go straight over?

Yes, let's do that.

They explained to the boys and away they went. A town like this once again the gossip was about and you had to keep it under control so when the two girls were seen shopping it did not take long for a drift of some sort to be about. Then when they were walking down the High Street to the coffee house, they heard a few growls in all but nothing they could not handle. Walking through the Café door a few welcoming barks came from here and there when they took seats with some other pooches and the screen came up, a few excited barks came about but it was only natural with the girls all being apart but the questions started to embrace the air and Keeley called out,

Lilly is that you?

Yes, yes Keeley.

Keeley turned to Aseena to tell her, see that dark-haired beauty down there? That is Louis's sister, the guy I told you about who works for Wards, you know the high-end agent who sells all the high-end kennels around the town and so on.

Ya, I've had the hots for him for years, if I come back get me his number Lilly.

Laughter spread all about that matched the happiness as questions shot about and the two girls mentioned the photo-shoot with Ray and next week, well, the end of next week the discussion of their flight to New York for the promo of the Doggie ma Hoggi new style set called Joseph and the Multi-coloured Coats and Collars. And just the thought of being in New York was enough to get their tongues wagging.

Lilly, is Louis dating that Claire?

No, no they are lifelong friends and they work together that's all.

Anyway, if that's the case you get me in touch with that brother of yours and I'll see if I can get you on this wagon for New York, a straight deal.

The laughter was about as they bantered on Tilly spoke,

That seems fair, times in Deal for times in New York for a set-up of Keeley with Louis and themselves having a little dilly.

They had their says and it was said that Poppy had left earlier with the Tour and how exciting it was for all. Another bark came out and it was Aseena,s side this time, enjoying their talk. A call came out,

You two, you are wanted by Stella at the reception!

Right, we gotta git, we will speak to you next week okay, and Lilly don't forget.

This in a way could not have been a better time as in a way Tilly needed someone even though she was smothered all around with loving folk. Lilly was in the same way as Tilly and the same age and to be able to stretch out one's thoughts on your own door step was vital and enough to get you by and Lilly and Tilly both needed this and now. It was not just here in this community of a town that times they were a changing, it was all over the country. Cities, towns and down through villages the ways of living had become a totally different level from how their lives had been for centuries.

Everyone knew each other around them but now every kennel beside you lay empty, just used for now and then instead of having a neighbour.

Look for instance just now? Who would think we would be in a café sitting next to a Border Collie talking to Keeley over a large screen when it only seems the other week, we were playing in the shingles chasing each other's tails and playing ball? Now we are talking about motherhood and business. By the way do you want me on board as one of your staff, Tilly?

I will speak to Sally okay and let you know ASAP.

A few weeks passed and everything flowed with a passion of seeing others' dreams for each other coming true. Lilly came on board and sang away with all the other members of staff. The company just blossomed with their lives and at this time Bailey and so on were in Cornwall with wonderful thoughts, messages flowing back that reached all the members of the packs. As we said one doggie could be in the butchers barking away or another having her hair trimmed at Teresa's or Becca's, word or a bark got out and off it went, oh yes gossip always rules many lives.

Nanny Ryan used the same butcher as Darcie, Sally and most of the other mummies and so on. Well, what more can one say? Gossip and banter were on one's lips and snouts for many and much of it was not a drawl or a bore just good ole lip-smacking chewing slander. Like did you hear about Wellington, Birdie's Uncle? Well, he's got a slender beauty on his paw walking into the Dog's Mane? Yes, yes it did not take long for that to get out and most of it was down to jealousy with a doggie of his age with a blonde Afghan hound with legs as long has an eel, mind you he still is a handsome chap of his breed you must give him that credit, haven't you? Look at the location he has on the market with Wards, that kennel's heaven to say and to be sat on that porch with that pooch what more would one want to bark about? So, I take my collar off to him or any successful four-legged hound who has got it all.

Just a few weeks passed and now the Dogs Brush or Broom as some called it was at its peak with talk over taking on major blocks but Tilly felt bold and stern on the subject of don't complicate things and get out of paw and let it all slip away. A good ole banter was going on and Tilly felt with all the talk and natter from many a hound's advice her time had come to become a mummy.

She turned to Lilly and told her to get hot water, blankets and call the vet and Dylan to let them know what the status was. Lilly's natural language of Spanish soon broke open whilst gathering the necessities as she was all excited, this was all going on as they were at the Floppy Ear Hotel over at Sandwich and the owners were so much down to earth this was a beautiful thing to happen at their domain.

It was not long before the sound of yelping all around from a proud litter of eight puppies that broke the sound of silence but once again the guests loved what they witnessed and cherished this affectionate time. The vet was first to arrive and within seconds Dylan came storming through the doors. A lot of congrats and hugs, smiles were about as a bark howled from Town to Town about the grand news of the litter spread that one must see.

Me now a grandma can you believe it?

This came from Darcie and the ladies as normal got woofing that which pup looked like uncle Sam or that one looked like Bailey and so on but that's just natural to say the least, yes, the main escapade of barks could be heard from far and wide of the wonderful news. Bailey found out he's an uncle and Aseena and Keeley beaming in were shown on the screen at the Cafe the basket that held all the little folk that seemed to be waving at them? You would think the main topic would be on the photo shoot of Aseena as it blew the Barking Mad Magazine's sale records out of order and Keeley's choice of designs got as much say as Aseena,s beauty.

The media was all over them and they could not praise them enough and fame was now theirs. But the girls' thoughts were just on the litter and home and that's the friendship they had and always would have. You would think in this day and age compared to the past historical dramas there was more to talk about but no, simple happiness of good news was the most important matter. News travelled fast like ole times how it spread and how? Well, it is said the currents that flow from North to South, East to West the gossip would never end. For look at the English language that was written from the thoughts of Daniel Defoe on the views of the human-domestic creatures' behaviour of this town? Maybe mine now for this town's Northern background of the Yorkshire Dales settlers and the Southern Welsh, Irish Celtic clientele both breeds of wild coal diggers, raised from the deep underground and of course the Spanish and French and Romans, hadn't the countries and cities been at war with this southern breed all along the coast and mixed deep in its roots the Celts bred with seadogs, what are you gonna get? A savage breed of first-class smugglers, scoundrels that are still meant to be.

Anyway, thoughts and theories will always be out there, won't they? Now with more domestic-tame breeds of humans with their four-legged partners paying top dog for the kennels here the savage ways of living are drawing to an end but alas the souls and spirits will run wild around the narrow streets leading off the stroll along the front so one's thoughts will still carry on wondering, I just wonder what it was like in those wild times?

Only a few weeks passed on and the grand litter of puppies brought the joy of life to anyone or anything that came within their sight, just to see them smile as they played was heaven sent. Even the members of the Keep Ped Pros Club who were the biggest critics of the mixed bred and breed of the Sin Club could not help but smile with nice thoughts after seeing the little ones playing in the shingles working out the strange items the tide had washed up and even the fishermen showed a blind eye as they played around their landing bay on the Prince of Wales Terrace. The young ones would often be looking up at the tall ole houses and they could see heads bobbing about in the windows and just could not work out what they were.

Ray, one of the puppies who was named after the landlord of the Old Ship, asked his daddy,

Are those shadows moving about the ghosts of the miners, smugglers that the fishermen told us about and that is why it is called the Prince of Wales Terrace, because all the row of houses were full of Welsh Corgis or Welsh Border Collies with their partners?

Dylan replied with, yes, son, they wanted to call it the Prince of Wales and Yorkshire Terrace but it just didn't sound right my boy.

With this Dylan looked at Tilly and all they could do was laugh to each other thinking look what they are being told already.

Tilly spoke with a stern bark in her throat,

As long Dylan as they don't start telling them about the scoundrel kennels of sin that once flooded every street and its never-ending tails of despair as all of those dark-deepened times that gave our now tame town such a bad name in the outside world where all the terrible words in their speech of us rhymes.

Talk about behaviour of sin, I must tell you one that has just hit out that you will hear about Tilly, so I'll tell you now as I was told at the base yesterday about it. You know Mark, who runs the shady historic looking abode of the Waterfront Hotel on the front?

Yes, what about him?

Well, he had a problem with Ann, you know Evie's mummy. Well, she was told that Evie has been hanging out with Megan and Haley, you know Frank the Crank's daughter and niece.

What from the Waggy Endings Parlour and Spa?

Yes-yes. That is Frank's pride and joy and Mark is his shady partner and Ann's life time friend. Well, you know the famous Great Pedigree Chum Train Robbery? You know the famous detective who was on that case? You know the German Shepard who was the one that charged Frank and Dean from Hackney as part responsible for that robbery?

Yes, what about him?

Well, that was Ann's daddy and Ann was his buttered beauty of a daughter who could do no wrong. Now she's the same as her daddy over Evie and to find this out. you know the clientele Evie's keeping well what can one say?

Well, she hit the bottle and you know what that leads to with stories of the past, she got turfed out, well she was asked to leave Arno's Wine and Delectation on the High Street. She turned on Andrew, Arno's boyfriend and Yoko and Toto their two pups. Andrew then gave Ann's son Joaquin a call in London to tell him to get his ass down here ASAP over his mum's behaviour is outta paw. Joaquin, everyone knows him as Dan and his boyfriend Harry had to put everything on hold and come down here and ease the war zone. First to remove his mum from the high stool at the Waterfront as it was getting to a stage that Mark was running low on his top shelf supplies, plus, get answers of what to do next with Ann were running out. And he knew as well what was on Ann's mind and what she would do.

Dan arrived and Ann's thoughts became as calm as a summer's breeze along the Channel, talking about gentle memories, Mark hinting with his eyes looking up the staircase as if to say let's get her to bed? So that was the plan, step by step they coached her to beddy-byes with soft talk and it worked as she took the last sip of top shelf that Ann was drinking then Dan walked her towards the staircase and slowly up the stairs where Ann's slurry words were these famous steps of sin brought shame on many my son and the dogs of the night and the women of the walk for centuries did their thing here, shame-shame on them all. Don't let your sister take that road okay. By now he managed to get her into the Pedigrees Parlour suite and she was out like a light and then he made it back down to speak to Mark.

Right Mark I'm going over to get Evie okay.

Do you want me to come with you Dan? This was Harry's words and just then Martin arrived, Ann's brother and Mark looked at him with a nod as if to say you missed it all.

No, Harry it is best I go over on my own and I'll talk to her.

What if Leo and his brothers are there?

Don't worry I've already called over to the Dolphins Parlour to tell them you are coming over Joaquin, these were Marks words so that is taken care of. Martin?

Well, he's still as eccentric as the town's history.

He took a seat at the bar on the high stool and started the banter of the history. As don't forget Mark, Martín and Ann and all grew up together and he laughed out loud when he was told what this was all about and his sister was out cold in one of the famous rooms of sin.

Mark, tell me, were you threatened with the talk of being accused of being a part in the robbery and your secrets are kept silent on her lips about your partner's history is still kept with her in the dark?

Yes, yes you know the score I understand I've heard it all before.

Joaquin then mentioned that he was heading over to talk to his sister and like many a man in thought he was best left alone. He just started to wander down Beach Street down towards the shady side of town and then turned down Dolphin Street and who was coming out of the Waggy Mehaggies Parlour, none other than Frank himself and who was with him but Alan the Basset Hound the historical judge of Kent and for 50 years he wore that famous cloth and guess what his most famous case was? Yep, the Great Pedigree Chum Train Robbery. Also,

Hudson was with them, you know he was the judge's loyal side and butler for as far back has I remember. He moved in with Paul and Jamie. Paul is the judge's grandson you know? They live on North Street off Alfred Square and who owns the house next door to them, none other than Giggly-Staffierea Staffur. She was the long-time mistress of Frank back in Hackney. They say she keeps that house for her profession you know. High end customers looking for a good time away from all the light of their businesses shall I say anymore? No one would dare say anything on that subject but she's down with them from the smoke as well.

Come off it, if you had any knowledge of the town's history what is a person supposed to think seeing this? All these vagabonds in company.

Dan just slipped into a doorway and let them pass by and heard Frank mutter you know that barmaid Hudson? Do you think she was sent over by anyone? She asked a fair few question's didn't she?

Na it is just a coincidence really.

He watched them share that gripping type of barking chit-chat until they reached the Farthing House and opened its mysterious door and they all kinda wobbled in and Dan being the way he is watched a while and guess what? The lights of next door came on and, Ya know what, no one went through that front door so how did the lights get turned on?

He looked carefully through next door's window and he could not believe who he saw, yep Dean'O the East End Dodger gang leader who was supposed to be either dead or living in South America. He recognised him from all the newspaper clips and so on over the years and there he was in Deal. What was Dan supposed to feel and think? These thoughts were whirling around in his head when all he could hear then was all the yelping and laughter. It was Teddy and

Trotsky with a whole gang of pups and all because it was Tom's 18th so it was time to party and do a little pub hopping.

They were two litters younger than Joaquin, so he kept in the shade of the doorway, then when the coast was clear, he walked through those famous doors of the shady pad of many a story. He looked about as he was approached,

Why hello, my darling! came a welcoming bark.

Sorry, love you're not my type.

Shame-shame came the response from the blond, red-crossed lab.

He then looked around and Elie saw him and with shock and dismay up she rose. Dan, Dan what are you doing here? She took his paw and walked him over to the table where the girls were sitting, before he could say a word, Haley said,

Look, take a seat and let us explain as I have a feeling why you are here.

No, no I don't think you do. Anyway, I'm willing to listen to anything that makes sense to all this blarney ado.

Right first of all don't think just because of who my father and uncles etc are, it does not mean I follow their doggery-dodgy history okay?

Looking around him he replied,

Well, this is shady O'Grady's. You've chosen a fine place to meet and talk, haven't you?

We were called here by my dad as he was in town passing by and had some news about a location that we have an interest in, because we want to open our own fine clothing shop with Elie and for some reason Dad wanted to speak to Elie over some matter. For some reason he was asking questions about your grandaddy. Why, I don't know, but it looks like we will get the go-ahead with the keys of the shop on the high street and we are ecstatic about it. Look, here are some of our designs.

Dan kept looking at them and back up to his sister and company and said, I'm well impressed; these are beautiful. Let's not get too excited but I may be able to assist in marketing some of these back in London. So, all the mayhem and so on is all panic and all in all, the salarnie is untrue?

Girls, do you mind if I have a quiet word with my sister?

Of course, not.

After chatting away and explaining where their mummy was right now and why; after listening to the saga, Dan had to go through what people were saying. Evie was mad but at the same time she had to laugh about it all. They laughed it off then she turned to Joaquin,

Come on, let's get outta here.

Walking across the famous floor that had been walked across by so many generations in all types of action, one looked around and quietly thought if only these walls could talk of who was seen in this abode etc etc a person would make a fortune on briberies.

She then explained to the ladies, I must leave now as something has come up, okay bye for now, Elie, we will see you soon with the results of the keys.

They started making their way to the door when Betty and Bella came strolling in with some very high-end guests all in great form. Dan knew their faces straight away and man did his thoughts fly in his mind or what? Betty and Bella? A pair of heart-breaking Boston Terriers. Yes, this pair of sisters have they broken some hearts like chewing a beef bone on one's day off. They ran the styles and services of The Leash That Led to Leisure for as long as a conger eel as they say.

Come on, Evie, we've got to go.

Heading outta the door that red-headed blonde Labrador managed to get one last word to Joaquin, you ever change your mind and ways, ma boy, ya know where to find me okay.

He smiled and said, I will, and headed out of the door.

Walking along the street onto Beach Street, Evie spoke,

Now you see, Dan, what small towns are all about with slander and gossip.

Yes, but Sis, you have to be honest about the girl's family history. It is only natural souls will talk so be careful, okay.

Walking up, they passed Snouty Mc Gowtie's bar and all the party mutts on Tom's 18th were in there and Dan spoke,

Looks like there will be a few sore heads in the morning!

They laughed along the way then reached the Waterfront Hotel and through the door they went, looking about they got the looks of confusion and curiosity and of course uncle Martin had to have a go,

Busy, young lady?

She glanced at him then at Harry and asked, Can I get you a drink and you can tell a tale of what the drama of a small town's chat can do to one's reputation.

The drinks flowed and the banters glowed and they knew a session was ahead as their bond together just laughed on and a melody of happiness through the company that they were in was ahead.

Mark, with all this chit-chat isn't it marvellous there is still no confusion about where it comes back to? What name comes out of one's mouth whatever shape, breed or size they know this establishment, whether it's the Waterfront or Waggiest all bring laughter galore.

Yes, the morning arrived and many a confused, sore-looking shapes and sizes were about. The first eye-to-eye contact was Ann and Mark. There was a little confusion about Ann's thoughts and reality started to come back to her; how and why was she at the Waterfront hotel?

Just to let you know, Joaquin and Evie are on the way down for breakfast.

What, Dan? He's here?

Yes, he and Harry came down yesterday. Here, drink this and I'll fill you in on a bit of the action over the past 24 hours.

Ann's thoughts were rolling around a little confused you could say until Mark filled her in on the drama. Mark in a way was trying to keep a straight face whilst explaining the facts. He took a quick glance at the clock and said, Right I gotta get into the kitchen. He got up and she slowly looked up at her old friend with a little self-pity but she wasn't going to get any from him that was for sure.

Dan and Harry had stayed at their mum's house with Evie last night and were making their way back and whilst walking along the Strand nodding to folks he knew when he met Dylan and Tilly with their new regiment leaping with joy all over the place. Harry got so excited with the little ones because being a care worker it just came naturally.

Are they?

Yes, they are ours and what a bunch!

Someone told me you have done well, Dylan, on your training and studies.

Yes, yes, I have and I'm delighted and on Thursday I get my diploma and intro to the first of my full-on action studies. Dan, how long are you down for?

Joaquin gave a quick glance at Harry who just nodded as he had a feeling there was something up.

We are here for a while, Dylan.

Maybe you would like to come along to the presentation night?

I'd love to.

Okay, I'll put you down on our guest list.

Dylan, just one thing; do you remember as kids we used to dream about cases of crime-busting and the ole banters we heard about and hunt for clues?

Yes, we used to pretend to join your daddy and become detectives, didn't we?

Well concerning something lately I've witnessed, I'd love to get your view on it. Why now you are really in with the line of duty it would be interesting to hear what you have to say.

Tilly gave a little nod herself and he said, Wait a sec.

Harry just naturally started to help with the litter of love with Tilly whilst Dan and Dylan had a brief chat sitting on the shingles on the front and out it came about the sight he'd seen with the whole pack together.

I honestly feel my Grandad's blood and history is coming out of his grave and into my veins if that's possible? I'd love your opinion on what you know I'm thinking of. Wow, what is one supposed to think with a historical case like that related to this ole town of ours?

He looked over at Tilly and said, Look I'll talk to you at the academy, okay but I think you know our thoughts would agree.

Time moved on and the joy of life just grew with the essence of love of the choices each member of this group made and look now, in a short spell of time how far apart they are in miles but in love and thoughts they were beside each other and that kept them together. Dylan's introduction into his academy went amazingly with the pride of all around him standing and just watching with love and joy.

Poppy's tour? Well, you would never have guessed it over one night of such a buzz of happiness with the band and from the crowd she got up and sang and the whole place stopped in awe just to listen to her Celtic soul voice that no one had any idea had been there. Now she was up on stage with every gig they did and her confidence grew by the day.

Aseena, well the girls were just climbing that ladder of fame, whilst their photo shoot in New York was going on, they were invited to a shoot in New Orleans and with the essence of the aroma of ribs, steaks and wild blackened chicken and the music, they found it very hard to leave the wonderful feeling of the south. But something strange happened one day at a shoot on the Bayou, an amazing blues band with the food matching with the sun going down over the river they were joined by a local hound, Pixie, the black Pointer, and she was invited into their company with the photoshoot based on a southern fashion. Well, they really hit it off and it found it was so much easier to express their inner selves when they were feeling comfortable.

Anyway, it went so well that the promoters asked Pixie's daddy would he mind if they offered Pixie a contract? And he accepted. But this is the best part of it. They were invited to a Barbeque with her friends and family and got talking and they found out that Pixie's grand mammy, Deloris, walked the catwalk with Daisy. This was just so hard to believe.

So, what needed to be organised was the next beam-in meeting at The Hope and Lane café is to make sure Daisy was there. Just to say that Aseena and so on wanted to say hello and how things were going on with their introduction to the face and fashion world. Don't let on what it is about just bring her along, she would enjoy that anyway.

Aseena was sitting down at the dressing table with Keeley and they were reading their charter ahead for them and straight away they read each other's thoughts that in October there was a week that was not so hectic so they jumped at the chance of a request, to go home for that week. They had not asked for anything and stood by the hard graft and proved they were ready to match anything thrown at them and do all the team proud, so they wanted this one request honoured. It was brought to Stella's attention and she contacted the head office, Mrs McDonald nearly snapped to her old ways and realised her dreadful errors of her past demands and calls, so she honoured the request and put it on the table.

Back home a week passed and the banters and everyday life were going on but once again it was about the changing ways of the town and had a little excitement to it. The company of the Dogs Brush was growing as fast as the puppies that had become the town's delight to see. Dylan met with Joaquin to discuss their views and it came out quite clearly that there was a great interest from them both but they knew all that was going on in their personal lives had to come first and they would return to that case of the sight of such a questionable unsolved adventure of those vagabond's on that dismal night.

Speaking of that night, do you remember the youngsters? They were all out on the town for that birthday tour of the bars. Auntie Marion got a visit from Teddy, you know, Colin's son. He slipped away from the pack of hounds because he was upset with what was on his mind. Had history and fact been known in the town if you had a heartbreak problem, Auntie Marion at the Hairy Tail Bar, was the one to go to, to listen and put it right.

You see Teddy had his first crush and wanted to ask Treacle out on a date. Well, Treacle was big Skip's doggy daughter and the apple of his eye and Teddy was Colin's Doggy son. With big Skip being the head honcho doorman in the town's wild days, he turfed Colin out many a night including the mad 53 Club and to be booted out of there… Well, say no more.

Big Skip said no, no you are not going on a date with that lad. If he has his dad's blood in him, well what more can one say? And by the way, he's a bloody DFL, isn't he?

Treacle wouldn't speak to her daddy and locked herself in

her room, note not basket. She had her own room, spoilt or what? Anyway, sloped over the bar, both paws spread out around a glass of Hound Dog ale, all his sorrows come out to wonderous Marion. Marion was a lifelong friend of big Skip and some say they were very close at one stage, Mm? But anyway, she said she would speak to him on this matter and see if sh. could sort it out; give the benefit of the doubt, and give him some leeway.

We had all been there in our lives and had these feelings but for him, no one had felt this type of love that he had for her. She was the love of his life and he couldn't go on without her.

Well, back to that night; Trotsky the Jack, curly Teddy, Ralf, the Shih Tzu, Megan's pup Paddy and Basil the Terrier, all got tattoos while being under the influence of the Dog's Tail ales and the shots set up by Ruefully Randy, the rampant bartender of Shady O'Grady's, the Boston-style bar which belonged to guess who? yep, Frank the Knash and said to be the lower end of the Waterfront's Waggling End hotel. Now do you see why all in all, the slander and blasphemy of gossip carried around an ole smugglers town like this?

Now, Trotsky's mummy had been told that her son was seen heading outta Shady's with a proud grin on his snout. And she being a doctor and in the public eye, certain breeds could not wait to tell her who they saw coming out of that house of sin they said on that cold old night. Yes, I understand that things were still unsettled around the homesteads, mostly the mums, for they were rampant at their son's behaviour around the town but the dads were all for it. They knew what it was like being 18 and full of it all and wanting to prove it. Well, how true it was or not of what I'm to tell you next but I'm all for it and know it is the truth?

Trotsky's mummy and Debbie, Basil's mum and Kaye, Teddy's and Paddy's mummy, Gill, got together about their sons' tattoos on top of their left legs; by the way, they were all the same and read d-o-d 2021 and what that stands for, who knows? Anyway, they got together and started to head down to Victoria Road to the tattoo parlour owned by Martin to give him a right ole mummy's ear-bashing, when behind them they could hear a frantic bark,

Ladies, ladies please stop! It's Lucy, Tom's mum. Look at these historical facts and listen to this person with me? She is one of the original members of the first Cherry Pickers society who belongs to and runs the little museum inside the Time Tower Museum on the front of Beach Street.

Good morning, ladies, a pleasant morning it is, Lucy stopped them outside the town hall where there were benches for the public to take a seat. Just sit a while and listen to me and it won't take long to explain what I want and need to say.

Well, the ladies took a seat and it did not take long for Lucy to begin explaining the history of her tribe as you may call it and what happened on that dreadful afternoon whilst just merrily picking away,

There was a dispute with a certain tribe, the Caistors. They believed the camp where my ancestors settled on Victoria Dock, as it was known then, belonged to them. The tension built up then bang! This savage-looking hard group of whatever you want to call them, wiped out the whole of our young and old who were just picking away, and that was it. Well, that tribe was the Caistors and what is the man's name you are going down to give a piece of your mind to, yep, his surname's Caistor. It is said here in these leaflets and book, they are of Anglo-Saxon origin who were taken from their wood homes in Lincolnshire and deprived of their native life and living ways and cast onto the Roman ships to row them to wherever demanded, whilst chained up. The name Caistor is a word of olde English pre-century that means ceaster, the word for a roman camp or fort.

Anyway, the time came and, in their despair, they broke loose of the ship as it ran aground on the notorious Goodwin Sands and they killed the whole of the Roman crew and jumped overboard. It was too late before the rest of that Armada realised what was going on as the currents changed over the dreadful Goodwin Sands and saved the savages' asses. They could not sail after them as they would have met their fate like many a past ship. But they opened up with their archery teams and arrows flew through the air but alas the arrows that hit them, they just pulled at them and spat them out, then just kept swimming away and no one got caught.

When ole Julius Caesar heard about this himself back at his old nook in Rome, he sent a special batch of troops, his best by the way, to find those culprits. But do you think they could find them? No way, they were a little embarrassed to return empty-handed so they say that is where the block on the Strand came from, just a pleasure prezzie to the people of Deal from ole Jules just to say Hi.

That is why you see many archaeologists along the front searching for historical arrow heads and so on. Some say that is how the small tribe at the bungalow came about in this town, searching one day for Knick knacks and bang! What did they come across in the shingles but hidden treasure belonging to a tribe going way back to when the smugglers began? I've tried to get the truth outta Nick, that's Bampie by the way, a few times about this question and is it true? But alas I can't get him to grass.

Anyway, back to what I'm trying to tell you, that breed settled and once again they bred with the coastal savages and what do you expect to have, an even more wild breed of savages that used to eat fishermen and anything else they could catch. They have been in that location on Victoria Street since their ancestors put rocks and timber together that washed up on the shingles and defended it harshly. Once again is it a myth or a true story?

Now then, about their trade; it started with the smugglers and fishermen, they would trade their skills for rum and whatever they'd fancy if they could not pay cash for their artwork. That is where the name of their business came from with all that was going on. They called it the tribal nations, trading with the world's tribes. One long, deep banter is said that way back when Middle Street was all one, before it was bombed in the war, you know as saying before Lady Hamilton was kept there. Well one evening one of the guardsmen related to the landlord of the Ship Inn, you know he's an ex-sea dog of generations from Scotland? Well, the guard took the lady to Victoria Street and Martin's great-great grandad was requested to give the lady a tattoo and on top of her left leg, that is where it was by the way, and it said: This lady loves Nels.

Some say she often said in a brief social chat even though there is only half of him left and the way he treats me, I still love the ole blighter but who knows if those words are true? But they still tell the story and it ends up feeling that it is true, just like the banter about the ink and so on they use. The ingredients in their recipes the Caistor tribe used, is it true? Do they really come from hidden secrets and some from hell? They say what makes their tattoos so unique is the paint-ink they use; they say out the back way there are magic pots on the shelves, special pots of the colours they use and what and how do you think they make them so well, the skin of their captives of the human breed that they feed on by the way, look next time at the shades, there are black, yellow, two shades of brown and red which of course comes from you know what? And they say the green comes from the Irish captives but I don't know about that. Look, just take a peep the next time you walk that way through their window, just look at them in there. Amy, JJ and Dan and their leader and empress Alison, see how they look and study you, and do your feelings turn to gel?

There was a certain vibe of silence whilst the ladies sat on the benches and sort of looked at each other with concerned thoughts, then Tonya spoke,

Oh, please forgive me I've just realised I've forgotten some prescriptions for that retirement home. I promised them I'd have them ready to be delivered today.

Oh yes, I said I'd pick up some honey to make a barbeque sauce for the guests at the B+B, these were the words from Paddy's mummy. Anyone fancy a coffee on the way back? Okay, let's pop into the Hope and Lane.

They reached there and sat down and thought a little while and one spoke of you know what, I've been thinking maybe it is best if we stay away from that Tattooists as if word got out that we Mammies were in there complaining about our boys being in there getting tattoos, the Town's gonna think they are right wimps, aren't they?

A little silence of thoughts then Gill spoke.

Yeah, I was thinking the same.

In the future, these youngsters will look back at that wild night and laugh about it. In years to come memories, good ones, are important in their lives and the night on the town in Deal when they were young pups will be one to keep. Wherever one ends up in their fate or destiny it was Deal they started their journey from and learnt how to laugh or cry or thoughts of something they tried to figure out, like whose idea was it to get the tattoos done and who was to blame?

A few days passed and the mummies could not resist walking down the other way to town to do their shopping and that route was Victoria Road and they took a peep through the window of the Tribal Nation's station just for their own curiosity. Anyway, Amy picked up on this and after a while as it was every day they were peeping, she mentioned something to Cynethryth, Alison's real Christian name. They called her Alison as it was more civilised being in a modern town. They named her after her ancestor who was Queen of Mercia, wife of the great King Offa who ruled in 715 AD.

Anyway, the next day, Tonya, Kaye and Gill were walking down and just turned their heads to look in when they noticed Cyn and Amy coming to the door and did the ladies move their butts or what? The girls popped their heads out of the shop just to introduce themselves but the ladies were gone, so they just shut the door and that was that. The mummies never walked that way again.

A few days passed and as we said many a time even though times, they were a'changing, news got about and Kaye was walking down to the Black Pig to collect her meats from Lizzy when she bumped into Winnie the Jack Russel and the banter began. Well, Winnie is Marion's half-sister, you know who her son was talking to the other night on that drinking binge, at the Tradesmen's bar.

Anyway, after telling her how upset he was and what it was about she could not help but feel for him but how could she approach Skip over this matter? Well keep it quiet, but Skip was Kaye's first date all those years ago in the Snouty Loutie's bar where all the bands played. They had such a wonderful time and the promises of their future were open-glazed when Kaye's daddy found out Skip had taken his daughter out and drinking and she was underage. well did he let fly or what, as being a headmaster at the Dog Handlers and Mandlers college he wasn't having any of that behaviour.

Skip was banned from ever approaching Kaye again and they said it broke his young heart. Well, Kaye had a plan in mind to tell Skip who she was and to remember what it was like all those years ago, how their young hearts were broken as they had believed that they were meant to be and not given the chance. Well, now she would somehow have to explain who she was and why she had traced him and what was the nature.

The next morning arrived and taking a stroll down the High Street with good mornings and so on being passed by folk and hounds of all shapes and sizes, big Bailey was coming down with his daddy from the park after giving the squirrels an ear-bashing and showing a few youngsters what was the best way to catch the blighters.

But Dylan had heard those words coming from his snout when he was a wee pup and they still got away and up the tree to poke their tongues out and so on at the doggies on the ground that really wound them up. As you know Dylan's brother's Bailey as well so that is how long-legged Bailey got his handle, from his legs. The whole town loves LLB because of his nature in life.

Are these the young ones, Dylan?

Yep, here they are.

Well, they are a fine bunch I must say. Before leaving to head up home, he said, just let me know, Dylan, when their first class is due for their first chase and it will be on the house, don't you worry.

Dylan just looked at Tilly laughing and headed off on their way. Nods and smiles came from all angles again when they met Alison, Dylan's mum and then straight away they walked straight into the path of Nanny Ryan and Bampie shopping.

Good morning and the essence of Alison with her first grand puppies and she was beaming with delight. Tilly, just to let you know, Poppy called last night to let me know they will be home in a short while for a week's break so I thought I'd let you know.

That is great news because on Thursday, Aseena and Keeley will be beaming into The Hope and Lane from the States with some news they said we would all want to hear.

The Thursday arrived and they gathered together at The

Hope and Lane for the chat with the girls abroad as the chit-chat was going on the next thing, they heard was Lulu demanding a little silence because there they were beaming with delight and excitement,

Don't forget on Tuesday, Tilly popped into Jilly's to let her know, could she please bring Daisy to the café as there would be another surprise for her? Keeley had her paw around Aseena and Pixie who they introduced and then the shock of her intro to the crowd in ole blighty of her grandma and oh my, how Daisy felt once again to see someone from so long ago there in front of her with a beam of love and delight upon her face.

Hello, Honey, were her first words to Daisy and away their chat began.

Then Aseena and Keeley were all fired up then explained that, after such a hardy introduction of their intro to the States, they were being rewarded with some time off and would be home in a few weeks and of course, with excitement they explained Poppy would be coming home has well. So of course, this put everyone into a wonderful mood so with the time they had left on the screening the questions were flying from all over the place then the bye-byes, see you soon came about and everyone's thoughts were just so dear.

Yes, there was excitement about the town with the feeling of the girls coming home. It came from all directions but the best one was from Daisy. She explained to all how she felt in her day when all the lights were on her; she wanted those lights to be switched off. So, when the girls come home yes, enjoy your reunion but let them rest, it is important and that is that.

Another week passed when the time came for Dylan to be called up to the academy of scent, nicknamed the Snouts and Grouts Pit. Why no one knew but the finest team members came out of that camp. Dylan sat beside his dad with his litter who were a great boost for his father's thoughts and condition and as lively as they were, it did him well. Also, Dylan wanted to explain to him who he had been called up by and once again the delight in his father's eyes was a wonderful sight.

The next morning in the early hours, Dylan woke and Tilly was watching him with concern and asked, what is it are you okay?

Yes, yes, my love I just want to go for a little walk along the front.

And she knew this was what he did as long as she remembered going back to when they were tiny puppies. The litter were all asleep and somehow, he managed to walk to the door and slip out. It was a beautiful spring morning and there was a nip in the air coming from the North side and he just walked up to the front and stared out at the mysterious Channel and its moods and ways.

Its own life tells many stories doesn't it, my boy?

The voice that spoke came from Mike from the Waterfront, he being an ex-serviceman knew the boy was deep in thought just like he himself was many years ago.

I was thinking, Mike, if I'm to be called up in years to come and something happened to me, who would take my position to look after my family?

Don't overthink things, my boy, like I did at your age. It is a wonderful way to take responsibility and think of others but you must think of yourself as well. But let me tell you now, you should know this whole town has the utmost respect for you and every door to every castle would be open and that includes mine, Dylan,

Mike, I didn't see your lips move when you spoke then.

The two peeped over the wall and it was Cooper. He being an ex-marine's sniffer, overheard them talking as he was sitting behind the wall on the shingles just chilling out with his thoughts. This seemed to be a local spot for thoughts from Doggies' and folks' feelings for some reason. And Mike, being a landlord, witnessed many shapes and sizes sitting at this spot as that was where the Waterfront was based and its windows witnessed many, many sights of centuries of history and those famous words, if only walls could talk what would these tell? And most of it would be happy and bright.

Right, I have to make it back. As Dylan was making his way off, he just looked back and spoke to the two left there and said, Thanks guys, thanks for listening. He knew in his own way they had been in this depth of thought themselves but really no one had the answer for another's thoughts. Advice, yes. But thoughts, mm, I don't know.

Walking back, Dylan viewed the scenes he often strolled past just taking things in for some reason he then reached his home.

Morning young one. This time it was Shelly from the fish mongers as she was out delivering. How's Tilly and the little ones?

They are all fine, they are fine Shelly.

Give 'em my love, Dylan, won't you?

And off she spread with her thoughts and she always seemed to be in good spirits. Walking through the door, he found the house was up and in full swing. Tilly knew her sweetheart too well to question him in any manner and really there was no reason. The puppies were in full uproar, one under the table and one after another one's tail, just madness. Dylan smiled to himself as he looked about and felt at home.

There was excitement about the town again as the girls' coming home brought this upon everyone, plus don't forget there would be guests with Aseena and Sally and it seemed a little strange that one of them was coming to meet Daisy and from so long ago. What with Mrs McDonald and Nellie; either way, who cared? It seemed that it was meant to be. Anyway, what Aseena enjoyed so much was learning to express her heart in writing a letter. She found like her mother who used to love to write home whilst on her journeys with the joy and love of her life, Aseena, s father.

Through countries they travelled and witnessed such beauty they loved to explain their feelings of how they felt whilst being around these grand offerings of joy about them and to just look at a dream. Anyway, the letters Aseena wrote home to Margaret and Daisy, Daisy kept hers solo whilst Margaret would sit in the kitchen with the staff and read them out loud and the joy would spread around the room filling the air with lament like Aseena was beside them and they loved Aleena's art of a doggy being able to write in feather with a paw style. Everything a family would express or wanting to share was in these letters for each other's thoughts, they felt it all around them.

Leleata, the young Greek maid, you see she got attached to Aseena like a big sister and it shook her up when Aseena explained to her that she had to go away for a while. But it was not something new to her because her family was used to moving all the time as they were travellers. Aseena's father took her to a new home of joy after witnessing a terrible fight behind a village back in her native land and her father was killed. He took the child in his arms and promised he would protect her just like his own.

When we get back, are we going straight home or staying overnight in London, Aseena?

Well, to be honest I thought it would be best when we land on Thursday to stay in London and why not wait until Monday to travel home? Then in the few days we can show Pixie and Nellie around the sights of London just like the reception we got in New York.

Okay, let's do that and I'll leave it to you to explain to those at home that that is the plan.

Keeley's back stood straight up as she realised, she had walked straight into Aseena's plan and that it was she who had to explain to folks back home they were not coming straight home. Aseena made it to the door with Pixie. Reaching the reception room and looking at the magazines of the fashion world spread across the tables, the Dogs Coat, the Long-legged Snout and of course the Snout To The Tail. Yes, Aseena and Keeley were across the front of them all with the design matching their beauty it made a wonderful image of how friendship and business can mix, but not complicate things.

Back home in Deal, Dylan asked, how are you feeling, Tilly, about the girls coming home?

I can't wait to tell you the truth as we have so much to catch up on, and how about you with Bailey? He's coming home as well, isn't he?

I honestly think it is a family thing, Tilly, but Mum is a little nervous as well.

Why?

We just want to know how he has been with Poppy. We know he would not treat her badly but he being as independent as he is having someone with him 24-7 is a different matter, isn't it?

Don't worry your thoughts, Dylan, he will not shame you.

The two weeks passed and the youngsters grew by the minute, never mind the day, and they were a constant job to watch over but a joyous one.

Right, how are the girls coming down and where are they staying? Keeley of course wants to spend time with her mummy and Aseena will be taking Pixie and Nellie to her Grand Daddy's and Bailey for most of the time is with us. Hasn't it been a strange time for Daisy over this past year? What with the drama of London and so on and now her friend from so long ago? I find it amazing, don't you?

Yes, yes, I thought all the drama was supposed to be based around the world, not Deal. But how long has that been said, what with ole Ceaser and the rest of histories past. By the way, don't you think Bailey is best staying at your mums as the little ones will pull him apart.

I think he mentioned he may be staying at Bernie's? You know their sound-light engineer. His folks have a location in Kingstown. I think they have a location on the front. You know who his dad is don't you?

No who?

Where we said before who needs TV or so on when you have the Dog's Tongue to tell you everything one desires? Yeah, his dad is the one who owns all the haulage companies around the port.

What, the big bulk and so on?

Yes, yes oh not again!

What?

That is the company they said unloaded the Pedigree Chum raid off the trains all those years ago. It is just a spectre once again and nothing was ever proven, was it? Anyway, Bernie is so laid back that he doesn't care who is who?

The girls arrived in London with their guests and it was best to get everything unloaded instead of hauling things about so they got forever faithful Tab to take them home first to their pad in Pall Mall. The girls were all excited to be home and hosts as well flew through the door with Pixie to show her about and with Nellie talking to Tab and laughing about the youngsters' behaviour when Tab's words said it all, we were all there once, weren't we?

Everyone got along with Tab, he'd been with Mrs McDonald since it all began and he'd seen it all. He worked with Skip in security for many years as they both witnessed the rise and fall of many stars including the Stardog Dust Band, Lady Lurcher and the Labradoodles and so on, they took care of them all in all types of despair.

When it calmed down, Tab called Keeley over,

Ah sweetheart, great to have you home. Stephani was here earlier to let you know there is an invite that I had to look at twice. Just look who it is from, just peep and don't look shook.

As Stella glanced, she saw straight away the seal on the envelope was royal. The younger litter of royal corgis were major fans of Keeley's and Aseena's styles and their fave video with the girls starring with the Lady Lurcher's whole band was enough for any young hearts to act in despair and it was not long for them to find out the girls were in town so they had been invited over to the gardens for a tour.

Daisy will be here by tomorrow as Mrs McDonald heard what is what and has given me the keys to the apartment in Earls Court where Nellie and Daisy can have some privacy and go and do their own thing before coming back down to Kent. I've got an invite here as well from The Flease.

What the store in Dogstands Arcade?

Yes, it is an invite to their private studio. Apparently, the owner who once again goes back to those cha-cha days of style walked the catwalk with Nellie and Daisy and wanted to know could they pop in if they have time to do so?

Bloody hell, this is more than the Queen touring herself, isn't it? A little laughter fell about and then they got back into the pattern of the field of this high life of glamour and who's got the look.

My, hasn't life been ablaze this past while, Tab?

Tab had driven down to pick Daisy up in Kent rather than have her travel by train. She being with him they had time to talk of what was going on.

So much had happened in such a short time and now another one for me meeting Nellie after all these years? She's a wonderful gentle soul, isn't she?

Yes, from what I remember. I've spent time with her whilst unpacking after taking the girls back to their place. I love her accent, Daisy.

What, that southern tone?

Yes, I love it. The girls if I could get a word in edgeways were telling me they met Nellie through Pixie and it turns out that Nellie's her grandma.

Well, they chatted away and before they knew it, they were in Earls Court.

Pulling up and walking Daisy to the door, with Nellie waiting at it, it wasn't long before Tab was ignored by the chatter of the old friends' barks, so he left them at it.

How the attraction of friends bonding into each other's company when meeting after such a long time and it did not take long to open up to each other and share their world of adventures of ups and downs through the life they lived and where they found their peace of mind and life to settle down with their own thoughts of love and life and there were no words to compromise how they felt to cut it short about each other. They reached the part of the chapter that separated them so long ago and of course, love was in within other reasons which took their legs to open doors of life and how long would it take to understand the roads to love and what type and what sort?

The morning arrived and visiting the sights, of course a person would want to see, being from abroad and they then made it over to the Dogstan Arcade and as they arrived, the public were looking on at the two being escorted to the door.

And of course, this made a person feel important whoever you are or were. Daisy smiled at Nellie and they felt like little girls at a fair for the first time and all the rides were free.

A tall elegant figure spoke and welcomed the ladies to the store with surroundings of the Victorian era with the balconies swaying over the edge. Glancing about and taking in more historical notes to pass on, Nellie, could not keep from looking back at the host who welcomed them, feeling or knowing that she knew this person but where from she could not recall. However, it was there in her thoughts and heart that she knew her.

They chatted with the staff of the fashions of today that surrounded this open world of desire when one member of staff seemed to stand out and she asked the two ladies in person. A little nervous at her age, she said Mrs, before she could say another word.

No, no, none of that Mrs, we are Daisy and Nellie okay.

Once again smiles were all about when she started again. In your days what with so many styles and all that you witnessed, can I ask you what your thoughts are on this design myself and Keeley have put together?

Nellie's eyes lit up; did you do this yourselves?

Yes, Nellie, the silks and satins with lace to match is just beyond its beauty but just one thing, the fine straps must fall from lace off the shoulders for it will carry anyone's heart to their heart and make any hot-blooded hound's desire stretch from his snout to his tail, young lady.

Oh, how the small Boutique burst open with wonderful laughter of the words to describe the dress, and with Nellie's southern accent, it all just felt perfect. They shared a grand time at the classic shop when Tab mentioned something that he kept a little silent but they too had been invited over to the Palace as two of the original dress makers were still practising at the palace and were on the last show Daisy and Nellie walked together at the famous Catmandu fashion show that was held at the Dalmatian's' club.

They arrived at the palace and were being escorted and when they spotted the girls with the young future generation, they were in sheer delight at each other's company so they managed to slip by without being noticed and then snap! Nellie remembered where she knew that slender lady from. It was back in her day at the Dally's. That is what they used to call that top brass club. Anyway, in one of the changing rooms she noticed this beautiful Saluki with her heart broken with tears falling, sitting in a chair with a tall suave gent barking at her. He looked back at her and shut the door whilst looking smug and gave her the snub.

She had never seen that woman since today and often wondered what was wrong and what had happened to her. And now after all these years, here she was in her presence again but she seemed to be much happier in life. When she got the chance, she would speak to her but not now. Now would not be appropriate but she would want to know, did she remember Nellie and what had that all been about?

At the Palace, the questions passed back and forth like the finals at Wimbledon and a dog's desire to chase the ball. The two dress makers explained that day at the shoot they were approached by a spotter themselves for their standard of stitching and to their surprise were ask to join the royal staff. What a wonderful offer to be given in life and since that day they stood and gave their services to the Queen's requests and never travelled outside their status.

They spoke many times to each other when they saw either Daisy or Nellie on a magazine or the TV and gave their wonderful blessings and do you know what? Not once was there any criticism of any of their outfits. That was how gentle their personalities were to this day, what a wonderful way to go through life without criticism, it makes you wonder doesn't it?

Could you go through life that way Nellie?

Are you being serious daisy? How can one live without giving your view and having a good ole bitch? Sorry, that is not for me. The thought of never, never being able to think of what's going on there and not being able to nose in with your big ole snout.

They stayed the night as guests of Corgarita. The elder sister to the Queen in Waiting's side dog realised that all the talking that went on rolled into the early hours and asked the staff to set the guest rooms for the two ladies and of course the royal baskets for the young ones as they had tired themselves out and a warm basket was ready to greet them all. Just as Nellie was coming out of the bathroom into the hallway the next morning, there was the tall elegant lady, carrying some coat hangers and Nellie introduced herself. After introducing herself from that time many years ago, the tall lady, Sallyandra was her name, explained what had happened that awful time but it did not last.

She fell for a bad barker's promises of fame and so on and paid a hard price until she finally released herself from his jaws and built a whole new life away from badness and filled her life with joy and created her designs and was the leading designer-supplier for the Dogstan Boutique that dresses the Queen and her first staff and found true love herself and there he was. She turned around to be met by a tall, gentle Red Setter.

Hello, my name's Windsor. Pleased to meet you, ma'am.

Sallyandra, I leave for Kent this morning but I'd love to talk and listen to you more and just to hear how your journeys of life's offerings brought you to where you are now? I could just sit for who cares how long it would take, I just would love to know. Can we exchange numbers?

Yes, let's do so and with this, she passed her Dogstan business card on with a smile and no words could express their joy of this intro and of all the time for it to happen where they both were in their lives. A joy to hear and listen to such simple happiness that put that terrible time in her heart away to the past.

The ole gals were talking when Nellie spoke,

Daisy, can you believe it of all times? My Granddaughter gets to meet Aseena, etc and one thing leads to another and now look? Over half a century has passed by and here we are in a dream of joy of meeting and so on and then I meet Sallyandra and knowing her life led to love is a joy just to be and feel alive. A complete wonder, and now I wonder what roads these youngsters will take and face in their lives? Just amazing to imagine what door will open and lead to what passage. I just feel fascinated by it all and mostly now knowing there is joy in the end because of what I was saying I never forgot that expression on the stranger's face in that changing room, desperation of sadness and heartbreak, and now seeing where that road took her and, in the end, to find true love. Simple, just simple she is or must be blessed.

They returned to their rooms in a hurry like hurrying to the Christmas tree on Xmas morning to see what Santa had left. Most of the packing was done beforehand because they had in mind the reunion with family and Poppy coming home as well but most of all in general being home, so they made sure all their collective items about them were packed to return to Kent. With Daisy on her own, the buzz was of going to be introducing Nellie to her settlement in life. Of course, the youngsters were all on a buzz as well as they met new friends at the hotel, the staff and all and who were the same age as them and yearning to get the chance for a break into the world just like Aseena's and Keeley's souls.

They said their farewells and goodbyes and the doors shut on the mini bus with the windows left down for waves of their thanks came about and the thank you's and the sound of joy carried on until the racket of the traffic overtook that sound and now the small convoy of barks and excitement fizzled down the way, they were still on a high as now only it would be the matter of hours before reaching their loved ones at their settlement where they set off from to find where their dreams lay and to find their goals.

Margaret called earlier Aseena,

I thought I'd let you know; she called the hotel as she wanted to know who was with you and I said Pixie and Keeley and maybe Stella?

Yes, the stern thoughts of Margaret's expression were mixing with Aseena's thoughts and of course, that was only natural if you knew Margaret. But at the same time knowing the feeling of being safe in her presence was a wonderful feeling and that had always been there since Aseena's childhood with her parents both missing. Luckily enough, there was no sob-harsh story like she had been put in her stepmother's care and locked in a cold cellar or whatever, if she had one that is.

Anyhow, the chatter-joy made the journey easier and carried the trip even smoother than expected with a gentle flow of chatter then Tab barked out as he signalled to turn off and onto the Dover Road into the Manor and down the driveway that led to the house that stood so proud with Grandad and some of the staff at the doorway, who could not hold onto their feelings and flew for Aseena and Keeley the minute they stepped down from the mini bus with Pixie, Nellie and Daisy. Oh, the embraces and so on filled the air and feelings were out. My, how the staff missed having Aseena around them day and night for she breathed joy and happiness and as the girls stood back to look at each other, to pass compliments upon each other, a good job Birdie was not there wasn't it? Anyhow, they could not help but notice Aseena's maturity into womanhood and beauty and with the sophistication of Keeley's proud stand, they could not wait to get them inside to their rooms to unpack their hearts and thoughts.

Through the double doors they flew after Aseena's Boston strangle of love on her grandad as that's what he felt it was and into the hallway where Pixie could not help but look about in awe with a feeling of an embracing welcome.

Hello, and you must be Pixie?

Yes, ma'am, came the nervous reply. Yes, I am,

Jennie the young maid spoke again with a nervous edge in her tone, Hello I'm Jennie. And that was that, heaven was made.

Then she felt Margaret's presence nearby.

Welcome my Aseena, welcome home.

Aseena just could not help herself again and flew into Margaret's welcoming voice and paws, and stepping back, Margaret looked at her,

My, how you have grown and matured.

Before another word was spoken, a sound came along, yes, of course, it was Crawford. A nod and a smile came from him,

Welcome home my child, all is well I presume?

Margaret looked at Aseena as she kissed him on his cheek and said,

Good to see you, Crawford.

Likewise, my dear likewise, came the reply as he turned with a gentle but stern stance and walked away. And carried about his ways until all was laid.

Up the stairs they flew with Stella smiling on, a little nervous in Margaret's presence but feeling comfortable through the essence of the house's aroma of love and it beamed with a joy of history of care. They could hear the girls upstairs with Aseena showing Pixie her room with excitement and Margaret spoke,

You'd better come with me, my love, as you won't be safe in that mayhem, you will be staying in the Eastly room if that is okay?

Oh, please don't go out of your way for my sake.

No, no my love this is how the house has always been. I must say Margaret, Aseena has left a major mark on the fashion world out there and what a joy she has brought about to many including myself may I say. I'm really pleased to be able to witness where she gets it from.

Margaret looked up to the left wall and Stella turned around to see what she was looking at.

That was Aseena's mother.

A little silence and Stella spoke, My she was beautiful, wasn't she?

Yes, she was and you see where Aseena gets it from?

Just then Grandad walked in. Hello, so you must be Stella? It is nice to meet you in person now as my granddaughter, Aseena, has mentioned you to me many times. This was a way he had of introducing himself, Grandad, as everyone knew him.

I've been trying to put a face to you as the girls never stop talking of their Granddad and it is nice to have one. I understand you are a magic one as well?

Oh yes, yes, I am. You can ask Margaret, Daisy's sister the spells I put on them. A little shock came to Stella when she heard that Daisy was Margaret's sister.

Come, come, Stella, I shall show you to your room.

Walking along the house's aroma filled the air and it was not long before it welcomed yet another nice guest to its security and Stella sensed this all about her.

I've sensed in Aseena's voice she has become fond of your company?

It did not take long before Stella had to reply with excitement as she felt secure speaking her mind around Margaret, I think it is vice versa or my feelings are stronger as I must say the girls, they have brought such joy back into my work and job and made me wake up before it was too late, to what I was sinking into. And between you and I, I've noticed the same with the woman we work for. Meeting Daisy and the girls has made her think a lot more in different ways and thoughts, why and how I don't know, but it has and it has done wonders all about us and it has affected the turn out and quality in every manner that reflects the company. I've noticed the response of the postman to whoever visits us, there is a new vibe about them. It is a nice feeling to witness, Margaret, after so many years; something created an uneasy presence and now none of that is about us and your family, if you don't mind me calling them that. They have removed that horrible word that surrounded us - sinister.

The staff's mixture with the guests and kin flowed about each room and once again Stella could not help but embrace it into her life and glow from it. It was so easy to embrace each other to say goodnight has the excitement of going to bed and wake to a new beginning.

The morning arrived with her gifts of life and the first question ask to Stella was how did you sleep, young lady?

I slept like a puppy with wonderful dreams all about me. I think Aseena was telling me porkies as she told me the house was haunted.

It did not take long for grandad to cop onto this chatter and in he came with, oh yes, it is my dear. It goes way back to when this was just a vision in one person's mind to build here and the spirits who lived in the woods were not happy with my ancestors and the building ideas so it is said there are a few of the builders who disappeared from the site as it was being built.

A little cough came from Crawford and he said, young lady,

come with me. I shall escort you to the dining area to meet the others for breakfast.

It was only a second, she stepped into the room and voices came from all angles of good mornings and so on. The foods encountered were met with the hunger of young hearts ready to be fed with desire and one could not help but feel the only thing that was missing was the Irish wolfhounds at the fireplace, ready to be thrown the carcasses and growl at each other. Margaret looked about and was happy with all that was being served and, in the manner, it was presented. It could be a guest with a boiled egg, to the full set, it had to be done right, and that was that.

Aseena, all excited again shot some words across to Stella to explain that she would like to take her and Pixie down along the stream that led to the inlet that led to the Channel, where she told them the smugglers used to operate. This shall we say in ways, were their needs and businesses of everyday life in the ole days. A walk around the joyful Manor like through the ole barn and so on, that is why there were old clothes left aside in the rooms for the girls to use not to ruin their attire. Later, if they had time, they would go down-town but first Aseena wanted to introduce her friends to her life as a pup and how often she spoke of these times and places, her wonderful memories came from. Keeley was all set and she had explained last night to Pixie about the cultures that she may find confusing when someone may be trying to explain to her like the smuggling-mugging in all.

So, if confusion comes to mind, just ask. Jennie and Annie, the house maids who of course were like, well they were family, should have headed off to do their own thing but the girls being home, well say no more as the day was to be with them with tales, and adventures to tell of their own as they grew up through Aseena's childhood with their opportunities under Margaret's guidance. In a way you could say the house was or is a heaven to fall into if given the chance to give back the love you received and prove you are worthy and want to be proud to be placed and sat.

The table sang with joy of laughter and looking sideways at Margaret, Jennie and Annie got a little fright as she called their names and they thought they were to be asked to work but no, it was visitors who had come to call. Margaret invited them into the side hall and said she would come and fetch the two of them.

You see, Margaret mentioned that grandad brought it to her attention that he had taken a great interest in sheep herding and looking for a dog to join the house. Annie mentioned that their friend who was a Portuguese Sheepdog had moved here and was looking for work and her background was just immense in the line of that class.

She arrived with Llewelyn the German Shepherd from Wales who she worked with on an estate in Canterbury who escorted her here. Just then, Grandad came out of the study, a little confused at first but when Grandad saw them both, he introduced himself to them and asked what was the status of them being there today?

The reason was explained to Grandad and it could not have been better timing. Llewelyn was now living in Canterbury as a guard dog, carer and gardener and being raised in the Rhonda Valley, that was his surroundings and background, yes of course, sheep.

Dollie, my what can one say but what a beauty and the awareness of a panther on the hunt. It was brought to her attention that you may be looking for a sheep dog and she explained her background across the mountains of Portugal and driving the flocks as well as assisting her brothers in goat and cattle herding. Well, Grandad was so impressed with them both, that after a little chit-chat to them, yes, they were now a part of the abode. But Llewellyn don't forget was only visiting.

Well, another part of fate you could say, with all the

excitement they got stuck in to assist in cleaning the tables with Stella feeling freedom in her veins she got well stuck in. All the knick-knacks were put into collar bags to feed the birds along their walk. What was going to be a stroll with Pixie and Stella had now turned into a pack, like a pack of wolves hunting. And of course, Grandad wanted to join them for the reason really to watch the two who had just joined them even if they did not know it. They would not turn down the hospitality of the surroundings and the security they would be offered with content.

Out of the back entrance they made their move and Crawford was asked would he like to come along? To which he just nodded, that he had many a chore - sorry responsibilities - to take care of before such matters of walking the estate. Down the old path steps where the grounds team had walked for centuries, it was not long before Aseena and Keeley started to describe their childhood. Along the stream and as the stream got wider, the banters grew bigger like inlets of the old clay pipework from fields joined the journey with its offerings of spring water into the stream then into a river then flowed into the Channel then the oceans of the world.

What a wonderful feeling to embrace this bond of sharing a friend a walk and thoughts, to help one feel relaxed and get to know who you were sharing the world with; what more would one want? They reached the part of the stream that met other inlets and yes, the fables or facts came out of the monsters and ghosts who lived in them. And all of the smugglers that crawled through the ways with their wares and tares then swam out to the waiting ships to unload or load through the darkened, stormy nights and warnings to others not to show their presence on their territory were made clear and then sent.

One's mind could not help but enter a world of mystery of thoughts to just embrace the adventure of your own view of wondering what they looked like and so on, but just wonderful to open one's mind.

Grandad spoke to Llewellyn, tell me young man, what brought you here? To Kent I mean?

Well, my family's history travelled here along the never-ending walks with many others in search of a better life in the coalfield line of work. My great grandad was a military dog and I heard so many old yarns of those walks that I had to see what the talk was about, so my first visit to Kent answered my curiosity and I moved here. I was asked to join the Coola-Daly estate to watch over it to start with, but wanted to be closer to the water's edge.

Before he could say another word, Grandad snapped at the opportunity and offered him the position on his abode and that was that. Just as they smiled in chat he looked over and just could not help but feel Aseena's presence. Keeley picked up on this as did Grandad but the two looked away before the famous saying of a dog's tongue and tail says it all.

Right, let's make it back to the house and sort a few things out. If you want you can stay at the house until you decide what to do. Let's not rush it but I will offer the lodge to your contract to live here. Dollie will live with the staff of her age that are with us now as I've found that the comfort of one's company is very important to one's class of services. That is just my view and it will be one's own choice. When will you two make it back to Canterbury?

Well, we have two days off.

Once again Grandad spoke, if you speak to Dollie and you two want to stay with us on your break then you can join us here.

Just then both sets of eyes met again and along this saga of a journey what would happen next upon this wonderful mystery of a Channel town and would it be fate at one's door once again had come to call?

Dollie, the call came from Margaret, can we chat please? A little nervous as they walked to the kitchen and out onto the patio, sit please, came her words. Grandad feels very comfortable with you, tell me how do you feel being about the house and its livestock and ways?

It did not take long to reply with an extreme answer of comfort. After a few other questions the one came, how would you feel going into training and going to the sheepdog trials beside Grandad with just the two of you?

Margaret, I was left alone on the mountainside back home to make a choice of my own to bring the stock down and I impressed my owner and the village, so being with one person suits me fine.

Plus, you would be his number one companion walking the estate, in short words what I'm trying to say is, I'd like to make you an offer of joining the house and the family as we call it.

The joy of Dollie leapt out and the question was answered. On the other side of the lounge, Lewellyn and Grandad had their chat and that was sorted without even considering second thoughts, so now within a few days the Manor's clan had grown again. It was just the matter of picking up their belongings from Canterbury and joining their new home.

Well, reality reached the next morning and the town's mobile feeling of joy just by simple shopping was going on and Bampie had to pick up some parts for the happy car so whilst he was doing that at the garage, Nanny went on a walk-about and thought she would pop in to introduce herself again to the Hope and Lane.

I'm doing a little shopping in the town and thought I'd have a coffee.

A few regulars were inside exchanging chit-chat when Nanny was talking to Danny and Lulu and heard the chat and thought she'd introduce herself.

Hello, are you Nanny Ryan?

Yes, I am, came the reply. By the way, happy Saint Patrick's Day to you.

Why thank you, young lady, and the same to you.

I thought I'd let you know Poppy called this morning.

She being young replied, all excited, yes, she called me has well Nanny.

She spoke to Nanny as if she had known her all her life but that's Lulu's personality and why and who she is.

Well, you know Poppy is home Thursday and I was thinking would it be better to be the Friday or Saturday for this get-together? With the girls being home from the escapade of their world's journey's and all our family and friends can have a few days to sort out who they need to contact for maybe puppy-sitting, etc, etc.

Perfect, let us hold it on the Saturday as I also can have a polite notice up that we will be closed to the public for a private holding and we can all get the boost for our gathering that no doubt will be one to remember at our domain.

Nanny smiled away with an embraced feeling of contentment after meeting Lulu and asked Rory, the other manager, about the closure for Saturday and sorted that little chat out as well.

Hi, you look glad, Nanny?

Yes, you know how I feel when happy results are about me, Nick.

He just smiled and felt glad to see his other half smiling away contentedly.

Nick, how would you find it to bring your guitar along on Saturday to strum along with the guests, as we just agreed that it would be the best night overall for everyone to get together for the reunion with Poppy's and Aseena's friends.

By the way who's 'we'?

I just met Lulu who is the Manager of The Hope and Lane café and she's a wonderful lass, plus by the way, Oscar the cross hound Lurcher and Arnie, the pair of Lashy boys are in town so that means the Fiddle will be out. These are ole friends of the family and in a way, it could not be a better time for us to rejoice in a welcome to see what these days of travelling have done to the girls' lives. I can't wait to tell you the truth. First of all, I was nervous but I think it is coming to terms with the fact that it is not losing someone when Poppy said she was leaving, but gaining as she will now come back with stories of her own.

I got a call as well whilst you were shopping. I mentioned to Oscar one of the Lashy boys what had been happening and you would never have guessed but they both know Aseena's Grandad, from the early days of National Service and they played together at the marine base and local hound hang-outs, jamming and just strumming along. You know what, I'm gonna give him a holla to let him know they would enjoy meeting him and would he have it in him to tag along and jam the night away?

Nanny Ryan was quite surprised by this chatter as Bampie mostly kicked back and would have left this type of gig-banter to the youngsters, but right then he was on the ole blower to Grandad and whilst explaining what the call was about, he had a grin on him like a Cheshire cat and winked to say Grandad's joining them.

Along the High Street, another introduction happened. A sturdy Staff Terrier that every type of living article in the town seemed to say hello to and welcomed just to say good morning, a little eye contact and a brief question asked.

May I ask, are you Nanny Ryan?

Yes, I am.

A little confused with her intro, she introduced herself, I'm Nanny Sky, Tilly's Nanny.

Well, hello! At last, we meet as your name has been brought to my attention through Dylan, Bailey's brother.

Nanny Ryan explained what had just happened at the Café and Nanny Sky knew about Bailey coming home, so they now had told her of the gathering that had been put on Nanny's card for the Saturday night. They parted content and admitted to themselves, I have a feeling this could be a bit of a night of blarney and see if we can get everyone's heart and passion going with a bit of Puccini in the mood for a bit of sway.

Dollie, can I have a word?

It was Llewellyn and they had a chance to have a little chat about what exactly had happened in the past hours since being on the estate and the company they had met. After a brief chat they both agreed that it seemed to be a little too good to turn down, what they had found and been offered.

Do you think we should go back and put our notice in straight away as they may feel back in Canterbury that all is well and if we just go back and give notice, it may get a little tense? I don't think a chance like this will come our way again or at least for a long time. What if I make a howl back to the Coola Daly Manor to explain what the status is? And I'll say that I've ask you to join me?

No, there is no need for that as I can hold my own.

Really Dollie, I know you can hold your own but if I say that I'd like you to work on the estate with me, then they can't or will not get uptight if you know what I mean?

The head game keeper back at the Coola Daly has a bit of a bully's reputation but he's not gonna mess with Llewellyn, is he? Plus, wouldn't it be best to be here with this reunion and get a view of what is what, and who's who? Or shall we work our notice out?

I think it is a good call for us to stay here, so you do what's best, Llewellyn.

Just then Aseena came through the door with a smile upon her face as she had just left Grandad's company and he had explained that Dollie was joining them. With both paws out,

Please would you come and join us as we are on the patio looking at some wares.

All excited off she went and as they reached the doorway to the patio, Aseena could not help herself from glancing back with those puppy dog eyes to I wonder who?

On the patio, Dollie got talking to Pixie about her ancestors who were taken by their masters at that time to the new world for a new life and worked the new land and its ways. They sent stories back to Portugal and for generations they would sit around the fire listening to the new life and adventures they were witnessing and many followed their tales.

At the same time, Llewellyn was on the old blower and got hold of the person he needed, to explain what was going on. The owner totally understood and gave his approval and told Llewellyn he was making changes himself as an offer of the land he owned was in demand and he may not be able to resist it. So, come and collect your belongings and please come and see me before you leave.

Just then, Grandad came about and Llewellyn explained the good news and then popped out to tell Dollie and then they explained to all that they would be back in a short while and they both felt that this was their ultimate dream.

Well really it is turning into a soap opera, isn't it? This came from you guessed it, Crawford.

Margaret glanced at him sideways as the reason he spoke such words was whilst outside on the patio he heard Pixie speak to Aseena and Dollie and used the words of expressing the estate as a plantation and what a mighty fine place to live. Crawford being such an Englishman hearing words and an expression of this manor being reduced to a plantation.

Well, what can one say? He said with a tut but also a laugh.

Margaret in fact could not wait to tell Grandad of Crawford's expression as she nearly choked on hearing it. But Grandad did not take it personally due to his understanding of human and doggie behaviour of speech so he just carried on about his business.

It did not take long for Llewellyn and Dollie to sort their belongings out and as promised, he popped in to talk to Collie O'Dore, the landlord of the estate they all seemed to be leaving and thought it would be best to explain to him personally the problems of his game keeper and if he was going to keep the estate or purchase another, not to let this happen as it affected the standards all around.

Well, here is my personal reference for you to carry with you anywhere and at any time, if anyone needs to speak to me, just tell them to give me a bark, okay? Good luck Llewellyn and keep safe and good bye.

On their way back to the estate, they spoke personally about their future and how they were feeling at that moment. It just felt natural to them both and they could not help but express their views on Margaret and Crawford and just loved their outlook and the gentle manner of Grandad and how much they were looking forward to working with him and the challenge ahead of them.

It was Hamish, the wire-haired terrier who got staff to drive the pair to Canterbury as he had the run of the Mill for many years and his main concern was defending the estate's poultry and stock from being stolen, or poached is the better word to use and having the best knowledge about every local and visiting fox or badger or roaming mutt he knew their whereabouts and driving back, he explained this to the pair and he just felt once again very comfortable being in their company.

I just want to say whilst we have a little time, I've been waiting for a long time for the right ones to come and match up with our team and I have a feeling you two will fulfil this quest.

They just carried on with the banter of the past and so on and Hamish explained to the pair about the town's surrounding history and of course much of it was on the old days and how times had calmed down a fair bit since then, but it was still out there and with interest, it was a great pleasure protecting our abode. Llewellyn asked a few questions and Dollie asked one for her own curiosity and that was, How long have you been here, Hamish?

25 years, young lady, and after a certain time here, watching and feeling the seasons and weather changing, you will understand why I stayed. Oh yes, and of course my wife! You will meet her soon as I've told her you two may be joining us and of course, she will want the pair of you to come to dinner one evening. I'll say this to you both on the side as she's not here. She's a JK, Jack Russell and lives up to the name of one, so the questions will be out with curiosity so try to keep a straight face whilst being interrogated by her, okay?

He had a happy grin on his face as he then explained how happy she would be having such a handsome beast as you about the Manor, Llewellyn and with this, he was a little embarrassed but they could not stop from laughing to themselves knowing that many more wonderful times would follow.

You will stay at the Manor for a few days, that's both of you but you will be taking the lodge, Llewellyn, you know about that, don't you? I feel it's a little better explaining it this way as you can gradually get the feel of where you are, plus with so much going on with Aseena being home and guests about, plus no doubt you may have heard already the gathering on Saturday, as the gang as I've always called them will be getting together; it has been their first parting as young adults and Poppy will be home. Also, a strange bit of news got out that relations and old friends of the older generation going way back, will be joining these youngsters as well on Saturday.

I'm looking forward to it myself as there is going to be mighty fine music played on that night, you mark my words, plus a wee bit of a dram will be flowing as well. Yep, it is going to be one good evening if I may say so.

Pulling up at the back courtyard of the Manor, they stepped out and within seconds they were set on by Aseena and co, who were just walking over to the stables, as once again she'd been showing her guests around and asked would they like to see the thoroughbreds of beauty, the horses that she was raised with and gave her the comfort of sheer love whenever she needed it. And three of the old retired ones just knelt to the ground with joy knowing Aseena was home and to greet her guests.

Aseena saw Dollie back again and this got her even more excited with all that was going on.

Dollie, you will be staying with the staff at their domain.

Two of the staff were listening so spoke straight away, Dollie let us help you unpack those bags and we can show where we are and you can join us.

It was not worth trying to interrupt them so Hamish just left them to it and smiled at Llewellyn and said,

Come on, boy, you come with me and I'll show you your place for a little while and off they strolled along the corridor, past the stables, down along the hallway to reach the stairs. Just then Llewellyn got a back hair upstand as of a sign of defence as a large creak came from the corner, from a very large, old wooden doorway.

With all the chit-chat going on that was filled with sheer delight from all this new friendship and adventurous opportunities flying through all their hearts, one could sense the aroma in the air and just then the glance came about from nature's feelings as Llewellin's Celtic spirit sensed Aseena's chemistry once again. He looked quietly over as she was making her tracks through the doorway that led to the stable yard and into the entrance for the old coach pick-up station where the guests and so on would exit the Manor in the old days. It was too embarrassing at this stage for both of them to stare but alas, fate could not hold the growing bond between them. Hamish sensed it.

Come on, lad, let me show you to your room? he said with a smile.

All seemed to calm down and Dollie settled in with the staff who greeted her like one of their own. Little meetings happened like Margaret, being Daisy's sister, organised Daisy to be picked up and brought over to have a chat with Pixie about her grandma and all that they went through together in the ole days of the catwalk. As they sat on the veranda where the musicians used to play in their day, the first words from Daisy were,

My you are the double of your grandma, Deloris.

They embraced each other and all Pixie could do was smile with delight as Daisy had some photos and programs of those old days and how the veranda could tell the stories of the past, this was what Daisy was doing recalling the wonderful essence of their time on the road through that era of style-music and what a time it was.

So, you will follow your Nanny's career then, young lady?

Yes, yes, I've been given this opportunity by Aseena and Keeley and what a way to start by being invited here and all to Europe.

I feel you have so much of your grandmother within you and

before we go any further, do you have an idea of what I'm about to say? But you are strong enough anyway to understand as no doubt your grandma talked of matters that we witnessed?

Yes, being of such beauty in those days and being black was a brave stroll to take but she did it and love and dedication and belief got her through and they are facts. She often told me she could not have done it without you, Daisy and as I'm sitting here, I want to thank you from the bottom of my heart, thank you, Daisy.

The smiles just gathered with the banters that Daisy talked about and the laughter from Pixie was ecstatic with the answers she was given to the unfolding questions she asked Daisy as she was a little too nervous to ask Deloris but one was very important to ask;

Who is the gent, the real handsome fella, who always seemed to be within my grandma's company wherever she is? And I noticed in those photos he is there again and he is handsome, isn't he?

A little hesitation in Daisy's voice and she felt she had to tell Pixie that he was the love of Deloris's life.

Reggie the Retriever was his name and he was from Galway in Ireland. He was called up for war duty as it had to be in those days and I myself still feel it now when he left, your grandma's heart was in his. And then one day, we were at one show and we were getting ready for a show and it was a new style of military wear and a telegram came through to her. I was beside her and felt a terrible sense in the air before she opened it, I had a feeling I knew what it was.

Oh no, cried Pixie.

Yes, my child, it was the loss of Reggie. The letter told us what he did through bravery. He carried through the trenches 7 soldiers and dogs to safety and the last one he went back for a shell blew the whole side of that trench out and that is how she lost him; it blew him up.

I see the angel ring you are wearing; Deloris gave you that didn't she?

Yes, how did you know that? That is what his last request was before passing away in that cold old trench to the two Border Collie medic dogs beside him, one Welsh and the other Irish. He asked would you pass this Cladder ring on to the love of my lifetime and to always remember me in good times to carry on through life, then that was that. You see those two dogs being Celtic, both knew how important it was and to make sure his request was honoured and it was.

Daisy placed her paw on Pixie's and for a second stayed silent. Then with words spoken with a smile she said, You are very lucky to have someone like Deloris in your life.

The two gave the ring a little glance.

And now then Pixie, I'd like to see a little bit of your strutting to see if you have your Nanny's art within you?

It was still early enough for them to be on their own before walking back over to the others. So, Pixie stood up and with the conversation she had just listened to, she thought of her grandma being back home sitting on the porch in her rocking chair and got up and my, did she strut herself or what? It was posed with such passion that all Daisy could do was smile with an open gasp of reassurance and just then a round of applause came from behind Daisy and it was Stella, Aseena and Keeley who made it over has Aseena still wanted to express her feelings of where her delight of love comes from and now showing it to the ones she was working with felt important to her and her delight.

Is this where the musicians would play back in the day? asked Stella.

Yes, replied Grandad, who was there with Llewellyn showing

him around some more. You would swear he was his son, seeing how proud he'd been since meeting the handsome fella.

I remember, young lady, my father standing up and walking over to my mother often just to ask her would you care to dance, my love? Of course, she stood and honoured his request.

And then out of the blue, Grandad turned around and walked up to ask Daisy to join him for the dance. It just came naturally to him.

Her thoughts just drifted with wonderful thoughts as she replied, Yes.

Then Llewellyn walked over and asked Aseena to join him and the rest joined in as the sound of the music coming from the kitchens was backed by the Collared Doves and Song Thrushes, Chaffinches and all the birds of the Manor joined in just like the old days. This brought such a feeling of pleasure it carried into the air of the circular winds that carried the wonderful bond out to the unknown and wherever it landed, it would open the music box and the charm of the sound would just fill whatever space they were at and bring such joy that all you could do was get up and dance with whoever you were with and if you were alone you picked up the broom or anything else you managed to grab hold of and dance, dance and dance until your world turned bright.

Thursday morning arrived and yes, there was a sense of joy and affection and it flowed around the happy lodge when the gate flew open and yes, Poppy's home! Nanny of course had both arms open with the embrace of her love trying not to show the affection of how she had missed her granddaughter but that was just natural to witness just being about them. Poppy turned to Bampie and flew into his arms as well. Nanny took two steps back when Bampie spoke.

My, you are looking well, my sweetheart.

She then called out to Bailey who was over at the camper

van. Is it okay for Bailey-?

Before she could say another word, Bampie spoke, Of course, my dear, of course, he's welcome.

Nanny Ryan felt a little shocked as she glanced at Bampie sideways. Bailey walked over and kinda nervously said,

Hello, as he walked into the garden. These are for you Nanny Ryan. They are from your native arts and crafts because a lady in Cornwall who was from Ireland had a stall and made everything out of items that washed up onto the beach in Falmouth and when I saw the flowers, I had to laugh about the time we first met!

This really hit Nanny Ryan's humour and she replied with a happy thank you Bailey, thank you.

There was a lot of hype going on from all the excitement, so Bailey said, I'll leave you at it Poppy as I've to go and visit Dylan and Tilly. He just nodded and said, I'll be over later, okay?

He sensed Bampie's eyes watching him as he walked over to the camper van and as he glanced back, they just felt there was an understanding there and it could grow from each day. Getting into the camper van, Lenny, Lizzy's brother from the Black Pig butchers, was in the driver's seat and leant over and said,

Buddy, I was watching on and I must admit it seemed to me it went better than imagined? Bailey, where are we going now?

Come on let's get this curiosity over with seeing Dylan's mob? Let us see if any of them follow with their uncle's looks! They both burst out with laughter as they drove off.

Arriving at Dylan's place, he could hear a racket that only a happy bunch could make and as Lenny opened the gate, he was welcomed with an ambush of the manicure stampede of waggly tails and yelps. Dylan looked up as did Tilly who was nursing one of the youngsters, who had just pulled a tooth on a bone she was told not to chew.

Anyway, in walked Bailey and a little silence at first then it was the hug time when Dylan introduced the litter, Kids this is your Uncle Bailey. A little hesitation then the attack came and you could not get a better introduction from anywhere in the world than from your own blood and looking about him there was plenty of that in every shape and way.

Finally, calming down a little they sat down to spin a few yarns and so on and then Bailey just before sitting down, picked up a leaflet based on the cleaning business, my, what is this?

Yes, what can we say but we are close to turning down work because of the demands for our services.

Bailey looked over again as Grannie Angie was on board and most of the pups were around her as they knew they would be onto something, a walk or chew. Whatever, it was always good. Sammy, the eldest of the litter came over to Bailey with paws crossed and just looked up at him and as Dylan looked at him, he said, yes, I knew it, he's the one that reminds me so much of you Bailey. Climb up, come up on my back?

Tilly was just going to lay into him to say, don't teach him your habits, when Dylan caught her eye and said with a nod, just let it lie for today, please. The chat went on to explain where Dylan was with his training and offers to both squads, teams and how pleased he was about this.

Yes, yes, well done, Dylan, I knew you would make it and you have.

Tilly just then walked over to Grannie Angie to say something about the day ahead and Bailey turned to Dylan and asked, How's Dad?

He's fine. He is getting about. Mum knows you are home and expects you over, okay? This was said with Dylan's stern status bark, so it was clear what was expected.

Well, well what, the tour and Poppy how did it go?

Just amazing, everywhere we visited was out of this world. At the last place we were based in Cornwall and whilst we were in Falmouth, we were approached by Bongo the Bulldog from the Pedigree Pro Promotions with an offer. He was so impressed with our inside energy and how we got the crowd behind us in great spirits over and over again, he brought others down to watch us and how they felt around us and so on. The main guests who came to watch us were Hot Doggie and the Bonnie-yoos. Well, he just could not praise us enough and asked us would we consider being his main support band as they are going on tour through South America and then onto the states? Dylan, he just said look, this is an offer from the heart, H.D himself in front of me asking me, how do you answer that? He said they are taking a two-month break and just going to jam and get ready to put the tour together and for us to think it over and let me know. I've mentioned it to the band and Poppy and we are home now and we are all going to discuss it right through and now we are home all the feelings will be out on who wants to go or not. Do we decide to take the offer?

Wow, it is something you really gotta think over, haven't you?

Yes, yes and discuss it with everyone involved in our families, Dylan replied honestly. But if I was in your paws, with an offer like that, how could it be rejected?

Back at the happy shack, where Poppy was raised, the chat was going on whilst sitting in the back garden and Nanny Ryan just could not help but say this trip did you well didn't it, Poppy?

Yes, yes, Nanny, and it made me realise how much you have done for me and still do and I will be forever grateful to you both. You know how much I love you both, as you both know, don't you?

Of course, and if your mummy could see you now? Although

she is looking over you in mind and spirit, she would love to see how mature you have become somehow in such a short time. Now then, with this party on Saturday, you know some other guests who are coming who myself and Bampie go way back with in our younger days and did not know they were living in this area and related to your friends.

Well, Grandad was in a local kennel college band where they used to bark away at the Dock and Duck on weekends to make a few wads for treats. Anyway, names were passed around and one snout led to another's tail and they just could not believe it after all these years that we all now live so close. Mind you, Frank, he's not close as he is the head of a dog team that drives the large flocks of sheep over the plains in Australia. Well, your Bampie will be getting up and jamming with a few of them. It will be interesting, to say the least Aseena? And look how this has come around? Look where we are, the first reunion get-together of your crop.

Back at the Manor, the banter was going on from Albert, one of the bloodhounds, and a question he asked was,

Can you feel and sense the ghosts of the estate watching us? These were stories told to Aseena who was raised with yarns like these over and over. The ghosts will question you in their ways to see if you are a friend or foe. When they sense you are a friend, you will never witness a welcome like it; it is wonderful! There's that wonderful feeling about the air as the aroma and scents carried the vibes of the nice tales of the estate over the centuries and what a feeling to have about you. But if they sense an enemy then what more can I say? They say for instance when Oliver Cromwell himself was staying here, he could not break the spirit's presence and he tried apparently. You see he stole two dozen King Charles's spaniel puppies from a little girl from one of his raids and loved to have them at his feet. Not one, he had to take them all from the young lass.

Well, after attacking our Manor and trying to damage the house and its loved ones, he failed.

The loner ghost who lives down beside the brook, you know where? Was the concerned question from Stella.

When you ask, Lass, about the table that is set up beside the stream? Well, that is set for the loner ghost from a wives' tale that if not set to keep him happy, then bad weather and bad luck will come our way and everything would pop.

Why did they believe that?

Well, one day whilst ole Crommy as they called him then was out walking this mob, the loner ghost thought let's teach this baggabond a lesson not to be spiteful, and he gobbled up every one of those poor innocent Kingies and used a brown trout's fish bone tail to pick his teeth!

The guests looked at each other whilst listening with a little concern and Pixie asked, So, what type of food do you leave this ghost at the stream and how is it that all the others living around there don't steal it?

They know better my dear, not to touch it or upset him as they know he will only seethe.

Back on the patio, the local birds knew the banter was a worrying one, so a skylark who had just landed to hear what was going on started a tune and all the songbirds joined in. Llewellyn thought why not? He walked to Aseena and asked, would you care to dance?

The response was beautiful and the others all just commenced in joining them and yes it was a wonderful sight. Aseena's eyes dropped as the birds mellowed their tune down and then she lifted her eyes once again and that was that. Llewellyn knew there and then he was in love, without doubt in all he knew.

You see Llewellyn was very close to his father and his father never let a day pass without explaining or expressing his love for Llewellyn's mother and this made everything about him blossom and she most of all. Are you okay? Aseena asked.

I could not be or feel better was his thought, he answered with a Yes, I'm fine, Aseena.

Whatever it was, he made a wish as he stood there with his thoughts, please never let me lose this. They both looked at each other then they were interrupted and he stepped away as Grandad called to him as he wanted to introduce him to the main gun dog.

Llewellyn, this is Algernon.

I say, ole chap, you carry a broad Welsh name there with Llewellyn, don't you? And off he started with his banters of old. I remember the autumn of 65 or was it 66? at the Queen's estate shoot held at the Lord Treyern estate outside the city of Cardiff.

It did not take long for Algernon to introduce his character and those who knew him knew within seconds if he liked a person or not.

Come, come with me. Let's walk and chat.

With this, he led Llewellyn away flooding him with questions from all angles. He looked over his shoulder to see if Aseena was annoyed taking this maybe sweetheart away. And he saw her smile and just slipped her paw into Grandad's side and she just glanced with another smile and walked away. Back to reality, Llewellyn's thoughts were of his mischievous puppy days and where he was first introduced to the birds, if you may use that expression?

Oh, yes, yes, a wet, wild day was the ideal practice time and he and his two best friends when they were wee ones headed to those woods of mystery on the Treyhern Manor and everything they had to- well wanted to learn about the birds of pleasure with the one long tails, it was there, sniffing, poaching, snapping it was all in their task.

It seems that Algy has taken to our Welsh guest as many others as well, my dear.

Aseena smiled with a little embarrassment at Grandad's question as he looked at her. My, you remind me so much of your mother each day you walk this planet of ours. You carry all her love and beauty she had to offer on glow. And now a young lady yourself, you have the world at your feet and the audience awaits your every move, my sweet. With so many doors at your feet open, I ask of you one thing, my dear, stick to your instincts of what is good and what is bad and go with the right one. I see many guests follow that fame and fortune at their feet and paws and greed was their downfall and the wrong crowd, so stay with that good side of thoughts within your heart okay.

She followed up with her look of truth and said, Grandad, I've seen enough already to teach me what is going on in the high life of the catwalk to keep me on my toes. Even in our surroundings, I've seen what is going on and what leads who to what. So, my guard is aware and there are good folk around me on the road. Ahead is all about the beauty life offers and the rest is all a show.

The chat ended with Algernon nodding away with his conversations as in a way answering his own questions. But really this was to do with the approval and Grandad's choice. Aseena looked over and caught Llewellyn's eye and that daunting look enticed him back to her side where he stood proud.

They make a wonderful couple, don't they? These surprising words came from Margaret to Stella who somehow found herself assisting the kitchen staff, after helping one of the girls carry back one of the large trays and so they met Margaret in her tracks and she asked could she assist in anything as she was heading back out to the others.

It did not take long for Algernon to make up his mind in choices as he got talking to Grandad about the estate and what's next on the agenda of fixtures?

I say, old boy, where did you find such a fine young chap as this Welsh bred specimen of a breed? He must be the one for the position may I say. With this, Grandad glanced back over to find Aseena at his side again and he just could not help but flow into a thought of his own daughter and understood that the two must not be copied in his heart as the same story of hers would only carry heartbreak.

The one road of everyone's life must be their own destiny and fate and even if the road is long, the journey will be a wonderful one to learn the offers of life's gifts and to embrace the lessons learnt and leave that back door open to let the bad times slip away and let them travel with the winter's wind back to where they are not wanted. Life can carry on in good company not needing those hanging on like icicles trapped and longing to melt and flow into waiting streams with wonderful stories of life's journey just for your own sake.

Well, it hasn't taken long for Algernon to decide who he wants for the job.

Grandad was at Llewellyn's side again chatting away about the estate and once again, Aseena glanced over her shoulder whilst chatting away to her friends and guests where she just slipped her thoughts to where she wanted them to travel and that was straight into the heart of Llewellyn and landed right in the middle of where it was aimed for.

The day just could not get any better with the flow of the local and distant breezes carrying wonderful feelings about with them to all the guests and staff and the sun shone on with watching her eyes slowly fall to the west with the glance and sense of a grand feeling for all to adore.

Would you care to join us back on the patio, Llewellyn?

Yes, let's stroll back up.

As at this time they were still listening to Aseena's childhood stories of adventure.

Need I say, my boy, but it is yourself everyone feels comfortable being around and about the Manor and with Algernon non-stop talking about you in such a short while, I'd like you to join us here as gamekeeper and so the offer is to your choice okay.

Looking all about him again, Llewellyn could not but feel something of great interest that the land gave him. Mind you, with a beauty such as Aseena walking the fields of golden crops and green fields that reminded him of an emerald he once set his eyes upon that was full of beauty, it all made sense why he could not turn the offer down. Reaching the patio, well to us it was more like a courtyard, Grandad bowed his head once again to the company of Llewellyn and explained to the youngster he had to join other guests who Aseena was modestly chatting away with. Llewellyn joined Algernon and others and with his natural personality carried on with the chats of life that were gifted about them.

Yes, eyes were locking from everywhere and seemed for some reason to travel back to either Llewellyn or Aseena. Maybe the guests and folk could sense the next grand love affair that this place seemed to create within its walls and ways. We cannot deny it but it carried on for centuries and hopefully will do in its history with playing with love and its journeys may there be many more to travel upon its trails and tours and happiness be at the end of the track.

A nod came from Grandad as he joined the group and he knew his granddaughter was listening and spoke to guests about the offer he had just made to the proud, gallant youngster that he knew he would only regret if he let him slip away. A little embarrassed, Aseena bowed her head as she stepped away from the company to speak to Stella.

Well, how do you feel now whilst witnessing what I told you about on our journeys about my feelings here on this strange but beautiful land I was raised on?

Stella's reply came from the heart and she spoke of her feelings and sensed the love that travelled all about from every corner of the estate and maybe one day she would be gifted to be given a page upon this story that will say her name in the way it has given others over the centuries of the blossoming feeling of sharing the special gift of love. But wherever it is upon this land may it always be carried with the love being carried from way back.

Back at the happy house, sitting on the patio, Bampie was in a silent thought and Marietta picked up on this and asked,

Everything okay with your thoughts my dear?

Yes, yes all's well. It was just then my thoughts were upon my memories, watching that Robin who has made our garden his home and Mrs B, the blackbird that is, who goes around checking all's well like a lady in the town doing her daily shopping and seeing the townsfolk, do they have any new gossip about them? Here we are all these years ahead meeting with old friends from way back. Look how much has happened, Marietta, since we first met up. It is a wonderful feeling now thinking about it and I've realised I've done too much thinking, well worrying they call it really and it has never done any good to anyone's mind. It is time to chill out and get a little bit more practice with this ole guitar ready for Saturday. I think as it was said the other day so much has happened within a year, well, what can one say?

Now as one was saying all these little groups were getting together and it all related to love with the next generation and where would the path take them? Would it be as adventurous as ours and as loving? Who knows, but it would be very interesting to see what was to come of it all. Just looking out across to the Goodwin Sands its stories of centuries of its drama, if only they could talk, can you just imagine once again the questions they would be asked. But surely, most of all would be why did you sink that one? Or that one? History of two lands separated by nature's arguments that split the land in two with such anger and force. My, it forever intrigued and fascinated me!

A bustle in the hedge came about that changed the mood and got things back on track and they ended the chatter with a generous smile of affection and a little strum on the guitar's feelings in general kept in motion and seemed to be in tune with the breeze's gossip and the main one was the get-together this coming Saturday and of course who is invited? But it was not like something of a main gig or fame in the town although it felt and seemed that way with the buzz, but as saying you will get that in places, they still call a town. Bampie, like his guitar, felt now in tune and ready for any type of fate that was ahead of him.

Grandad and so on seemed to be practising in the barn back at the Manor. I wonder who would not let them practise in the Manor itself? Were all their songs in tune as well, plus the youngsters seemed a little balanced and ready for all the questions they were more than likely going to have thrown at them. The local newspaper kept their promise by not putting anything in the paper but they had been given a private invite to the evening as this way it would keep all the annoyance at bay.

Yes, the morning of the gathering arrived and it was a beauty if there was ever one. An Easterly breeze with the southern chorus joining in with a melody of a tune that settled in with the mood of the day's adventure ahead. At the Manor, word got out to all, about their new gamekeeper and what a fine choice it was. You could tell in ways there was a settlement of the choice by the tunes the birds tended to choose from the full height of the Buzzard soaring over the estate, to within a small hedge, a Jenny

Wren with her chirping tune. Across the fields, a Pheasant squawking within a scream. Then the Skylark's tune of a loving ballad with Finches joining in to harmonise the chorus, it just sounded as if it came from an opera written just for this time. Yet how many times have you heard someone say when they have heard a wonderful tune, oh that must have been written at the Manor? It is just an expression because it is beautiful that's all, the saying goes way back to even the hardy sailors, smugglers, fishermen and so on, before a trip they would request, could we have a song that comes from the Manor just to bless us with a warmth that it will be a safe trip? And we ended it by returning to our loved ones and gifts for all.

Once again, was it banter and buff? Whatever it was, it was a nice feeling to have a flow about you to capture one's pleasant thoughts.

I must say, Aseena, I tried to imagine the feeling of your words when you often spoke of your home to me, these were the words of Stella expressing her thoughts now she had witnessed the feelings of the walls of the house's offerings to those it cared for. Now experiencing it how could one explain the feeling except with a smile and joy?

Pixie explained as, Well I know it was only a short time ago that we met but your words of home brought so much peace to my mind, I just want to say thank you. Thank you from my heart, Aseena, for sharing it with me and others.

Dollie entered then to say, Ladies, I must say I'm looking forward to tonight and I've a message from Becka that she's coming over at five to check all coats in all. Plus, she wanted to know are we wearing any of the classics?

Dollie looked a little confused with that question and Aseena put her thoughts at ease, The classics are my mother's dresses, Dollie. I told you of the night we were invited to the dance on the Strand and that was the night I got chosen to join this modelling bizzo. We walked in wearing my mother's gifts from my father who had them made from the finest wear of the world and as we walked in, we were embraced by the whole media for guests could not stop from enquiring who made such beautiful attire for our call?

Right here it is, all the instruments were taken down and put aside for safe keeping. Aseena, Keeley and Poppy came down a little early so they could welcome whoever was to arrive and get an introduction to those who they did not know. Nanny Ryan, Bampie's guests and so on were all excited, to say the least.

Well, Aseena, would you mind if I got a shot with you and the band and team to take home for memory's sake as I've got a feeling it is going to be one of those to remember? These were the words and feelings of Pixie as she just felt it in her blood of the south, soul and passion she would have a treasured capture here. The band were already there so they all posed in front of the set-up with their treasured smiles. Bampie's guest arrived, Dongo, he knew straight away who it was, by his feature of a tuft of hair on top of his head that was still there after all these years. It just carried on from there that the door then just welcomed wonderful guests to this amazing gathering. I must say every shape and size of a mutt arrived and if you had seen the confused expressions passing around, it was a sight for anyone's thoughts but most of all it was the wonderful memories of the older guests checking out who was who, and what feelings were and are there now. Plus, the new ones that were to be created. Just a wonderful expression of thought was around.

Darling, who on earth would it be or what party would be complete without, you guessed it, Birdie. Dressed to the hilt, in she strolled on the paw of Wellington, who somehow got introduced to Llewellyn. The two stood proud as Wellington was introduced by Algernon who Llewellyn arrived with. Wellington was at the Officer's College for a spell with

Algernon plus they were at boarding school together as pups. In conversation, Llewellyn was in silence as he kept glaring over to the left corner.

Algernon spoke, It is beautiful, isn't it?

Yes, yes, I found it with its owner in a back lane sitting with a one-eyed mutt outside a back-alley bar in Spain playing it. It's a beautiful Spanish guitar that was the object of the chat. You never would have guessed something like this would be the conversation but its beauty just captured one's feelings. It was placed upright ready for its other half to join in and harmonise together and bring joy to all.

Just then, Aseena was standing beside it chatting, as by now many guests kept flowing in that was building the aroma of the night. Skip and Taxi were guests as they being daddies to Teddy and Bobby, watched the door just by instinct. Anyway, as the band were chatting with Scamp who was over from Australia, Aseena was talking to Bailey and that is how she was next to the little stage set up where the guitar stood. The two beauties, one being an instrument and the other Aseena, they gave the word beauty credit to the ground.

There's a wonderful flow, isn't there? A twang to the bark as this comment came from Scamp and he being away from ole blighty for so long and living down under, carried this accent. He was talking to Tuppence. Now, Tuppence being one of the oldest legends of the town, an ole Staffordshire who backed a lot of the old howling bands and by Christ, could she howl or what?

Did you ever marry, Scamp? she asked.

Na' the music and the road have always been my love, Tuppy.

This was the name he had on her since way back. They say, once again the ole tales that they were a pair and when he set sail, he asked her to join him, but she turned the offer down and never loved another again, not like the love she felt for him that is.

Before it gets outta hand would you join in, if we jam later?

Let me see how many of these long-tongued trotters I sink before I answer that!

The trotter was a drink renowned at the Hope and Lane, made up from the banters of drink smuggled into the area in the old days, it was said to take away the pain of either a broken heart or a sea-going injury. Either way, it worked and was carried on from one member of staff to another. I got wasted one night out on it the night when Snouty M'Gowty won his beret and we had a wee bit of a session that day. That's the weekend they say One-eyed Jack had it out at the back of the Runny Snout with two-tailed Tobby. That fight, ya, the two mutts both North End boys, it went on for three hours you know.

Before this night was out the bark and banter of chat like this would be plentiful, to say the least. No doubt a lot of memories and thoughts would be brought back to one's mind and heart and mostly it would lead to a smile. Just then, the first song began and of course, it was the beginning of many more. Introductions kept coming in with all the compliments flowing as don't forget it was a gathering of friends to welcome the youngsters back who had reached a lot of achievements since they parted to go their own ways on the road to their destiny in the outside world and tonight was the first time the town really got to know about what they had reached.

Then the idea of the older folk getting together, well, what a bit of destiny and timing it was. Because as soon as the music got introduced, its affection would follow everyone's feelings. It came from everything you could imagine but mostly in song. Tunes flowed one after another to the point where breeds and folk were flowing from all directions and this had to be controlled. The last thing they needed was to give someone something to gossip about, last night there was a disturbance at the gathering of that group, blah, blah, let's just let them do a write-up in the paper or from the tongue of good things to grow.

Oh, how the night just flowed with everything that could be imagined. Tilly was looking over at Dylan whilst talking to Pixie, who she really took to after being introduced to her. Yes, that is my sweetheart as you say, Pixie.

I heard him talking to Llewellyn earlier about how he is at the College between the police and military?

Yes, yes, he just got his diploma, Pixie into anti-terrorist, bomb disposal.

Wow, isn't that interesting to say the least. Are you nervous Tilly?

Pixie explained that her father was with the Anti border patrol squad and when the troubles broke out in the Middle East he was called up and from that first day away Pixie's mum used to sit on the patio with silent thoughts of her own but her main wish is that Daddy comes home and he did. What was alarming to say the least is Daddy is as black as you say there could be and when all breeds from all over the world were found by his nose, he had some strange looks and some hard words and views shouted and barked at him. It is understandable why, isn't it? He told me his two partners, a honey Labrador and a golden Retriever, not a word said to them, but him, he got the tail end of it all.

The guests arrived like the way the current and tide play along the front, you just didn't know what breed or who was next to turn up. But what it did was bring so much joy to so many because when one guest realised who was who, it brought so much happiness to many thoughts and feelings. It seemed to assist in many guests' emotions, as one could not help but overhear some people say, well the last time I saw you was …

etc, etc. And the chit-chat went on from there.

As we said, some of these guests had not seen each other for over forty years and more? And to hear the chat as one was saying just brought a warming feeling. Aseena was talking to Poppy about Poppy's tour and where the next step was of the band being offered the contract. They had already had their main chat between themselves and they had made up their minds that they were taking the offer to go.

How can we turn it down with a chance to go on tour and be paid for it? It does not happen normally, does it?

Aseena was explaining to Poppy, how much she was taking to the clothes' side of the designing section and herself and Keeley felt themselves really falling into the depth of what should be worn.

We are sketching each day in little ways of our thoughts into rustic wear and what suits the human creatures' fashion, to suit the four-legged companion who's beside them. We keep coming up with such an open flair that no one else is doing, or ever has tried, and we want the style to come from our hearts and it is going to be our call.

You see, how many times have you heard in conversation that some Mutt or high-end Ped says that their partner embarrassed them last night or yesterday out walking with what they were wearing? We have been there ourselves, haven't we, that we are not happy with the attire that our partners are wearing so that is why I've been thinking why not do something about it?

Aseena really caught Poppy in a very strong point about how she felt about her views and she was just going to say something when she heard her Bampie being called to the stage by another guest.

Nick, you are needed with that tune you had in mind from earlier when they were jamming on the patio with that Spanish guitar. Will you give it a go with us?

Nanny Ryan gently smiled and whilst doing so Poppy was weighing up what she was wearing.

Making his way through the crowded bar, Bampie gently smiled as he picked up the guitar and strummed out a tune with Scamp the Auss joining in by saying, do you remember this one? The crowd did not take long before joining in with a humming kinda introduction that really harmonised with the tone of the evening. Yes, the younger guests and all knew these tunes as the parents or partners were often playing them away on the deck or the radio. Whatever way about it, the tunes brought a wonderful joy to their abodes and their minds and thoughts were often left just glaring.

What are you looking at, Poppy?

Oh, it's nothing, Nanny. I thought you dropped something?

You know what it was, don't you? That chat with Aseena had not left her thoughts and mind and they had triggered her little secret hobby. Just then, Tilly was in front of Poppy and she had that worn chiffon scarf around her neck, the one she was given by Jilly at the graduation way back, for helping her with the store. Tilly used to assist Jilly in stocking the kennel sheets, blankets and towels. It was her weekend job that Jilly gave her whilst the barracks were open and the blankets for the horses and dogs were never-ending and it was such a joy to drive up on the back of the pickup and deliver and drop off the freshly aired and washed blankets, smelling of the scents that Jilly had made. They were wonderful times that she would always remember and adore.

I have to say, Aseena, Keeley, this is more than I expected. I often longed and thought of what it must be like to have a bond between family and friends and you guys have shown me from first meeting you both, that what I believed in is out there and it's around me all the time. From just meeting Daisy to

Granddad, just the shopkeeper to the street cleaner there seems to be a bond and I'm learning from it. There has been heartbreak, to say the least, but that bond has helped one all through and gathered all the lives back together.

I have seen from Mrs McDonald and from our designers, etc, etc what they lack in a certain part of their lives. For if there is a standard of feelings to assist one through one's life's path, then you have flight of air to fly you through it. This I see is wherever you are in life and on what path, if you need each other then you will call out and help each other along, and that support I feel will be there forever.

Keeley looked at Aseena then back to Stella and knew what she was trying to say and explain. Ever since they were puppies, looking out from the Front, watching the traffic flow of ships from the small fishermen's boats to the mega-sized cargo ships they listened to banters that were made into stories of such sagas of the smugglers and so on. Yes, at the same time when you think about it now, those stories we were being told with such drama because of the danger of its destiny. You look at it now, what made it so interesting and inspiring was who was telling you these historic stories or banters shall we say, for you to believe, they were told by a marine fisherman or a ruddy miner who are now your teachers at school and who you are going to get any sense outta.

When you think about it, these three crazy breed teachers giving out these lectures had everything a wild man would want in a town, didn't they? a different pub for every day; the winds from the wild to carry you anywhere you desired; kennels filled with the wild felines with the finest coats; ships that would take you anywhere you desired in the world but held its own passion of its own character to keep one amused day and night. Many of those tell tales are gone now but their spirits still haunt the wild, windy, narrow streets off the Front and if you wanna listen to one of those sagas you'll still find a bent-up, snouted-nosed mutt to tell ya.

Can I ask you something girls? This came from Stella. As we are all here together now, can we make a vow, or a promise if you want to call it that. Can we meet every once in a while, here on a date we will all choose before leaving?

They looked at each other and even as young as they were, they understood the words and all agreed and said let's do that. Every dog has his or her own path to follow but what these girls had reached in such a short time was amazing to say the least and had set an example to many who wanted to find the courage to make that one break and hit the wild open road to find their own fate and may they find it.

Entering back into the party, Bampie was talking again to Grandad with Scamp and Sloppy Joe now with them. He was down from Bath where he held a gun dog club and news got out to him through the weekly paper The Howling News, and he said to himself these are my old buddies they are writing about. So, he got on the wagon and made his way here as well.

With all the excitement going on, Aseena put both paws out to Llewellyn and fell into such a happy madness of laughter, she gave a little bark out,

You will be here when I return, won't you?

This came as a little shock to Llewellyn as he had no intention of leaving after just taking on the position but it did make him realise that it was only a matter of days now before she left.

So, he just smiled with his pleasant presence and replied, Of course, I will, of course. He knew now because he was in love.

There was so much going on just within this small but enlightened area of a gathering of just wonderful hearts and minds. Some had only just met whilst some souls went way back when. But it was all beaming with joy is what one could say. Just let this capture be within their souls young and old and forever.

I don't think I can remember such a joy of breeds of all shapes and sizes, tones and modes of business and so on being together for so long Nanny?

Lilly was here and the swaying with all her friends from way back as well was in the tracks of the music that filled the Hope and Lane. Personalities of one's heart just could not help but flow into such thoughts and feelings because of the company of grand memories and guesswork trying to remember one's names. This had helped every state of mind and thoughts not really knowing it had. The girls being home and getting set for the new shows ahead, the calming of the older folk now knowing that their worries were at ease because they had an idea of the company and status of who their loved ones were with. Then were the ones who stayed at home and all their thoughts and love were safe with the above.

Burt caught Tommy's eye whilst Freddie spotted Paddy chatting to Basil and what laughter came about when Paddy could not help but pull back the fur on top of his leg to show off the tattoo they had all had done just a while ago and what did he start singing- well howling a little - was The Wild Rover and by Christ, the five just walked over to each other in harmony's smile and sang along with others joining in. My, it was a grand atmosphere to be about, I must say.

The evening carried on until the final whistle was blown on the party when a certain breed started howling, Take Me Home Country Road and the rest joined in with the song. Lulu looked up at Rory and then back at the clock as it struck 3 am, it was time to call it a day. Many, many smiles kept flowing as the music faded. Instruments were placed down and the last two were the Spanish guitar and the mandolin, held and played by Bampie and Grandad.

Lulu said, Leave them here. Just place your instruments to

rest after such a grand show they have put on. The place will be locked up and we can all pick up whatever belongs to us tomorrow. The nods carried on as the small crowd said their goodnights or mornings shall we say? Then a switch was pressed down to turn the well-earned lights off and the old lock was turned around and all was put at bay.

All the hearts that made one were at the same level of thoughts by the time they made it home or to wherever they were staying and the questions to each other could not be held onto. Like, did you recognise, blah/blah? Or did you know who that was? Just wandering thoughts were all about that made the evening so well to be within.

The older folk really enjoyed themselves, didn't they? Aseena could not hold her thoughts when they reached bed. Talking across to each other in their beds, my, what did you think of my Grandad on stage with the others?

I wish I had a Grandad like that, said Stella.

Questions were flying about as the adrenaline was still flowing within their blood. I see you were in deep laughter with Basil, Pixie?

That embarrassed her but a proud expression of a girl came from Pixie that the others picked up on and looked around at each other but held their tongues, for another time would be best to get an answer to this response of one's feelings?

Well, it seems love's been playing in the air and all around it just seemed to have sprung from all over at the right time for all to be about, so let's just say enough said!

Breakfast appeared to the sound and mode of the sun that seemed to have captured everyone's thoughts from last night. Margaret overlooked her glasses whilst strumming around the kitchen when Grandad walked in. Another little silence then a word muttered,

I understand you stole the show last night from the other youngsters who were on stage at the Café's gathering, is this true may I ask? She looked at the young girls who had somehow beat Grandad to the breakfast table and Margaret winked at them all with a little smirk upon her face.

Grandad's reply was, well, word seems to travel fast as usual around these parts.

Pixie was trying her best to behave in the manner of a guest but like Stella she could not help but feel they were like little girls at bay with new toys to play with.

Who was talking may I ask on this fine morning, Margaret? asked Grandad.

Oh, it was the Postie as he was dropping mail off this morning at the butchers and he could not help but overhear a batch of bats putting in a thank you, not a complaint, but a thank you to the council for last night's entertainment by local musicians as well. The main bat, Barny, was talking to Danny, the Scot at the Black Pig butchers. He recognised Grandad as four of those bats lived in the loft here at the Manor before it was insulated with all that chemical stuff. He was saying when he heard the wonderful tunes, he recognised some of them and when he popped his head out, he spotted Grandad on the guitar and the harmonising just came with a flow from all involved as their hearts were all about. He recognised Bingo, one of the oldest Jack Russels in town with a history of playing the mandolin whilst on board one of the fishermen's boats that struggled to get ashore when a storm erupted. She used to sail out each morning on a different boat to carry the spirit of safe sailing to all involved. This once again came with many of the other ole wives' tales that left the launching decks.

You see once again when news needs to get out, someone's listening. Bingo heard of this gathering whilst at Chewy Moggie's the tuck shop at the castle. He told himself he's not missing that for anything and who is his grand pup but Basil. So, he just coddled along with the flow that night; he was just visiting his daughter so it seemed and thought he'd take an afternoon stroll with his grandson pup but he knew well where he was going. That evening will certainly pass on down for a while with a well dog-tongued tone of how much everyone enjoyed themselves from the back street mutts of all around, the feisty pack of hounds and then onto the long-legged lurchers.

Well, I'd like to be on the desk of that councillor when that comment arrives. I think what is unique around here is that a lot of the facts have really got out about some known things still going on here in ole Deal, like how would someone deal with a note that you need to follow up on that comes from a batch of bats, Mm? Kinda strange isn't it, one might say. But alas it will pass by and be taken care of. A camera check will be viewed as I'm almost certain there's one along that St George's Passage. So, when just harmonising along the wonderful feeling of the clientele of the evening, shall we say one notices half a dozen bats clapping their wings to the mellow dramatic tunes whilst sitting on the telephone cable on such a passionate gathering.

If one did not know some passed-on secrets of the town, you'd swear someone's pulling one's tail, wouldn't you? Some of these banters like the one of the six-legged Corgi or the two-headed terrier, I just don't know. But if I can, I'm gonna get a view of this vision of the bats. This story has to be joined up and listed along with the long history of the many others of many a year past and present.

The morning carried on and Grandad's enjoyment, sitting around the large welcoming table that had hosted centuries of guests of all shapes and sizes that carried good and bad news. You would not know where or who to start with if you tried remembering when or who.

Right, Margaret thank you for my well-fed frame and now I

must pop down to the Café to collect my guitar and so on.

Grandad, please wait a sec? I'd like to come with you to sort a few little things out.

The others just naturally turned to help Margaret clean up and how much they enjoyed this start of the day.

We will be back in a while, okay? Said Aseena as she made off with Grandad, as Harvey the handyman was up with his pick-up van delivering items ordered.

Driving down to the town, Harvey had already heard banter about the gathering of last night and what a wonderful feeling there was about the gossip.

How's your dad, Harvey?

He's well, sir.

Once again, one thing that still held around here was the handing down of trusty positions to those you could trust, like Harvey for instance. His family name, Handy Hand and Paw Extraordinaire, went way back at the Manor and now it was his turn to prove himself for the position. Down through Kingstown and onto the Wellington Road, looking out over the Channel,

Just look at that, for instance? This came from Grandad, commenting on the view and there was a break happening on the Goodwin Sands, the tide played with the neighbourhood's edge, the lips of fate, some poor fisherman may sing those words in a song of the deadly point of history's spot that gave sailors a hammering.

Arriving in the town after a mellow chat along the way, they parked in the market place and just walked the few feet to the café and the aroma was nice, just nice to feel a sense about one's body language from only the matter of hours ago of what was going on. Of course, the butchers were in action prepping for the restaurants and all and the tune of a few chaffinches and sparrows were giving the air a nice expression that all was well. Rory was on the site as a delivery and a clean-up was on its way. Also, there was Jess. You know, she's Steve's wife, the Scottish lady who plays the fiddle.

Jess, morning! Came the welcome. My, wasn't it a grand evening and the turn out! Well, there were guests there I never thought I'd see again. It will be talked about no doubt for a while.

Can I get you a coffee, Sir?

No, no I feel we need to get outta your way plus we just had breakfast. Mind you, a to go coffee would do me well, came the humble quest from Harvey.

Grandad picked up his guitar as Bingo strolled in with a quick Hello and no doubt one knew where he was heading with his loyal mandolin, yep over to the launching deck to join one of the fishing crew.

Grandad, I do hope that, as you said this morning, some things do carry on to keep the character of the town and its ways. Like who will carry on such a responsibility as what we just witnessed? Will it just become another myth of the town, or what?

One just doesn't know. I suppose you have heard already about the neighbour's request of last night Rory?

No, I have not. What is wrong?

Rory, a little worried, was somewhat set back until being told the fact of such a happy bit of news as the dancing bats. He smiled so much after being told and he just looked up sideways at the small hole entering the roof of the Black Pig and he was almost certain he saw a pair or two of shiny eyes peeping down on him.

Grandad, I wonder if we should offer them their own gig night of say an open mic to play away?

Grandad just smiled and said, Sure I'll pop down and join in with them maybe.

How long are you home, Aseena? asked Rory as his sister Tania 'wanted to know. She was in school training classes with Aseena and grew up with her but could not make it last night. She would be back tomorrow from Battersea dogs home where she's a nurse.

Anyway, tell Tania I'm home all next week so we will catch up in the next few days and that is for cert, okay? If I knew it was going to be that good last night, I would have had her down by flight but no way would anyone know it was going to be that entertaining, yes it was one hell of a due.

Lulu, there has been nothing but compliments throughout the Town, Lass, and I must say you managed and handled a magnificent evening. This came from Granddad with Aseena praising on. I will have a word on the committee, Lulu, for any of our future meetings and you can host them here. Don't forget, he, Grandad, belongs to all those little club-like groups. The Chatta-ma-Gatter group that has anything to say about everything that goes on, or if you were applying for whatever; that's them.

Walking out of the Café they received a fair few nods and shakes along the High Street from the crowd shopping. Harvey said, Christ, what did I miss last night? This came from the body language and all the complimentary signs from many a folk along the way.

Right, let's make it back to the house and get the day rolling. Walking along they met some of the others who were heading for the Front with a nice flow as well. Last night, Bailey had been invited for breakfast. It was at the late stages of the night when a little jamming was going on. Scamp with that Spanish guitar worked wonders and as the tunes were going, Scamp was strumming when Nanny Ryan asked, are you coming to breakfast Scamp like the ole days?

I would not miss it for the world.

Would you like to join us, Bailey? Asked Bampie who was maybe feeling feisted up. But the request was a little shock to Nanny and Poppy who looked at each other with a smiling fray. On arriving, they then sat around the table and with its Celtic feeling of sharing like from the beginning of time this was the main way to start a day.

Bailey spoke, Scamp I must say the sound of your guitar brought so much joy to my feelings last night. It made me write some songs in my head to be honest. I think it was the first time I'd felt that way and written.

Why, young one, let me tell you something and you must make a promise to me has well. Here, take this and treasure it with care and when you become famous you will offer me tickets to where you are playing big time. It will be very awkward for me to carry back again, so I would like you to have it and I'd love you to find and write a beautiful song that's been created from its heart by you.

Bailey put out his paws and embraced it from Scamp's hold and said, I promise you, Scamp, I will honour your request and everyday listen to the tunes of the world.

And when you hear that certain melody song and sound, you will automatically know where it's coming from, it's coming from this Spanish guitar, from that wonderful night's memories where we all got together to celebrate the wonderful gift of family and friendship that will always be true.

Back at the house, there was that same feeling when they returned, the feeling of care and concern and a bond of natural love. The girls were sharing the wonders of the house just assisting in this and that. Stella had a smile on her face that had a concerned expression.

Grandad spoke, Right, you must excuse me as I've many a thing to get rolling on the estate as Llewellyn will be up soon.

Yes, Aseena's scent was aware of the name just spoken. Aseena's excitement was telling Margaret of the bats and where they lived now, and the shock of seeing them again. A little whispered reply was said under her voice, it was not a great loss when they decided to move out as they were above my room in the loft and they were forever up to something. When I told them for their own safety it would be best to move, I offered the barn to them but they chose to be closer to the Channel and town.

Anyway, Grandad was out of the room now and Stella spoke, Aseena can we have a brief word?

Why, of course.

They sat on the kitchen patio and quickly Stella mentioned,

Two of the designers were on the bell, to ask politely, when are we back? Mrs McDonald got that contract on the Miami Motion Move, a style that they all put a touch in to create and now it is on the cards. I didn't want to say anything but thought the sooner I told you the better.

Stella, don't worry you are only doing your job.

No, Aseena, it is more than that, I wanted to tell them on the phone what to do with the contract but I held my tongue. I did not know I'd find these types of feelings within myself, Aseena, and want to thank everyone. If anything, it has given me more to think about and maybe go for more, as now I feel I've things that I must do for my own sake, if that makes sense to you?

Yes, yes, I understand for let's be honest, look what has happened since being back here, Stella? Maybe it is a lesson in our lives to learn and benefit from and what we want to head for. Tell them we will be back next week and we will not let them down, okay.

DEAL'S PIER OF FEAR!
Marrowbone Channel Way
Birdie The Bitch
Johnny Dealy Dingo
Little London Dave
Deal's Dodgy Dave
THE SOUTH DOWN CATAHOULA Smugger's TRIBE

Aseena's Beauty
Poppy sings The Blues
Frank the knash rules okay
Pippa's Pram

Just then who came strolling in but Llewellyn and of course with all that was going on, there only seemed to be two souls in the room as the girls had just walked back indoors.

Morning to you all, a little shyness to his tone he asked, Is Grandad about?

Yes, he has just popped out to the workshop, Llewellyn.

Okay, I'll pop out to find him now. Bye. With this, a little glancing was about with a little fluttering of eyes, shall we say?

I myself would not like to be the one to speak of the news they had just received, that they would be leaving next week, as let's be honest it was their introduction to the Miami status and they had great interest in their attire as well as the modelling of it. But it was not parting with ill feelings, it was with joy and what a beginning to many new doors opening with beautiful songs all around that had been composed and as yet unsung.

That evening there was a charming feel to the end of yet another wonderful day of sharing the Manor's manner of her feelings to those who she welcomed under her roof. Whilst all that was going on, Grandad and Margaret were just walking into the kitchen and Aseena came in from the stable side of the entrance and felt that, with the pair together, she could mention the news she had just received and told them that it was next week they had to leave.

Grandad said, I gathered that with all the calls coming in.

Just then who walked back in but Harvey, who had also really taken to Llewellyn, as now he would be working beside him and also Harvey could really show him the nooks and creeks of the estate. He looked at Nanny to say that the staircase banister had now been repaired, coming up the kitchen steps to the main back entrance.

Just then Keeley said, Margaret, where shall I put these straw, sweeping brushes?

Let me show you, Keeley, said Harvey because if anyone knew where they went, it was him.

Oh, my word what's going on? These were Margaret's thoughts as she then scented the capture between them both. Yes, another pair of young hearts about her and it was Harvey and Keeley and with all that had been going on since Aseena had been back, with such a flutter of romance with her friends and Cupid and love with all their hard work, what would the answers be?

All the species separated in a flutter with one going one way and another going the other way, when Keeley came in and was told of next week's plans about leaving. Wow! was her response on hearing that they had won the Miami contract. She had designed a lot of the new types of styles that she found would suit the clientele of the area, set upon with a chic look and she had put so much drive and passion into it, she found it hard to leave the sketch board and it was only two days before they left that she asked Aseena and so on for their view of the style? One may sense that if this came through, then it maybe her day to go her own way on the road to her own label with her dreams in all paws with her passion in heart.

Right, it looks like we need to sort a lot of odds and ends out within this week, so anything that matters, make notes of it now okay you lot? This order came from Margaret who I sensed was getting a little too emotional with the girls being around the Manor and the house felt it as well. From the kitchen to the hallway, young excitement of feet and paws, barks and rants all about was a nice vibe compared to its stillness before they arrived.

Harvey was making his way to the exit door over to the stable side and turned around as his natural, nature's feelings could not resist Keeley's chemistry for him to respond and it did. The whole room picked up on it to be honest and what more can one say but what an open plan to everyone's future this holds and when they all go their own ways what will be the drive within their hearts to the next quest?

Evening arrived and it was a cosy one because of the main fires being lit in the lounge with the beginning of the embers of flickers from the logs sending out magic messages for each one looking into the twilight flames with their own thoughts whirling around their hearts and minds. Margaret cooked legs of lamb that were a gift from the Black Pig as a going away prezzie to wish the youngsters well. Poppy was invited down with a few others and it was just a girls' night for them to chew and chow and that is exactly what they did in front of that burning open fireplace.

Over the years, so many thoughts had been shared and some of the most important decisions had been decided on one's whole future. Crack and clicker was the sound of the fire and Aseena mentioned that the name Crack a Bam was for the flames trying to tell them things but it was a guessing game that the girls made up and called it and loved to play.

They explained this to the guests like Pixie and Stella and so on, that what they had to do was guess what the fire's heart was telling them and give an answer back. I love this were the words from Pixie who said she just made a wish that she's not going to keep secret and it was that in ten years' time she wants to sit here with all who were here now and each one with a smile upon our jaws and speak of happiness and that is all we had to reply with and say.

Do you know what happened next? With the contentment all about their thoughts they all fell asleep under the protection of the flames that kept them warm. Grandad came to the doorway as he was going to play a few tunes so all could sing along to but seeing Margaret's smile and expression he turned around as she turned the light off and stepped into the doorway and left the door open.

A low light was left on in the hallway to give anyone who woke a focus of where they were and where to walk if needed and the both of them walked to the staircase with smiles and a little guess of their own. Who will be up first when the kitchen's action will be in flow once again? Nanny Ryan, Annie and Jennie were given a call to say Poppy, Evie and Lilly would all be staying the night and where they were at the moment so don't bother driving over unless you want to join them yourselves. A little laughter was in Grandad's voice as he put the phone down after talking a little to Bampie as he wanted to ask Grandad about maybe now and then getting together for a little jam, after the fun they had the other evening and he'd love to do it once a month. This just put a wonderful feeling into the air with care and contentment.

Are you okay? This was a question to Stella from Pixie. They both woke in the middle of the night as they both seemed to have heard and felt the presence of someone speaking to them softly. Whatever it was or who, it was very trustworthy to their thoughts.

Stella, shall we say anything of the sounds last night in the morning?

Let's see how we feel' was the reply.

There was a little flicker coming from the wonderful fire and chitter-chatter seemed to be coming from the remaining flames. And they were kind words. I can understand Aseena's passion and love Stella for this place now especially after what we both witnessed.

You have to admire her, don't you? These were Pixie's southern thoughts coming out. Now we know more and meeting this wonderful heaven of hers and staying here at her home as well, how she is in life and how she looks at it with her views, we can understand now why.

Just then they both looked at each other after hearing a fox with that horrid screech they send out that could pierce a rock and they made it back over to the fireside and they just smiled, curled up and fell back to sleep. Aseena woke whilst they were chatting and just listened and watched the pair. She didn't want to acknowledge she was awake but she did respect and liked the way her friends spoke of her and she then fell back to sleep herself entering into a wonderful dream which was widely woken by the Manor's morning crier, an observant, mannerly, timely gentleman if ever there was one, Roderick the cockerel. Roddy as he was known by the ladies; Rods by his official friends and then Roderick by all the others in line.

The lounge became alive with glaring, joyous vibes but still a little bewildered eyes from the gang who stayed the night. Grandad spoke first by telling the girls that he had called the folks of whoever was here last night, to let them know they would all be staying the night so not to worry about that okay. Everyone's thoughts were catching around the aroma and scent of guess what? Yes, the kitchen. Like trumpets from a military band standing high whilst howling out the King is Here!

The girls' snouts were up in the air with the wave of wonderful aromas floating around them. Yes, you guessed it, Margaret's magic formulas to her menu. Walking along the hallway, past doors open to other rooms, they felt a sense once again of security. Whatever it was, it was here and a wonderful feeling to its company as it seemed to mean well. Maybe that is what woke the girls last night whilst within their dreams, who knows?

They arrived at the kitchen door and Llewellyn and Harvey were just leaving by the back exit, picking up a neck parcel pack from Mollie, the second in charge of the house. Yes, there were eyes and smiles crossing about but it was not hard to understand why. The smiles and nods were sent over from the boys that were returned with that special girl's look of a shine.

I know we have only known each other a short time but I must say I can see we can really give this a go, running the estate as top priority, you know. Plus, if you don't mind me saying, is there something going on between you and Keeley?

I don't know really, came the reply from Harvey. As to be honest, I was going to ask you the same thing about Aseena.

They laughed openly as they walked across the courtyard heading for the stables where Trotter spent most of his time gathered with the horses, the two main ones being Solo and Solitaire a pair of retired jumpers owned since they were foals by Aseena's mother. Trotter being a pointer and head gun dog, leader of the hounds extraordinaire grew up with them and my, did they have stories to tell or what?

But let's wait a while before they start leathering them out. You know the girls leave next Thursday, don't you? This came from Llewellyn to Harvey just to inform him in a way of the status of things concerning romance.

Yes, yes, I know it's Miami, isn't it?

Ya it is, it's some big fashion contract they have won for their company, you know they are big time, don't you? You know the Big Catwalks, the Velvet Paw, the Dogs Dinner, those magazines? Yes, that's them all right. Myself and Aseena are going to keep in touch on a monthly basis as it would be nice to share what is going on out there and I know being where I'm based, all the news from here and what's going on.

You could feel the pair really were trying to tell each other, God, I wish they were not leaving.

As they reached the stable doors, the tops were open and they could hear Solitaire telling someone off because of the way she was being groomed. No, no was the stern outlet. Yes, yes that's better? It was the young squirrels and kittens, they had been given the job with small tough brushes to climb and run all over the horses and with this deal, they were being taught how to climb and scramble in a hurry to get away from danger and the horses would have the best rub down they could possibly have, as there were places that no human could reach but the youngsters, with four little legs on the move, what more would you want?

There is another retirement location with a wonderful team of groomers and we'll see if we can get you to witness their work, okay?

Hello, Trotter, came Harvey's intro. All the heads turned around with Solo weighing up Llewellyn. Come in, please come in. Trotter this is Llewellyn the new game keeper.

Hello and welcome on board our grand home of happiness.

Here she goes, came a comment from Solitaire.

I heard you are from my ole land of song, Wales, and what part would that be, may I ask?

Tiger Bay, ma'am. Many a many a memory I have of the old bay as we did the Eisteddfod every year from the docks' march to the Castle for the yearly parade of the changing of the manes in honour of all the horses and ponies from the mines and from the war field, stories that carried on that could leave one in such a mess of grieving.

Peanut, that's Trotter's real name by the way. He got the handle Trotter from the horses and staff hands from being 24 - 7 around these fine animals it just came about and stuck on him ever since and suited him may I say. Just then a stern but wonderful orderly bark came about. It's Heidi, Trotter's wife the equivalent of Margaret. Here, take this lunch pack for yourself.

Harvey then said, hello, Mrs Wagtail, this is Llewellyn the new head gamekeeper.

Morning, ma'am, came a word from Llewellyn. A nod came the reply then a look up and down to weigh the lad up.

You can tell she welcomed him as when she spoke again it

was to ask him, have you eaten, Lad?

Yes, ma'am, I have.

She then spoke again by telling him, you must come over for dinner once you have settled in. Married boy?

No ma'am, no I'm not.

Okay, once again welcome on board. You two listen up. Toby, the wire-haired red terrier who shared the estate's running for 30 years before calling it a day and moving to Gloucestershire, well he will be back here on Friday. As soon as his name was mentioned, even the horses said oh my, time to lock up your daughters! Back in the wild days from the sets of Terriers and Hounds, he was the head honcho of the Terriers and lived it up to say the least. After he left, they would share visits as Trotter would make a break to Gloucestershire and vice versa. The best of friends if there ever was and by Christ, did they stand their ground or what? You will hear banters of those times and the fights like the one in the Flea's Snout.

The pub was over in Kingstown used mainly by the farm workers, huntsman's dogs and the miners' dogs and so on. Well, one day Toby and Trotter took the team out to say thank you for such hard work that the estate's team had done that season. Well, a load of the dodgy staff and poachers from the other estates were in there and yes, the ears and tails were up and yes, it had to happen with the booze flowing and feisty tales being told, the fight broke out which is still being talked about to this day just like many others in the town. Trotter and Toby's team got the better of them and once again pride was at its post to be held. It carried on over tables, bars and the outside areas and so on. Bites and barks filled the air and the sound seemed to travel for many a mile and in respect, the Police dogs kept away until they knew it was time to just check it out.

The best part was what started it and when the truth came out all on both sides laughed until they dropped, as it was caused by floppy-eared Fred, Toby's cousin, accusing short-legged Luigi, the French bulldog crossed pug of stealing the estate's finest rainbow trout.

Anyway, Llewellyn, come on and I'll show you around a little more.

The waves came about from the manes and tails of the ladies and listening to their mutters of, well they found a fine young stand of a lad there, haven't they? If I was a few years younger, I'd make a move for that lad to say the least.

Trotter gave a side glance with a chuckle, just to let you know you will be getting a lot of that chat around here, Llewellyn. Come on, let's go down to see, if intentions to poach are on the cards, where the main spots are.

Llewellyn's thoughts were becoming very clear and feelings of contentment spread, knowing that he would enjoy being here at his position and with that, they headed off down to the woodland all happy and contented.

Back at the Happy House, Nanny Ryan caused a little shock by asking Poppy what date is this grand tour going ahead and which band and promoter would it be with?

We have a meeting, Nanny, in fact tomorrow morning with all of us involved, to ask who should we really go with and why? But once again we will have everything in writing in front of us to be witnessed.

Good, great to hear the way you are going about it. Bampie is still talking about how much he enjoyed himself that night at the café, and he looks forward to another jam with the lads.

In fact, Nanny, some of the band asked me to discuss a matter with Bampie and that was would he consider being our roadie-manager on the tour, as they really liked his outlook and tone. They asked me was he a hippy, you know back in the days of the long-haired mutts with the hey man type of bark chit chat.

I wouldn't ask him but I wonder what he would say if I asked him to join us?

Oh, I just don't know, Poppy. How could he leave his plants and all?

No, not that, the main question would be how would he be able to leave you? Unless you came with us as well?

I don't think I'd find the time to be in a te-pe or a caravan and so on, Poppy. We will be better off keeping this castle of ours under protection from all those invaders out there. Nanny Ryan was having a private natter to herself thinking of sharing the road with a band and a mass crew of musicians travelling from town to town, city to city, country to country. How would I come out of all this at the end of the day? A little silence to herself and a silent thought then, well, it would not be a bad thing to have one last crazy time out there in this world of ours with all its offerings and so on, would it? Then she gently turned her head and looked around at her domain and with a contented thought from her heart to her thoughts, she smiled once again and said, I think I'll stay in this keep of mine that has been built to make my home with solid cement.

Back at the Manor, on Wednesday morning, Margaret was talking to Stella to make sure she had all the details for next Thursday when they leave and how was this all coming about?

Well, there is a car coming for us as we will be back in the public eye, Margaret.

Good was the reply. Because, Grandad, I don't want him driving around any mad, huge London airport with you lot and then trying to get back out again.

No, no the chauffeurs will be here with all the works to get us on that plane. That's Mrs McDonald's policy, don't you worry. I will miss you, Margaret, and this place.

Nonsense, Lass, now you know where your home is and an

anchor in life. Watching you since you have been here, you have found yourself a family as well. So, when it comes to the seasons like Christmas and so on, I will set another seat next to Aseena's for you, okay?

Oh, yes please! came her reply then a large hug for Margaret as Stella just could not hold on to herself and what lay inside her thoughts and heart.

The next few days were hectic to say the least, with the gathering of things as the band met about the offerings from certain promotional agents and so on and they chose Pedigree-Perfect Proms and the Hot Doggie and the Bonnie Yoos. They just could not wait to adventure into the music world on a different level.

The feelings around the Manor flowed like the melting of ice flowing down a mountainside and finding an ocean to call home but keeping streams open to swim in. Yes, they really enjoyed meeting Toby and his visit to say the least as he stayed at the estate, so more banters came their way and were shared around the fireside.

The main story that really captured the listeners, especially the girls visiting, was about Michaela. You know she owns the wonderful bijou salon at 40A Stanhope Road. Note the A? Well, her shearing of fur and hair styling was so unique that there was a six-month waiting list to try and get her to look at your coat never mind cut it. Well, the main situation was beneath her Salon, Number 40B. That was her parents' dentist, the Knashing-Begashing practice. It was so legendary that news of it was known throughout as far as you could imagine.

Michael, Michaela's daddy by the way, was best friends with Toby and were both from a tough part of London who came down here one weekend and that was it. Once again, Michael fell for the beauty of Geladine, a local dentist. Michael, a half-bred Boxer-Terrier was a charmer and a tough cookie, to say the least. This cocky, dark-furred, handsome devil had a lot of choices, but there was only one for him. It did not take long for them to be floating over rooftops in love and Michael settled here and Toby? It was not long after he and his wife were Geladine's best friends.

Anyhow, one day in thought, Michael mentioned an idea of his to set up a Denture Centre. Geladine was from a history of dentists of ole stock. You know the type? When a fang had to come out, two big galoot mutts held you by the tail and paws and whack, out they came and no questions asked and then you were sent on your merry way. The practice, that's the dentist by the way, went back to the 16th century you know, maybe longer, but on record, they had the Navy's contract for pulling their knashers. Geladine's great ancestors worked outta that famous coal pit and no questions were ever asked.

Anyway, Michael brought in the plan of the Dentures and my, did it kick off or what? All the wealthy devils out there, like the Sandwich Doggie and Sailor's Retirement Club and the one in Kingstown, not one of those ole blighters had a tooth in their head and the next minute there they were with these big shiny fangs on show that gave them major confidence in everyday life, and were a pain in the butt to every pretty gal out there. Well, it got outta hand when Michael brought in another idea of Upper Market Knashers, real fangs. But where were they gonna get them from?

Michael was great friends with all the mob heads from back home in his native plot and here along the coastal towns, it didn't take long to sort this problem out. Yep, Frank the Knash and his fellow culprits were earning even more dosh by mugging some poor, four-legged doggie who was just out taking a wee stroll. It was never solved, once again like many a case around here, who the devil was mugging and pulling the well-toned doggie's knashers out? But yes, many had an idea. The town was nicknamed Sweeny-fanged-town.

Michael's two brothers never followed in any of that baggabond way of making a living you know? One followed, that was Carl by the way, his dream of designing beautiful shoes but his main passion was his music and it is rumoured that he may be joining up with Bailey to go on tour. And Deckery? He always liked to play the part, didn't he? So it was his destiny to head for the sunny side of California and become a famous actor, you know he was in Lassie and A Dog who had Two Tails, that mega smash hit film. He's Michaela's twin brother you know, Dean? Michaela's sweetheart.

He knew right from the beginning where he stood if he fell in love with the only daughter of this type of dog breed. And if he did not obey the rules, what could happen. But he held his own and behaved, that is why he can still smile with a full set of fangs when he opens his jaw wide.

Tilly was thinking things over with Dylan and mentioned a plan that worked. It was a clever but thoughtful quest to ask guests of young and old to get together over these next few days, because everyone was making a move and going their own way in life, on business or so on. Llewellyn and Harvey came over as guests from Trotter's wife and that went down well.

Then Margaret who seemed to organise the matters of the older guests, she invited certain guests who would not be offended when the old banters were coming out with the barking type of talk of those days. Grandad enjoyed the gatherings, as his memories of that era were so happy and he took his stand at the fireside whilst one spoke again about, Oh, do you remember this one or that one? Yes, the short time they now had left was coming to an end so the family were making the most of capturing memories of these wonderful times of new folk joining their domain and ways, and once again the estate could share its heart, gathered times on its land for everyone to make a grand new start.

After the wonderful days, they all shared and the weather stayed on their side to smile over and glowed with everyone's feelings. The first departure was Toby as it was time for him to return to his sweetheart back to the beauty of Gloucestershire, Lucy, her name was and the reason he left the estate and learnt to love so much was because of her. As tough as the little devil was, just the mention of her name could calm any storm. He came out to the old courtyard at the back of the property where a bunch of youngsters were cheering on one another but over what? Within the group he noticed Kipper and Shelby the delivery dogs for the Hope and Lane, they were cousins. Kipper lived on Middle Street by The Ship and Shelby in Walmer. Both Cocker Spaniels, one red and the other black. With them as well were Elissa's and Terry's litter. Chloe, Logan, Noah and Sonny as they were in the practice of yet another secret art taught from the Manor's history, catching, sniffing out and retrieving speciality eggs laid out from the pens from their wandering prize birds. It's a game to lay the eggs in secret places and who was the first to retrieve them all to keep them apart.

Adelealoola, from the Scooter and Cart Art Shop, was within the group and enjoying a day off with her friends. You see she had been working on a secret project and it was really coming together. Lulu and Rory got talking one day about rewarding members of staff, as if it was not for a certain pair, they would have come to a standstill. So, Bully Benson, the bulldog was having a coffee the other morning and got talking about the beauty and skill put into what Neil and his niece had created. So, with her ears pointed up she was listening and got a cracking idea and ordered a super bike-and-cart for Kipper and Shelby as they had run so many deliveries in rain and snow without one complaint. So, that was going to be a present and their reward for their sheer hard work but just you wait until you see it, when it is brought to their call. The artwork over the sheer body was just amazing. You see, Adelealoola and Lulu have always been very close since their puppyhood, sharing the same basket as their mums belonged to the same nursing kennels and they had known each other since they were small.

You couldn't help liking the pair, but Borris the Boston Pug and his step- sister Frier, the Jack, oh Frier? They are from Dover you know, and it's a good job she's no Dobermann as she wants to fight everyone. Some say her ancestors were Romans, but she had to be Celt you know, as she was a savage. Borris? He was so laid back, he always kept her at bay and the gentleman he is, he knew how to un-rattle her temper. My, she caused a lot of heartbreak in her time as believe me she captured the hearts of many a mutt.

How and why? Well, many thought they would match her wild heart, but alas, she's still at large. A few days passed and on the Saturday with the families of the band and everyone else involved with their world, were at the Manor as guests to say their farewells. They were all spread out around the main garden and all open to embrace each other with as many hugs to last a lifetime. It was such a warming feeling to embrace and share one's thoughts and what a time for this to happen, as you had to look at it, look what had happened since the girls had been home. My word, you could write a book about it all to say the least. The bond between them all had just grown and it really was a wonderful thing between them all.

Before leaving, Grandad spoke to Bailey to say I will consider, just like Bampie, going on tour with you so just give me a few days to think it over and I'll catch up with you to let you know, okay? Bailey really didn't know how to react until Margaret barked out, oh don't be such a blaggard will you and get inside. With this beautiful day coming to an end, it brought folks thoughts at bay with the sun falling asleep over the west end view with a beautiful coloured crest.

Yes, the few days left passed quickly. You see, all the tack belonging to the band was kept in the Manor's storage sheds which was ideal so they could load their tack and still share their time with everyone. After loading everything, there was time to just stroll along the beautiful grounds and share the little time left and then it came to a head, time to leave and the final hugs and embraces took part. They slowly mounted their transport that in their future history would tell so many a tale and wonderful ones they would be. The final hug passed over and a wave from he or she came out and the sentimental looks were shared as glancing out of the windows and then off, the transport started to move. Then Tilly and Dylan stood there with Nanny Ryan and Bampie as the small convoy of Deal's dogs started heading out to play their own rhythm to the world and with the two pairs, they looked at each other with gentle smiles and said, right, let's plan it now, when will we all meet up again and share our world's lifetime adventures and all be back within our special nest?

Nanny Ryan silently looked up at Bampie with a sigh as if for comfort as the fading reflection of the indicator on the back of the band's transport disappeared into the world's wonders and she thought, well there she goes. With her heart fired up, she had to speak and Grandad was beside her.

When does Aseena leave? Were her opening words to Granddad, as he stood chatting away to Llewellyn.

It is Thursday, Miretta, so we have a few days left.

Hello, came Miretta's introduction. You must be Llewellyn?

In towns like this, chitter chatter passes rapidly, my Celtic friend. I'm from Ireland and my father held a lot of dog shows in your native country and he took me to many of them. I found it a very beautiful place to be about and of course, you feel the Celt when about one. With this statement, the pair could not stop from laughing to each other and then carried on about their ways.

The handsome devil could not hold onto himself and Nanny Ryan picked up on this and with her experience, she took a quick glance at Grandad and he too knew of these feelings that were floating about the Manor. Now, really all that could be done was to share the thoughts and times that were all about.

Hello, Aseena, how are you feeling now that one set has headed off? And it is only a matter of days before you will be on your way too, won't it?

Yes, came her shy reply but I do look forward so much to us keeping in touch, with me on the road and you on the estate.

She spoke of Stella and she was feeling so happy, Llewellyn, because of Margaret's statements to her about her status here on the estate? You know when I come home, etc, etc, it really boosted her confidence in life's journeys as it was important to feel and belong somewhere and now, she did. Let's be honest, where else in the world would you want to be offered a location to call your home, other than here? Yes, the smiles expanded and yes, the eyes were about of course.

Aseena, can I tell you something? I'm so honoured to be chosen by your Grandad and given this opportunity and believe me, wait till you see the little touches I will introduce here but not over extensive. It will be a feeling that our hearts will all be at bay.

Nanny Ryan glanced back over to Bampie as if to say it's time to make it back, so let's say goodnight and make ground. The gentle understanding words were shared with Grandad and Margaret then on their way to the Front where there would be a strange feeling in both their hearts into how would it feel walking back into their castle without their princess being there?

Shall I drive, Miretta?

Please do, that was an emotional time, wasn't it?

To be honest I find it could not have been at a better place and the company that was there was more understanding and seeing how content her company is within, she made me feel content.

Bampie had a little joke as to say, Mind you, I came close to jumping on board with them with my guitar and Grandad came close too.

Nanny Ryan just smiled with a glance and off on their way they drove.

Little Binko knew the way home himself as he too had emotional ties with all this. Binko, that's their faithful little car by the way. He too had things running through his little engine as he witnessed Poppy not being in the car and it felt strange. But it was all with a nice care.

Arriving at the house, there was a south-easterly wind breezing down the Channel with a whisper in her voice. It was like history repeating the tales it was going to tell, like the days of the sailors, smugglers, fishermen, whoever and whatever. It was ready to tell a tale of her life's experience and view. Stepping out of Binko, he smiled and said goodnight to them both and parked up for the night.

Fancy a glass on the upper patio?

Yes, let's do so.

Sitting down, the wind just harmonized them both instead of chatting away and that was ideal to suit the mood and the way they were within.

Grandad and the company were pretty amazing today, would you say?

Yes, and to witness that new feeling that I find will grow between the pair of youngsters, is there, isn't it? Mind you, Llewellyn, he's a handsome chap to say the least and a gentleman to match it.

Just then a westerly breeze joined the conversation after

gathering all the scents off the Front from all the plants blossoming which were in such essence and spoke to say, I'd just like to let you know, well, with Poppy on her travels, we will watch her ways without worry, okay?

Nanny Ryan looked up and raised her glass to say thank you, what a wonderful thing to say. This is our way of saying thank you for all your time and heart, thoughts into what you have done for us here with the blossoms and scents that fill our lungs and thoughts that mean well.

This was just amazing, to say the least, for the way Nanny and Bampie felt and how contented it made them. We would like to say thank you ourselves in reply. We have more scents to offer you with the new bushes that will join the others soon so be prepared for their bedding. After a little while, the wind moved on as she had more chit-chat along the coastal front, off she went with a harmonizing song with the lyrics to match and wonderful tales to tell.

The morning began with a bit of a banter going on out on the Front. No doubt a young seagull getting too cocky for his own good and trying to mess with the set of Ravens that had been there since time began. They tolerated each other's company but gulls and ravens, friends? No way is that gunna happen and that is that. Smiles passed about the house as the smell of breakfast was around. It was such a grand morning that you have to clear anything bothering you by having a dip, just to stroll and wade in where many a smuggler landed 'it was just rewarding to the soul and mind with so much going on, it worked wonders. You will quite surprised in who you would spot wading in or out of those famous, mysterious waters?

Back at the Manor, things were taking heed mostly on the sorting out of items needed because the girls were leaving within days, so yes, of course, Margaret was in full swing. But you try telling a group of beautiful people who raised you' No I don't need this or that it will be given to us? Just nod your head and agree with them because they will tell you they know best.

How are you feeling at the lodge, lad?

These words and how they were spoken said it all about how Margaret's thoughts and views were on Llewellyn.

I'm fine, Margaret, and I swear I could hear the strangest sounds throughout the night that it was an adventure of its own just to listen to them. It is obvious that I will hear all sorts as it's a brand-new location to me but some of those sounds, Mm, I certainly would want to discuss the Manor's history with someone.

Leave that to me, my boy. Once you have settled down, I'll introduce you to an ole friend of the estate who goes way back and she can tell a yarn or two, believe me she can. Delila's her name. She was married to Droshky, the main gun caddy and used to live at the north keeper's house and my, sometimes after a night's stroll checking the manor's ground, he would return bemused in thought swearing he'd seen this or that, or heard that or this. Just a shake of his head after trying to explain what's what, and back then to reality, which often left Delila shaking her head in her thoughts of yep, those nights after shoots and hefty glasses of rum he shared with all those other hearty mutts had finally caught up with the ole boy and yes, he'd lost his blonker.

But one evening, she was walking along the bridle path down the north end where the downing stream meets the river and bridge, she swore what was underneath that bridge that day was not human? And after slipping down the bank, knocking her head on a stone, you know the large one the puppies used to jump off into the river? She woke to find herself safe and wrapped in a beautiful blanket that she still uses to keep her paws warm. She looked about her and sensed the warmth of a spirit of the two-headed Wolf that apparently roamed the woodland for centuries and still shows up now and then. What do they call him? Siolence the Sleeper 'or the sleeper to locals, Word is that there are still sightings but I've never came across his path again and to be honest I don't know if I want to, my boy. So, let's just wait until I can introduce you to Delila and she can tell you many a yarn, including this mystery.

Just then, walking out towards the courtyard, Aseena appeared with Stella and yes, the shyish, embarrassed eyes fluttered away towards the gallant newcomer and the smile of Margaret passed away with contentment.

Oh yes, by the way Aseena, Michael called to say he will be up at 10 am to pick you up to take you down to the house to meet Gillian.

Michael was an ex-captain in the Royal Navy who taught Aseena and the other girls how to swim just beside the Pier.

They always remembered their first lesson paddling to the North and back to the South, different areas to get used to the sheer change in currents of the Channel. There was many a banter as he, being from a naval family of centuries, who would not have anything to do with the smugglers, so he got a hard time from certain families and clans whose children would try to pick on Gillian's family but they held their own, don't you worry. They lived on the High Street and after a lesson of swimming they would walk up from the Front all excited as Gillian would make her own lemonade and no one could make it any better, you mark my words.

Well, being a man who travelled the world through its waters there were the wives' tales of safety and the curse of the captain's cat. And of course, a town like this with the smugglers, fishermen, freighters and all there were bound to be banters and tales about him. Did he have a cat? Was the question asked whilst listening on to yet another classic banter. Yes, in fact he had two, Freddy and Maisie and they were who Aseena was taking Stella and Pixie to meet.

The curse of the captain's cat comes from many a year back that the care, love and protection of the boat you were on would be blessed and carried on board by the captain's cat. The wives would give them a cat when they first met and each time they set sail, the cat was brought on board to keep away the curses of the deep until they returned to land. In fact, Captain A.J Hailey, Mick's ancestor, captained the RMS Empress. One day he was ready to set sail for a certain section of land that they heard was full of treasure and gold. Well, the pussy cat that was travelling on deck looked at him and hissed and blinked and sorta said don't go! They later found out that six tribes of cannibals and many savages were waiting for them and that would have meant certain doom. Who knows if this is banter, but Mick's family who followed the seas always set sail with a cat on board?

Freddy was Michael's first cat and whilst in South American waters they were harboured in a small port when a wee wench of a girl was in such danger of the terrible traditions of the tribe of that village, that on the last night of the anchor they set sail in the early hours with the young girl on board to take her to safety and she smuggled a cat with her who then became a part of the crew and Maisie was her name.

It was a little strange, being doggies, but the girls after the swimming lessons would go back to Gilly's house and the pussy cats would tell the tales and yarns of all the ports and harbours of the world and their ways and with each story, they would wrap themselves around the girls' necks to comfort and talk away. The young girl? Well, she become Gillian's second daughter and they raised her as one of their own. The pussy cats looked over her like a pair of tigers and the same with Aseena and the others. They were told through the stories that Gillian and Michael's house was magic and still to this day the happiness of facts of those stories within the house were true in

Aseena's heart as Pixie and Stella would soon find out.

By the way, I'm going to call Tilly to let her know I'm going to be down at the pussy cats' house as she too learned to swim there and not just the doggie paddle.

The pussy cats were very old by now but when they found out Aseena would be down, all the pruning and so on was on full alert as they saw the girls like they were a litter of kittens and that was not going to change whatever happened. Aseena got all excited and straight away got on the bell and yes, Tilly could make it and would meet them at the house on the High Street. With all the hype of the chit-chat, Michael arrived at the Manor and Aseenas's excitement came out again with the hugs and so on and they set off in the car. With this Llewellyn could not help but smile away and with Harvey arriving, he was going to show all the setups of the Manor, starting with breeding points of all the hunting game.

After the tour, many questions were asked of each other with many exciting ones, to say the least, and that was about how they wanted to make things better all round for the Manor and how to run it. Harvey felt that he got a huge drive within himself being around Llewellen but if only he knew it worked both ways, because they both gave each other a great drive. It was a wonderful thing to witness a new friendship that meant well in life and drove one's dreams to reach a wonderful future that they would share.

Back at the Pussy cat house there was joy from all corners as questions came from every angle like what were you wearing at the show in London? etc, etc. These came from Maisie being the stout one of dress code. Mini coats, high heels Mm? Stella most of all just fell in love with this response of care, joy and love that was shared within a few miles but once again as wild and wonderful the history had been there had always been a connection, like a village type zone within the ones who were cared for.

Tell me something when do you leave, sweetheart? Keeley answered to this one Thursday mam'It is Thursday we have leave has we have to meet the rest of the team to get everything rolling,

We leave on Thursday ma'am.

Yes, came Aseena's response, as we are heading for Miami the place you often spoke about whilst you were on your tours.

Gillian came in then with more of her special lemonade. Tilly was questioned then about how she felt about being a mummy?

It has brought so much out in me, Gilly. (That was the name the girls had always called Gillian.) You will make a fine one, don't you worry, a mummy that is. And that handsome devil of a Dylan, is he pulling his weight?

Yes, yes, he is. I meant to ask you about that by the way. When Michael was away at sea, what was your best way of coping? You see he has been chosen for both the bomb and drug squads and he may often be away.

Never forget you are not alone, was Gillian's main answer. If you want some time to yourself, just bring them down and we will take care of the little blighters. In fact, we could set up a swimming class, couldn't we?

Tilly spoke then about Poppy. Yes, she learnt to swim with the gang. Tilly explained about the singing contract she had won and she had left.

Well Nanny Ryan is feeling a little lost and she will be taking the pups on and her main thing is swimming lessons. Maybe it would be interesting if you guys set up classes together? So, I'll give you her contacts, okay. But mark my words, the main concern in their lives at the moment - that's the pups, Gilly - is to play.

The energy and so on is amazing but my main thoughts are

that they are so observant of each other and share a bond of love that is wonderful to watch and witness. They are telling me already that they want to be vets! But Lisa, that's the eldest girl, just watches the current and talks about the North and South winds and their desires and the stories they tell. I don't know if it is in her blood to travel the seas or is this just a spell?

After the chit-chat around the pussy cat house, a question came out,

Does anyone fancy a stroll or maybe a dip?

Oh yes, let's do.

Gathering some odds and ends, away down one of the side streets they rolled when Stella like a child wandering into thoughts, she could not help but look about. As they walked along, a one-eyed bulldog barking away opened the door of a corner kennel that startled her and she stepped back a little. He looked on and bowed his head as if to say good day. He was opening up for trade as he was the landlord of the One-eared Mutt pub.

Gillian spoke out to Stella, are you okay?

Just then the landlord spoke with mumbled greetings as he recognised Gillian.

Morning, Tom, came the response.

On they walked and after reaching the Front, Aseena spoke out to her guests,

Now you see all the mysteries of the Channel; this is what it is all about. Looking North to the South with all shapes and sizes of boats travelling back and forth this has gone on for as long as time began that one could sail and will keep doing so.

Gilly spoke, you see, Stella, you know when you were startled by the pub door opening?

She pointed out a certain spot where you could see France and all, then the Goodwin Sands etc, and spaces.

Well that bulldog Tom who barked, his family were said to be mainly the head honchos of a smuggling gang that used that pub as their anchor. Oh, many a time it was raided by coastal forces and police but they never proved anything. Many say Officer Timmy Two Ways, he was a Spratt Waffler if ever there was one, who tipped the gang off in time to hide away their stock but who knows? Many an evening he was seen with a wobbling walk coming outta that domain with Crocky O' Dockty the old beagle and large smiles were upon there snouts.

Stella once again was hooked on these banters and loved to listen to the many yarns. Tilly's smile spread when she heard a call come out as a fishing boat passed by,

Tilly, my sweetheart, how are the little ones?

Fine, fine Sammy, came the reply.

Sammy? He owns the Snappy Crab and as been friends with Tilly's family from way back. Off the little boat trugged, through the currents to see if their luck was in for a catch. And yes, if you looked at the small cabin, you'd see Goofer, their water bond pussy cat sitting at the front window giving the water a stern look to keep away its curses.

On through the shingles they walked and just sat and paddled and shared their wonderful time together and as the sun played a little shining game, they realised that it was time to make it back as yet another little gathering was set for that night with friends before they left.

Aseena, Tilly! A call came out from the walkway and then a shuffling rush came flooding down to meet them.

Quickly Gilly spoke, Stella you say how much you love the local banters? Well, here is another one that may be on the brink of the top of them all and it will capture your thoughts, so get ready for the greeting then I'll tell you the whole saga of their escapade that you just can imagine witnessing and the drama just captures everything you could put to words and add more each time of your view to it all, okay?

Molly, Freddie and Milly, the three choc spaniels and you know their mummy, Maggie? She owns the grocers on the market and has done since time began and once again through generations of adventures. Yes, before you say anything, Molly has only one back leg and obviously questions you will want to ask will come out of what happened? But wait until all is settled and we will discuss it then.

We heard you were home and have not had a chance to call or whatever but how are you?

Oh, we are fine. Yes, yes the flow of excitement was all about once again as they were very close to Aseena's parents and saw Aseena like their own daughter after what happened to them both.

My, you are looking well my dear.

Then Aseena explained who was who with her and when they would leave etc, plus the reason they were down this way today and explained how much had happened and what they needed to do before leaving Deal to set onto this main show in Miami that topped all the main fashion bouts.

A calmness passed with joy and hugs and then knowing they had to head off they said their byes and set off on their way.

Now then Stella let's sit, in fact, we don't have much time left until Thursday's parting, so let's walk a way up to the Strand? I'll explain to you some of the town's history including the story of how Milly lost her leg.

They strolled along past the Pier and along the front of the Prince of Wales Terrace, explaining to Stella the days of the trade when as small as the town dockside was, it matched all the main harbours of the UK's trading cities like Plymouth, Bristol, Southampton etc.

Along the castle keep and the beginning of the Strand every

five feet or more fishing boats were being hauled onshore with their catch and non-stop you would hear the sound of the little diesel engine-run trugs pulling boat after boat ashore. Hardy fishermen of all shapes and sizes shouted out orders of this and that. All around the town, the large houses that were now care homes, they once belonged to the families who owned all the traders' stores and so on here. You would see and smell every chimney pot's smoke coming from the open fires burning Kent's finest coal that the hardy miners who travelled from the Valleys of Wales and the moors of Yorkshire dug up under the deep dark pits here. These hardy breeds did the famous walk from their homelands to Kent from their home villages after listening to the talk of better money and so on.

Deep in thought they walked on a little further while Tilly spoke when they reached Nanny Ryan and Bampie's domain.

This is where the couple you hear often about live, that is their welcoming home. The Clan William House built in 1878 and it too carries so many stories under her roof?

Anyway, they strolled then they reached the Strand and of course, the monument that is set to explain where Julius Ceaser sat his butt down when he first arrived in this native country. Then to point out the location that Gilly was looking forward to telling the keen-hearted listener about what happened on that dismal day to Maggie's family.

Let's take a seat for a while.

So, on the ole large cans of old cooking oil used to loosen the wire cables or a recycle bin nicked from outside one of the houses in the town, they sat a while.

Well, one day out with the family for a stroll, Maggie got an urge to go for a swim. So, she just ran with all her strength and leapt in, splashing about for the others to join her. Then they heard a massive splash and who showed his big ugly mug, but One-eyed Greg, the croc who made his way straight for the mother. Looking on were the pups, so in they dived after barking so much for her to come back ashore. Greg reached the spot where Maggie was using a railway sleeper as a raft and he bit it in half with one snap that flew her into the air.

The puppies reached the mother then a little confused, Greg with more on the menu, snapped again and had Milly in his gob. She let a yelling scream out that was heard by Finnigan the cross-lab doodle and partner Bob, another ole fisherman who were out on a daily stroll. The two without hesitation swam out and it is said with an almighty bite, Finnigan snapped and got hold of Greg the croc's tail and he squealed out loud but let go of Milly and then Bob with his old fishing skills grabbed some netting twine floating by and wrapped it around the blighter's snout and all six swam in desperation ashore, dragging poor Milly back to safety. The croc was so frustrated trying to release himself from the netting he could not do anything to stop them but vowed he would one day get revenge mostly with Finnigan. You see this ole croc lives under the pier but who knows?

But now, Stella, another story that you can take away with you about this ole devil of a town's banters. Maggie for many a year could not forgive herself as she blamed herself for going in the Channel but you can't do that, because these dips went on day and night and it was just bad timing that day and whenever the story's told now, it ends up with a big doggie smile.

Stella by now was engulfed with so many stories she herself felt like a local who could not wait till she could tell a tale to others of these historical times.

Aseena, we need to get back.

This was just a reminder as the time was passing so fast and if they went any further, they would not stop from wandering on with adventure in mind.

They explained to Gillian what was what and started their gentle stroll back to the pussy cat house.

By the way, Gilly what is Zadadier doing now?

This was the daughter that Gilly raised after Michael rescued her and brought her back, to save her from being sacrificed.

Well of all things as you know from growing up together, she loved to heal things. She became a vet and a doctor in one and decided to return to that native island she was rescued from to assist in building a more civilized life within her native tribes. She is the president of Zuckalatta and has set up a whole new way of living and day by day it welcomes more humane ways but she knows there is still the odd sacrifice going on deep in the forests but she can only take things slowly to explain that the tribes have been doing this for thousands of years after all and need to know this is being unkind.

They enjoyed so much natter walking back and little things being pointed out like things of simplicity like the blackberry buds, budding to turn into the best blackberries in the world.

Gilly spoke, maybe next year you can visit, Stella, on the date when they are ready to be picked and I'll teach you how to bake the best blackberry and apple pies?

Oh yes, let's make a date on that, Aseena.

Smiles were all about when they reached the pussy cat house and shared some hugs and Michael drove them back to the Manor where they parted with him driving off with a hoot-ta-toot wave out of the car window.

On to the back entrance and into the kitchen where looks over the shoulders came with greetings and of course looks of where and what have you been doing? But of course, that was Margaret all over.

Right, ladies, how was it?

All excited once again the banter of the day's ways was out when Aseena asked Harvey who was in the kitchen, and don't forget he is from a historical fishing family. Harvey, what do they call the engines belonging to the boats along the Front? I keep forgetting for the life of me, it keeps slipping my mind. You know the ones that pull the boats back to the shore?

Winches, Aseena, winches they call them. Always think of wenches or witches and it will come back to you.

Aseena was trying to think of the name when she was telling the story about the attack from Greg the croc and how busy the Front was with the sound of so many winches chugging along with their smoke-filled diesel engines, as it kinda sounded like a form of the choir of the fishermen singing in their local bind.

The time shared getting ready for the evening's event was as exciting as the more chit-chat which came about on who was who and what their status was or is. They were to meet Aseena's father's family who lived down next to the barracks and for centuries in the large house; Beachlands Court was the name of the abode. Built in 1830 for a serving officer who bred the finest company dogs who sat with the finest horses that belonged to the officers of the barracks. Many wonderful things started here, like the way the horses were groomed and it was only here that the horses were groomed in the special ways. The chaff finches and other small birds used to peck a poke all over the horses' beautiful bodies until they were spotless and the wonderful thing that made it special was the harmonising of the birds singing in tune whilst they did this.

It's a little strange as another part of the town there was another special set of groomers yet to be seen anywhere else in the world. Grandma Grady, Grady that's the surname by the way of her Daddy's Mummy.

Aseena, with the travelling part of your success in your job do you get the chance to see much of what lives around here?

Because she loved to visit the world's corners and see how the creatures out there in the world lived when she was younger. She travelled with Grandad when he visited his trading spots around the world.

Just then, Lucy came in whilst the chat was going on.

My, Aseena how you have grown. I must say you are the cut of your mother and carry her beauty well.

Lucy was introduced to Stella and Pixie and the nods and smiles were passed around. Lucy had been with the Grady family for 60 years. She was from the North end of the town and Marciana, her grandma, met her at the market one Saturday morning whilst trying to choose a new blanket for her mother's birthday. Lucy explained one design and who had made it, plus why she would want to pick that one. Lucy was Rosie's mummy; you know the doggie who I introduced you to who looks after the cemetery gardens of the Saint George's church on the High Street. That small park's own beauty that shows the colour green off in the melody of the grass and trees that harmonise nature with her breath-taking view.

Just take a stroll in the morning and feel the breath-taking dew dampen the greens to quench the thirst and the reward for this was the wonderful aroma. The morning birds from the robins to the song thrushes, sing a welcome world melody just to say good morning to the world then everyone could join in so in life what more could you want? Life's gifts are still out there with all that we have done to the world she won't give up on us yet. Each time just to go for doggie walks with her mummy or daddy or a sweetheart walks a loved one, you can guarantee the tails are wagging and tongues are sagging with joy as snouts are wide open as sniffing goes on and you would never guess what scent belonged to what, or who or where it came from as you wouldn't have a clue.

Grandad, with his gentle, tall elegance came in with his embracement around Aseena, his pride and joy.

I look at you, my dear. You must be breaking hearts left right and centre?

Grandad, I only left you a few hours ago.

Yes, Aseena being all embarrassed again with his charm just fell into his welcoming warm fur that he carried from his breed. Yes, you can see why Marciana, that's my Granma's first name, fell for him in his day. He then turned to Aseena's guests and of course, the charm came out with them as well.

With all the chit-chat going on, Aseena asked Nanny Grady a personal question.

Nanny, do you want to go in the morning with me to visit the resting basket?

This was a section back at the Manor where loved ones were laid to rest. Before she left, she wanted to visit her parents' graveside but would honour it more if Nanny Grady was beside her.

Oh yes please, we shall do that.

Lucy could not help but overhear and said she would like to join them if they didn't mind and she would get Stevie to drive her up in the morning to the Manor as he had to pick up new fencing posts for the allotments and the builders' supplier was on the way and passed the Manor.

Okay, I'll see you at 10 am.

They once again had a wonderful evening and just settled to the tune of their talk about this and that, but Stella had to say she'd like to have a peep for her own curiosity at No 40 B just to look and imagine what went on under that hair salon?

I'm heading that way in the morning as I've to pop in the fishmongers to pick up the order of the day. You know the catfish and all, you can come with me as it is only around the corner, said Harvey.

The morning arrived and the wonderful gift of life was on offer and all life's breath of chit-chatting was about 'Lucy arrived and greetings of excitement was set within the air,

Are you ready?

Wait a sec, wiping herself dry, Margaret said, I'd like to join you.

With little bunches of flowers, they had picked along the way they reached the ole arched gateway, lifted the latch and entered the small graveyard. The words were kept silent but the sheer gentle thoughts were wide open and you could feel the vibe between spirits as they placed the freshly picked flowers of forget-me-knots, bluebells and daisies and the spirits could sense Aseena was home and that brought even more joy to the visit. They all spoke a few silent words and then stepped backwards out of the graveyard with content.

They just joined paws and hands naturally and gently strolled back down to the Manor.

Thank you both, Aseena, s emotions were up' Margaret and Lucy.

You have nothing to thank us for it is our honour to visit here with our memories, came their reply.

Just then a skylark began a tune and it was perfect timing as the emotions that were being felt needed a little lift. Entering the house, anyone who was around just smiled and carried on about their business. Grandad was out again with Llewellyn which as you gathered, he had taken a great liking to. He wanted to show him the old building that kept the fur and woollen coats dry. Whatever the chores were through a day or night shift the harsh winter time, you would wrap in the huge woollen coats to go on your way to check the estate's assets and stock and then when you returned, you would step into this building and the huge fire would be roaring. It is still in use but not as busy as back then. As the fire was burning away, the sheepskins hanging from the curled hooks, high up off those thick beams, it seemed like they were dancing. And you just could not help but feel and embrace the air-feelings of what the building was about. Just one's silent thoughts of what it must have been like in those busy times of the estate and your feelings were lament.

Just walking about, Margaret was looking out of the kitchen window and approached by Aseena, who was wondering what Margaret was watching?

You know what it is, Aseena, Llewellyn is the son Grandad always wanted but never had. Just look at him/That lad has brought so much joy to the ole codger that he's like a child with a new toy.

Aseena put her paw out and Margaret just held it and watched on as the two made their way over to the kissing gate. Aseena had a little flutter of memories as those kissing gates were so important to her because every time she passed through them, a kiss to her parents had to be given to be able to pass by.

There were still traditions around the Manor that were cute to witness if it was new to one; such as the large bell being rung when dinner was near enough ready to be served.

Do me a favour, lass, came the request from Margaret, Ring the bell for me.

Aseena just smiled and caught hold of the long, loyal rope and swung it back and forth with a wonderful smile matching the sound of the bells' sides in a way ordering everyone to make their way to the kitchen table for feeding.

Come on lad, let's git over before we get in trouble with the old lass, said Grandad as they made their way over and through the door. They let on no one was watching as Margaret's humour was ready to have a dig at Grandad.

Everything fine out there, lads?

Yes, yes came the reply from Llewellyn's Welsh bark. I was just being shown the dry room as I call it and to be honest, I could live in there.

Just be careful with your behaviour young one or you could

end up there. Margaret's tone looking over at him with that famous glance made him sorta laugh with a nervous edge to it not knowing whether she was being serious or not.

It didn't take long before the table was full with the day's chores in mind for many and Stella spoke about earlier when she joined Harvey for a walk down to the town Fishmonger's and they strolled down past the No 40B location. She had to for her own curiosity and yes, she felt the presence of what she was told happened there over those years of history.

As we were chatting a lady was saying who was just outside 40b that her family, a fishing family as well from the Spratt Wafflers' time believed up to this day Geraldine's nickname was Madusa. Just like every other pretty gal outta that family and tribe of theirs, there was one called this.

Why? Asked Stella.

Well even up to modern times with her pretty charm and looks, she would entice the toughest, handsomest of them all back to that northern end of the town with promises of eternal love and they would wake up the next day lying in the back of a fishing boat or on the shingles penniless and toothless etc, etc. Shame, shame upon her, she kept muttering as she walked away down the road and on her way to the Strand.

Then walking up Western Road that meets Queens Street, Harvey wanted to point out where the tough mutts of all shapes and sizes met in the past. They reached the Hole in the Roof bar that was the notorious Swan Inn hotel in the days of wine, women and song and before he could say anymore, we got called on by a cab driver named Mark who slammed the cab door in a rut shouting out enough is enough!

We heard a little shouting and other drivers pulled up.

Harvey, good morning and what brings you this way? And I say, who is this pretty one beside you?

This is Stella; Aseena you know from the Manor, she is her agent and I've been showing her some old parts of the town and where all that harsh banter comes from, the stories I was raised on. Oh, my dear I could tell you a few about this ole hangout. Anyway, what is all the shouting, and ranting about?

This was said as more cab drivers pulled up and Matt, Samantha's sweetheart since time began and with the patience of a saint, he came out of his cab as he had finally lost his rag this morning with Sammy.

Why?

He just replied with, I cannot help but feel I come nowhere but second best all the time at home and so to the dogs, you know Poppy, Noodle, Little Man Louis and Reggie? Well, he stood up and ranted and barked out, enough is enough let us stand together and protest to our rights!

The five doggies looked at each other, then over at their mummy, Samantha, who owns the Deal Cars taxi rank on South Street and she's a tough cookie who will hold her own.

Well, are you going to back my heart and stand with me? Matt shouted out proudly.

The male doggies looked at each other, then at their beds and luxuries and then looked at their mummy again then back to Matt and sorta told him,

Sorry it looks like you are on your own buddy. We got it too good here. Poppy and Noodle live life just like Birdie, everything a woman desires are in their basket. Yes, they had always been in competition with Birdie's dressage lifestyle and it was always fun to watch at a dance who tried to outdo who outta the trio.

Matt thought right then my fellow drivers, they shall stand and side with me as they have been treated the same.

Yes, they stood their ground but now were homeless with no

baskets of their own. They travelled down to that watering hole that could tell many a tale and through the door, they burst. The chit-chat started and the news got out and back to Samantha who got thinking and then called about on that famous radio that many barks were sent out on.

She turned to the doggies' sweethearts and said, fancy a drink and to tell all those daddies we still love them and not to be so batty.

The other Mark, one of the long-term members of the taxi rank, looked on and watched with a chilled-out vibe and thought, you know what, my single life with Bo the boxer, that's his side hand who just loved to take a stroll whenever and do as they pleased, let's stick to it and not complicate things. The reason he was thinking this was Mark had been seeing a Gal for a while now and the other day she moved Bo's bed over a little from the fireside and she just lifted one eye and dropped her kissing lips and snout down a little with a sigh. But then she moved Mark's chair over to the right from his basket and fireside and the both of them locked eyes at each other Mark's thoughts were identical to Bo's and both agreed in silence, she gotta go.

Back at the Manor, there was still a build-up of thoughts as the parting with the girls leaving was close and Harvey asked Margaret,

Shall I mention to the girls if they want to hear how those generations related to the ole smugglers and so on used to behave and take them down to the Swan Inn hotel? they can listen to the banter of tales. Samantha and the rest of the wives will be there so what do you think?

Why not?

So, Harvey turned to Aseena and mentioned it and don't forget she knew the history of the domain and asked Stella,

You know what you witnessed earlier down at the Swan? Do

you want to pop down and see how the gathering of the lot has gone on and see if it's solved?

Stella did feel in her thoughts, I just wonder what it will be like when the wives and sweethearts walk into that inn? Where will their thoughts be? Will there be any lee-way etc, etc? Could there be an answer to solve it all?

Lucy was driving that way home so she told Harvey and the rest to gather whatever and she would drop them off. Margaret looking over her glasses, wondered once again what would they come back with this time in thoughts? Lucy looked at her with a nod and a bye with her load on board and to say we'll listen to the facts in the morning of what was to be said.

Down they drove and coming off the Tor Hill you could look right out and it was clear to see all the coastal area of France and the current of the Channel was travelling low to the North and you could see it splashing and tiggling the Goodwin Sands for gossip. Stella's interest in history could not help but assist in talking about the devilment of both the Channel and the Sands and the dammed in life they created together, like a pair of lovers you often read about and the doomed lives that they chose, or one of the classic movies such as Bonny and Clyde. But this pair were active and still carried on day-to-day enticing any boat or whatever they could to visit the shore with the wind as their call.

As they arrived at The Swan, there were a few drivers outside chatting and letting off a little steam and I wondered what it was about? Matt was outside when they got out of the car and straight away, he noticed Lucy who was old school.

Hello, my love came the welcome, with a kiss on the cheek. Fancy a drink for ole time sake?

She thought, why not. And then she walked in with the youngsters both left to right into the old wet house where her father of all mutts gallivanted. Memories of seeing him perched up against the bar - he had only one ear as the other was chewed off by Lofty the lurcher in a brawl over Lusha the greyhound in a rant over which one did she love? Lucy's mummy left her father in the early days as she was the leader of the Cherry Pickers pack and he was just a wild dog of the sea. It was a wild romance but doomed. You know who the other leader of the Cherry pack is or was don't you?

Yes, Lilly, that is Daisy's mummy. Like many breeds around they just lived for the day and the next generation looked on. Today was a good lesson to learn from, as the different generations and many of this clan, pack or whatever you want to call them, were related. So, Bob's your uncle after thoughts of your own by what you see in today's behaviour and sight.

Aseena! came a call. It was Noodle, Samantha's young one who knew Aseena from the play kennel they were at when they were puppies. What brings you here?

She did not want to impose by saying she wanted to let her guests and friends witness the habits of some of the savages of the town's behaviour in life, so she quickly answered,

My friend here has a great interest in old property so I'm showing her some listed ones.

Stella copped this on as Lucy did as they were introduced. Just then more mummies, wives and sweethearts came through the doors from all angles and the bar staff were looking on like: what the hell's going on here?

The grooming and bearhugs were all about when Lucy once again had time to explain to Gertrude, the German Shepard crossed landlady the misunderstanding with the male side of this pack's problem and how they became homeless for a few hours. Just then the one and only Samantha walked in and straight away gave a smile to Matt and said,

You big softy we at the house will always love you, and she embraced him like a dog being reunited after thinking he or she was lost forever, never to see their loved ones again. So, you can guess the rest. The barking to the juke box started as the water of sin flowed about like a flood out of a reservoir with all its might.

Lucy gave a quick glance at Stella and told Aseena,

Look, I'm just taking Stella over to where I always drink and admire just to see her response as to how she feels about its structure okay. We won't be long so if anyone asks where we are, which I doubt as what we are witnessing now with the mode and make-up mood going on, it was a sight for sore eyes. Stella, come with me as you don't have much time left here in Deal so I'd like to show you a little nook I use often that you will admire.

A little confused with the rush of everything she just followed and out of the door they strolled, down some side street and just like 40B underneath an ole building, they took some steps down into what seemed to be a cellar of secrets. A nod from here and there from guests and then at the counter a nod came from Chowlie, a sleek Afghan hound welcomed the pair and said,

Your usual, Lucy?

Yes, please and make that two as I'd like our friend here to try our tastes of Deal.

A wonderful greeting and then a well-spoken English Bull terrier introduced himself,

Blachfords the name, me love.

He looked like something straight out of Oliver Twist and his name, whatever next? You wonder how he learnt to speak so proper? With one large black patch over his left eye, born that way you would think his lingo would be pure Cockney. But no, a gentleman if there ever was one and a wonderful manner to witness and see.

They introduced their chat of everyday life and when

Governor said he was involved in Medical and a Physiotherapist in practice,

What bones? was Stella's humour as she burst out in a fit of laughter. Sorry you must forgive me.

No, no please it is nice to meet a gal with humour.

Just then the phone went off and he answered with,

Hello, this is Blachford Clark.

After the call he hung up and Stella had to say your surname's Clark? You are not related to Sophie Clark, are you?

Yes, I am, she is my mother. Why is that may I ask?

That is a woman who will be in my heart until I die. You see we had a major show in London and it was the big one for me, my first as a manager in fact. Well, the stage collapsed with sheer chaos all around us. Out of the audience came three doctors and one was your mother who just shook her shawl off and got stuck in and saved so many models' careers by cracking this and that, and she did it with such ease and gentleness. We were under so much stress we would not have coped in any way if it was not for your mother's skills and heart. I will never forget her for the rest of my life.

They chatted on with such ease of each other and then Lucy said,

We'd better make it back, Stella, as they will be wondering what's going on and where we are.

They explained the status and knew it was best to bypass Blachford's offer to walk them back up. With where they were heading to and Blachford's accent and so on, you would not know what the response would be.

Please, Stella, before you leave on Thursday can we meet for a coffee tomorrow? Please even if it's to chat a little bit more about what happened on that day you just mentioned about my mother.

Walking back and chatting away,

Well, that was a little strange, wasn't it? How in anyone's name could have that been you mentioning to leave for a little while and how it ended up in a conversation like that?

You see, Lucy, Aseena and Adele's friendship and understanding in life helped me so much to realise what I was becoming and what road I was taking, little important things like the bond between them all, Tilly and Poppy etc, etc all sharing their hearts. Like, look for instance what goes on back at the Manor every minute by the way. An exception that they all share can only come naturally and it is wonderful to witness. One can't say where the anchor is. I'd have to say, Margaret. But whatever it is, I'm honoured for this to be brought into my life and I owe you all.

Lucy stayed silent as they reached it back to The Swan and as they came through the door, a lot of singing was going on from hefty drivers and by this time other shapes and sizes of many a mutt heard the boys were up in paws at The Swan so they popped by and that was that. The words of a renowned song rang happiness all around as it was blasting out. It went: in Deal's fair city where the doggies and gals are so pretty, I first set my eyes on the sweet Aseena and Poppy and Adele, for they wheeled their Spratt barrel through the streets short and narrow singing Spratters and tatters and live your life like you are from hell.

Just the laughter of it all broke out as the girls joined in with the volume of all the make-up time that had been shared over one little tiff and barking your heart and thoughts out did one good. Nanny always said do not keep problems inside, it's too dangerous having it trapped and it will build up like a volcano that is gonna explode one day. The singing and so 'well it just rolled on like many good times of the past and this was a good way to end the trip to Deal, because in a short while the girls would head back out into that world of fashion.

Stella stared at Aseena and Adele in paws with a hefty driver beside them who's friends with her daddy, they raised their glasses and barked to the top tone they could and just let everything out as high as they could. The smiles came from every angle as the landlady racked what had to be Rum for the honour of their ancestors of the waters that all their lives were involved within. Whether a fisherman's doggie, a partner or smuggler's guard dog, they sang to their memories galore and reached the point of just sheer joy of all making up with their sweethearts. Many a thought came at bay in the end but the main thought was how in the name of anyone are we all going to get home when all the drivers of the town were in this drunken cockle shell?

Yes, they reached it back to the Manor with the help of a late driver's delivery. A package business van at the train station. The Swan was next to the station and he was picking up a load of boxes from the London express for a couple who had just bought a house there on the Front and he would be storing it for a little while until they settled in.

I think it will be a while as they are having so much done to the house, you know the old fishing bait house? They have gutted it, Dylan.

By the way Tilly and Dylan heard the banter from mummy B what was a going on and could not resist the crack and came over to join it, Tillys mummy had taken the reigns of the herd as she now called the pups' Anyway, Dylan's friend, Luke, was passing by and saw us in the car park and stopped for a chat. He then explained,

If you don't mind waiting a little while whilst they load my van up, I'll give you a lift home.

He was telling Dylan about the old fishing bait house opposite the Royal Hotel. It's a three to four storey house and by Christ to have it gutted, wow what would that cost? Anyway, what has brought you around the Swan Hotel at this time of night?

Yes, yes, the ale flowed into the early hours with the craic still going and Dylan explained what had happened earlier and what the gathering was all about.

It was one of those, was it? That was Luke's question knowing the type of gallivanting that happens at events that were not planned, like what goes on you certainly don't want the news to get back to your mother!

In the state they were all in and trying to climb about in and above the cargo in Luke's van they could only laugh out loud and thought when they reached the Manor, to tell Luke to stop at the gates and they would sneak in past the eyes of Margaret. But let's be honest and think how they could pull one past such a woman? Sneaking down the driveway and giggling, they slipped in and up the stairs. They tried to keep quiet as they crept.

Margaret's abode don't forget was right next to the driveway and it was said even the ants took their boots off when trying to pass her domain without being noticed. It was such fun trying to keep quiet and to get to their rooms, that the more they tried to hush, the more noise they made. So really the innocent ones were the ones to be entertained and knowing it was close to the parting, it could only be understood of their behaviour.

Yes, yes, the morning arrived and the feeling of essence was all about in the kitchen and around the table, the odd glary stare at each other and a hard task not to burst out laughing when you got eye contact and then looked at the lady of the house's movements around the room. With her back against the youngsters, she said,

You find something funny this morning? The words coming from herself as she slowly turned around.

Yes, yes, we are a happy bunch this morning aren't we. We need to keep the humour up as I've your chores today as we are desperate for assistance and short of staff. Aseena, Adele and Stella, if you would you can give Harvey a hand to clean out the stables and hen house which I can't see being a bother?

Before another word was said, Margaret had the answer as they thought they would get out of the chores as to not having the right clothing.

Don't worry about ruining your fancy wear, we have the ole clothing overalls for you all to get changed into, so after you've all finished your breakfast, just follow Aseena to the loft as she knows where to get changed.

Yes, yes silence was about and they reached up and placed their breakfast bowls in the sink and tailgated it out.

She was joking, wasn't she? asked Stella.

No, she's not and there's no way out either so let's just get stuck in.

Oh, how much did they take to the feeling of the stables? A little delicate with a hangover, but rewarding. The birds helped as they sang a tune or so whilst the horses chatted away with the harmony.

Stella, by the way Blatchford called me this morning. It looks like you left an impression last night?

Harvey looked on listening and, in a way, felt relief as he had eyes for Adele and them being together on the tour, Stella and Adele, that is, could anything be awkward if he was to ask Adele could they keep in touch.

Blatchford asked me could I get you to call him before you leave, he wants you to meet his mum. What is that all about?

Oh, it was an amazing thing to find out that Blatchford's mummy was the heroine of an accident that I witnessed and she saved so many lives and careers that day and after all that time,

I get introduced to a charming gent who ends up being this lady's son. In this town, I just find it stout.

Glances were looking a little nosy as of this date, shall we say, but it changed when Noodle, Samantha's daughter came to call for Pixie as the two were talking yesterday about another mystery of the town down into St Georges Passage and how castaways became about. You see Ralph, that's Susie's son, was best friends with Noodle and he was telling Pixie about the beauty of his mummy's hats, caps and clothes that want to make you dance and all the other items in the shop and how it was created. Pixie you see, adored hats of all types and all that was going on yesterday. In chat, Ralph mentioned the saga of an Ancestor Historian searcher he hired to do a search of his mum's family for a present for her birthday and just a reminder of how much he loved her and to say thank you for all that she had done for him. Well, when the searcher finished and sat them down, this is what he came up with to show us would you believe?

Well now I have you both sat down and what I'm about to tell you may come as a shock to your ears, okay? The two looked at each other intrigued and ready to listen. The gent started to open this rolled-up script and began.

Well, your Great-great-great-great-greatest Granma Sushilleshar was about to be burnt at the stake as she was accused of being a witch for no good reason. But alas a sea witch she was born. Well, she managed to free herself from the pole and fled down through the village with all the tribes chasing her shouting and ranting she must burn. She managed to jump off the cliff face into the dark, deep Channel and somehow banged her head but managed to climb aboard an old canoe used by the Pearl searchers in the harbour where she used to play.

Anyhow, she passed out and when she woke, she seemed to remember being dragged over strange, rounded stones that we call shingles now. She remembers sorta savage-looking people saying can we eat her? No, no not yet?

Then she passed out and woke to find herself in a cave with all sounds around her of things being moved about? Day by day, she got her strength back and built the cave into what is now, 7 Saint George's Passage. She gathered things around her that the tide brought in and made hats of all shapes and sizes and with a smile, she gave them to the strange-looking savage people and dogs and so on about her. A wet, dismal in-hole from the Channel was the abode that became her home and what became the Bibbity-bobbity Hats House of Happiness for everyone with the intention of carrying on smiling with joy for every day's journeys and each generation they added more joy to their design of wearing a hat or cap on arriving or when one had the sadness of leaving.

Noodle had to say something to Ralph that concerned him.

You see she was ear smuggling as her mother, you know her mummy? Samantha the cab owner lady? Anyway, she was talking about what two concerned drivers had witnessed the other early morning. Well Mark once again was driving home after a long night's shift and giving Bob a lift as he had a puncture, when a small group of about 8-10 women, some faces he knew as of his time in this town. Well on the base of Sandown ruins there they were dressed in strange kinda outfits with these strange kinda wands with strings like a cat's whip or whatever. They pulled over to the side trying not to be noticed and a shocked Gavin said, Mark look, I would recognise that fair mane from anywhere, that is Steve's wife Polly. You know him, he makes all the magic, beautiful red shoes on the High Street, Anyway, Polly's paws were up and over and chanting all these strange sorta tunes, spells you could even.

Next to her was Sophie, you know the bone maker? Susie, that's your mum by the way, was in the middle jumping about shouting out messages to the wilds. Dewi O'Dooley from Beautiful Homes, that's the guy who builds and renovates luxury kennels for the yuppie pedigrees. Anyway, his mummy, Sonya's her name, was jumping around like a Skippie doo and Nicki? You know she's with Bright Properties on Victoria Street, she was in double paws with Tanya, you know her from Rooks butchers on the High Street, but I never thought I'd witness the day that they would be jumping about like a flea up a mutt's butt. I know there is talk that for many years she was from the Tribal breed out of the Black Horse. You know the pub that was on the High Street as well and what went on there was to say the least … Her grandad's the one who had it out with Frank the Knash on whose ancestors ran the main tunnels out of the Prince of Wales boatyard in its day.

Then the shock; who do ya think was in front of this group with a wand howling like a banshee? None other than Steve Comfort the director of the Bone House, that's the physiotherapy practice on Clanwilliam Road, you see the Road Clan. That word, what it means in the Celtic l, and all this type of behaviour going on with them. Yes, oh one more thing, the other fair maid with them, that was sweet Sammy the receptionist from that practice. Well, she was sweet you know? A few others we couldn't put a name to. Oh yes look, that's Lee's wife Haley from the Carpet Shop on the High Street as well. I bet she is the one who makes the magic flying carpets Lee sells and they do fly honestly! Anyway, it's the wands we were worried about. It looked like they were made outta fish bones, rats' skulls and skin.

Yes, Bob's memory came back to him. Mark, now I remember who the other two were. That's the pair of cousins, Stacy Shar La La, Bracie from the 123 High Street Studio. You know, Bramble, the wire terrier? Stacy's his mummy and her cousin from Margate, Lisa La Loo La. Stacy has that collectors' shop, you know where over the centuries her tribe collected a vast amount of all the herbs and ingredients for many of her antidotes and remedies, they say that no other practice could cure. Why? Well, they say it's the ingredients of the recipes. They were collected from all over the world you know and oh just to feel and wonder of the many a item you would find in that cave of hers are amazing.

They say she, that's Stacy, has the ingredients of the contents to the recipe that goes with the treated bone but who knows? Brambles were barking out quietly one night over some fine Cognac in The Ship Inn, to Stacy's sweetheart William about his aunt. Yes, Lisa La Loo La. Well, when she comes to visit shall we say with her comes those secured-iced up boxes with 'handle with care' written all over them. Well, they always go straight through into the secret lock room inside the shop plus you know there is a special ingredient needed for the main antidote?

Well, for a few hours Mummy and Aunt Lisa disappear and the strangest aromas travel from underneath the floorboards and all the cracks and crannies. One day I just managed to peep in there whilst coming down the staircase and all I could see were these real old pots and pans and bottles; and out of the pots, I thought I could see legs and arms, toes and noses. But I think I may have been in a dream or so?

William looked at Bramble sideways and said, Wanna another top up?

Yes, I will have one for the road, Wills.

Since that chat, William never once stepped outta line you know? That is my honest opinion. And yes, I understand now more why these recipes are kept hush-hush and how they are locked up until moved in their black boxes. Back at the shop there is another trap door under her staircase that enters her cellar and leads straight under the other buildings and one tunnel to Woods the butchers and into the arms of Tanya and Ben the bill; and the other tunnel to the south goes to the Bone

House but I don't know about that.

William spoke then to say, maybe if I keep quiet there is no need to contact next of kin?

Back to the cab drivers; they thought something more on their level of this behaviour they had witnessed. Mind you they could have been drunk and having a bit of a hen night finish off, but they could not help but feel was this witchcraft. Anyway, let's keep this quiet okay, as mum will kick my ass for eaves dropping and telling, I think after witnessing what they were chanting to the weather gods and good luck for their businesses and loved ones.

After can doodling all over the place they just bowed down on their paws and kissed the feet of that wizard and then the ruins and embraced each other and skipidee-dooed out of there. Well, we have feelings that Susie is the leader of the female breed of this Tribal movement. And Tanya, she being in front of this strange kinda behaviour can make sense as don't forget her tribe of centuries goes way back, they often saw them clambering and chanting with the devil's brew outta that cave of theirs, the Black Horse.

Mark was silent for a while, then they just looked at each other and let out a big fit of laughter that could be heard a mile away. They did mention one thing, I've seen Samantha with a few of those wrenches in the past, I wonder if she's got something going on with them? This concerned Noodles and why shouldn't it, as she loves her mummy. It could only happen around here my friend and we had to witness it!

Dewi's friends with my son as they did S.T together at the cadet station. S.T, that's Sniff Training, by the way. Do you think I should say anything to him concerning this?

Na' don't bother as it is not doing any harm is it?

I hope it isn't as I'm wondering now, did they see us and put a bloody curse down on top of us? Plus, what if he thinks like me that mum's losing the plot and calls the specials in? You know the ones with those long white sleeved jackets that they tie up behind your back and then leave you in a cold old kennel without a care or a bone to your name. Let's just keep it low and see what happens and maybe if it gets outta paw we will talk to the priest, you know Mike the parish prayer? You know what he went through and why he retired? Well, the one thing you cannot control if it is meant to be in this world is falling in love and he did and do you know who he fell for? Sandra the nun.

After this beautiful happening occurred, they both went with their own thoughts and set up their own way of praying for the future and that was for nothing to stop the reason to fall in love. They were given blessings from many cultures and faiths; they say even the Pope himself gave his blessings when he heard of their wonderful creation and that is a little heaven to visit if you feel you are falling in love. The place to visit is the Kissy Castle in Walmer. After visiting there you will know if you are in love or not?

Anyway, back to this cult that is about us, we can discuss this with Mike as you see he knows all about these things as to being from the mountains of South America which has these types of cults and behaviour in their ways. You know he may be able to do one of those exorcist things or sing a voodoo chant to get rid of this cult with outgoing tones.

Whilst we are around that part of the town, I'll explain to you another fact of the past, and nowadays ways. Just up the road is Water Street and that is where the water pump tower stood and it was crucial to what was going on there. Plus, something that was not supposed to be happening by law but it was. Just two doors away from Neil's bicycle shop, number 190, the Lion House. No, it was not a pub but Eddie's hardware store run by Eddie the Light House and yes, he was known for his smuggling of everything you can imagine but most of all the finest rum you could find. The amazing set-up was on Middle

Street because there was the Shining Star pub that later became the Greyhound pub. Ya, it shut down in 1920.

Anyway, from the west to east, they burrowed tunnels that led from the waterfront into the Shining Star, then down underneath where there were the horse stables, then yonder into a lean-to at the back of the hardware store that kept Eddie the Lighthouse smiling from ear to ear. Don't forget whose store is two doors up on the street and had a bit of a name from his fatherhood's breed for a bit of movement of items the government was interested in, Neil's Cycle Shop Mm? And underneath in the cellar and the wooden panels in the bedrooms, where did these doors lead to? We shall say no more.

So, you see, Pixie, if your thoughts go dingo into thinking what was going on between these ole baggabonds, just put two and two together okay and let your mind do the rest. If any questions stroll astray within your thoughts, just jot them down and we will talk to who we feel we will get an answer from and it will keep your imagination walking with more and more wonders of what was going on and see if we can solve some of these unsolved cases before you leave and maybe we will get a reward?

Pixie just started to think and replied,

If we got stuck into this, as there was so much going on, I feel we would be here for many, many years would you say? But wouldn't it be so intriguing to try and solve so many a banters or facts and get a reward for it? I have to think of this profession of Noodle's and maybe we can set up together and become solvers in historical cases of smuggling and muggling quests?

The one concerned thing I have on my mind is that geezer, the wizard with them, Stevie boy Comfort. Well, my grandma used to say in the ole days of that practice, you know in the wild days of savagery around here, his ancestors used to sell real special treats. For instance, owners and successful businesses would purchase as a reward to their staff for their loyalty, like the staff from the Tattooist would purchase them? Because you know what they were? Bones, they say, human bones that only once in a lifetime you had the chance to chew on. Well in the town's banters you still hear how gorgeous they were, whatever they marinated them in; once tasted that was that, you were hooked. You know whose family had a big part in that don't you? Ben the Bill, the guy from the Rook butchers on the High Street.

What, where Tanya is?

Yep, that place. I tend to let my thoughts wander sometimes and it do in some cases like Ben the Bill's history. Do you wanna hear his background?

Yes, yes please tell me.

Well, way back when he was a pup, only 12, he was getting outta hand with mixing with the wrong breeds you know. Well, he was playing about in the shingles under the Pier when snap, Greg the croc was out prying and he got hold of the crab line Ben was playing with off the pier and started hauling him in for breakfast when the ravens saw the boy in despair and flew down and picked up the biggest shingles they could carry and flew up an dropped them down on top of Greg's head and he let the lad go.

The other ravens picked the boy up with all their might and carried him to their cousin's domain, Rooks the butchers and he's been their ever since. They raised him like their own chick and he earned his keep in every manner. His family you know was another tribe from more inland who used to take loads of you know what, tobacco and all from the smugglers to London, carriers they called them.

Anyway, one from his tribe many years ago was the carrier from Steve the Comfort's practice on Clanwilliam Road. One of their tunnels led straight underneath Rooks and if you look carefully there's still a trapdoor in the corner. Well, the most special treat of all given to loyal doggies and so on that belonged to the town was carried through that tunnel to whatever location and traded. Do you know what that treat was and maybe still is? A good ole human bone. Yep, and it is said the art of the flavour between the Comfort physiotherapy and Rooks, plus the 123 Studio is still in practice and the only order that can be taken has to come from upstate. You know like the 100th birthday card from the Queen? It can only be prepped by Ben as that is the curse not to be broken. They say if the price is right, you may get one of these never-forgotten treats but I don't know about that; is this just banter?

Pixie had to ask one question and that was,

How do all the other staff feel about this chit- chat or fact being about them? You know under the same roof as they say?

Oh, they don't mind because to tell you the truth they are hoping the trust of learning and knowing and historical art may be passed on to them is right under their own snouts and they may be the one to be blessed with it, maybe under the Christmas tree given to them from Santa?

Pixie just let her imagination flow and thought of her family back in the ole USA, what would they have to say if they got a telegram from me saying well, I've changed now from the carrier of modelling to crime and ghost hunting? Wow they would certainly send out a search party to see what in God's name was going on? But how is one supposed to feel with so many stories of this exciting tell-tale town of Deal.

Just then they were walking down the pathway of Middle Street and Aseena with Stella came off one of the side streets after visiting the Pussy Cat House to drop off some mice they caught and off the chit-chat started and Pixie felt she'd better hold onto her thoughts of the partnership with Noodles and come to reality of what she had recently learnt about local history that once again just made your thoughts wander.

Whatever or whoever you are, you can't help feeling your imagination travelling to places in your thoughts after listening to so many stories in such a short time from one town, can you? I can only say that one can only lie in bed with the thought of what, why or where did that happen? And your dreams would just slowly set sail into yonder.

The days passed and when it reached the eve of the girls' leaving, they gave visits and had them as well to those who wanted to share the great times they had and new friends they had been introduced to and what a wonderful experience it had been. But ahead of them was Florida. This contract in itself was one great honour to be given, as there was so much competition out there and we were the ones who got asked. What can one say?

Stella took to personal chats with Margaret when she had the time to talk. Mind you, there could be 1,000 guests about and Margaret would still manage to answer you back. I think it was the childish ploy in Stella that had come out since meeting her new grandma? Who knows, but it had done wonders for her feelings to be relied on and to bark about. The boys were getting the feel of the girls leaving as well and what would be the thoughts in their hearts when they were gone? Not seeing them around the estate would be a little strange in itself to everyone but the joy of thinking about when they would return made the smiles lift up.

Llewellyn was just coming out of the side stables as he had really fitted in with the surroundings and Aseena was there collecting the eggs from the ducks and chickens like she did as a pup. Basket in the mouth and knowing all the secret spots where the birds would lay to try and hide their eggs, these memories don't leave one's thoughts and it was cute to watch.

Mind if I join you?

No, no, please do. Go in there and check behind the water trough.

A little telling off from a few hens and some pecks and Llewellyn showed his snout with a few eggs inside. He placed them in the basket and Aseena said quickly, I told you so.

The pair just started to walk the buildings with yes, arguments coming from the ducks this time around the left side of the pond but they got no pecks.

Llewellyn spoke openly, I shall miss you not being around, Aseena.

Yes, he was shy saying so but glad that he told her.

Yes, and I shall miss you and not being about but it is not like I'm leaving forever, is it?

I just want to let you know, Aseena, I'll be here when you return don't you worry.

Margaret was looking out of the kitchen window with yes, you guessed it Stella assisting her with the chores.

They look well together, don't they?

Yes, they do. This reply came from behind them as Grandad just walked in. I promise you both this from the bottom of my heart, I will make sure that nothing goes wrong out there in this wild world; I will make sure in the best way I can that all is well in our journeys of life so we can all return to the essence of this little palace of joy and to all that we have shared within this flurry.

Back in the town, Evie made a call to Dan, her brother Joaquin, to let him know that Martin, their uncle would be down in the morning and wanted him here to meet someone. This was interesting to say the least as don't forget Evie's interest in what she called gossip was top of the list for her. So, as they were chatting away, she thought well what could this be about? She had a feeling as she had been listening last time to the chit-chat of course about the Pedigree Chum hit and after witnessing what Joaquin saw last time, he knew a good bit of what was going on.

How have you been down in that ole bagga bond town of yours, my dear sis?

That's Dan's humour of course,

All's fine, came the reply, and yourself?

They had a little natter and then kisses to say I'll see you later, love you. It was only natural Dan was thinking, who is this that Uncle Martin wants me to meet? He had a feeling what it could be about and, in a way, he was a little excited for the morning to arrive.

Do you want to come along, Harry? You can see If we are going into the Sherlock Holmes saga again.

I would not miss it for the world, Dan.

They made it down that evening just in case there were any complications with traffic and it was always nice to see Mummy Anna, sitting around that evening.

It must be serious this matter of yours, said Anna, for Martin to get all raised up like he is and I know him better than anyone, shall we say?

The morning arrived and Evie was all about having her family around again making her feel full of joy. Uncle Martin arrived with this youngster beside him.

Do you guys want the front room to chat or the loft lobby? This is the room that was made out of the attic into a private space for privacy to commence. It was a great call as it has served its purpose time and time again. Making their way up to the loft as that was their choice, Evie asked do you want me to bring anything up?

Yes, if you would, just a good pot of coffee please.

Joaquin, this is Josh, Josh the Jackal Wheeler as I call him.

A feisty, young, up-straight officer with a look that I'm here and mean business; that was the impression he gave of himself. Anyway, they had a great vibe about him so it did not take long before they all felt comfortable in each other's company.

Anna and Evie brought up assets to enjoy and tried to hang about until they got Uncle Martin's friendly but stern stare, can you please leave, before Evie could bark anything out, they made it downstairs with both, mainly Evie, frustrated, to say the least, that she could not stay. And anyone who knows her would know she was so used to having it all wrapped up and today being in her own domain, she could not have it her own way.

Just before the door shut, she gave a glance back that made Martin and Dan want to laugh but they held it well.

Right, Martin stood up and put his briefcase down, opened it and passed out paperwork to the others around him. Since the sighting the last time you were down concerning the judge, Sir Alan Carey and the company he tends to keep, like Frank the Knash and so on, it would not leave my mind and so I made arrangements with the S.H branch, the Sherlock Holmes branch that is to bring to mind that we may be able to reopen a major case and I will come out of retirement to assist in solving this historical crime.

After reading the paperwork passed out, they were so impressed with the evidence given them, it had to be asked, where did this info come from?

Well, I was given an open 3-month investigation case to prove that it was those culprits all the time and prove justice will be returned and the shame that Sir Alan brought to the law will be uplifted and we will be the ones to bring this matter to a close.

After a little while and after serious thoughts calmed down, Dan asked Josh,

Where did you get that handle from, the jackal?

Well, since I was a pup, if anything was given to me to find out I'd work on it so hard they said I was like a pack of Jackals all in one; not wolves hunting a prey but a pack of jackals and from those days the handle stayed on me. Back at the station, they would say oh let the jackal sniff it out, etc, etc if there was a problem, he will solve it. Well, I was often reading up on cases and to be honest when I read all about the Great Pedigree Chum train robbery and what happened within the case and verdicts, how can one not be obsessed with finding out what really happened? Most of all the cheek of each anniversary of the case, a can with the order number gets sent through to that detective living here. Let's be honest about how that must drive the mutt's mind crazy, it would with me but I must say I do laugh, how can you not?

What are their names?

Yes, the pair of detectives?

Why, one as your name, doesn't he? Mushy Martin and the other, Nosy Ned. I feel after all their work we just can't shut them out. We will give them the benefit of the doubt to bring their choice to join us from their nose?

Okay, I shall give them both a call and the rest is up to them and we cannot be more than fair on that matter, can we? I want to get onto this case ASAP don't you, Dan?

Yes, I do and the first thing is this; Josh you are local, aren't you? Who do we contact to get search warrants? With a situation at the same time, we can take suspects down for questioning. Look since that stormy night and what I witnessed, there is one thing I have to do, like Mushy Martin and Nosy Ned said before they pass away, is to bust this case. My peace of mind is to wipe that smirk off Hudson's snout as he knows something. He's bound to after serving 40 long years with that dodgy judge.

Lads, you are going back to London, aren't you? This is my

view so hear me out. When you get back to the ole smoke, if we can get warrants to take in Deanio O'Dalio with Staffieria Staffur and at this end, that foursome of bagga-bonds Paul, Jamie and most of all Hudson and of course, Frank the Knash and his mob, one of them will snap or crack? Jamie and Paul will be loyal but when we lock 'em up and tell them withholding vital evidence from a major case they will be looking at a 40-year stretch. Just think you will be slurping outta an ole pot for the rest of your life instead of a cosy cottage in Deal, by not telling us what you know, you will only begrudge.

Martin was listening to all this and could not believe how switched on they were with ideas, great ones to be honest. Just then Evie came about with a knock on the door and a quick entry. Still annoyed, she said,

Mum sent me to say dinner will be served in five minutes so make your way downstairs, or would you want me to serve it here on a silver tray?

She was trying to look at the paperwork on the desk but alas it was covered but she could see on the folder, Top Secret, which got her even more wound up. Yes, she really got it into her head that whatever was going on, she wanted to be a part of it too.

Thank you, Evie, we will be down in a moment to join you both.

As they were folding up, Martin said he would enquire about what was needed plus if so, he would get the London board to contact their Kent branch about warrants.

You will do no such thing, came the response from the Jackal. I'll take care of that.

And fair play to Joaquin, he gave a look to his uncle as if to say well, that is telling you, isn't it?

They made it downstairs and yes, the looks from the

feminine side of the family were not that pleasant but, in a way, it had to be laughed off and slowly the share of great food and company started to spread around the table and the girls' tempers slowly calmed down all seemed to be at bay.

Yes, the spread of good-hearted food and the joy of great company helped calm the mood, but then Anna and Evie were letting this meeting end and did not know what it was that had brought Martin out of his dwell.

Just like many questions that were not asked on cases that were never sorted, the pair would find a way to get the information that dwindled within them. Evie would work on her brother and Mummy would get stuck into her beloved baby brother. Yes, they would get the snail outta the shell.

When do you go back, Martin?

In the morning, Anna, as I've to get so much sorted out.

In a way it was a little wind-up using words like that but he knew he had to leave as now the answers were there in the light, he would have to put in for Joaquin to be registered to legally operate as an officer of the Law.

The morning arrived and the chit-chat was going on again as Josh popped in to say hello and he was in uniform and his coat was on a shine to make his status. Martin said to him straight away,

You know after all the paperwork is done you will be out of that rig up don't you?

Martin watched Josh look at Dan as they laughed at this question and he could see the bond and the beginning of a cracking team and then wondered would they crack this case together with contentment and all, paw in paw?

Back at the Manor things were being packed away ready for the departure on Thursday as that was the given date now. Aseena had a thought on her mind to make a call to Tilly, so she got on the bell.

Tilly, this is Aseena, how's the gang, meaning the litter?

Crazy but all well, came the reply.

Would you like to come over with the pups tomorrow? Margaret met your grandma this morning in the town whilst she was shopping as she had to pick up some odds and ends. Nanny Sky can come along and we can take the pups along the river and around the farmyard to look at other creatures on this planet.

Yes, they would love that. I'll call Nanny Sky and I wonder should we invite nanny Ryan, because with Poppy gone now, she may enjoy the company?

Yes, I'll do that, what with Bailey being the puppies' uncle and Poppy beside him on tour, she may get a reading of being able to get to know them?

Okay, I'll get straight on to it.

Putting the howler down, that is what the phones were called in their lingo, she got on to calling Nanny Ryan. She was going to ask Margaret to call but thought no, she would do it herself.

Yes, Nanny Ryan accepted the offer and the morning arrived again and all chaos was out there once the litter arrived at such an adventurous location as that of the Manor. They made straight for the gent standing at the Manor's entrance with a basket full of all the necessities to calm the storm. It was Crawford, not Grandad, as Margaret came out of the larder's side to empty a trough of leftovers, she had to look up and gave a smile as every day there seemed to be more amusement and joy about.

What a wonderful sight to see once again! Said Stella to Pixie. Could you live here, Pixie?

It is wonderful to witness and feel but as Aseena feels about here being her roots 'home' I feel the same about being born on the bayou. The sound of the river's current and the aroma of blackened chicken and so on. My grandma barking away and the sound of hounds in the far distance is just out of this world to me. I will never forget here and will return but the bayou is my home. Nanny Ryan seems very happy being about Tilly, you could feel it a mile away and I could see it helping her with a little pining going on for her beloved Poppy. I can see invites for those puppies up to the front house coming about. Bampie, I don't know as he does like his privacy but who knows?

Sally was about with her feelings as well as she was in this mode as feelings were high as it really was just a matter of hours before they departed. She looked over and Aseena caught what she was watching?

Why it's Harvey with Llewellyn in chit-chat over the land. Yes, the flutters were up in their paws again as it was just natural to them both. The two handsome hounds made it over to the ladies in waiting and started to bark away on their discussions on the matter of the estate, Showing off you could say. Pixie was over in chat and Harvey asked her,

From your neck of the woods, where you are from, Pixie, have you ever been to Miami as that is where you will be based isn't it?

Yes, it is we will be based in Miami itself. But no, I've never been there before and that makes it more interesting as to the adventure. The weather with the seasons changes so much with its history of storms, Harvey. Where I'm from just like your country Wales, Llewellyn, it is always raining. Mind you it is the same with other parts of the States. In Seattle the rain never stops. But the word Miami, Florida, it just says it all, doesn't it? It all happens there. It is those new designs they have come up with in the new coatings, I can't get out of my head; I just want to feel and express them. New coats to suit all seasons and styles of the whole dogs' world will be coming out of that show and we will be a part of it. Wow, what can one bark about that this is being offered to us on a plate?

All the feelings of sharing were around this personal gathering and I think it was to do with the girls being so close to leaving that the chat was emotional and personal. Whatever, it was nice to witness and be a part of.

These times were important for the heart and memories, because any negative feelings about these wonderful times would shoo them away. Just then Nanny Sky passed over Lilly, one of the puppies, to Nanny Ryan and into her paws she jumped. Yes, the tongue was out and kisses all about and I sensed this was a bond starting with one that would become her favourite. Out then came a call for the youngsters to learn an old game for the pups to stand on two legs and see who made the most hops?

It was a wonderful, social day and a nice thing once again for the elders to get to know each other as by now Dylan's mum was up as she got a call to join in when she had time, so all their stress at what had gone on could be barked out for a while.

Kinda reminds me of when we were young again, doesn't it?

Yes, it does, Grandad, came the reply from Nanny Sky.

The thoughts of their close ones on the tracks of their lives' journeys had been on their minds as well so this gave them time to unleash a little.

I'll be honest, once the girls hit the road to what Nanny Sky calls the new world, they would become all at ease. Sitting in the barn having a little break, Harvey was in his own thoughts whilst sitting listening to a pied wagtail telling a few banters about the girls the other night trying to con their way past Margaret coming home in the early hours, behind him, a bark came out lightly,

Gonna miss them, mate? It was Llewellyn speaking his Celtic

thoughts.

Yes, yes, I am and I'm not ashamed to say so.

I am as well, believe me I will but as I said before, we have only known them a matter of such a short time, haven't we? Even so, we will have a lot to take care of between these new projects in mind and the board giving us the go-ahead after viewing them. Don't forget that the meeting is tomorrow morning so make sure we are both switched on to that, okay?

The Manor just flowed on with the guests at play 'and the workers at their chores they each said their good afternoons and made it back to their own kennels of home to rest. These meetings were a wonderful beginning of something of a reunion to make sure communication was within and this would create a bond between them that would only bring pleasant times. Stella was certainly getting personal as she spoke I myself would really like to know what it is with Nanny Sky and Grampie? I'm glad there's no friction or whatever you call it? Whatever the feeling is, it's a wonderful flow of gentleness shall we say.

When you think of it, the two have been through so much in their lives haven't they? This was Margaret speaking. They both lost their loved ones very young, witnessed the world at war, and they both raised families; it just goes on, doesn't it? But I've never seen a negative choice in their outlook.

You and I, Margaret, have been about this before, haven't we? This was Harvey speaking and we have been asked in different eras by different generations what it is between them? They stood their ground, did what they had to do and maybe not see each other for months then bang! they bump into each other again and then Bob's your uncle, it starts all over again. Bitterness never had a chance or tried to enter their hearts as they knew it would be a losing battle even after their loss in life but I wonder now with things calming down would they give each other a little thought of setting up their own nook?

A little thing happened the other morning as Mark, you know one of the cab drivers who witnessed the seance the other day? Well, he was driving down along Beach Street down past the Sandown ruins and he noticed Mike from the Loving Parish? It looked kinda odd but he was there with a crate of bottles and so on and some herbs and he was just spreading them about and barking strange sorta garb and I'm sure it was to make those goolies shoo?

Well, you know what he was doing? A batch of locals asked him could he do something about a problem with our local gals, to make sure they were not cursed in any way? He seemed to be looking up to the sky then all about him then he'd say a few words again then smile about. It is better than many years ago when the wee lasses were put at the stake and set fire to.

A few days later at the Department of Scents where Dylan was at class, and Dylan was called to attention for a discussion with some head honchos/

Dylan, can we discuss an issue that has come to my attention? This was the main head of the department of the D-B squad 'please take a seat.

Looking a little confused and nervous Dylan sat down and looked at the officer and those with him then after shuffling some paperwork around, the captain started barking away,

After all the discussions between myself and the other departments, we want to make an offer to you and to think it over, okay? As we are based so close to Dover with access to London and France and so on, we would like you to work with both departments, the police and military and it would be you calling the shots with the small team we want to put together. This way, Dylan you will be based here as you know the town and ways so well. We have a small holding in sight for you and the team to build into what suits you and all your team to do your job and to get outstanding results. This way, Dylan, you will be able to in my eyes be able to get a great response, plus your young family? You will be about them.

Before the officer could finish, Dylan's thoughts jumped out.

Sir, I don't need to discuss this with anyone, my answer is yes! What more would I need to open up my career with such an opportunity as this? came the reply from Dylan's heart and honesty.

Being fired up most of the day, he could not wait to get home to express this news to his loved one. Well, the understanding came quickly to Tilly's heart and thoughts as she was nervous, wondering if Dylan would have to go overseas at first and like anyone's love for someone in service that thought of being sent to war was a frightening act in life.

The building they had in mind was none other than the old church along Middle Street where as a pup he and Tilly and the litter they played with used to hang out, as this was their quarters as they called it. Some said that it was supposed to be haunted as well. But who knows; was it yet another mother's tale that would frighten you with strife?

Over the oncoming weeks the team members were chosen and hand picked with excitement and then walking through the building was so opening for them as to where to put what? like desks, racks for coats and blackboards for notes. It just went on and to know all this was beginning now was a dream to this pack of only six. It was put together with thought, you could tell that just by seeing them all, a bond was growing of never-ending friendship and trust.

I don't see any tunnels, Dylan? This came from Johnny which brought out such laughter as everything that was built in this town was made for smuggling and that was that.

Maybe we want to start our own as you are a Jack Russel and used to digging out rabbits and badgers and so on, aren't you? But now if one could say the best sniffer in the bizzo to be honest is Johnny Jupiter and he's on our team here in Deal.

Yes, I'll get on with it just catching wild things for another while came the humorous reply.

The looks came about from the other breeds with joy as it was a great feeling when all your dreams come together and here it was on their doorstep.

Just then, Josh the Jackal stuck his snout in as he was passing by and saw the door open and decided to see what was what? And to find out what was going on inside was a joy to him as well as don't forget what was on the cards for him in his department, this could not be a better time in life and it was all coming true.

By the way, talking about Josh, he had a little tip-off as a friend of his mum who had known him since his puppy days and also Josh was close to her son Floyd as they were in behaviour school together. To be honest The Jackal looked after Floyd as he was bullied by locals and stayed friends ever since. This old mate's mummy known as toothless Tessa the Tell-tale, had news for him? Yes, Josh's mum as mums do when proud of their young ones, got talking and told Tessa her boy would now be based in Deal instead of London as Dylan offered him a position to be a part of the team and as you know what these towns are like for gossip, it did not take long for this news to get out. So, what Josh did was plan a social intro walk around the town and this way it didn't look straight clear he was heading to Tessa's. So just strolling along the town introducing himself and making his presence known and then slowly making it to Tessa's and of all locations where does Tessa live, but Alfred Square which is off Middle Street and crossing over to the east side that leads on to North Street, and who lives there, but you know who?

Walking along and passing the old Strawberry House where another legend lived which I will tell you about later. Then down to where the Ship Inn came in sight, as he strolled past, he took a peep in to see Goldie getting ready to open up for the day. Now then, when we mention banter, you wanna sit down and hear a few outta that hound! His kin even have a street named after the family's history of, you can guess what? What's his nickname? and one of the streets off Beach Street that marries up onto Middle Street, do we need to say any more?

Also, way back the same ole thing happened with the romance of those days. The pedigree of a beautiful Golden retriever who was his ancestor going back hundreds of years from the Vikings, fell for one of those feisty wired terriers out of the North end and what do you have? A certain pack of dogs that did no good shall we say. They were called Goldies and were ancestors of the notorious pirates, not smugglers; they say they mugged the smugglers shall we say anything more? and over the centuries they held their own, the raving wired coats of the terriers mixed with that blonde of the retrievers, oh they caused some heartbreak and romance with the boys and girls in generations past and present. Yes, the Gold Sack pack is what they named them.

Anyway, pop in one time and have a natter with him.

Josh then carried on strolling down the way when he reached to turn left into Alfred Square and into Tessa's domain. With a warm welcome she was standing on her kennel doorstep that in fact was a butcher,s in its day. Anyway, Josh looked about to see who had their snout out and watching with a question and that was, what's he or she doing there at Tessa's? Yes, there were a few tails just swaying with curiosity wanting to know what was up? Then he took a quick glance over to North Street and there was the house in mind they were planning to raid. It was only seconds away and if they planned a look out, what more would they want? His thoughts just looking at the other house were stuck like glue.

Hello, Mrs Harris, how have you been? Mum told me you wanted to have a word with me?

Yes, yes come inside my boy. You have grown since I last saw you.

Yes, it's all a part of growing up, you know. Where's Floyd?

Oh, he's gone for a swim in the Channel. Yes, the proud mummy talk came out. You know he's applying for the Life Paddle and Guard Team? He is just keeping himself up in shape, just like his daddy was, you know his father was a life guard?

Then just in time before hearing the whole nine yards, Floyd came in. He had a good shake down on the front but his mum got him a towel and this broke the saga story of hearing all about his dad from Mrs Harris.

Floyd just laughed and asked, how have you been?

Fine, I'm fine. I just left the ole church as it won't take long before the news gets out who will be taking it on. He explained about Dylan's team and Floyd came back with,

Wow, what can one say and what an adventure to be in amongst, what a dream?

Josh spoke back on the visit 'Mrs Harris I understand you want to speak to me? Mum mentioned it to me 'Yes 'yes take a seat'

Well, my boy, across the way, you know of the houses on the right side of North Street? You see I've seen some strange kinda behaviour coming out of that one cottage that Staffy owns. You know the one and the type of DFL she is and the neck of the woods she's from, shall I say anything more? Anyway, the two who she brought down this weekend, I am sure I recognise the two well-groomed hounds from before? I'm certain I've seen both of them in The Pointed Ears newspaper. You know that right-wing paper? I'm sure I've seen them on the front page. You know the posh one I read from the Smoke?

She had to get that in even though she was talking to a local hound.

Anyway, the others visiting there I've seen as well, with this she brought out her daily diary of all the times and dates and so on of everything that had moved around that pad.

What it is, Josh, I would not like for someone of that breed, you know, bringing back the shame that this town was in before. How and what exactly does she do for a living may I ask?

The way she barked this question out to find out more about this one dog, in general, was enough to frighten the biggest Rottweiler, but Josh kept his cool by answering,

She owns a shipping company, also a few restaurants in Manchester and the capital and also a lawyers' practice that takes major business clients on with their overseas trade and business and so she came across Deal through an invite and liked it so much she chose this town as a getaway kennel place. You often see her at the functions as a sponsor for run-down areas where Mutts are given a chance to step up with their ways and make something of their lives and also if you watch the sports channel, you will see her sitting with a pack of her greatest friends, you know? Including the royal corgis for instance when they attend the most famous dogs' race.

Oh really?

I admit Josh had to get this out as of his humour and Floyd tried not to laugh at his mum's Standard Poodle status. She muttered on a bit and then came about with other local news.

The other matter, Josh, is on your walk about would you have a word with that group of mixed breeds from you know where? As she showed a picture taken with the dogs all playing in the shingles and up came the tails and down came something else. And not picking it up time and time again, they tend to act in this manner from that area, lad.

Here it goes the ear-bashing chat of we have worked so hard for us to live in comfort and these common breeds from all types of areas come about and do this in our town. I just do not know what to think anymore. When you lot were pups, we taught you …

Just then Josh's radio collar went off.

Officer Wheeler, come in' Officer Wheeler come in. Sorry for this, he barked gently, I have to leave I've got a call in. Replying to the call, he also said that his mum sends her love and wishes and he would look into this behaviour for her straight away. He looked over at Floyd who was trying his best not to laugh but it was hard. With this Josh made it out of the door and thought he'd walk along the Front and strolled across Middle Street onto North Street and onto the Front. Looking back down the short narrow road, his thoughts came about that one house there that had seen hundreds of years of history pass by and would be the making of a whole future if a raid went ahead and which way it turned out would be one's fate, good or bad.

Josh was on the Front when this time it was his phone and it was Dan.

Hi, I thought I'd let you know I'm just leaving to go back home to sort things out and to make arrangements at my end, so I just want to say it has been a pleasure meeting you and what a way to be introduced to someone in this manner. I hope you can forgive my mum and my sister?

Of course, I can, came the reply. If anything, it was entertaining. As soon as I'm back I'll get set up with everything this end, okay. On my walk about I popped in to see Kev and Johnny from the Cyber Shed on Victoria Road. As all the friggin high tec limbo you know back at the station, they will sort that out and I've asked them what is the best way to keep you and I posted, one-on-one? John's coming over when I'm ready and settled in my office to explain to me all but at the moment, I just want everything to be kept hush-hush. Not a soul must know, okay? I feel I've to pop over to one of the detectives to explain what is what? But I'm going to sleep on it for a few days and then decide what would be best.

Talk about the Cyber Shop, back at the Snug and Hope coffee shop, they are the ones who asked the Cyber Shed to set up the connection for the girls, so when they are abroad, they can contact each other from all over the world. That is what my sister was talking about before she got vexed up. The girls leave on Thursday and with the whole group now all over the place, they will be using the set up so I'm going over to see it in operation in the morning as they are meeting tomorrow when Poppy will be beaming in to touch base. She can talk to the girls from the Manor, plus Bailey will see his brother's litter again as Dylan and Tilly will be taking them down whilst on their stroll along the Crest.

By the way, do you remember whilst talking to your uncle he mentioned Elmo Cosimo, that Italian Spinone who was a detective in Italy and over here? Well, your uncle said he had vital evidence at that time for the case as Frank and Deanio and that mob of theirs had their hang-out in Milan? The Kenneloo de'velloo Chateau. They would use this location as a getaway. But I don't know why, because it was in the media and press every day. Anyway, you will never believe it but I got introduced to him today as he is visiting his sister who lives in the large tall house by the Royal Hotel, anyway his sister Bella la Buxxumoo was on the Front sitting on one of the benches and spotted me. She barked me over and introduced me to him and me being in uniform, he mentioned about way back in his time he worked on the Great Pedigree Chum Train Robbery. He saw my eyes go up and he said a few things about that case and sure enough, out came the saga of it all and the parties that were held at the Kenneloo de'velloo. He said wait there a sec, as he raced across the road to his sister's house. Within seconds he was back as he had some old photos from those days, because he used to send to his sister pictures of all the famous snouts who used that domain, like what is that singer's name known to all for being involved with gangsters like Barky Baboney and all the rest. Yes, Frank sin Barko and Elvis da Pawris, they were both there in these main photos and who do you think is right in the middle of this mob? Yes-yes only the judge himself, Sir Alan Carey.

Oh my God, Joaquin, how is a mutt supposed to keep his head on sensible thoughts after seeing this?

Can I make a suggestion sir' what I suggest is this, I'd like to invite you to meet at our base, there could be one or two detective's who don't forget may have worked with you before and explain that we are gonna open up the case again, and put their dreams at ease and bring these culprits to justice once and for all. I think it is an amazing idea, that is if they agree to it? By the way, whilst growing up, I asked my dad why do they call Bella La Buxxumoo that name? He did not mention to me her assets then as he knew I'd slip up to Mum. But I do have one question, does she still wear those type of dresses that show off her best assets, you know?

Josh could not help but laugh at the question that came out and yes, was his answer to Dan. A buxom full madam if there was ever one and I do know now why your dad kept his tongue quiet on the answer to give you way back. If the wrong bark came out and it would be easy to do so, many mothers and wives would let fly so let your imagination and thoughts learn about life every day and let your own answer grow.

The morning arrived and Josh was just walking down through St Georges Church gardens as he was heading to The Snug and Hog, he watched the bond of mums and dads strolling with all shapes and sizes and laughing to themselves at their doggy's dream of catching one of those Grey Canadian Squirrels who kept their habit of tormenting the local pets to chase them and then climbing up the tree and poking their tongues out and calling the dogs all sorts of names whilst they barked their heads off with rave and madness telling them you come down here now and fight. Then the squirrel picks up a conker or an acorn and just throws it with a head-on hit just to add to the torment.

The doggies then got in conversation with each other and said,

When I catch that blighter, you know the one, I'll show him what is what.

The same thoughts each day would just wind them up even more but that was the little blighters' game and has been for as far back as anyone could think. Josh carried on with ease of delight whilst a gentle breeze played away and blew thoughts and sounds to his ears and that brought a lot of new and old feelings about the town's streets where shops of new and old gave out their aromas of offerings that would suit any scent.

Out through the east side gate and across the road he passed and then entered into the Café where there was a nice essence of the aroma of coffee and feelings as around there was a gathering of friends getting ready for the beam-in from Poppy. Dylan was there which helped Josh feel not outnumbered by all the blondes, brunettes sitting around. Dylan looked up and saw Josh and called him over,

Josh come and join us. You know Tilly, don't you?

Within seconds he had a very welcome warm warmer sitting on his lap, one of the litters making himself known and giving Josh a feel-at-home lick. How could you not smile with this feeling about you? Tilly was just going to say something of an embarrassment to one of her sons when Josh picked up the little fella with his front paws and lifted him high in the air and said,

Well, who is this then? She glanced at Dylan with a smile and just sat back down. My sister Isabella has six young ones, Tilly, so I'm used to this welcome alright.

Have you any of your own, Josh?

No, no I have not found my Cinderella yet.

Oh yes, the flutter of fleece came about as the young maids were checking out this handsome devil sitting in their presence when they heard his comment and they included, guess who? Evie, Dan's sister. The girlie eyes were checking each other out as to who would make the first bark into introducing themselves? And just then, the sound of music and so on came about and it was the screen lighting up with Poppy and the band about them as she was onstage being filmed live in action.

Hello, hello everyone at home, how are you all? As you can see, we are onstage getting everything ready for the gig later, because we have been asked to stay an extra week here at this festival on the North side of the island of Jersey and what a beautiful place! A spotter from the French coast was watching us at The Dogs Duet in a small town there and loved the way we mixed with the mandolin and so the next minute we were asked by him to play at his festival and that is where we are now. Just then Bailey showed himself and the pups all started barking up at the screen and everyone found this funny.

Hello, hello you all. Can you believe our tunes and barks have reached this level and height to listeners and we just can't believe the response and welcome we have had?

Aseena, hello, Keeley, I can see you, Poppy got all excited and barked out, when do you leave, girls?

Tomorrow, it's tomorrow we leave, Poppy.

Yep, we head out all the way to Miami. Do me a favour? See if one of those head honchos can slip a few tickets this way and I'll be on my way there to you if you like, A place like that I'd have no problem finding musicians to get our tunes rolling out to entertain you all. A big fit of laughter came about in the Café as you could feel and sense their bond all about what was going on in their lives. What a way to share everything that was happening to all involved in such a short time was just beyond anyone's thoughts and to assist in everyone's contentment was just full of passion.

The joy and thought of all that was going on in each individual's life was just amazing and as one was saying, it had all happened in such a short time from when they were playing chase on the Front. To now look at what was going on with such contentment of all different careers in the steps of their lives. Just then hairy Ben gave a big blast out on that sax of his and all about was the excitement of what was ahead of them onstage.

Guys, sorry this has to be a short chat as we have got the roadies on our butts and the head honcho, he's barking away at us. Aseena, Keeley touch base with me when you arrive in Miami and we can set up a date to roll all the beam-ins with John from Cyber.

A bark came out, Poppy, get that mike set up here in front of the drums. Gotta go! Was her call before all yaps broke out around them, Bye!

Back at the Café the smiles were all about and Aseena said,

You can tell she is really happy, can't you?

Dylan responded with this comment to Tilly, because don't forget he was worried about what would be between Bailey and herself being together like that all the time. Well once again only time and essence can answer those questions and put peoples' thoughts at ease with a sigh.

But to witness what we just viewed, answers any questions out there, doesn't it? I think it is deja vu that they are helping each other on these travels and not knowing how much they have needed each other to get by and once again an amazing journey in life. The finest of music, food, company and other countries to share all this with, well say no more. I only wish I could be there. The Café kept busy with the delight of chatting about Poppy's success in her choice and feelings to go with this tour and the next thing Becca stood up and barked out,

Everyone, please can I have your attention to let you know Aseena and Keeley and their special guest from the States, Pixie, will be leaving us on Thursday as well so can I have a round of applause for their company and sharing it with us since being back and if anyone does not know, the second weekend of every month we will be meeting here with the whole team beaming in from Miami and wherever Poppy and co are, to see where the road of life has taken us all through trouble and strife.

After the yaps and the wagging of happy tails and so on, the Café became empty apart from a few, the likes of Tilly and Becka. Dylan took the litter home with the assistance of Honey who was visiting for the day with Bobby her other half. Lulu looked across and said,

Well, I wonder what will happen to us all in life between as we stand here now and the next time, we touch base and bond together again? Will it be anything like the first introduction to these new steps in our lives? A little tension in each other's thoughts travelled about the room when Pixie spoke with her broad accent and said,

Well, I do hope I'll be one of the lucky ones to be chatting away about what you just said, my dear, as it's been a mighty fine time for me and I'll sure miss here and all about what I've learnt. But mostly the stories of the gools and so on. Even if I did not meet any of them head-on, they have sure been in my presence all the time.

With this, a spurt of laughter came about from the remaining friends as they made their way out of the door.

Walking out, Aseena said to the little group,

Who fancies a last stroll over to the Pier?

Ya, let's see if I can get a good look at that vagabond, Greg the Croc and I want to ask him one question; around my way, the swamps are full of his breed and so is he any relation to these beasts of the snarling waters of my homeland?

Yes, come on let's walk, came Becka's call and out they stepped with a glare of delight at the company they were in.

Some usual faces were on their business deliveries and nods of have a safe journey etc were about and then they walked straight into the path of Mike the Preacher on his early journey back from his last spread of special spells to rid anything nasty left from the so-called sea witches of Sandown.

Aseena, would you and your company have an hour spare so I can take you back to the temple and share your thoughts and cares with the local travel spirits as they want to share their thoughts of travel and protect you? A quick look about and, please?

Yes, we would love that! came the excited reply again.

The girls gathered into the estate car that was parked up and off they sped laughing to each other until they reached the house of Joy and Hope of Love and through the door they walked with the feeling of what it stood for, love. The joy of just being inside felt very safe to the girls and they had the strangest thoughts and feelings about them. Around them all the beautiful souls in their lives and their love and thoughts came about including new love. And I'll give you three guesses who was on Aseena's thoughts and heart? Could it be a tall handsome Welsh newcomer? Is Keeley's heart floating a little to a certain gent? And Evie's heart, could it be playing games about with a certain pack animal? All these flows and rushes came about whilst inside this ole building and may it stay that way.

Come on, I'd better get you back to the town as you must have so much more to take care of or say goodbye to certain souls. Come on, let's get on our way.

Stepping out once again a wonderful sense in the breeze about them filled their thoughts with joy until they got back down onto Beach Street and as Mike spoke, he wished them all well and told them to hold onto their dreams and thoughts and his thoughts would be with them all.

He didn't want to drop them off at the Manor as Crawford and some staff felt a little odd towards Mike. They often wondered if he was involved in witchcraft himself? You know why, don't you? The wonderful thoughts between himself and Sharon created what the girls just witnessed and that in the old days of their ways about were not really recognised. And if you were not at Mass on certain nights and you were elsewhere, did tongues start wagging or what? Oh yah, noses were pointing, tails were wagging, ears up and eyes staring at you from every doggie who had his leg cocked up on a lamp post or the side of a fishing boat angle you can just imagine it can't you? Not fair really as if you knew what was going on all about you, you would think twice before giving poor Mike a hard time whose thoughts were in the happy, glad vibes. Anyway, a good part of that generation still felt that if your thoughts are not bland, then they belong to the ghouls.

The evening arrived and they spoke to Margaret and Grandad to ask something different and that was to let Aseena and Keeley's friends stay the night as it would be a while before they saw each other when the morning arrived and it would be in the early hours that the car would come for them to depart. So, each one chose their favourite coat as autumn's nip was about and they got changed, wrapped up and you guessed it gathered around the large open fire to share their time and thoughts until yes, that famous rooster gave them that cry out in the morning to get your butts up and set you on your way.

There were nice humming tunes being played from a few of the picking birds, the chaffinches, pied wagtails, sparrows and a skylark came about to sing a few joyful songs and then some gentle lullabies to put their minds and thoughts at ease and that is exactly what happened. The darkness of the night set in and the tunes mellowed with the flickering flames' harmony and all around, including Margaret and Grandad fell into a beautiful trance of sleep and as Crawford popped up and put his neck out around the door, he took a peep about and smiled to himself and turned the low light off to put it at bay.

Nature let them all sleep until that big beaked bird got the pleasure to shout out, get up the lot of you! He made it clear that they all heard him as he climbed up onto the large flower pot then hopped up on the window sill and let out the biggest yell, get up! Margaret was in a little shock herself to find where she was. She looked around and a beautiful feeling flowed about her from what she could see, as heads started to roll and eyes open. Grandad's sort of shocked look joined in but he could only smile about it.

Right, how is everyone? The movements of bodies were taking shape and Margaret said, come on, let's head for the kitchen before anything and get our gnashers into action.

Well, when they arrived what a sight to meet? Crawford and the staff had everything spread out with a feast that would set an army into battle.

Oh, the flow from everyone to enhance this sight and share it on this beautiful morning as it would be the last time for a good while so they would treasure it in their thoughts. Their feelings were something no one really could explain but they were just magic. They feasted with flair and a few birds were in tune and their reward was to join in their choice and eat well with joy. All were fed and then all headed to their rooms to collect any magical items that were given to them, everything they had with them was packed away the day before. Then after all washed, tails and ears all polished up they headed for the big city without a rattle.

The gravel on the front of the Manor was making that famous gritting noise and Keeley and Aseena knew that sound well. Yes, it was the sound of the cars coming to pick them up. The gents, their bodyguards etc were in full style to open their smiles and feelings just by seeing the girls once again and having them about them. You see most of their clients were kinda bland business people or political figures, but within the girl's presence there was joy and adventure and they found it a pleasure to be about this even though their job was to keep them at bay and safe.

Hello, hello ladies, they even got a hug from Clancy which put Margaret and Grandad at ease, seeing this safety around them. They knew they were in good paws but it was still nice to have a reminder of certain things.

Over to the right of the driveway, Llewellyn and Harvey appeared from the courtyard with a few of the gundogs and this helped hide certain emotions that they carried within them. Big Clancy felt something as he looked over and sensed the expression of the lowered eyes of Aseena and then Keeley to the two handsome gents standing aside. Right that minute and it could not have been better timing, Daisy arrived with Jilly, Michaela and Teresa and it was a wonderful sight. The truth was the ones who had felt love at its element sensed what was about them, and they were Aseena, Llewellyn, Keeley and Harvey's presence of their feelings.

Daisy's smile brought everyone around from the little flutter and managed to get a big hug before the parting. As the girls were getting into the cars, all the staff and friends held their own until the comment Teresa made. A tut came about and then the famous statement,

Well, I'm not happy with their hair in that type of mess and to know they are heading for London what would the fur dressers honestly think of us down here? Everyone just looked at each other and burst out with laughter and their thoughts were full of well-being.

After the final hugs, Clancy once again spoke just like when he first met Grandad and Nanny.

Here we go again and you know they are back in safe hands, Margaret, one brief question, I don't want to look over but are they the girls' boyfriends over to my right? Margaret leered over her specs and then back to Clancy to answer,

It just could be, my friend, it just could be.

What's to happen on their journey of life, I just wonder? The looks between those youngsters of who will wait? Will one or the other fall in love with another along the winding road of life, we will just have to wait and see.

The departing from the Manor had a strong vibe about it like many a parting from the past generations. The staff followed their chores back into the flow of their positions and guests started to make it back to their domains as the two flash cars were making their way out of the property and heading for the Big Smoke. Waves were barely in sight with certain heads turning back to get a last glance just for old time's sake. Harvey spoke out first when the cars disappeared,

Well, that is that over and done with my friend. If anything, he took it better than he thought as there was a positive response from both him and Keeley with no promises to each other but just wonderful aims and thoughts for each other's future, and that was the best way to part without saying goodbye.

I have a strong inclination there could be more deeper thoughts from his Celtic friend's feelings for Aseena after watching their body language and he maybe was feeling, oh well another parting in my life, but why?

To be honest, he knew better than that as he did not have a

clue what was going on here at the manor before arriving? But it was for us to imagine, I wonder what would have happened had she stayed? Alas we have to have our imagination don't we. Plus, it keeps a cracking gossip chapter on the post for staff and so to say I wonder what it will be like when they meet again? Oh, yes the gossip had started already.

Come on, let's go and check those pens down the southern side of the woodland, Llewellyn looked across and for some reason Margaret passed a smile over to the lad which he returned and then carried on about his business. Heading across the courtyard there was a nice embracing sound of a tune coming from the elderberry bushes and yes, it was the local birds and to be honest this made the two hounds laugh as they both thought the same and that was the berries were in full season and as looking at the bottom of the bushes there seemed to be many an empty acorn shell facing upwards which was embedded into the soil to make them solid, I wonder why? And what was going on here? Then one of the birds seemed to have tripped up and fell off the twig he was roosting on. A song thrush with a little wobble to him and two sparrows balanced the wee blue tit to its feet and back into song he began. Oh, the wonderful sound of laughter came about and there were certain birds that did not agree with this behaviour and stuck their beaks up to this. But the wine began and the birds sang to the last sound of the cars' driving the girls away through the Manor's hard grit.

Several days later, it did not take long before a very polite, professional message came through from Stella to say the journey to Miami went amazingly well with no difficulties at all plus the girls were in full swing and setting an amazing example of their skills in every manner. The main thoughtfull message was to say thank you for such a welcome and help in her own life to everyone involved and I'm sure we will see you again and share all the wonderful times of joy again. It was signed off with, next time I'll make sure I catch one of those ghouls around that ole town and Manor. Grandad laughed at this comment as he read it out to Margaret. A few magazine clips and photos of Aseena strutting the floor were enclosed and they were printed and put up in the staff room for all to see and once again this made everyone smile.

Back in London, Joaquin had become extremely tucked into the information he received from certain colleagues about the case's history and what he found very interesting was the feedback on Deano O'dando all the way back from the sixties to the recent date, a real bad mutt if ever there was one, I must say. He had a meeting with the board's special branch on visas, search warrants and so on plus his own license to operate.

Yep, all updated licenses legit to operate on such an epic part of criminal justice to be brought to reality. He called Josh just to let him know all the good news that had come through and the board of control would like him to visit them within the next week to introduce himself as well has hear his update on this matter.

Yes, I'd like to do that but I need to ask you something? At that meeting, should we invite your uncle and this Italian detective from the old case, to show respect to their hard work and any little matter that may become vital to our case? Sleep on it and get back to me by the morning so I can let him know. Is he willing to travel or does he just want to keep it this way and just observe?

Okay, mind you I must tell you something, I was out the other evening heading to meet a friend and past the Chewy O'M'Guwie's steak house and I just glanced through the window and who do you think was sat around that big ole oak table that is only set for VIP's that goes way back, they say Nelson's butt sat there with ole Henry the Eighth discussing boats But this time it's the Judge and with him Paul, Jamie and

Leo, Frank the Knash's son and of course munching on a fillet of rare steak was that vagabond, Hudson. Oh, how I wanted to pop in there and batter him around the head with that cut of fine meat but I thought please hold your tongue and temper, as no one must have any idea at all about these meetings because all will fall into place in another while and justice will be.

The phones were placed down but the thoughts were up and my, were they flowing wild or what? What would one expect from anybody's mind with all this going on? That is what helps to live in a location where you can just go for a stroll and ask the wild wind whichever way, she's blowing to talk away about so many questions and turn them into answers and if not blow them away, give a person a clear mind once again. The next few days were chill time for everyone, apart from the media. Anyone from the Manor who was out shopping the response from the public around the town centre was obvious as they wanted to know, have you heard from Aseena and the girls? Yes, yes, we have as they are blowing the catwalk apart.

You had to remember the ones who asked many of these questions meant well and never had the chance to travel so you had to be fair in your reply. Humour helped in these times being trapped with a mutt staring you in your face for a reply, you'd just say, oh, they send their love and thanks for asking. And then they walked away smiling and left you alone.

The next morning arrived and there was a visit and what was grand was on that morning Josh was walking down the High Street to the Town Hall when who was straight in front of him but the fine ole visitor Elmo-Cosimo.

Good morning welcomes came about then Josh said to himself. I've got to ask him myself. So, he said,

Sir, do you fancy a chat and a coffee? And with a reply of yes, they made it up onto the Front.

I've been thinking these past few days about meeting you and what a pleasure it has become.

Just before he had the chance to bark another word, the gent said, I spoke with Richard the other day as he heard I was over and vice versa. Life has treated him well, but we often kept in touch as we go way back when we worked together on a case. I was to return to my native land tomorrow but he mentioned to me a certain breakthrough over a matter going way back and some young lads have taken a great interest in it and want to put it at bay once and for all. He feels these young-minded adventurers will have it sorted in a short while with a cracking plan they are setting up with a great tone. You don't have to worry, young pupeano, he barked in his native lingo, you do not have to tell me about any secret case you are working on, to strike at the right time. I'm going to stay here in Deal for an extra few week's and if anything comes to mind then just ask me and if I can assist in helping you, then I will with pleasure. And as for the trip to London? Yes, I will join you as I'd like to see if some of those fine restaurants are still there and the one fine, four-legged beauty that walked with grace. The thoughts that my heart still pants over after all those years, oh how my thoughts are still there with a shine.

On these thoughts, Josh left with a contented mind as he seemed to have so many questions answered without asking them. Anyway, after leaving his fine company he gently strolled down Middle Street and reached Dylan's project and stuck his snout in to have a sniff about.

My, it is coming on well, isn't it?

It sure is, my friend, came the reply.

Josh then walked on down to the old chemist which he was using as a safe house office just to sort his assets out and got straight back on the blower to Dan with the content news he had just got without any complications. When did you say you wanted me up there?

Friday came the reply and of course, you know I have a guest with me?

Yes, Uncle Martin told me. I have some great ideas, Joaquin, and look forward to discussing these with you.

Me too, so let's get it ready' take care and I'll see you on the weekend.

A little while after sorting matters out, he shut everything down and called it a day. The next morning, he said he'd visit the fine house on the front of Beach Street belonging to a certain Mediterranean lady, Cosimo's sister and as he was walking about and down who was on the corner of New Street but Hudson? Yes, a certain sorta glance, stare passed about but you don't want to give certain thoughts to one's head, do you? Josh played away by acting he was on his blower and made his way to his destiny.

As he arrived, he gave the door a knock. The grand lady answered the legendary old door of those front houses with a way of welcome and the door answered with a creek to it as well. She being a fine buxom lass of her days, welcomed Josh in and gave him a fine check eye over and called out to her brother, Elmo Cosimo, you are wanted. She left the room with the impression that the house would welcome you anytime young one and her brother walked in with his smile,

Hello once again, by the way I spoke to Martin and yes, I'm clear for Friday. Another question answered before asking again.

Can life stay this simple he thought? Then he explained that a cadet trial course team would be leaving on Friday morning for London and they had mentioned that we could climb aboard if we liked, as Sam, their instructor, would be taking them to the test centre and he's located at the townhall next to where I'm based and he was in discussion with the driver of the trip with the students or cadets as they preferred to be called. Anyway, that is sorted and they will return on Monday morning.

Can you make it to the Town Hall on Friday or will you need to be picked up here?

No, I shall meet you there I'd say.

Then as their main chat came to a halt Josh said bye, I shall see you on Friday at the town hall. Has walking down the high street who of all shapes and sizes came out of a store none other than Birdie, with all assets of shopping. Just then Josh's phone went off and a call came in and he did feel once again the radio saved his tail and was becoming a great friend of his and a life saver to his own show.

The few days passed with a nice flow to them and Josh on his walk-about kept popping his snout in to check with Dylan's project and a wonderful buzz was going on there I must say. But his main concept was his thoughts on the new project they are going to be working on and the visit they were going to make.

Friday morning arrived and the trip to London was on and it carried a lot of chatter along the way and then they arrived at the college and they all piled out. A car was waiting along with Martin and Joaquin standing beside it at the drop-off and with their welcome they then headed off to Joaquin's which was best so as to keep a low profile and not be seen coming out of the police station, especially in London as you never know who is looking on? Every second of the day you are observant in the line of duty and if your backs not covered by a good coat then you could be doomed because if an ole mutt with a good snout picks up your scent, never mind how long ago he or she sniffed you out, you know it is all over as they will first check why are you here? Then all the hard work goes down the drain and they then laugh at you as they see your work as a joke.

After reaching Dan's pad, they chilled and headed out for dinner and of course, it had to be Italian for their main guest.

The service and feel of the location they chose was wonderful and Elmo Casimo even felt he knew a few faces. I think it was just an essence of the joy and company that brought this on. After a grand evening, they all made it back and sat a while. It was the first time really Joaquin and Josh felt very mature in their chat as they sat with a fine glass of Cognac, slightly heated from a dog's breath, that's what they call the presentation of making it, then when you present the drink, it is an honour to say good luck. Anyhow, it was a wonderful welcome and very easy to go to bed that night and feel content.

Over breakfast, just simple but refreshing, they got stuck in as Dan had built an all-purpose office pad out of the spare room which was ideal. He showed what he had gathered in and what he felt was important in this matter of putting an end to this historical case of the Great Train Pedigree Chum Robbery and giving satisfaction to many from the past and present. Harry, Joaquin's partner you know he's a chemist, don't you? Anyway, they can do all sorts and he enlarged all the photos that had been given to them and addresses too that stretched way back to modern times for tracking as each one now had a postcode.

The files and folders were neatly stacked and across the table were some enlarged photos of the wild ole days including the days at high top ends where the hot dogs met including the Kennillo de-velloo Chateau And there straight in front of him within one of those enlarged photos was Frank the Knash with his brother Basha Boozer and who was there next to him? Only Mike and Teddy!

Josh just spoke out and said,

Look, Cosimo, isn't that the vagabonds with that woman, Helen? And look at the date? Isn't that the date you said Frank's brother disappeared?

Dan then asked why Josh was asking about that pair of old mutts? Before he answered, Dan asked his uncle, Martin can you come here for a sec? Do you recognise this pair?

Why of course I do, that is Mike and Teddy, they were Frank's side paws, they did everything that needed to be done like running items from kennel to kennel, etc, etc. Just like the old smuggling days you know.

Why do you ask Joaquin?

Josh butted in then by barking out, well, I was only talking to that pair yesterday in Deal.

You couldn't have as they are in Manilla.

You want to put a bet on that? I was talking to them. They were with a slender type lady named-

Before another yelp was said, Martin barked out, not Helen?

Yes, why and what made you say that name?

Her mother was a juror on the jury that called the not guilty verdict all those years ago. She went by the name of Helen of Joy. Tip offs were given back and somehow from the jury but they do not know who and how they were sent?

Oh, my word, Martin's thoughts were flying wild in a gesture given to him all those years ago that Helen senior was the daughter from an affair that the Judge had, but this was only an off-shot from a young officer who lived locally and knew the gossip. Nobody really listened to him of what he had to say'

Wait a sec, where did you see this trio?

Why they were coming out of No 4 North Street.

No, no this cannot be as you do know who owns that don't you? Only Alan the Judge Carey.

Don't say that Helen junior is his granddaughter? That makes her Paul's stepsister. Look we can't make this any more complicated as we would have to go back to the board for another warrant.

No, we leave them out of it until it is all over and if we feel that we need to pull them in, then we will but only if all is okay. Getting back to the London end of things, Dan showed where they stood with Deano O'Dando and his mob, their bases, dates of the past visits and so on and there was plenty of evidence, to say the least, to pull him in. Once we pull them all in, there has to be a blockade on the Judge as he will get a tip-off from someone inside and either head for his place in Manilla or Brazil and we have to be able to stop this.

I've already taken care of this, said Joaquin. Because, as we are going for the Big Boy, if he gets any bad sniffs or tip-offs, he is going to head for the hills so my instinct was to ask those head honchos for their advice when I applied for the search warrants and they told me to make sure you have all ports and airports covered for those suspects being observed and cannot leave. The thing is he is a master at whatever suits him, as he has got away with everything since way back and now we, a pair of pups are on his tail who you may say and think are naive in the manner of cases like this, but believe me, nothing will be left without us going from snout to tail for every detail there could be for us to pull this off.

One question I need to ask is do you remember introducing me to the banter on Goldie and his family's history and background, mainly the smuggling of piracy and how they moved items from one place to another? Well, are there any tunnels from the two houses in mind? The two both belong to the judge on North Street, Number 9 and Number 4 and could there be any tunnel from Jamie and Paul's pad and Helen's leading to any other street? One slip-up and we are back to square one, guys. So, give me Goldie's number so we do not give anything away with me calling at his kennel or popping into The Ship. I, d like to meet him out of town somewhere to get some more info on those outlet tunnels. Let us make sure all is clear so that once we strike, the rest of the case with us watching on will only be bliss.

Martin, I have to ask you one thing, even down to the Romans and Vikings and those bloody Celtic northern miners, why is everything around here based on drama of something naughty? Is it something in the water that makes the mutts and so on get up to no good? From the finest dressed pooch to a scrawny fishing mutt, they are or have been up to no good. There must be an answer somewhere.

Martin gave this some thought and burst out laughing as it was true what Josh was saying. I'll give it a good thinking over and ask some old folk what their thoughts are on this matter, okay? Let us see what their replies are and I'll be honest, I look forward to their answers. Right, let us get this on the roll and what date all this can go ahead and we strike?

Let us go down tonight to the west end and there is a location of old style with the finest ribs to chew on, called Boney McGown's and it has a cabaret sort of Casablanca feeling to it and I think you will enjoy it, Josh, as it gives the days of what London was like with a nice vibe to its mature offerings.

After finishing all the necessary matters, paperwork and so on, they all got shaved up and groomed to the hilt for a nice evening out with just a grand flow for walking down through the historical streets of a totally different scene compared to Deal, past the One-eyed Jack pub and then on past the Bowl and Basket and into the West End where they could hear the howling coming out of pubs to the matching sound of the piano.

They passed doors which had a sorta large-looking host on it, their eyes would weigh you up and it was their call if you went in or not. You knew well when it was time to shut the snout and keep quiet when one of those big galloots gave you a certain glance. But if you knew the feeling of respect and the manner to behave, they soon gave you the respect you wanted or deserved. Martin, don't forget goes way back and tales of many a story could be bantered about him and his position being in Top Dog helped, but they all knew he was clean and if you were straight with him then you got back what was served out.

Before reaching Boney's, they were just walking along and a bark came out from across the street outside Snouty M'goutie's and with her flame-red mane, the lady yelped out, Martin is that you?

He could not resist it as they had an hour and a half before their booking so they crossed over with him saying come on lads let me show you something?

Walking through the historical doors with a few chewed up chairs and tables around the room, looks came with nods pointed at the foursome.

Gentlemen this is Brettsie, the longest landlady from the depth of Southern Ireland. Nods came about again then Josh lifted his handsome chin up and just froze over. It took just one glance of this lady's granddaughter and yes that's all it took was this one big bite.

Martin introduced his guests and mentioned they had to make way in a short while for their booking but it did not stop Josh introducing himself and of course with charm as he asked Brettsie, is this your daughter?

Of course, it was returned with,

Actually, she is my granddaughter.

Oh, how charm works its ways. Straight away a connection happened and the youngsters were chatting away, of course, he wanted to keep it a little silent to mention he's a cop but Shannon said she was the Head of the south side of Battersea Dogs Homes and runs the reconditioning program for dogs to walk the streets again. My, what a challenging program I must say.

He then spoke quietly and told her he had a great interest in that line of work. What was said next was just too much as in just a short while she found it very easy and trustworthy to yap away to Josh and she mentioned her working life really as being about Battersea Home as being born where she grew up she took a little stroll away at times from mum's safety and mixed with the wrong mutts and was put away. This is where the shock came in. She mentioned she did time at the Barking Boarding Home for bad-mannered dogs and when Josh mentioned where he was from, she told him,

Well, that is a little strange because in the young pups' offenders program she did time with who they called the Bitch who was from Deal, her real name was Helen and she was doing time for constant smuggling of high-end bones from parts of Europe. Even that young she chose to follow her family of high-end packs and followed their trail in life and to be honest she should have got a lot more time but alas, someone was watching over her. Shannon straight away took to the programs of offenders and built a career to bring a better life to a dog's walk and which way to head for, what tree to lift your leg up on, if you know what I mean?

She then mentioned she never felt she wanted to get to know Helen for some reason but could mix with all the rest. The last time I heard about her whereabouts, she was running a chateau for high-end breaks in the wilds of a French luxury spot. But who knows? I love my work, Josh, as it brings great satisfaction to me seeing a future in a dog walk when he or she leaves Battersea's North side and goes over to the South side for the humans to view and hopefully pick them to take home and become a part of their pack and just lead a wonderful life away from the strolling of the streets and biting anything or anyone. Just great to live a normal life and keep the parks and sidewalks, happy and clean.

The company and chat were just immense and when Martin apologized as he mentioned their booking, it was hard to leave but just before they walked out, Shannon thought why not? She asked,

How long are you in London for, Josh?

He glanced at the team and yes, they had small glees around their jaws as they looked on then Shannon spoke again,

Maybe you would like to join me for a walk-through Hyde Park and I'll show you our program?

He had to answer yes, as something once again started to stir. Maybe this goes on all over the world? But there seemed to be a lot of loving or falling for it going on between the lot of this pack involved. So what? Let it be if it is meant to. Walking out of the mature famous location, there were a few glances upon them from bent-over heads with their ears trying to prop up to get a wee listen on their names or their meaning of being in their local.

Yep, just like old time's sake and great to witness if you are a part of one side or the other? Walking along and down a side alley to Boney's, Cosimo spoke to Josh,

My, you cannot turn that offer down can you, my friend? As what a fine figure of a lady she is if there ever was one. A shy embarrassed expression came from Josh but he knew he was right in every way.

At the Boney M'gowny's bar, they shared a wonderful evening just embracing such quality in their prep of the ribs and the evening flowed by. It was obvious there were looks about from some tough-looking customers but more of curiosity but many thought it was a pair of fathers taking their boys out on a graduation dinner. You see this neck of the woods one has to know your bizzo and that is that. Josh could not get Shannon out of his head and his inside smile loved the expression of his feelings about her honesty in explaining her life in such a short introduction.

However, of all people she had to mention Helen.

How can this saga be of all the tail-ended beasts out there in this country, from John O'Groats to Lands End it had to be this individual we met up with? It had to be fate! Picking a career through your own errors and standing beside a rowdy scruff ball and then seeing where you may go wrong in life, you changed your stride into a mode of smiling instead of biting at someone. Then working with a wonderful team and building futures for nasty mutts, yep great teamwork and satisfaction all around.

After such a great time, they let the ladies walk on and they were strolling back to their pad and a little bark came out.

Are you gonna see her before you leave, Josh? asked Joaquin as they were strolling a few feet behind the gents.

Yes, my heart has told me I have to or I'll only regret it in life. Changing the chat, do you know what my thoughts are when walking these smog-filled streets and how tough they were? It still reminds me of Jack the Stripper. He was a well-known culprit back in the days of old and he mugged the wealthy of the finest coats, bit-bang and it was over. Coats of the finest gone. He was never caught you know? But one thing I give him is he never really hurt anyone of his victims. Left them a little shook but that was it. They were a little embarrassed walking to their destination and telling the host my fine coat got nicked but maybe that time they walked the wrong street and then got lost and astray.

They made it back to their domain and in through the door, they walked and wiped down their dampened paws with a warm towel,

Right, I'm ready for the sack and basket so I'll see you all in the morning.

Breakfast, just came naturally and the light barking started of the past few days and after breakfast, we have to take a stroll down to the Thames River to meet two certain dogs that are apparently very important to them within this case said Martin.

What is it about?

I don't know honestly. But it must be to do with the case as it has been pointed out that we can't meet them at any station or so on. They finished breakfast and then popped into the Chemist to take a little peek at the photos and so on from what Harry printed off and enlarged again.

The newspaper front pages and all the clips on the robbery in general were amazing and it felt very primitive compared to today's covers, you could not help but pick some of the clips up and study the shape and form of the dogs involved in and around the case. A different shape to some of those these days but you could tell by their structure who they were.

My, Martin, be honest is that you?

A little bow of the head and yes came the reply.

My, you were a handsome devil of a mutt if there ever was one, weren't you? A smile came the reply and another question came out,

So, who is this who seemed to be beside you in a few shots? A long-legged beauty who in the style of the '60s wore the jacket type coat, a mini suit that showed off her top pins in only a model of class could wear.

Why that is who they called Wag the Hag?

Why was she given a handle like that?

Well, she would drive you insane with questions and like a mum nagging you, she would get the answers she wanted from a bad culprit just by driving them crazy with the constant nagging 'questioning she called it. So Wagleatta ended up with the handle Wag the Hag.

What, she was a cop as well was she?

Yes, she was and the best there was if ever there was one. By the way when I said she would nag the truth outta a suspect? The other thing she used was those pins of hers. She knew when she turned away, they would be weighing her up and hoping if only I could get a date?

A little laughter about as the boys sensed something from Martin that was personal so the questions ended there as a call came out that they had to make their way over to the Scamp's Bar and Restaurant to meet whoever it was that was important to their case?

Folding over some of the files, Martin glanced at those historical clips and with a smile closed them for now. Joaquin looked at his uncle with a gentle smile and left him in his thoughts and said to himself, I wonder if there was something going on between them? There must have been as to express a look like that? just for his own curiosity he will ask Martin what happened? After clearing everything up and put things away they strolled down through the historical streets again and down past the famous cinemas and so on of the West End and reached Scamps to be met by the host in his fine set of a coat that he wore with pride.

Good day, have you a booking, gentlemen/ Came the next question?

Yes, he gave the time and name given to them to meet here and the host gave them a curious look after reading who they were guests of and said, please follow me. Leading them through the famous riverside tables of the building, with the guests looking on and for them to be escorted by this person led to a lot of glares.

Do you think we wanna be writing a diary with all this fame of looks we have received since being in town? Elmo Cosimo laughed at Dan's words but they were true.

They arrived at the table and sitting there was an elderly, smartly dressed gent with a welcoming smile. A younger, groomed gent stood up and said,

Please gentlemen, welcome, and then he introduced the host of this drama. This is my father, Sir Giles Chappy Chewler, the founder of PC Petfood's, the owner of Pedigree Chum.

He started the conversation with, oh, I do love this Hampton Court it is a far cry from my native Yorkshire town where my puppyhood was spent. Please take a seat, please do.

A gentle breed if ever there was one were the guest's feelings as being introduced,

The waiter arrived to take the drinks order when a smartly dressed lady arrived and was introduced there and then.

Gentlemen, this is my wife, Wagleatta/

When Martin lifted his chin to this name, how was he supposed to react? After all those years wondering to himself what would he say or do when he met the woman, he walked away from who loved him all those years ago. There was a silence for a sec and for some reason, Joaquin sensed the strangest float of air about in the company. The waiter returned with the order of drinks which assisted in lifting the slight uncomfortable vibe which was about.

What weather we are having I must say, said Julian, the son. My two other brothers wanted to come along but had to pop back over to the States where our main office is based.

I thought I sensed an accent within your bark, I've always wanted to visit the States you know.

Well after today maybe we can arrange for you to visit my homeland.

Yes, the youngsters hit it off with their chit-chat then the two of the company once again lifted their eyes that locked over into a deep, thoughtful stare.

The older gent then spoke again,

Right gentlemen, you must be wondering what this meeting is all about?

They had a feeling about them what it could concern after the intro of telling them who the host was?

Let me tell you now, ever since the day my folks decided to walk out of that cold, old cottage and my dad coughing up dust from pulling the carts outta the mines of Yorkshire, he vowed life would be better for all once we arrived on better soil. I watched him try his paws at everything and his desire and passion in life was to create a meal that was to satisfy the hungriest hound out there and he did it in respect for all those who had the drive for a better life and do whatever it was, as long as it was legit then that was fine.

Dad had an awful set on any con artist out there and mark my words there were plenty of hounds out there who would bite your snout off for a quick buck. Well, keeping it as short as possible, a bunch of dirty mutts did that to me and my staff and mainly in my mind, they hurt a few doggies who were just trying to do their job and I vowed as long as Pedigree in capital letters is written across my cans, I would bring those scoundrels to justice. When that Frank the Knash and that other vagabond and his gang walked away free after that court trial, I knew there was something in justice going wrong and I vowed to find out. So, I want to know which one of you was it, who brought that judge to the attention of the law?

Josh just lifted his paw to say it was he.

Well, I thank you, young pup, as in respect a high-end officer approached me recently with a request to open the case again and after I asked why? He told me the whole nine yards and I just took great interest in what your thoughts are? And why do you want too re-open it as well? I gave my approval and asked for this meeting to be put together to let you know anything you need in any matter to solve this case you use this? It's a gold tail to collar credit card open for the case to be solved at any expense.

Julian, the son, butted in,

Just one thing. If you have any notion to head for Las Vegas with that card then count me in, okay?

A round of laughter followed this comment and took the tension away when Giles spoke again.

Just to let you know, Gentlemen, my wife worked on the case in her days as a young police cadet and that is how we met.

How were four furred hounded minds supposed to think after this was said? Casimo broke the ice and put the charm in by saying to her that must have been so interesting being a youngster and brought on to such a serious case?

It was, my friend, it was, she replied. If you need to ask any questions do not hesitate as here in this folder are my direct contact numbers and please if possible but not to complicate anything, keep me updated.

The meeting then dropped the conversation of the case and got to the social side of what was in line for the rest of the day.

Well, if you do not mind, I've arranged a day out for you lot in London which I've spoken to your higher up honcho about and given him my request before you guys go into full gear and end my plea.

Sir Giles stood then and said,

I hope you do not mind but I must make my way back. My son and wife have asked to stay on, if that is alright by you lot?

Josh and Dan said why of course they can and one nearly said, right let's get this day rolling but his tongue held on as maybe he was learning to wrap it instead of barking it. After Gile's chauffer drove him away, the youngsters got talking and Julian really hit it off with the other two and they stood up and said, come on let's head down to the west end.

Their first stop was the Golden Fleece which carried so many stories of actors and singers in song that you could cut the air in there like chopping a steak. The three youngsters popped out onto the patio as the cigars came out to match the chat. Casimo, just coming back from cropping his leg at the gents' pole felt he just he wanted to leave the two for a little while, so he said oh, I forgot to tell Josh something that he just got an email. A text into his collar and it was addressed to the pair of them. He needed to speak to him about it, So, he left the pair alone.

Well, what can I say Wagleatta but you are looking stunning and it all turned out good for you didn't it?

She released a wonderful smile that embraced both of their thoughts and she said,

That day when you told me you could never love me the way you would want to, she knew already but tried everything to ignore reality but it was there in front of her. When you stood up and walked away, she felt the whole of her life disappear and when you walked out of her life the first thing, she found was the comfort and security within the case she was working on as she was sniffing out the train cabins and Giles was on the scene that day and spotted the beauty and ever since that day he set eyes on her, it was she he wanted in his life and he invited her out and with her heart feeling the way it was for comfort she accepted. But she knew however long it took there would only be one in her life who she loved from the heart and I wonder who that is?

He smiled just then as the boys came back all excited as the messages were the date and warrants were at the station of the Kennalarano department in Camden Town and there to be picked up as of tomorrow onwards for our use. Yes, the craic had started and by now Julian was full on it and bounded up with the way they were acting even though in many ways he had no idea whatsoever what had just happened or what was said about history and fact. So, with all the happiness and smiles about, Joaquin made a jest of,

Come on let's head down to Gooffee's Martini bar as they have a blues band and we are all set for a cocktail, beer and a bone!

On arriving, the laughter lit the room with barks and larks from all shapes and sizes and just then the band started to play and that classic song of so many memories began and that 's Me and Bobby McGee. Oh, what a wonderful tale for a song that can only make one smile to the lyrics.

The day went on and turned out to be just bliss. One of those that was not planned but just wonderful. A few sore heads were the cost but nothing more.

Right, we need to get back to that old smuggler town of Deal, came the words from Josh to Elmo Casimo over the kitchen table back at Martin's. First, let us take a walk down to pick these papers up and so on and see what they will allow us by law what we can do? Then let us make tracks. The cadet pick-up will be at 1 o'clock so we should have time also on the way down to the station to pop into Snouty Mg'Gouties to say hello to a certain lady. Anyway, let's get things rolling.

All the bags and so on were packed and dropped off at the pick-up point so there was no gallivanting about over that matter and so down they made it to see what this paperwork was all about. In they stepped and some smart Alec tried to become cocky by not letting Martin and Cosimo into the station offices but that was soon sorted by a gent who came out of the SS department, Secret Section.

Sorry about that, gents, just a misunderstanding that's all. If you'd like to follow me this way. As sitting down, I'll explain what we have. I want to keep this as short as possible as you know how you are going to do this as you know the team and town on your end. Dan, this is your paperwork for the London search and Josh, we have given you an extra warrant for that certain lady who has been brought to our attention. Why? We want her as well on this end as you know of her younger days doing time. Well, she set up her own section of a pack of hounds called the Flutter Eyes, a group of beauties if there was ever one who struck the rich at the private kennel clubs and so on and one of the head honchos on the board got bitten and he wants them brought to a close. He feels she is working with Steffearoio shall I say anymore? Anyway, if you can find anything whatsoever for yourself and us, we would be very grateful. I have another batch of paperwork here to pass to someone in your area who I understand has just been approved and passed to operate with you, Josh?

Curiously, Josh opened the file to find Dylan and his team had been given the go-ahead to work with us as sniff n backup on the strike. What a wonderful bit of news for Josh to be given before he made it back home. Also, there is a personal letter here from Sir Giles Chappie-Chewler wishing you both a very successful operation that will put everything where it belongs at bay.

They gave their best wishes to each other and started to make it back to the pick-up point and then past the places they had been entertained since being up here and a wonderful time it had been.

Wait here, guys' as they reached the pub. Walking in, he got a few looks as normal then made his way to the counter with a thank you card addressed to the pub, not just for Shannon. Oh, this boy had his ears clipped right if there was ever one thinking. He barked out a little to say farewell and he would be in touch soon. He said he could not stay long as they were waiting outside for him and he just wanted to say thank you again for the welcome. Just as he was turning away Shannon called out to him,

Josh be careful out there and I'd like you to have this. It's a wee cladder pendant to wear on your collar for good luck and safety. He said his thank you, he made his way to the door with a smiling glance returned by the most beautiful smile there could be.

Out he came and Martin said, feeling okay Josh?

Yes, I am, thank you,

Come on let's get you guys on the way before you start another bloody soap opera.

They got back and it was time to unwind first after their escapade in London. The first thing Josh did was to ring Dylan.

My, that was some shock for me, Dylan, to find out what's going on? I have your paperwork mate and to think our first case is together and what a beginning to open everything 'what can we say mate?

Tell me about it, came the reply, when can we meet? Let's get this over and done with Josh, let's meet at my spot tomorrow morning on Middle Street.

Josh gave Elmo a call to ask him did he want to sit in on the meeting which he replied yes to. The morning arrived and, on the way, down to meet Dylan Josh called at Casimo's then they strolled down to meet Dylan. It's a little fresher to walk along here compared with the past few days, isn't it? They had a little laugh and then Josh had to ask,

What was it with Martin and Wagleatta?

You could feel the immense affection a mile away and Casimo felt he could trust Josh not to slip up and understand what he was about to tell him so he did just that.

Bloody hell, what drama is about us Casimo, and I have to say I find it very sad for both sides there and after so long how can it be that it had to come to something like this to open it all up again?

Talk about romance how about yourself? That lass back in London is a beauty if there was ever one. I must say you looked wonderful together and is there an open door and I feel that is a stupid question to ask you?

Yes, I will be seeing her again and once this case is over, I will be inviting her down here and share the banters we talked about and then she can see for herself where the sagas come from.

Dylan welcomed his friend and guest and had a table set up amongst the debris of their settling in movements. There were a few chewers about who he did not know and Dylan did not take long to introduce them. This is Ludwick who specializes in under cover smells, they called him Ludwick as his daddy of all crosses is a West Islander married to a Russian mutt so some brainy boffin came up with his name. A nod came from him then Cinderson was introduced. A cocker spaniel and Josh knew him as off and on a lot of files he read and he was one who worked on the first raid on Frank the Knash's pad. He'd seen everything crewed away over one verdict. He worked with Cosimo as he barked a few lingos so it was ideal for communication.

Then over to the left was Stephine, a Silken Windhound. Her breed developed through them sniffing prey within miles as of their long nose picking up the scent of something to eat. They could follow or trace anything once they got the sniff and that was that. We tested for ages can it be done within the cities to pick up a tail end of a breed and trace it to the spot where it was hiding? And yes, 98 per cent they were found within two inches of their hideaway. Another nod came and some glances from each other came about and then both Josh and Dylan explained the case.

Then the guests if you can call them that had to look twice as Dylan introduced someone to them both who he interviewed whilst they were in London and Dylan had to hear about her ways of working underground and on major open areas of tracking? Bercy is her name and she's a Hungarian breed called a Koondor.They were bread for defending and driving sheep out in the wildest conditions so scents and tracking is just an art to her plus being able to banter a few different lingos helps don't it. One could not help but stare at her coat because you would swear, she had it done for some reason as her whole coats in dreadlocks but it is her natural coat? Anyway, they all sat about with a wonderful ambience about them. Josh passed out some files and had to explain the lot as quickly as possible to get the team to understand the tension of what the survey of the case had reached in their time on it. How do you think I honestly felt guys when I was in London and the head honcho told me about the team, he wants me to work with? Be honest it would shock anyone wouldn't it to take in all at once? But it is here and what more do we want. A light applause came around from all involved and what a beginning to their carrier.

Here we are now at its peak and we have been given an open timetable when we want to strike and that is what this meeting is about. Dan in London is ready for his bite at the action and now it is up to us to give the date. I say we could be ready by Friday, do we all agree on that? We now have three houses to operate on, one is owned and run by a female and that is Helen's house. It is vital and an asset to our plan and if you are comfortable, Steph, you will be dealing with entering and interviewing her 'under all what is going on are you are you okay with that?

Yes, yes, I am. And she explained she was looking forward to it as she was the one who busted her sister in the bone marrow case way back in Chew- Chew Town and sewed that up with a piece of lace.

Dylan, I have a vital question to ask you and I want your honest opinion on it okay?

Yes, go ahead mate.

At my time in London whilst sitting with the head honchos, I brought up a major thought of mine which is the gamble on my call. I told the board there will be no charges on the scene on the ones taken in for questioning' The reason? We want to make the head honchos sweat it out and hopefully with the ones we take in, one will grass. If not, the head barkas may make a run for it, for the likes of the judge and Frank the Knash and that other bill-a-bong, Deano O'dando. When they do, we nab them. My reason is this; although we have everything covered from paw to tail, is there a big shot insider in those offices in London? With Johnny O'Jingo set up in the base of the Cyber Shed, he is listening to every comment recorded and if the grass makes his move, we can nail him big time.

The cover card that Mr Chewler gave us covers all the costs to operate the type of scanner that the Jingo set up and it is amazing. Anyway, what do you think? A little sniff let out by Dylan and then, Wow! What a gamble to take? I honestly feel you have made the right choice. You know the older Yupuppy mums knowing their young, yuppy offspring's are put in cold old cages and being questioned hard, in time will they crack just to save their warm, cosey butts? I think one of those zobos will and when they do, we have the head honcho in a written statement, signed, sealed and in our paws.

There is a lot riding on this, guys, and how do you feel about the plan and striking on Friday?

Nods came all around and everyone agreed that the longer left, the easier it would be for them to make an exit and run for the hills.

Right, we have everything in paw, yes? I'd like Dylan and your team to sit here and go through everything; anything missing, get it sorted and we strike, okay?

Excitement spread around the room, Josh walked over to the window and gave a whistle and down came Swinky, the Swallow.

Are you leaving for your winter break in Africa like you told me yesterday?

Yes, I am' I'm leaving this afternoon, why?

Well, when you are passing London could you pass on a very important message to someone for me?

Of course, just tie it here on my leg. He flew away, with the last words, See ya next summer, guys, and good luck.

Within seconds he was out of sight and away into the height of the skies. Josh was in deep thought about all that had been put into this operation; it would be just around the corner that they could go into action and strike. Within hours, Joaquin received the details of the time and date of the strike and the reply was returned to Josh's team by Pedro, the racing Pigeon who was passing by through London and stopped for a break at his cousin's. Perfect timing it was as he sat on Dan's sill and was asked to drop these reply papers to the team in Deal and with a yes reply, they were ready to hit this end and bring those baddies in at last with the law.

Josh got up to stretch his legs after a long sit down, focussing and he made it to the door with Dylan.

By the way, how are the pups and Tilly?

Oh, they are doing amazing, Josh, and growing by the minute.

They walked outside and Tilly was there with Sally and Emma coming down from Beach Street after just finishing a large house on the front and two of them cleaning the offices at the lawyers' set up.

Looks like the company is going well, lass.

It is, it is, Josh. Maybe we will get a discount on this place?

Dylan started to laugh, then asked how his sweetheart was.

Just to let you know, Josh, Aseena and Keeley will be beaming in on Wednesday from the States and Poppy and Bailey will also be touching base from their tour. They will be connecting in as well so it should be a good bit of fun and chat.

Okay, Josh replied. I'll make it over as I'd love to know how it is all going for everyone.

The girls headed off down the road when one of the girls asked Tilly what the boys were doing in there, she told them they were helping clean the place up to make a puppy club of some sort which was the quick thinking of Tilly.

Mums got the pups so come on let us make it back. I'll see you later, Dylan. Take care, Josh, and off they strolled down the way.

They walked back indoors and got back on their tracks and mentioned the beam-ins from their friends abroad and it really made it interesting but to be honest, what would they think if the facts came out on the status of what this pair were just about to do? It made you wonder sometimes, could anyone predict one's ways in life, because look now, look what is going on in these tracks of young lives who in reality have just begun the long winding road to their destiny? It keeps one's thoughts active, doesn't it?

On Wednesday afternoon, they met at the café for the beam-in. First on board was Poppy and oh, could one read the joy of what this tour had done to her life? It had brought the full bloom of life's blossom out in her like the flower she was named after. It stood for so much in life and history and now she was making her own.

Dylan and Josh managed to slip away from all the action as Dylan wanted to speak to his brother to see how he was coping. And after seeing them both with the company they were in, answer anything one would want to ask.

Then up on the screen came Aseena and Keeley as one mentioned just a while ago about a certain flower, now we have a pair of blossomed roses, that just one glance upon them you could tell and feel how much they had bloomed in life.

Hi, everyone! How is everyone at home? Pixie then showed her face with Stella and what fun it was to see them all in such joy and I did not know who could get a bark in edgeways, but it just flowed. Keeley asked Tilly how the business was going as she was going to join them before being asked to fly her wings with Aseena.

Look, Tilly lifted a local article written about the young company and what more can one say but the item said it all; they were here to stay.

Look, it was Keeley showing her first design in the rural style of more inland living of upmarket doggies that suited the European set of dress and it was getting attention all around.

Aseena spoke about her first main walk out onto the catwalk here in the depth of Miami and the silk and satin expression of beautiful coats she carried just like her mother did all those years ago. It made a woman feel like a free spirit to just flow the way she wanted to and of course, be glanced at with grace from every eye looking on. Every eye in the fashion world was on her and the critics could not express it any better than to rank her with the highest models in world history, from Cleopatra to now the highest out there, Legglee la Loola the lurcher the most desired of all to walk the ground.

The time to shut down came about from both ends as Stella's call came to the girls,

We must make a move; they are waiting for us.

Then some mutt's head, a roadie called Johnny, came ranting out at Poppy,

We need you now on the stage for that tune? Johnny has got the tone for you to follow, come on now before he loses it.

I gotta go, bye!

Then Bailey barked, Dylan I gotta go back. Take care and give my love to Mum and Dad.

Aseena didn't mention she was online to the Manor to keep the whole house hold happy and they could tell as well the joy this position was giving her and this helped to calm any negative thoughts or worries, they had for her.

She spoke to Llewellyn as well and just the expression to

touch base was enough for them both. With Miami sorted, she was telling Margaret that the next major show would be held in New York, in aid of the poor and needy, and Kennels for the Homeless, and it would be held in the Bluwie Chewie club where Twiggy held her first walk and coat shows. What a pleasure it was for my ears to hear this as you know the way I am with my hero of all who worked in the top class of glamour.

Just then there was a blur on the screen and then some quick bye-bye barks, then gone as the screen fell silent. Smiles were all about as contentment was within everyone's thoughts to carry on so they all made it out to get back to the flow of their own lives. Dylan's contentment stood out and Tilly sensed this. Don't forget, he felt concerned about his brother's behaviour being out there on the road with a woman under his protection for the first time and for such a long period. How proud he felt that any doubts he may have had, were proved wrong and that we all have to admit sometimes we are wrong to judge another's habits.

Talk about judges, walking out of the café, Josh did not want to make it look obvious that he was strolling with Dylan, so he walked down St Georges Passage to have a chat with Lizzy at the Black Pig butchers, just 9 steps away from her doorway was the entrance into the Castaways salon, you know the lady there, don't you? She's one of those supposed to belong to those sea witches based down on the Sandown spot. I understand Mike and Susan from the Loving Thoughts Chapel chased all the baddy demons away and left a cracking impression about the town's clans and cults and breeds and mutts; in other words, those who go praying for goodness as many of them still thought Susie and Mikenello were from a high mountain tribe that did a lot of things that were naughty. They even said they were doing sacrifices under their cult to make their ways well, but after it, it all came out that they were nice doggies. So never mind listening to those barks from bad snouts that can hurt you like a hammer.

Josh made his presence known then headed off with a little gift of a chew bone from Danny from the butchers and made it onto the High Street, then double backed through a side street onto Middle Street to meet Dylan at the base. Just as he walked through the door, Ludvik said,

Don't get too comfortable as there is a message from Johnny O Jinglo. He's got a cross line he wants you to listen to.

Okay, anybody wants me you get me by text, okay?

Making his way down to Victoria Road, it could not have been a better time as Cimino was walking down after shopping for his odds and ends and whilst Josh was in thought, don't ask why but he asked Cimino to join him.

Through the door there was the little narrow entrance that led down into the cellar where John was on top form because he'd connected to the main lines to what they'd been after. These important lines were the ones belonging to the head honchos and now he'd got them. Putting his bags down and looking about, Cimino's spine froze when he saw a certain name scribbled on the board which was joined by others on the wall of calls coming back and forth.

Josh asked John, I understand you wanted me to come over

to listen to something?

Yes, yes please take a seat. Morser O Massa, that is my works partner here. A nod came from this active Welsh border. Well, he picked up a line connection called interneting to Frank the Knash's base and Dando O Deano's and this one track showed us it was coming in from a strange line both at the same time from the south of France. And the number connects to a bank of some sort with the capital name of Lady Chappriella von Beckinsdale.

This was the name that Cimino was concerned about written on the wall board. Before any confusion could start flowing, Cinimo spoke again,

Josh, you know when we were in Scamps Restaurant and just before we left you to ask something of the case, when all the serious chat was done with and you asked about the photo shots on the wall beside us and you asked Sir Giles, why that is you, isn't it? Yes, came the reply they were taken many years ago when we sponsored certain conventions using his company name and they were held here? Yes, they were held here and then he mentioned some of the others in the photo and you said about the beauty in one who was beside him. He replied in a sorta sad way, yes that is my sister and the conversation ended there and then for some reason. Well, her name is Chappriella, Josh, the name on the wall and the beauty in the photo. Josh, with all the paperwork we've been going back over, I distinctly looked at a name that popped up and there is a name that I remember interviewing at the time of the case because it had connections overseas and mainly an Italian account that led to a Swiss account under a certain name, a Mr Bromley Barkinstale. They asked me to look at this as I spoke both lingos and I interviewed this chap who, guess what? He was the accountant for M.D.D.O.L, The Med Division of Dogs of Law. You know what that means, don't you? He had all rights to enter every detail of anybody's account and pass grades to view their details.

So, what is the surname of the account John is picking up? Oh my God, surely, they would not be that stupid to have an account with such details open?

No, no they would never think it could be picked up, not in this country anyway. But there is an error; there is a connection directly to Frank and Dando and they have left it open and given it to us by leaving it idle. This means if we go through all accounts, step by step, on transfers etc, we will have everything belonging to them and it would bring this case to its last season.

A little silence reigned in the cellar, until Cinimo started to applaud John Morsie's work and Josh joined in.

By the way, what sort of breed are you, young one? Cinimo had a habit of using this line to get to know whom he was dealing with.

Well, John replied, my dad's a bulldog and mum's a lab, so you can guess where the intelligence comes from, yes, my mum. Both breeds have common sense, well the lab anyway and by the way, my dad was with the D.D.D, that's the Dover Drug Division.

Cinimo butted in, Surely, he's not Jonzie O'Bonzie?

Yes, why?

He was on a case when we first opened this original one as they thought it could have been a drug traffic gang involved. But he put an end to that with his views of the way they raided the train at that time and he said it was just the cargo and cash they were after.

Now then I'm not going to say anything like nothing must be revealed of today's findings but just be careful and aware, okay?

John, I just can't thank you enough but now I must find a way to let Joaquin know, or do we just keep this silent and notify the head office to see what they want to do? I think they will contact the banks and freeze these accounts. I have a personal line of contact that leads to wherever I need it go and this is what we call the Sniper, as you never know where it is coming from.

You can use it now, John offered.

Thank you.

John and Josh got straight online to Dan and told him what had just happened and what he listened to and witnessed.

So, Dan can you get to the station of the Top Dog, as he has to be told to make sure we are not held responsible for withholding info.

I'll do that now and make it back, okay, to tell you it is sorted out. Josh, can you believe this, just when we hope to bring the case to its end?

I need to get back to the base to go through some details for tomorrow as we cannot and will not call it off, and that is that.

It did not take long for Dan to get back to Josh and explain what the head honcho had to say,

But just one thing, he could not stop from praising us on this major breakthrough and the slip-up of the tail-end of these vagabond's giving this away, or is it yet another tailgate trick of theirs? We will just have to sit' wait and see won't we?

Whilst Joaquin was explaining to the top brass at the station, he heard one or two emergency calls go out in different lingos and barks but it was all to do with freezing accounts here and abroad and to be held in silence without the clients knowing.

Are you going to tell Martin as he has to know, Josh, it is only fair, okay?

Of course, he is to know. By the way, how is he with all the drama that's been going on?

Josh in this startling news I had to think to myself, if this is all linked together and it has been Sir Gile's sister from the start in partnership with all the leaks to get those scoundrels in the clear, who will it be to tell the gent the facts that it has been his sister all along? Surely it is enough to make any dog's back bend?

This left Josh a little deep in thought and his first thoughts were how do you tell someone that their sister is an informer? Because of all the years past trying to work out who it is, who could have such information to pass on to the big shots and get away with it? Money is a big answer but anger is a different line one would take and you have to think about why.

Cinimo, can I ask you something?

Yes, go-ahead ma boy.

Could there ever be another informer playing games with us and leading us up the garden path with this care plan and all we do then is get more wound up and they walk away barking at us and laughing at the law again?

No, my honest opinion is this is more personal, Josh. Whoever is the main planner and feels there is no stopping them until they get what they want and also, those accounts are real, we are not talking about a bob or two in your account, we are talking millions upon millions, Josh, and now we have it all under watch. Would you take a risk of a prank to know you could lose it all? Na' this is the real deal, my boy, and we are gonna prove it. Come on let's take a walk and chill out a while.

And so, they headed out and the first snouts they bumped into were Evie shopping with her mummy, Anna, with their baskets all full and skipping along the way.

I could easily settle here with its ways, you know that, my boy.

They were sitting on the front of the other side of the Pier on a bench when who came walking by but only Jamie with that culprit Hudson and you would not think butter would melt in his gob but boy oh boy, he's a bad one underneath that brushed up coat of his. He gave a side glance at the two enjoying the day and sorta sniggered for some reason and Josh's thoughts matched Cimino's, like Ya, you wait till tomorrow Mr Smartass and we will see whose tail is wagging then?

Just then the beeper went off and it was Joaquin,

A quick word, got time to talk?

Yes, we are on a break.

I just want to say we are all set for tomorrow to take Dando O Deano's old biting strays in. How about you, are you ready?

Yes, one of them just walked past us with his tail stuck high up in the air.

Just keep your cool, okay? I still can't get over the news of what those boys picked up on and of all times for it to happen. It is just meant to be and that is that.

By the way, Peanut the Pointer who trained so many sniffers in the old days said he was talking to you the other day as he was down in Deal for some reason.

Yes, he came in to look at the base we have been given and he's offered to give lessons on the first way to pick a scent up out of the waters which is really difficult. But he just loves the plan and project that we have been given; also, you know who his daughter is, don't you? The woman working with us tomorrow, Hanna the Houndress.

Just one thing, how did he know about the set-up?

Well, he still belongs to the Hunters and Sniff'outters Club as that is how he started with all the hounds on those chases. He was talked about so much that he was invited down to what in those days they called The Pit, because there were so many smells and scents and so his magnificent career began from there. He really is such a gentleman and I love his presence; it makes one feel welcome in any manner. Anyway, my top hound dog boss asked him to pop in to introduce himself and lend his paw if needed and mentioned me and you and that he told him and asked him for his views on the project. Come on, let's make it back and the best way now is for you to relax and chill and try to just level out until tomorrow.

The morning arrived and everything was in place at both ends and they both agreed on the time as it was a perfect day to see everything clear in daylight.

The time to strike is 4 pm on the dot and now it is 11 am.

Josh, in fact, felt more chilled than he thought he would be and at 1 pm he took a stroll over to meet Dylan. As he walked into their base, he just smiled to say this is it. Are they going to be there or not? You see when the mind plays games on your thoughts and here it is the town in general, all those myths and banter about all those tunnels etc, had there been any tip-off to them and they had sneaked out of one of them leading out onto the Front and away to Europe?

He changed his manner by asking Hanna about her nickname the Houndress?

Well, I'm from Folkstone and was raised around the coastal towns as all my family are or were either coastal guards or police officers. As puppies, I'd hunt my brothers and any other one from another litter like they were my prey, and my daddy used to sing that song to me, the one by Elmis Prawley, You Ain't Nothing but a Hound Dog, and that was that, it stayed with me ever since.

You could feel a bond here as they found it easy to get along with each other just instantly and then Hanna asked how The Jackal name came on Josh, and he explained his story on the matter of his handle and they just burst out laughing.

I wonder by the end of this saga, Dylan, will there be a handle on you? And I just wonder what it will be?

The youngsters got to thinking then as they kept watching him and his movements and it was obvious the name to put on him would be a lively one. Now then this young outstanding team did not know their own forecast as to whether they would become the ones talked about after these next few days? Would they become the heroes of the next generation to be talked about and would their legend grow?

The time arrived and the radio code word was ready to set off from the Top Dog in London and monitored with Morsie M'gorsy and Johnny O'Jinglo recording every sound and sight both with all their might. It was so intense you know, the air and so on surrounding them but at the same time, it was exciting, to say the least. They had never witnessed something like this but who had? Then off it went, those words, Barko, barko, barko shot out. I just loved the way both gangs began the operation. They simply knocked on the doors like puppies playing ratta-tat-ginger and the culprits answered, not smashing down doors with paw rams, the rams with this team were Ramboo and Bamboo who were on site just in case there was no answer, but they just looked on whilst chewing carrots from Prentice's grocers who are on the High Street, as you know.

It was Paul, the grandson who answered first at Number 9 and Josh served him with the warrant and Jamie looked on after glaring at Hudson who gave a smurky-glurky look at Josh but he soon changed his expression when he saw- well, heard Helen ranting and raving at Hanna on her front door step of Number 4 when they cuffed her. I think she was on a date and all the cooking and so on was going to go to waste. She had bought some really expensive lamb this morning, as I had her followed to Rooks the butchers and Anita told me what she had bought.

Anyway, Number 10 was empty, so they had their locksmith open the doorway. Once again it was done with ease until the young officer, Pupoo the Poodle came to tell Josh they couldn't get access to the cellar of Number 10, so Josh gave the nod to

Ramboo,

Sorry to bother you, mate, but we can't get into the cellar; can you assist us here?

He nodded and told Bamboo,

Wait a sec, I'll be back in a minute.

He spat out his carrot and mumbled, damn, how is it he got the action?

The crew outside just laughed about his comment and the next thing you heard was a smash and down came the door of the cellar and the search all around began. As this had been going on, they led away the culprits in separate coupes and drove them to what they called the Keep and put them into the cages for questioning. Once again, they chose the Keep because its history is next to the castle and in those ole days, they shared the cages of putting away the baddies in those damp old cages where you can still feel the presence of the ones who never saw daylight again.

Anyway, on the other end of this operation, it was different as of all the luck, timing like listening to the chat from the cyber shed, just being in the right place at the right time and Joaquin was just in that because as he strolled into the old house of one of Dando's ole gang members, who was in there but the Dodger, the head sidekick of Deano and all around the room were iced-up boxes stocked and packed so neat and tidy and the crew that end looked at Dan, who walked over to one of the boxes and on top of it were the address and directions to a house, in guess where? Deal and it was one of the yuppy kennels called the Furry Ma Curly Manor owned by Minx, the Tibeton beauty and Ethull, the half-bred pug crossed with a Shih Tzu and also her half-brother Hugo, that's the one who sees himself as a bit of a tree-top lover. Anyway, his dad's a bloody French pit bull and his mum a pug, so what is he? Oh, yes, a Frug a Poo and believe me, in those parties they host, anything goes either way.

This pack of yuppa-puppas were all business partners you know and yes, they had some wild, wavey, swavey parties, you know the type, don't you?

Martin came in on this launch just in case he could assist in any way and then seeing the Dodger there and this cargo they found heading to this address, his heart and feelings joined in and sang and barked out loud.

Hello, old boy, how the devil are you? It is a long time, no see, isn't it?

Then over to the box Joaquin walked and he turned around to take a look at his crew then at the Dodger who was really staring at him and the others with him were doing the same, when Joaquin lifted the lid to see what this cargo load or whatever you want to call it, was all about? And what met the eye next was well, what can one say, one of the rarest, banned, expensive meats there is out there, rum marinated ostrich legs prepped into the cut for a King you might say.

My, oh my, what do we have here? It is not worth asking how in the hell did you pull this one off, bringing these into the country. Or could there be an Ostrich farm out there with such a fine demand for this type of order for the Yelpies may I say?

Anyway, with a sigh in his bark, Joaquin gave the order,

Cuff em, boys.

A few others were batched up as one or two were recognised by the team but there was no interference as we might have expected. But it was better to be ready than not. Martin just couldn't believe this and had taken to it a lot more than the rest, because he knew this geezer going way back over 40 years and now in a back street, London pad, they had met again, for near enough the same bloody reason as the first time. How are you supposed to explain that to somebody? I put it down to fate, as

I said before, if you do wrong out there and it is bad it will bite you on the butt one day in the future even if it is 40 years or so later.

Come on, let's head down to the Kennels and get these all tucked in nice and cosy into their baskets and get the ball rolling as we can read them their rights in front of witnesses and have everything recorded but the main concern now is look who we have in our custody and we can charge him with many crimes he has committed.

You are quiet, Martin, you seem deep in thought may I say? said Joaquin, looking at his uncle's deep, thinking expressions, one with a smile and the other sorta saying I just wonder?

As they reached the station and stepped out, some of the younger pups arrested were cobbing off ranting on about do you know who my dad is? You wait till he hears about this!

The reply came back from one of the older officers,

I know your dad and when he finds out how stupid you have been and getting caught doing this, I would not like to be in your paws.

But we were not to do with the ostriches, honestly!

Yeah, right. Who is gonna believe a bark you come out with? Being in a kennel with one of the biggest rouges about and getting caught red-pawed in the act.

They charged them and gave 'em a search over then placed them into the old London cages with a lot of history to them. Some poor doggies were put in there and were never seen or heard of again, you know? But what was the most rewarding thing of all was they were only to be taken in for questioning and now look? How do you think Joaquin and the team felt, everything that happened today had put their minds and souls right back on track.

The next morning back in Kent, Bear, you know he's that

red fox lab and was called in by Dylan for his brilliant instincts of picking anything up with his extra-scented snout. They made their way to North Street as they really needed to go through each house with a brush to find anything else in this raid, giving a little sniff to the air. They didn't want to seem out of the way with the neighbour so that is why they didn't put security on all the houses overnight but it was being watched, okay. Again, Ramboo was with them just in case there were any other secret tunnel doors leading into the other houses.

You see Ramboo got talking to the Bear as they were in Pertise's on Saturday night, dining. Rosie, the Bear's girlfriend and of all things, a bloody vegetarian; anyway, they love the menu there at Pertise's as the dining area is at the back of the shop and you can see them prepping all the veggies and so on whilst you order and they don't just do veggie dishes. I love the Chunko Chops. Anyway,

Rosie, isn't that Den, Janice's daughter, the couple who make the socks and ear warmers for the lifeguards and didn't they open up their own shop to the public a few years back in Den's name?

Yaa, that's them alright. Why say Den's name like that?

Well, they say Janice's folk and breed way back used to mug fluffy, hairy doggies for their coats and then make the finest items there were for the cold wintery wear and tear for the fisher dogs and humans and that is how they started the business. It was not good for modern times for folk to know this, you know, so they changed the title over, that is what they say anyway. Plus, it was not good for the Bear's career as well knowing he was dating someone with a past like that.

Anyway, after this banter, they headed into Number 9 and started going through Hudson's belongings and his own room but not a trace and they went through it with a fine fang and brush. Paul and Jamie's rooms were in the clear and the rest of the house and just as they were about to walk out, Bear got the sniff of something that caught his interest. He followed it out of James's room down into the cellar and moved a few odds and ends about and then he saw a cabinet up against the wall, with things like can openers, bowl stirrers, grub mixers for mixing with meat you know and a few cocktail shakers, etc, etc. Bear looked at Ramboo and both thought, that's strange having something like this in your cellar. Bear's snout got on the move again and up around the cabinet he got hit with a scent of some sort behind it. They looked at each other and then started to move it slowly and there in front of them was a trap door.

At the entrance to the cellar stood a young officer on awareness watch and they gave him a call,

Buster, you know Tilly and Dylan's friend?

Yes, he made it to the police squad as well and doing quite well may I say.

Anyway, Buster, give Josh a call next door to come over here straight away and do it quietly if you can and try not to get too much attention and tell him we may need his back.

Buster, you know now he's dating a hearty Ainu? She's a Japanese hound dog who he met at the dance at Snoutie's. Anyway, he set off into Number 4 where Josh was and gave him a little nip on the tail to get his attention.

Josh, you are wanted at Number 9 as Bear wants to bark at you over something?

He nearly slipped up with his innocence as ever but managed to keep his tongue in his gob. Josh put his special magnifying glass down and made his way over to Number 9 and down he went into the cellar.

What's up, guys?

This, Josh, a secret entrance to next door. We wanted you here as we open it and you can be another witness with that camera you have.

Ramboo was more worked up and said,

Want me to give it a few wollups?

Wait a sec, let me try it first.

Bear grabbed the knob and gave it a few twists and turns and then it opened with a creak. A dark room appeared and with their headlights on they shone about and found a light switch on the wall. Josh pressed it down.

Well, what do we have here, guys?

It was a room made up of such a classic design, based once again on Casablanca with its unique bar and martini tables and stools with a beautiful, long table running through the centre. The walls were full of pictures of celebrities and political bounders from all over the world. Yes, the judge was there amongst many but this was a personal collection, could it be used for evidence? It was just amazing to see and have a good sniff about and they really felt high and mighty about their find.

I wouldn't mind this myself, said Josh and they just kinda smiled at each other.

Then a major shock hit them as they looked onto the Cocktail cabinet and there with the original labels were five cans in a row. The first one, well it was only a Pedigree Chum can, wasn't it? Then a Chappie and so on.

They can't be, surely- surely, they're not what we are looking for, cans from the raid itself? Let's not touch anything, guys, this has to be left to the hairy-tail-team and get them in here right now.

How do they breathe in here, mate? asked Bear.

Just then Dylan popped his head through as Josh flea'ed him. This was a certain way of texting someone or thing with great privacy and hard to trace.

Fancy a Martini, Sir Dylan?

Why, of course, and you know how I want it don't you, shaken not stirred.

Of course, this was said in dry humour as nothing could be touched but, oh my word, what a find! His eyes scanned around the room looking at the clips of the stars on the walls and it all must belong to, of course, Staffieria, and all this was a memoir of her friends or clients, shall we say? All of this was just a shock to the system, like our ancestors, the mysteries of what they smuggled and what was the next cargo, everything seemed like an adventurous dream and we would wake to find it all blurred.

The forensic team was called over from Number 4 to get the items from this room packed and tested and taken down to the lab. By the way, these were in Jamie's folder next to his basket and they were clips of a certain part of Manilla, a collection of classic menus from the Pedeegredour, the famous restaurant renowned back in the day to serve Chum and Chappie la Prie. It was a dish all the yuppies dined on. What was he doing with these, for God's sake, especially the ones from Manilla?

Wait a sec, Dylan noticed something in the background photos of the Manilla clips. Isn't that the jet they showed us at the beginning of the case of the judge's lifestyle, you know his possessions and so on?

Staring at it, Josh brought his magnifying glass out and both pups' eyes glared at it and then lifted their heads with smiles all around with even more great evidence. I think we should go back to camp.

This handle, The Camp seemed to become the name of their domain.

Anyway, let's get out of the way of the boys so they can do their job and go through this lot with a fine toothbrush.

Dylan knew one of the team and called out,

A Sweepy, he's a Yorkie and from the hard Dales of the Yorkshire area of the mines, set in the old ways who got involved in sniffing for dangerous gasses before the miners went down under, so his nose was pretty good you could say. Anyway, sweep. If you need us, get us on the bell as we will get out of your way and we will be back at the camp.

Okay, mate, came the deep bark of his Yorkie twang.

Arriving back at camp, they walked in only to find Cimino waiting for them and a tall, hairy, well-groomed dog reading the boards of the team's work and findings on the wall and as he turned around, the boys just looked at him.

Hello? before he could say anything, Cimino apologised for being inside but he was excited over this old friend turning up on his kennel step. Gentlemen, let me introduce someone from way back. This is Nosy Ned who was with Mushy Martin and me on the first case.

He nodded away and spoke to say a few barks and said he chose not to get involved with this new case as it was too much. But in the end, he could not take any more of the curiosity playing with his mind about what was going on with it all. And this morning, as he was walking his daughter, Mischa, along the Front, he passed the top side of North Street to find it shut off to the public and when he saw the certain kennels 10, 9,5 and 4 involved, he could not take any more and needed to pop in to see us.

I just want to say what a great job you are doing and if I can assist in any way, then do not hesitate at all to ask.

The boys welcomed him with a smile, a little bit worried at first which is of course natural but as Josh placed his collar bag down, Ned noticed the photos and gave a little bark,

So, Mr flash bones is still living the high life then? This remark related to the jet parked up or whatever you call a plane when it's standing idle? Ned just spoke in his native old slang.

Mush called me that is Martin, by the way, from London and told me what had happened in their neck of the woods with the Dodger. And I just could not believe it, of all times to be caught and involved in something like that. Perfect timing. Do you know anything of that loving scoundrel?

No, we don't but we have time to listen and would love to hear any banter.

Well, going way back to say, he hesitated in thought then back to barking out a date. It was 1816 at the height of the notorious smuggling times and a baddie boner if there was ever one was on the coastal blocking case. His name was Captain Joe McCullock known as Flogging Joey. What he did to get information was bad to say the least. Anyway, cutting it short, Dodger is from that clan, and generation after generation there was one biting vagabond who sort of went his own way and did things his way as well. Centuries later, we had the Dodger generation and he decided to join the coastal Navy and follow the captain's sails and see the world and maybe chase a few whales. But na, he got itchy and started to scratch around the ear and he and another member of the crew started the old trade of smuggling. From the real expensive chewy toys, you could not get over here for some rich mutt for Xmas to then more serious items like what he has just been caught with, but to be honest there is no harm in him at all. His breed the Wheaton Terrier is an ancestor of Ireland so his behaviour as a blaggard is within his roots.

Anyway, that is his way of paw manners shall we say, but he will become an asset.

Just then a gentle bark came through the door. It was Buster, they had managed to get him on board and shall we say absolutely delighted about it. Once again, he was in the right place at the right time as with a new team being built. He knew the town like the back of his paws and being sent to the North

Street assault was perfect to get him on board. Anyway, in his gently mannered tone, he asked,

Does anyone fancy a cuppa?

Which was replied with nods all around. After a real nice chatta around this and that, Nosy Ned realised how close these pups were to maybe nailing the judge once and for all. And he was told about all the blockades at the airports and all and a little silence again until Ned asked,

Do you have a lockdown on Betteshanger Park? As something of importance was within his thoughts of a long time ago of what had happened with a slip-up. Could you get a vehicle guy for tomorrow to just check an itchy tail instinct I have? It could be vital for something that may be of importance.

There were only the three of them in the room at this time and Nosy Ned mentioned a long time ago that there was a private lock-up kennel or a hangar, whatever they call them in human lingo. Well, could it still be in use and many a thing tucked away to fill anyone's dodgy boots?

Look, Ned, Josh showed him the platinum collar-to-tail credit card that was given to them and his reply was,

How in the hell did you get that?

So, he said, if you really think we can benefit from getting a car or a van and visiting this place, I'll get on the blower now and have one ready for us in the morning and pick it up at the bay.

The morning arrived and they met at Sandown just a little walk along the front of Beach Street, just so it did not stand out with them being picked up at the camp. I honestly could not see the reason because someone's bloody nose would gossip and wonder what they were doing around there?

Anyway, the four lads headed out as the car was waiting for them to go over to Betteshanger to see if Ned's instincts would pay off. Buster was buzzing with delight now at being involved in this and he was holding his own in behaviour. Arriving at the gates, they gave their pass ID's and in they drove and got the go-ahead to enter the private old road that passed through the woods and over to where this old camp was, that belonged to the Army and Air Force combined and it had been vital in the Second World War, for spy planes. It was a good job they had a Land Rover as it was a little on the rough side crossing over. They arrived at where Ned was talking about and there it stood, this large camouflaged hangar or whatever you called it.

The large ole sliding doors stood proud of their history and Josh commented,

I think Ramboo would have problems with these big boys, don't you?

Laughter came about and security who escorted them there opened up the sliders and there all covered up was some type of flying machine. So, they just caught hold of one of the sheets and gave it a good tug and there in front of them, yes you guessed it, was smarty paws' plane. Looking at each other they could not believe once again the timing of Nosy Ned's turn up at their door.

The security looked at the boys and one of them seemed a little nervous for some reason.

Don't say he's a bloody part of the Judge's team?

Na, he can't be? But alas you never know do you? It is not what you know it is who you know. Now then what do we do with a Jet? We can't tow this into Deal, can we? Surely someone will notice and start talking with a smart-ass gesture. Let us contact Top Dog up in the ole Smoke and ask them what they recommend and feel. It is best to get a team down here or one from a local base and remove vital parts, so it is not able to take off.

Dylan made a comment, I know, let's take the spark plugs

out?

Yes, the laughter of tongues was wagging and sagging with joy due to this find and comment. They locked the shutters back up and Dylan had a brainwave with his position in the Army and called his head honcho who said he would have a special team sent over to secure the hangar and disconnect anything important. But he said there and then, do not let the security there know of this call, okay?

Commander Cooper got straight on it and had an SBC squad sent over and he called Dylan to highly congratulate him on his work. He mentioned Cimino's say on it, never the less Dylan did the organising within minutes to set it up and head over without bothering to waste any time with the head honchos holding things up.

Dylan took the call at home as he had some time to share with the love of his life who as you know was his family. Tilly's mature beauty as a mummy had just gone beyond with essence and wonderful to witness and be around. She looked at her sweetheart who had a contented expression on his snout.

You look full of joy, Dylan.

I am, my love, and what more could I ask for? He just looked around at the young ones running about biting each other's tails and just loving life.

Oh yes, whilst out shopping I bumped into Margaret at the Black Pig butchers doing her chop shop hunting and she told me Aseena and the girls will be home for Christmas and Bailey and Poppy will be home as well, so Deal look out. Oh, by the way, the SBC, that is the special bone crunchers squad, Annette, Hayley and Heather, they are from the history of folks' families of the famous Air Force Squad, the hill 112 of the Second World War operation.

The girls followed in their parents' paws, anyway they have been assigned to undercover, if you didn't know, okay? And they are not to be messed with if you know what I mean?

Dylan, they were at the training ground of your first Sniff Class, showing you the leads?

Oh yes, I remember them. They were fantastic and I learnt a lot from them.

After a wonderful afternoon and evening shared with his family, it was back to the battlefield and whilst sitting down, Josh mentioned that Joaquín had been in touch and the Dodger had given a fair bit out and the first thing was, a statement of the names and address of the organisation involved in ordering those top of the range banned items.

I'd like Buster to escort Ludwig to pop up there to that high-end love nest to question the hosts and I want to ask you and be honest, okay? Is Buster ready to hold his own in questioning those beauties, Minx and Ethel plus the bull himself, Hugo, will put out to impress him with offers of high-life parties and so on.

After a little hesitation, Dylan replied, yes, yes, he is.

Right here it goes, Buster come over here, mate.

Sitting down, Josh gave his orders out to both of them and said,

Buster, don't let anything pass your snout okay if they put the charm on, watch every move they make.

Ludwig looked aside when Josh finished talking to Buster and said,

Right then, let's go for it and by the way, lads, if you hear or see us in Monaco sipping on one of the classic drinks, you know they have charmed us.

A little laughter came about and off they headed.

You know where we are going, don't you?

Oh, ya I know all about the lifestyle they live and what they do up at that pad, don't you worry about that.

They arrived at the house and Minx answered the ring-a-ding at the door and after discussing what they were there for, the eyes of charm came out, then Flash-ass Hugo came outta one room and got really defensive and ordered, do not say a word until we have spoken to our lawyers.

Then Ethel spoke and apologized for his behaviour and said,

Darlings, can I get you something to drink?

The natural hound instincts came to them as they started to look about them at the scene.

They accepted and she headed to the kitchen and got straight onto the old bell to call mummy and daddy, who of course were in business with Ethel's folks who were high-end business hounds out there in the world. After discussing what had happened, one member of the family got really defensive as he was involved in shipment and close to a big contract with the Bonza Bedda Lalla company that dealt with the most exclusive baskets you could imagine and the contract he was working on was to supply the Arabian embassies all over the world. If his name came out in any disgrace, then he may as well kiss his tail bye-bye.

He got straight on his blower to Atailia Barnes and Wallis Waglar, the highest defence attorneys out there and ordered them both down to Deal.

Both barked out loud to their clients and told them to just say no comment to any question and wait until they arrived for their advice. The boys did have enough evidence to take 'em down and Buster called up the camp and asked the lads,

Shall we bring them down to the keep as you know they are friends with you know who?

Josh looked at Dylan and the others and asked a quick question,

Lads, having them all in the Keep wondering what the hell is going on could work wonders, so what shall we do?

The ole boys and the youngsters just smiled and said,

Yep, bring 'em down and let them wonder why.

Just then, Mushy Martin and Joaquin called to the boys for another reason to tell them something vital. When Josh told them what they had just done, they just burst out with laughter and said,

Right, at this end we have everything in top security so we are on our way down with our news.

Within hours, they walked into the Camp and were welcomed with hugs and smiles all around and yes, Buster got the brews on all around. They sat about with more calmness after laughing so much about the past few hours and the occurrences, when Joaquin spoke in a different tone.

Right, Josh, Dylan, we have something of great importance to tell you.

He looked up at Buster and then to the boys as if to say should he be listening? And Josh this time replied with his head to Dylan first then back to Dan with a nod of approval, yes, he should.

Well, here it goes. He opened up his briefcase and put in front of the boys a signed confession from the Dodger that with leeway to the arrest of himself, he would give the most vital evidence there could be on the Judge, Alan Cauden and of so many cases and bribes from the past, you would need to hire a tower block to go through them all? This would be enough evidence to see the whole lot, Frank the Knash, etc, etc go down. They would never see daylight again and could kiss their high lifestyle goodbye.

Silence was all about as they read the statement and then the heads started to rise and they looked at each other and the first to speak was Josh.

Gentlemen, I find this just beyond and with your pure history of cases you have witnessed from way back, can this statement and how we got this statement- could it go against us in any way whatsoever?

Martin introduced the new gent to them and it was Cooly M'Gooly. He was a top dog attorney who had seen many of the judge's cases that ripped off many of a poor mutt's savings thrown out of court, so there was no holding back on his end. He spoke briefly to say,

I have gone over every word on this case and the evidence that you hold, and there is not one letter, never mind a word out of place. Therefore, you can go ahead and submit it to the supreme court.

Applause rang out all around.

Everyone, can I ask something of a professional and personal matter that I'd like to do right this minute? Asked Dylan.

What is that, Dylan? replied Cooly M'Gooly.

I'd like to go over to the Keep and just walk along with yourselves and just to take a glance at these yuppy' puppy gooffballs who thought they would take a shot at us and tell us, not ask to let them off just because of who they are. After bringing in those really rare birds just to munch on, knowing there are so many fantastic dishes out there that one could legally order to feast on, they chose these poor birds? Just the ignorance of it all is what bugs me, mate.

Okay, let's go down and see what's what and make sure all is in order. We could let the North End gang out to go home, now we have this statement from the Dodger' Josh said, of course of the ones living on North Street, he was calling the North Spratt enders.

Anyway, no, not just yet, let us question them for a while as we are waiting, don't forget, for those paw prints mainly on those cans from what you found in that cellar in the Farthing Cottage?

They arrived at the Keep and at the drawbridge, sorry entrance, there was a sort of waiting room from the medieval days where visitors could change outta their armour, they say.

Anyway, the culprits who were held had their parents gathered around. Steve and Cathy, Ethel's folks; Emily and Steve, Minx's; Hugo's and a couple from the historical Walthamstow greyhound races who are guess what? Related to the Dodger. But why are they here, I wonder? They were the first to approach us but why? And how did they know about us? Well, they introduced themselves and explained that the Dodger worked at their ground and wanted to make it clear that they were nothing whatsoever to do with him and these play dog's games and that they were a very professional outfit and not a chase a tail around the bedroom type of business. The Dodger had now been struck off their members' or employers' list and books forever.

We are nothing to do with these hounds here. It is that somehow, we turned up at the same time, but the one geezer with his ears sticking out of his bowler hat, who was Minx's Daddy was watching them closely and seemed to be in an embarrassed state.

You can bet your dollar why? That deal with the Arabs, I'd say.

Anyway, let's get this sorted out. Right then if you could all write your names here, please in capital letters and then sign your signature please underneath.

After doing so, they were escorted to some tables with a few roughed-up baskets about, to place their butts down if they wanted to. Then their off spring were brought up, cuffed of course to an officer, and the first thing to happen was the rules of no touching, no holding paws, etc, etc and Minx's mummy burst out sobbing into a bark to her hubby,

Darling, they can't treat my puppy like this. I demand you tell them to release her now, you have your friends in that private club of yours, call them immediately.

Not realizing her words were being recorded, she was yelping out and was then told to,

Wrap your tongue now!

As eyes were looking and ears propped up listening to all as everything was jotted down. The Minx played on her innocence with crying wolf but they knew her game as she owned a heart as cold as ice, to say the least. Hugo got an ear bashing as words came out like who do you think you are? Daddy was not amused at all and just then, the big shot lawyers entered with commands to their clients, do not answer any more questions other than no comment.

Their time was up and so the sob-sob crap came out and they were led back downstairs. One of the guards could not but help say,

All right then, let's be having you all, you lot back down to the dungeon and back to your cages!

So down they were escorted with the yuppie folks looking on. Back in they were put and it was just enough time for the boys to walk along the corridor and peep in through the ole sliding peepholes and give 'em a stare and as they did, each one with a drooped down snout looked up at the little window and saw the looks from the team who put them there, laughing politely.

They knew back upstairs that as soon as the papers were filed and signed bail would be given after questioning so they got on with the drilling ASAP and yes, a few were shaking like the leaves in autumn falling from the trees at St George's Church Park. A few questions shook them up by saying,

Look you can tell us certain things now and you could be back at the fireside of your uppy-yuppie baskets but alas the call came out. They were granted bail and so they were led out of their chambers and let out to bark away about the torture that had been imposed upon them.

Huffs and puffs were about at the exit as they were leaving and words from the parents, mostly the mummies, were like, you wait till I speak to blah-blah. He or she will deal with you. Mr M'Cooly looked straight at everyone as if to say do not bark and bite anything out and give them anything to complain to anyone about, you guys, okay?

All the parents were together outside waiting with a Sanitizer cart from Linda's Store. As you know she is based on Queen Street and sold, you name it, she had it. From the ingredients for the spells the witches used to what the fishermen needed for their hunting. They say she used to sell harpoon cannons. You know, the big ones for hunting the big boys back in the days of hefty shoals. I don't know but they say she's still got a few left, but I don't know about that?

Well, the parents bought the infection towelling and wraps also from Linda's and had hired the staff from Bonne-Bombe's whose shop was just beside Linda's on the same street. The staff stood waiting and as soon as they stepped their paws on solid soil, the sanitizing netting was thrown over them, then they were all wrapped up and the next minute, zoom, away they were driven to Mike and Jane's Bonne-Bombe shop where the second they arrived, they were hosed down then scrubbed, starched, rinsed over and over until the parents said, okay, that will do.

Then they were thrown into the blow dryers until they came out looking like young dandelions before they flower. These puff balls looked like something else and looked around to see if anybody was about to witness this. It was bad enough being banged up in those cages but this was the final straw. Luckily enough, nobody was about so they all made their own way back to their homes. You see at Bonne-Bombes the most loving, scents and aromas of soaps and so on were created. The world cried out for them and even Birdie had her own style made for her there.

You know Eric, the ole playboy who drinks in the Spotted Dog and his sweetheart, Isla the lab, Linda and Mike are Eric's folks and Linda is Isla's mummy. They had been together for years and that blighter Eric, believe me, he was a player in his day. Anyway, anytime you wanted a good aroma about you, like going on a date or you had rolled over too much in something along the Strand, you took a hike down to Jane's, she would clean you up alright and get you into shape for the date you were going on. Just be careful of one thing. Coming outta their shops, watch out for the scoundrels that are about because they will be after whatever you have bought because they know they won't get whatever you purchased elsewhere and the ones to watch out for, were those packs who work for the fishermen, those packs of stinky, smelly, doggies are all wild strays.

Monday morning arrived and everyone had the chance to chill out for the weekend with their loved ones. Tilly got even more great news of the business that had just been growing and growing. Local magazines wanted to advertise them for being so successful and helping local employment, so she was delighted about that news.

The team finished collecting samples for testing at the properties of North Street and notified everyone that they could return to their domains. If they had any sense, they would keep their snouts shut if they had the notion to put any complaint in of any mess about in their kennels as they should feel lucky to be able to have the chance to chew a bone again. Someone did them a favour and put a good word in to give them bail and I wonder who that was? Josh contacted everyone involved to say how proud he was, with Dylan, for everyone's work.

I now feel we should meet at the camp and put together all that we have and organise a trip up to the old Smoke to present all the evidence to the heads to view it all and for them to grant us to serve Judge the Smudge with a warrant to join us for a little banter and a few questions of our own.

We will also organise a meeting with Sir Giles Chappie Chewer and give him the evidence that we have as well. But Martin, I need a huge favour and I want you to think about it, okay? Would you sit down with Sir Gile's wife or with himself and tell him about his sister and the proof we have? It is not going to be easy but alas it has to be done. We got more recordings of what was going on with that Swiss Account and who and where the deposits were coming from. Morsey M'gorsy called the other day to say he has more vital evidence relating to this case, that is the Swiss account case by the way, and it is to do with some video recordings on tape in a certain bank and who is on it? I was going to leave it to those high-rank bankers or Stock exchangers or whatever you call them, to break the news but even so there will have to be an arrest, won't there? Or do they have their own laws in banking? Either way, it will be going to the supreme court.

I have really thought this out and even thought that maybe an officer that he does not know would be better to tell him. Then how would he react if we acted in that way? You see he did put everything to us and I feel he may think we do not have the balls to tell him ourselves. So, let's talk it over after we arrest her, okay?

It did not take long for the lads to head back down to Deal as the suspense chilled a little and everyone seemed to be much more kicked back after we managed to get back. Maybe the few days' break did us all well in heart and soul, who knows but it had worked. With the first meeting, the files were opened as they sat around the table and each page turned with each paw and was proudly read out till the final one was enclosed in thought and mind. They looked around at each other and Ricard stood up to say,

That is that, lads, let's head for those big boys with this load from this magnificent team that has grown.

Yes, they discussed the matter of Sir Giles after viewing the info the boys had gathered at the Cyber Shed and my, of all creatures to see on that video how do you explain to someone it was those you trusted who were the delinquent felons moving these lump sums of dosh about? Yes, Richard said he would break this news, and then out of the blue, both Dylan and Josh said they would be beside him when announced. When they stood up to recommend this, Richard was very proud of their mature thoughts and agreed.

Well, shall we go now or first thing in the morning?

Let's go now and get this tension out of us because if we wait until morning, I feel we will cut loose on the town. So, let's get on the way and get all this off our tails.

Arriving into the City of Sins as Josh called it, they entered into the private parking and their visits had become so common that the big Boxer, Booty the security guard, another galoot nodded at them with a smile through his dribble and up into the building they entered. Nods came from different departments as the pack walked along the long winding corridors to the head state of cases, in front of them stood the head honcho with another greeting of a smile and he asked them to sit. After a little intro from the lads, he asked,

Okay, what have you got for me?

Well after going through so much, after they opened their files and one for him, he had to compliment them on their sheer determination in this case and he ordered straight away the legal status of putting up the laws of paperwork etc to address the Judge on this matter.

He brought the lawyer in to tell the lads the legal side of what they must do and to stick to the laws whatever happened. They were so built up in suspense that they even checked out the attorney by watching his body movements to see if he had any doubt in them putting trust into giving him this info. But when he started talking about his dad who was a Fish merchant from Deal, they found it hard to believe, so they threw a few questions at him and the answers were ones you could not guess or make up, as they were personal from banters handed down from the Sprat Wafflers and so on. Now then after this amazing meeting, the lawyer personally folded his file over and the boys felt this case was personal to him as well.

So, he said, right I will leave you to it lads and I'll get all this proof on the boat and we will set this case on with its sails.

They decided to stay in London as the adrenalin had drained their feelings so Dan invited them to stay. They got back to Joaquin's and just felt a flow of contentment so they got a little groomed up and headed out on the town for a little reward for the results they have received. Sitting in the Hanging Ear pub in the Soho neighbourhood, Josh had to mention that in the morning he was popping over to meet Shannon and really looking forward to seeing her again.

You are found of her aren't you, matey? This came from Harry, Dan's partner as he joined them for the evening.

A nice social evening, if anything it was the contentment to their minds that the head wagtails were, well, so pleased with the matter the boys brought them and found.

The stroll back was really enjoyable as once again it was the positive response they were rewarded with. Getting their tails tucked in back at Joaquin's they just kicked back and fell asleep contented.

The morning arrived and after the call to Shannon from Josh, they met up at the park they last walked in together and it was just a pleasure. A little hesitation from Josh and he told Shannon his status and that it was a serious case that he could not discuss and please understand that and of course, she did with respect.

Shannon, maybe when this has calmed down a little, you may want to have a break and come down to Kent for a weekend?

Yes, came the reply. Yes, I'd love to, Josh.

They shared the morning together and then it was time to make it back and settle the other paperwork on the Ostrich charges and so on, so they parted again after Josh escorted Shannon back and they barked off a little to say see you soon.

Back at the major London base, the matter of the legal files and paperwork was being set up and there could not be one error in it, because look who they were serving it to? The pack got back and the wonderful welcome to Dylan from his litter was just amazing and a joy to witness.

How did it go, Dylan? asked Tilly.

Better than expected, lass.

I could tell that from your body language to be honest as I can see you have released a fair bit of tension.

Anyway, we can only wait now for those head honchos to give us what we need and it will have to be spot on, Tilly, and that is that.

It was a nice feeling getting back as Josh wanted a little time to discuss a matter with Cimino and he really wanted to have Hanna with them for a lady's view on the subject. After explaining everything to her, they sat with Cimino and the question came back up; who will it be who sits down with Sir Giles and explains to him what evidence is in front of them?

Cimino said he had spoken to Richard up at the Smoke and he would do this but there had to be one main thing on the plate, the proof. And after getting another call from Johnny O Jingo on more news of the account, he felt he had enough to give us the facts to tell him.

Right, let us stick to this plan and we all feel our paws are secure to the ground. It will be very sad and disturbing to sit with him and tell him what we found out but I honestly feel the news we have in ending the reign and freedom of the judge once and for all, for him it will make up for the sadness his sister has caused him. He may want to witness it when we serve the Judge his paperwork. But it would have to be behind closed doors for him to view through a screen as it may not be legal to be with us when we give it to this vagabond?

All the tension now will be built on the time they take to give us all that we need to advance and end it all. With so many things open at the moment, from the old friends coming home, then there's Paul and the North Street saga, the Swiss account deal and the view of new love beginning all around and then there's the Ostrich case. There is so much to take in, so let's just lie back a while and see when this vital paperwork comes through for us to discuss. Then with it all in our bowls, we can sit down and put together a plan to serve the complete menu of all these cases out and what will be the most intriguing, interesting, tasty feast they have had for a while and it will come directly from us.

If this all goes to plan, then God knows how many cases we may be asked to solve. We will see after we have our results on all matters and what they will be. Only the true facts will be our answers and then which way will our feelings go. Will they travel like Aseena and Poppy? Or become content like Tilly, just staying at bay. Who knows? Whatever happens, may the road to happiness take us on the right journey and lead us up the right path and point us all in the right direction.

A light journey of life seemed to be at bay around all involved in such a saga of this open drama of reality, until John and Dave called Dylan, who was on the blower to Josh at the time, as they stuck those famous heads through the door of the base.

Hey, mate, we have a box of paper for you and it has to be picked up personally to be signed for, so can you get your butt over to the station to do this please, and when will that be?

Dylan straight away asked Josh who was up in the big Smoke,

Can you make it down tomorrow, Josh? There's the postman here now telling me there's mail at the station and it must be signed for. It must be what we have been waiting for.

Yes, yes, I will be back down this evening or first thing in the morning, okay?

Okay, I'll see you then mate.

Dylan then turned to the two and answered,

Right, guys, we will be over first thing in the morning to pick this package up, okay?

Sure, see you at the station, Dyl, and off they strutted in their usual manner.

Now then, what could be said of John and Dave? I'll try to put it in as normal words as possible, like many a banter and fact, this was their story and true as well. Back in history, when the Prime Minister at the time was William Pitt, who ordered every single boat for a two-mile stretch, a mile each way from the Pier, to be burnt to the ground as the government was losing so much in taxes because the smugglers were so successful and so he thought he would play the Griff's and mutts here at their own game. This operation was called the blockade of Dealy-Wheelies back in 1816. It was to be under the charge of Captain Joe McCulloch, mostly known as Flogging Joey.

Well, this went ahead and oh my word, was there corruption in the waters and land or what? Hell was created, for who could or would tolerate such behaviour as this? If anything, it created more problems along the English Channel. You see this Captain McCulloch was on a South American, Mexican mission before his long sail back to ole blighty, so you can just imagine what the crew and so on must have been up to on that four-year journey? Near enough the minute he docked in Plymouth, he was given the orders from the top shelf to get his butt here in Deal.

When arriving here, the crew wined and dined with the local savages just like the group that escaped from the Romans many a year ago. This was mainly around the Sandown marsh and swamp lands down the North End where in fact these two, John and Dave still live amongst those harsh wetlands of fear and mystery. Well, you see the slaves who were captured from abroad became members of the crew of Flogging Joey and those who settled here, yes, they started mixing with the Saxon ways of the breeds here. So, what type of turnout would there be? These mixes of Mastiffs Cioties who were captured from the Mexican port towns, the Bloodhounds from the southern states, Apatchoos from Nevada, Dingos from the northern state of Louisiana; all this harsh breeding created the Catahoula named from the Indian word meaning secret lake where all was held in hope for all we got.

So, you could say Captain McCulloch was John and Dave's great, great, great granddaddy, then?

Yep, sure was. They say, you know, the pretty lass, Keeley, from the bookies, she is from this Tribe. Also, the young James, her sidekick in there, him too.

Yes, I can see Keeley being related with that fiery beauty of savages, but James, I don't know about that. I'd say he's more of a Gentalow, that breed from Kingstown way. Now then here is another thing and how it has been kept secret I do not know. You must promise me that what I'm about to tell you goes no further, okay? But you know the famous dessert, chocolut-challure that is made from the eastern world's marrow, banned from everywhere. Guests will pay any price to have it on their menu and top dogs like Mike and Sue, Alan and Sue at their suave dos, they have the right connections to get it. Well, do you know where it comes from? It comes from the marshy swamps of Sandown from the Catahoula tribe and this is how: first, John and his cousin Dave, with their natural skills, growing up within the swamps of Sandown, swim out to the Goodwin Sands on certain dates and times of the currents to meet the French Short Haired Shepherds and the French Toy Bulls.

The teamwork is like watching the work of a special force operation. The Toy Bulls lie across the Shepherd's back and swim into the Western current that carries them to the sands. They dismount and paddle across the sands where they meet Dave and John plus LLD, Little London Dave who swims in between the pair and when unloading off the sands, he carries the cargo just a few feet over the water mines and barbed wire traps.

For centuries they have been there and deadly to those who do not know of them. You see once again that lethal current travelling south-easterly, it lifts the traps with the water's surf, so LD, that is little Dave by the way, he's a Jacka-whipperoo. His dad is one-eyed JR and his mum, Wilma, she's from the travelling fair dogs. Well after finding out the birth of Dave, he tracked them down searching town after town and found them and kidnapped him and brought him all the way back here and knowing he was a breed from the travellers, he stood no chance of any pack taking him in under their protection. So, what was he to do? Then one night on the way home from the Howling Hole on Water Street there was a mugging going on. Even with a snout full of ale and rum he wasn't going to walk by and see four onto one, so in he jumped and gave his best.

Not realising who he was assisting all you could hear and see was bite, bark and bruising and after the cowardly baggabonds fled, this feisty mutt invited LD back to his pad where they shared wine and howling many a song from the heart. Only when he woke, he found what he had been involved with. He had assisted the leader of the bloody Catahoulas and ever since that day he and the tribe's son, John was inseparable and then known as cousins. He earned his keep and position well and became loved by everyone. Now then any order for the Raw Marrow or the full Pate recipe made for an up-market duo they say comes from two locations to start with, maybe to test whether you are a Snouter or not? Customs officer, by the way, that's what a wet ole Snouter is.

I have to admit it I often seen the teamwork even if it is breaking the law, it's amazing to see how they do it. The two locations are Steve's Leather Lounge or pretty Keeley's at James's Betting Slipper. I'm only guessing mind? Plus, how they reward themselves for their time and effort. But I do admit just to think of when they leave the edge of The Sandown Castle remains and just disappear into the deep, dark swamps and marshes, na, sorry that's not for me. When we were younger playing down on the edge of the remains of Sandown, I bit John on the leg and he growled at me and said you wait till I tell my family what you did to me, just you wait and see. You will be put in the big pot just like many others and boiled to our liking, a feast of yourself will be to our jest. Now you see after telling you this about the rare marrow bone and so it is only fair to tell you the true fact? You see on South down street is the main Post office department, Well Dave, John, Dan'Menzy'Mark and tall Craig are all POSTIE'S and this as been a tradition since the first letter was carried way-way back when. Before the posties began what was one of the main incomes as you know they say with honesty 'Smuggling; Smuggling was on the agenda with the fishing an so. Well, all these families named got the positions at the post yard but the tradition was too healthy to give up so the post office was a great cover for them and still is. I must admit you just have to try that class of Marrow they bring in? it is unbeatable to say the least. There has always been one main family head as they call him and who will be giving his position up soon is Long ways Louis. For 45 years the in and out of the supplies through all weathers coming out of the swamps of South Down and the Channel he made it happen. You see him now just strolling threw St George's Park with a smile and a wag of his tail you wouldn't think butter would melt in his mouth, would you? They say when the clans meet to vote the next Marrow-Post-Father will be Craig but who knows? Anyway, what I have just told you keep it to yourself okay as it is very hush-hush.

The next morning, Josh and Dylan made arrangements not to go to the camp, but to meet outside the post office café and get the parcel and make it back, to see if anything was missing, they could get straight on it. All the staff were flat out at the yard as it was the early hours 'The boys were waving at Dylan as near enough everyone was in puppy training with him so the wave of the paw or nod of the head or a wag of the tail was just to say hello.

How are you feeling, Josh? Was Dylan's call'

I don't know what to say, really? Here we are like something from a book or movie and have this lot to read and once we sign for it and go over to who we serve it to and what happens then may I say?

Just then Martin arrived because don't forget he was on the first case. The two boys looked at him and both read each other's minds; Sir Giles and the case of serving him the proof of his sister's behaviour. As they were signing for the papers box, Dylan asked how was Martin's trip down from London?

Fine, just fine. But this is more interesting; I never thought I'd witness something like this. To serve the Judge with these legal papers as he thinks, or thought he was untouchable, to say the least, and now here we are ready to stick these lawsuits under his snout, and Frank the Knash. The last time I stared Frank in the face he smirked at me as they left the court with that not guilty verdict. Well, my, oh my will it be interesting to see his expression this time!

Their confidence was building by the minute and a nice feeling flowed about; the more they read, the more it was to their benefit. Then Dylan broke into what was a difficult question to ask Sir Giles. After explaining the status Martin answered with desire and understanding and agreed to announce what they were going to serve Sir Giles's sister with.

Do you think he knew of her behaviour all along' Martin asked the boys?

I don't want to say it but I think he did you know? When she saw herself in the limelight within the red baskets with all the big shots, yes, in all she loved it but I feel he doesn't want this splashed across the front pages of The Dogs Desire. That's the head newspaper and many a dog wags his or her tail when one of their reporters is about. Let's just see where she turns to wag with this around her neck and doesn't she deserve it?

After sorting everything out and what was going to who, they each let out a sigh of relief.

Shall I give Sir Giles a call, Josh?

Yes, do that and tell him we want to meet ASAP and have with him his lawyer as it is important okay? We must meet on neutral ground so it is easy to discuss any matter on this case because it is not every day you are told your sister screwed you over. Let's try and tell him this is the easiest way. Let us be able to give him a good sign.

They agreed to meet at the Green and Found, a delightful location opposite Deal Castle where they could sit on the lawn without some busy-body peeping over their shoulder instead of taking care of their own business.

Anyway, as Josh and Dylan were sitting on the lawn, you guessed it, Mrs B was sitting on the back of one of the chairs with one eye glancing over at the two boys and then Sir Giles arrived with his lawyer and of all other guests, his sister. Josh looked at her then at Dylan and then kept as calm-headed as he could, asking the guests to sit and join their company.

Mr Banks, the lawyer, said, I'd like to thank you for your detailed groundwork and what you dug up and what you are about to tell us will not be held back, we want you to tell us everything.

With this Josh opened up his file at the same time as Dylan. He then passed one file to the lawyer and asked Sir Giles if he would like one or would he prefer having it explained to him by Mr Banks? Sitting as calm as could be, it was explained to him the reason why they were there. The words flowed on until the whole case was explained and that took a while and as the last words crossed the tongues, the eyes just leered at the sister with a well what have you got to say expression?

Dylan got up and so did Josh and as the words were just going to come out, Sir Giles spoke,

Gentlemen, please I'd like to request a plea that Janice, my sister, be put under my custody until the court case.

He knew the boys were going to arrest her but with the lawyer there and enough hurt going on with Sir Giles's feelings they looked at each other and honoured his request, but they did get the lawyer to sign the arrest papers that by law had to be done if they were to let her walk away with him.

Sir Giles spoke again, I want to thank you both for your work even when it comes to times like this a fantastic job to bring justice to light.

Just then Martin arrived and Sir Giles looked up and greeted him with a smile. Martin could not resist but to look straight into the sister's eyes and ask silently, well why? Now it has been brought out, where has it got you? All were standing now and Martin knew Mr Banks and as Josh was talking to Sir Giles with Dylan beside him, Martin spoke again,

Tomorrow, Banksie, it is the judge's turn and I bet I won't get an ounce of sleep tonight thinking that the time has reached us now after all these years, not to mention Frank the Knash as well. Martin for some reason had a tone in his voice like he was telling the lawyer this intentionally, but surely the lawyer wasn't involved in this setup? Don't say he's been in with the Judge all along, it can't be, can it? Walking away they felt better than they thought they would; they believed the emotions would have been much higher, instead they had an empty cell with someone else having to take responsibility and not having to deal with that depression.

The morning arrived and what a beauty it was with a pure Eastern sunrise; being beside the Channel, it was surprising how the birds were in tune compared to the normal howling screech of the gulls. Maybe they knew as well that there was certain action taking place around the town and they liked the tune as well. Maybe it was to do with the buildings these vagabond's parked up on for generations no longer existed and they missed the banter they had with many friends sitting on those chimney pots? The ones being served today with legal matters were the ones who had those classic buildings knocked down. Who knows but there was a nice vibe about it?

Are you okay Dylan? asked Tilly as she watched him over breakfast and getting ready to walk out of their kennel.

The young ones were chilling a little, they too were getting ready to walk out to The Puppy Club which they had only joined a week ago and loved it. The Puppy Club was an introduction to schooling and could put one on the right road in life and give ideas about which way you would want to go. Anyway, they were all in class one.

Yes, yes, replied Dylan. We've just got so much going on, I want to make sure I have everything that is needed today as I've to meet Josh.

Just before he could bark another word the door went and it was Martin. Tilly knew straight away there was something in the air when she saw Martin calling at this time in the morning. Then not a second passed before Josh arrived.

The puppies for looking a little confused as to see this company here at this time of the morning? Bye, daddy, bye! Were there gentle barks.

All the partings went ahead and the pups were out of the door and on their way with the walker and the other students heading for class. Then Dylan got up and said,

Right, I shall see you later, my love.

Be careful out there, okay? Tilly replied.

Josh and Martin with their manners gave an open smile and headed for the front door with Dylan giving a little glance back and within seconds the kennel was empty. This was a rare occasion to have silence but nice in a way for Tilly's mind. Tilly looked out down the way as the three turned onto King's Road and out of sight. She knew something was on just by the way their bodies spoke but what could it be? Tilly took to the chair and on a rare account sat in silence which seemed to be impossible; she let her thoughts just wander into this bliss and then thought of what the boys were onto and she realised after thinking of little things she saw hanging about the house's tables, all related to the Judge and that time in history when he ruled with others in such a corrupt town and era it was a wonder any four-tailed mammal survived.

Arriving at the lodge, that's the Judge's pad, just as Martin opened the gate Dylan's phone went off and it was one of the crew who was on North Street outside you know whose house, talking away.

Dylan, I have a question. Hudson's not here but the other two are saying they don't know where he is as he's gone for a walk. Shall we wait or arrest these on suspicion of withholding vital evidence?

Wait a while and see if he returns and I will see what I feel is best to do with your end okay? All right, I will get back to you later.

Walking down the garden path Dylan told the others who had been looking on curiously, Hudson's gone, disappeared out of sight.

They looked at each other with a glance and tried not to smile but could not help but do so. Knocking on the Judge's door, Alison answered and taking a peep inside they noticed suitcases beside the staircase and out came Martin's question,

Going places may I ask?

Alison was looking kinda embarrassed, to say the least, as she looked over her shoulder to see the Judge scurrying about in the lounge and then Martin said,

Mind if we come in, ma'am?

Alison was too nervous to answer as the boys walked in. Opening his side pocket and pulling out a certain letter, Martin said,

Alan, Brans Goldin here on the 25.05.2022 I serve you with this and charge you with the breach of the law etc, etc. Okay, take him away boys.

He started to bark out who he was and who he knew and the big mistake they were making etc, etc, but after so many years one tended to believe he really did think he was untouchable in the line of the law but now we will see?

Then back to the boys,

Before word travels faster than sound, let us get our butts over to The Kooloo Kennels where the hip, flash tailors live.

As they entered the courtyard, who did they meet head-on making his way to a packed-up car, but the one and only Frank the Knash.

Been a while hasn't it, matey?

Yes, the eyes locked on again at each other as he too was served with certain paperwork and led to the Black Mariah, cuffed up. Martin turned to the boys and said,

Do you know how long I've waited to do that? And now the time has come. Come on, let's go for a beer.

Walking into The Snooty Mcgooty's pub, Cobbly Steve was sitting at the bar barking away to Harvey the hound dog, half cut, and he was saying to Harvey,

And you know those tunnels that lead from your place going west from Middle Street? They lead down to the old coal track off the railway station, don't they?

Ya' why?

Well, I would place the biggest bone there is out there as a bet that I saw those famous white ears and tail of Hudson sticking out on the Stanhope Road exit that leads into the post office yard with that beauty he has always been with, Tessa, and I was just wondering what they had with them? where they were heading and into what task.

Sir Giles gave Dylan 'Josh a call and ask could we please meet up just have a brief chat, so the boys suggested that he came to Deal to visit their station to see the location that helped them so much to solve this case once and for all. He agreed and came down the next morning where the boys explained to the team make sure all coats and teeth were polished up.Sir Giles wanted to thank everyone for such an amazing job they did even if some of the results were personally hurtful like the results of his sister but sometimes the truth can hurt. Dylan explained to the gent about there building and the purpose it was built for in the beginning? Josh explained we find it very important the surrounding are comfortable for the mind to do its best and get the results you want. Yes, I find that very interesting young man and keep the good work up but I have to say I can't wait until the court case next week to see the faces of those two main blighters and see what the judge as to say when he gives the final verdict? I hope you do not mind me saying but I could not help but have a little giggle at the scoundrel Hudson, just the cheek of the little mutt and you got to give it to him he had the balls to give it a shot. Now here is a little gift for you all to have a good night out on the town okay. Yes, it was an open card again for the whole weekend. Plus, the other thing I wanted to say was I can go back to my dads grave and tell him justice as been brought to light and his soul can rest that is what he wanted as of his vows before about bad people brought out. Now I shall leave you at your work and once again thank you from the bottom of my heart. He made his way to the old weather worn door and stepped out onto Middle Street and away he went on his travels home.

Well guys I'd like to say thanks for bringing light back to me and my thoughts of this profession. This was Cosimo saying how much he has enjoyed being in wonderful presence. Josh, can I have a word 'this was Dylan talking' I been thinking mate where we are now and there is no way it will be kept from the media and so. We will deal with it with a easy flow okay. My main concern now is we go way back to childhood and generations with the post office boys and knowing their both professions what do we do? Do we keep shut and with a blind eye mate? We need to think this over okay and see how we feel in the near future? The two looked at each other and then made there way to the door to start another day.

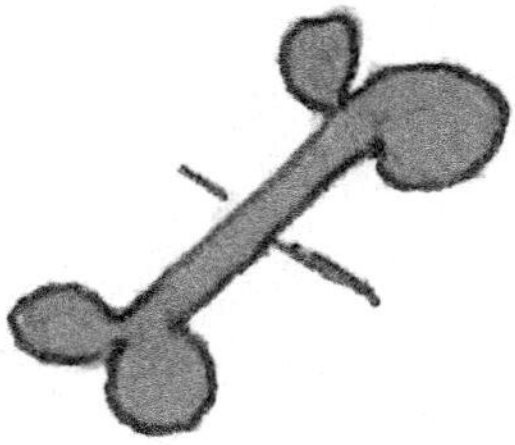

Thank You

Here's to the UK town of Deal in general and its characters of humans and doggies (whatever breed they may be) to say thank you for your support whilst writing and creating *Tilly's Tails*. It was a real pleasure for me.

The character and the personalities have really brought out this saga but as you must know the banter of the town's history inspired me the most – such as the stories of the Scot-Yorkshire and, my breed, the Welsh who walked here in those early days through all weathers to find a better life within the coal fields and mines.

There is always the crack from somebody saying: "Oh my… was that one of those who walked here and joined the coal business and later set up their own business?"

To the people of my upbringing who instilled in me the passion to drive on in every part of my life, I just want to say thank you for guiding my thoughts towards writing *Tilly's Tails*.

Take care.

- KJ -

Printed in Great Britain
by Amazon

37163128R10264